SHE LOOKED AT HIM
WITH GROWING DISBELIEF.

Roger O'Neil would never say anything so radical. Could it possibly be that the spirit of Brian O'Neil was trying to reach out to her through the flesh and bones of his brother? Her mind reeled.

"You're daft, lass!"

It came with the heritage. Gaelic superstition. Ghosts, goblins, devils, the Little People.

A stretch of rolling green lay ahead of them beyond the cotton crop.

"I'll race you," he dared.

She wanted to get away from him far more than she wanted to race. Now she was terrified. She put the whip to the horse's flank and Ginger shot away from Black Lightning. His laughter trailed off in the slipstream. Then he was in hot pursuit.

"Go, Lightning! Go!"

"Faster, Ginger! Faster!"

It had happened before. Another time. Another place. Reliving that wonderful day when she had been deflowered by Brian. So why was she so frightened? Because the man on her heels was not her husband Roger.

HE WAS A PHANTOM, A GHOST!

FLOWERS OF FIRE

STEPHANIE BLAKE

PLAYBOY PRESS

FLOWERS OF FIRE

Cover illustration by Betty Maxey.

Published simultaneously in the United States and Canada by Playboy Press, Chicago, Illinois. Printed in the United States of America. Library of Congress Catalog Card Number: 76-49400. First edition.

This book is available at quantity discounts for promotional and industrial use. For further information, write our sales-promotion agency: Ventura Associates, 40 East 49th Street, New York, New York 10017.

BOOK ONE

your hair is done. You'd better go and see what that surprise is now."

". . . The same way the English are keeping the Irish in chains. . . ."

The master, he was a fine one for speaking so hotly in defense of the Irish! The Duke of Ulster! Son of a wealthy English landlord who owned a twenty-one-thousand-acre estate by grant of the Crown.

Eight thousand landowners possessed three-quarters of all the land in Ireland, a majority of them Englishmen who had never laid eyes on their ill-gotten gains. The vast estates administered by usurious overseers and stewards and rent collectors. What they saw was the bounty—flour, meal, butter, lard, beef and pork and the tithes—shipped to England for home consumption or export. Meanwhile the landless Irish peasantry toiled and died to fill the foreign bottomless horn of plenty that was bleeding their country dry and barren; they eked out a bare existence on a national diet of potatoes and skimmed milk.

Rose's father was one of the half-million turned out of their homes and off their land in the year 1843 alone, out of English greed to breed and graze more and fatter cattle, sheep and pigs. There was no appeal; the Penal Law of 1691 had seen to that.

No civil rights for Catholics. No education for Catholics. The Catholic church was forbidden to advertise itself in erecting steeples on its houses of worship. Salt rubbed into the wounds—every Catholic had to pay a tithe annually to the Anglican church. A Catholic was forbidden to marry a Protestant, or even to buy land from one. And if one of the spare few Catholics who did own small parcels of land passed on, the English-dictated law said that all of his possessions were to be divided among his sons. With the stipulation that if one of the sons was a Protestant— some men out of desperation swore allegiance to the Anglican church—then all of the inheritance would be inherited by that one son.

That very year, Parliament had passed the Poor Act of 1847, cutting off relief to any Irish peasant who owned more than one-quarter acre of land. One of many measures of blatant extortion, calculated at seizing the last foothold the Irish people still clung to on their homeland.

Villainous rent agents could arbitrarily grant or deny a tenant to renew the lease on his land, and the right of renewal almost always required a fat bribe to the agent.

In the words of a tune that was popular among the young militant rebels, Ireland was *"the saddest country that ever you have seen."*

Condemned to a life of slave labor in the fields. Forever excluded from joining the world of commerce and industry by the English masters from across the Channel.

Rose had nothing personal against the Duke of Ulster, a far better man than his father or his grandfather, who had been granted the land by King George. Neither one of those gentlemen had cared enough to make the crossing and acquaint themselves with the poor "spalpeens" who toiled sixteen hours a day to line their pockets and keep their larders and wine cellars full.

Edward Shea Wilding had been different. He had discharged the overseers, stewards and rental agents and settled in Ulster to manage the vast estate himself. Twenty years it had been now. Married himself an Irish colleen—Rose caught herself, thinking that well, now, you could hardly call Vanessa O'Connell a typical colleen. Real gentry she was, second cousin to the great Irish patriot Daniel O'Connell.

O'Connell: The Great Liberator. Founder of the Catholic Association, the first organized resistance group to defy the English occupation, Daniel O'Connell was the first Catholic mayor of Dublin and the first Irish Catholic to be seated in the British House of Commons.

The way it was now, the Duke of Ulster behaved more Irish than English. For instance, what he had told Ravena: ". . . the Irish in chains." A good landlord, fair to his tenants and his servants, a decent man.

Ravena tapped lightly on her mother's bedroom door.

"Come in, dear," Vanessa answered. Her father was with her mother, standing behind her as she inspected herself in the dressing table mirror.

The Duke beamed at her and spread his arms wide. "You look ravishing, my love. I can't believe that dress, as lovely as it is, can make you appear so grown up. Yes, indeed, you are a young lady."

Ravena was pleased and showed it. She ran over to him and hugged him. "Daddy, more of the old blarney."

"No, I mean it. I never realized how tall you were."

"It's the high heels."

"No, it's the magic. Cinderella at the ball."

Ravena giggled. "I hope I don't turn into a pumpkin at midnight."

The Duchess swung around on the vanity stool, smiling. "Cinderella didn't turn into a pumpkin. Darling, please don't muss her up."

He laughed and bent over to embrace his wife. "All right, I'll muss you up."

Ravena loved her parents dearly and thought they were the most handsome couple in the entire world. Her father was a tall broad man with dark handsome good looks. Black eyes that fairly crackled when he glared at anyone in disapproval. The heritage of the Grand Shea. Black Irish.

The bloodline diluted by centuries of intermarriage with the English and Scotch. The Shea, six generations earlier, had been there with Red Hugh O'Neil at Ulster in 1599 when the Irish won their last great victory over the English. But after O'Neil surrendered to James I, Shea was taken back to England and imprisoned. It was said there was no prison in Ireland strong enough to hold him. Irish sod to Shea was like Samson's locks. Deprived of the sights and sounds and smells of Ireland, he became a lesser man. Wiser, perhaps, but without the spark that had sustained him in the repeated one-sided battles against the foe. With the exception of Ulster.

Granted amnesty and released from prison after he had sworn allegiance to the Crown, Shea married an English-woman, the daughter of an English lord; he'd met her at a rally sponsored by the Protestant Committee for Fair Play to Ireland. Eventually they had three children. Now after many generations the Duke had learned that one of those children was his great-great-great grandmother.

The Duchess opened her jewel case and removed a necklace, a pair of earrings and a bracelet. All solid gold.

The necklace, one of Ravena's favorites, was a chain of multi-colored jewels interspersed with golden leaves. She attached an earring; it hung almost down to her shoulder.

"There's your present, Ravena." She indicated a box wrapped in white tissue paper on the vanity. "You may open it now."

Breathless with anticipation, the girl unwrapped the package. Her eyes flared wide. It was a smaller replica of her mother's jewel case.

"Well, just don't gape at it, child," her father urged her.

Her hands shook and her heart beat faster as she opened the top very slowly, prolonging the suspense. It *was* what she had anticipated.

The very same necklace and earrings and bracelet that were her mother's! Proportioned to suit her age and size.

"Oh, Mommy, they're so beautiful!" She hugged and kissed the Duchess and then threw herself on the Duke. "Daddy, you too. Oh, you're both so good to me. I love you both so much."

He put an arm about her and pressed her face against his white waistcoat. "And I hope all people will love you as much as your parents."

The Duchess inspected her daughter with an objective if immodest eye. "The way she is going to look when she's a woman, I strongly suspect that men will be falling over each other for the chance to love and wait on our little Ravena."

The night of the ball, her introduction to the Viceroy's mansion was not the disaster that Ravena had envisioned. She was assisted out of the carriage by the most elegant-looking young man she had ever seen, wearing a green uniform with gold braid, a red waistcoat, white breeches and silk stockings.

"Is he a general?" she whispered to her father.

The Duke laughed. "Sorry to disappoint you, sweet, but he's the footman."

The butler, who stood at attention at the head of the broad staircase that curved gracefully to the ballroom, was equally as elegant. He cleared his throat and announced:

"The Duke and Duchess of Ulster. And their daughter, Lady Ravena O'Connell Wilding."

With Ravena on one arm and his wife on the other, the Duke escorted them unhurriedly. Dazed, Ravena followed her parents along the reception line. Just a blur of anonymous faces, except for Lord Clarendon. "Ma'ams" and "Sirs." Curtseying with the fixed smile causing a fierce aching in her facial muscles.

When it came to receptions, Ravena Wilding was not exactly unsophisticated or lacking in the social graces. She had observed, from the top of the stairs, lavish affairs hosted by the Duke and Duchess ever since she was old enough to walk. Handsome men and glamorous women, the highest caste in the land. But none of them had ever affected Ravena like this ball. Part of it was being a participant instead of an observer, but there was more than that.

Her own father was wearing the traditional evening dress of the upper classes. Top hat, tailcoat with a white waistcoat beneath it. A ruffled shirt set off by a silk cravat.

Many of the other men were similarly dressed. But the majority of the male guests were clad in dazzling costumes that rivalled the women's bids for attention. Frock coats carmine, poppy red, green, violet, pale blue, the wearers posturing like peacocks on the dance floor. Short breeches. Black silk stockings. Ravena imagined she was at the French Court of Louis XV. Swirling and sweeping around in a kaleidoscopic display of colorful designs.

"Civil servants," her father explained to her. "Sort of dress uniforms. That chap in the poppy red, he's a chamberlain. No, he's a prefect. Chamberlains wear the red."

Lord Clarendon came over and put an arm around Ravena. "The most beautiful girl in the room, and my nomination for queen of the ball."

Ravena blushed. "Thank you, my lord."

Lord Clarendon, a stocky man with sidewhiskers, was as popular among the populace as any Viceroy could be. Like the Duke of Ulster, the Earl of Tyrone and other landlords who accepted the responsibilities that came with their vast land holdings, the Viscount had lived with the Irish people for so many years. They all had adopted quite a different regard and respect for them than that held by the absentee landlords home in England. They represented the English conscience, which Irish militant nationalists like Dan O'Connell, Will Smith O'Brien, John Mitchell and John Blake Dillon were counting on to become their trump cards in the struggle for independence.

"There is someone I want you to meet, my dear." He laughed. "Or I should say some*ones*."

He led her around to the other side of the room. "I'd ask you to dance, Ravena, but I think you'd prefer a younger gentleman."

"I'd like to dance with you, sir," she protested demurely.

"Of course you would. Still—ah, here we are." He took her up to two young men in scarlet uniforms with black trousers and patent leather boots.

Ravena judged their age to be thirteen or fourteen. Actually they were twelve, and tall for their age.

The astonishing thing about them was that they were twins, identical except for their hair. Ravena couldn't help gaping in unladylike fashion. One boy had black curly hair, almost as dark as her own. The other's was a mass of golden ringlets. In every other respect they had been cut, as it were, from the same mold. The same intense green eyes. The same noble brows and aquiline noses. The same strong jawlines.

What beautiful boys, she thought.

They snapped to attention when the Viceroy addressed them. "Young gentlemen, this is Miss Ravena O'Connell Wilding, daughter of the Duke of Ulster. Ravena, I want you to meet Roger and Brian O'Neil, sons of the Earl of Tyrone. I have an idea the three of you will be seeing a good deal of each other this summer. Your fathers have both agreed to serve on a special committee set up to administer the distribution of food and clothing under the provisions of the Poor Act just passed by Parliament."

"Miss Wilding." Roger the fair bowed stiffly from the waist.

"Ravena, now that's a quaint name." Brian the dark inspected her boldly.

"Excuse me," said the Viceroy. "Lady Clarendon is stalking me. Maybe I can lose myself in the crowd." He left quickly.

"Ravena. It's a pretty name, Brian," Roger chided him.

"It's a Spanish name," Ravena informed them.

"Sure and I said to meself, now there's a Spanish lass the first sight of you," Brian said in the brogue of the peasantry.

Ravena laughed. "It comes from generations ago. My great-great-great-grandfather—or should there be another 'great,' I'm not sure—was an officer in the Spanish Armada that was wrecked in the Irish Sea. He was washed ashore unconscious and found by the daughter of the Great Shea—my father's descended from a line of old Gaelic kings. She nursed him back to health and they were wed."

Brian's eyes danced. "So you've got hot Spanish blood in your veins, Miss Ravena?"

"Brian!" His brother gave him a withering look. "Where are your manners?"

"Beggin' yer pardon, lass, he's right. I'm an oaf. You see me bruther got me own share of manners along with his own. In fact he's quite a dandy. He was born a half-hour before me, so that makes him first in line."

Roger's fists balled and he looked at Brian with such undisguised hate that Ravena was shocked. No love lost between these two, she knew.

"Your uniforms are grand," she said to change the subject. "What school do you attend?"

"The Royal Cavalry Academy in Dublin," Roger answered. "Second form. Do you go to school?"

She felt herself blushing again. "No, I have tutors. But I plan to attend finishing school when I'm fourteen. I'm twelve now," she lied.

Brian grinned and made a chortling sound deep in his throat, a belittling sound. "*You*, twelve years old. That's a laugh. Roger and I are twelve, and you're a child compared to us."

Ravena tilted her face in the air and looked down her pert nose haughtily. "You're right, Brian. You are an *oaf*. Roger, aren't you going to ask me to dance?"

He bowed and offered his arm. "I'd be honored if you would."

Brian made the deprecating sound again as they joined the swirling couples on the dance floor in a Strauss waltz.

"I wonder what she'll be like in a few more years," he mused, his eyes following Ravena until she passed out of his sight, by the orchestra stand.

And in that first meeting was established the pattern of the triangular relationship for many years to come.

Roger the fair was formal, courteous, a conservative gentleman in every sense of the term.

Brian the dark was a nonconformist, a crude, uncouth bully with no manners or taste. From that first night—and through that summer—he would take sadistic pleasure, it seemed to Ravena, in teasing and taunting her, even so far as pulling her hair and shoving her to the ground in outdoor play. At one and the same time, although she did not realize it then, Brian was always behaving outrageously to shock her and to impress her, especially in the matter of foul language.

One minute he would be laughing and full of fun, and an instant later he would be sullen and brooding. When she questioned him about his erratic moods, he replied earnestly: "I'm Irish, descended from Red Hugh O'Neil, the first Earl of Tyrone—you're not the only one with king's blood in your veins. A mysterious people given to dark dreams."

Later in the evening when Ravena went up to the powder room on the second story of the Viceroy's mansion, she discovered Brian eavesdropping at a door that was ajar. When she came up to him he put his finger to his lips.

"Shhh. They're in there with Sir Charles Trevelynn, Chancellor of the British Exchequer. He's a real bastard, he is."

She put an eye to the crack between the door and the jamb on the hinge side.

"It's him talking," Brian said.

Sir Charles was a tall, mustached man wearing the uniform of a Brigadier of Dragoons.

"I am personally opposed to the Poor Act. It will serve no better purpose than to encourage the natural sloth and indolence of these ignorant beggars."

"Sir Charles," the Duke of Ulster suggested respectfully, "it would be a good thing for you to tour the countryside, particularly in the West. My God, I don't believe there's a field in Galway that isn't an unmarked graveyard. They're dying like flies. Buried in mass graves. You can't drive down any road without seeing men and women carrying their dead on their backs to community graves."

A tall, broad-shouldered man with dark hair and a craggy face that looked as if it had been carved out of Moher limestone supported the Duke's view. "It's beyond belief unless you see it for yourself, Sir Charles," he said.

"My father," Brian whispered to Ravena.

"Last Thursday I passed a skeleton of a man crawling along at the side of the road. I stopped the carriage and asked him if there was anything I could do. He thanked me and said he was trying to reach the Catholic Churchyard half-mile down the road because he wanted to die on hallowed ground."

Sir Charles arched an eyebrow at him. "My dear fellow, surely you didn't let him ride in your carriage?"

"I did."

Sir Charles shook his head in disbelief. "You will be most fortunate, sir, if you do not contract some fatal disease from being close to a creature like that."

"Creature?" This from a man whose bent body and lined face bore the ravages of long suffering. "Is that how you see us, Sir Charles? In the same way as we were depicted in the *Times* editorial last week? How did they phrase it? 'Now we can rejoice that soon natural Irishmen will be as rare on the banks of the Shannon as are red men on the banks of Manhattan.' Is that your view, sir?"

"I wonder who the old boy is? At least he's standing up to the Limey," muttered Brian.

"He's stood up to a lot bigger men than Sir Charles," Ravena said smugly.

"How would you know, child?"

"Because he's my third cousin. *The* Daniel O'Connell."

He jerked his head in her direction, eyes round with wonder, mouth opened wide.

"The hell you say? You're pulling my leg, that's it. *Him*, Daniel O'Connell?"

Sir Charles confirmed it in his next words. "Mr. O'Connell, I certainly do not subscribe to that calloused and flippant opinion." He took out a small gold snuffbox and placed a pinch of the finely ground tobacco on the back of his left hand. Snuffed it up his long nose adroitly. Cleared his throat. "However, I do not think that we can altogether ignore a certain divine implication of the potato famine and the epidemics that are killing off hundreds of thousands every year."

"Close to a million so far and no end in sight," O'Connell put it.

"Yes, to be sure. What I think is that the Irish problem over the years has multiplied beyond the power of man. Is it not logical to deduce that the cure for the problem is being applied by the direct stroke of Providence?"

There was a stunned silence, broken by Lord Clarendon. "That is undoubtedly the most inhuman attitude I have ever heard expressed with regard to the Irish problem. Sir Charles, I don't think there is another legislature in all of Europe that would disregard such suffering as now exists in west Ireland or coldly persist in this policy of systematic extermination."

"Tommyrot, Clarendon!" snapped a stout, irritable man with a bald head. His accent was Oxford. "We're talking about savages, not human beings. At least, not civilized human beings. No disrespect intended to you gentlemen." He nodded deferentially at the Duke and the Earl. "People of your caste and breeding are as far apart from the peasantry of Ireland as we English are from the abominable Welsh and as the Americans are from the Negroes. Well, there's English blood in your veins. No, I am speaking of savages, fanatics, led into all sorts of disorders by cabalistic priests."

"Sonovabitch!" Before Ravena realized what he was going to do, Brian threw open the door and strode into the room.

The assembly within the room gave him full attention.

"What did you say, young man?" Sir Charles asked coldly.

The Earl of Tyrone confronted his son with the desperation and frustration that was afflicting him more and more as Brian grew older.

"What is the meaning of this, Brian? How dare you intrude on this conference?"

Brian smacked a fist into his other palm. "How dare *you* let this fat English pig talk to you as if you were a lackey? *You* an O'Neil. Old Red Hugh O'Neil must be spinning in his grave if he's ken to this conversation!"

The Earl's handsome face was drained of color. Chalk white he was. He hit his son with a powerful, sweeping, open-handed blow that sent the boy flying to the floor. He lay there stunned, braced on one elbow. A thin scarlet trickle oozed forth from a corner of his mouth.

The Earl stood over him and spoke quietly. "That was for the disrespect you have shown to Lord Clarendon and all of the other gentlemen in this room by your unforgivable intrusion. You are a stupid, immature, romantic child." With contempt. "Red O'Neil, indeed. Our family have been British subjects for generations and loyal followers of the Anglican Church. Now on your feet and apologize to Sir Charles."

It was on his tongue to say: *"Go to hell!"*

But the last time he had cursed at his father, he had been flogged so sorely that he couldn't ride for weeks, a worse punishment than the flogging. Brian O'Neil had been born to the saddle. More than the saddle, he was part of the horse. Big Red was his favorite, a black Arabian with a white star on his forehead.

Together they had ridden over most of Ireland. Over Kerry's emerald hills. Along the towering limestone cliffs of Moher overlooking the tumultuous Atlantic. Through the fertile valleys of the Shannon and Lee and waist-high in wheat over the fields of Leinster and Kilhenny to the outskirts of Dublin. The country had everything that is required for a paradise.

Never too cold and never too hot. Almost no snow. Even in the August doldrums, the late afternoon wind had an edge to it. But winter was the season that appealed most of all to Brian's dark mysticism. Riding Big Red along the desolate beach with the raw wind off the Atlantic numbing his face, watching, listening, to the angry winter waves pound the shore. Once he had been caught in a quick winter squall with mighty winds that bent ancient trees until their crowns scrubbed the ground. He was entranced by the sense of isolation that winter gave to him.

"On your feet!"

He got up a little unsteadily, touching a hand to his sore mouth.

"Your apology. First to Sir Charles and then to the other gentlemen, including myself."

There was no other way. Brian could tell it by the expression on his father's face. If he refused, he'd be flogged worse than before, and he might even lose Big Red. The Earl had made veiled threats in that direction when he failed the tactical course the year before. Now his grades were in the upper half of the class.

Swallowing, he wet his lips with his tongue. "Sir—Sir Charles, I regret having lost my temper and my manners and calling you what I did." He looked around the room. "Gentlemen, I apologize for barging in on this meeting."

There were more than a few muted expressions of amusement.

"And, sir—" He snapped to attention. "I apologize to you—" he hesitated as his mouth twisted wryly, "for being such a misbehaved and ungrateful son."

Father's and son's eyes met challengingly. The Earl shook his head wearily. "You may leave now."

Sir Charles looked after Brian with a faint, speculative smile. "Well, well, Earl, he does have a temper, doesn't he?"

"A hellion," the Earl admitted. "I've been thinking of sending him to another military academy back In England. The discipline here is not all that it should be."

"I don't wonder." Sir Charles' smirk said the rest. What could you expect from any institution that was rooted in Irish soil? The taint rubbed off on everything. Even an Englishman's son born and brought up in this accursed country. It was just that. Cursed.

An Englishman. . . .

"I've been told your wife is a de Moleyns, my lord?" There was mockery in his tone.

The Earl stiffened defensively. "That is true, Sir Charles."

"Her family is prominent in merchandising—Dublin, isn't it?"

"They are."

"Charming woman, your wife."

"Thank you, Sir George."

A case of subtle affront. The Earl knew it and so did everyone else in the room. Theresa de Moleyns' paternal grandparents had changed their name from Mullins to de Moleyns and renounced Catholicism for the Anglican Church. It was a passport to prosperity and acceptance in Irish high society, which was dominated by English land-lords, English administrators and the Protestant Irish nobility, of which the Earl of Tyrone was a prominent member.

"True loyal patriots, the de Moleyns?" Sir Charles' smile was sardonic. It was more of a question than a statement. A mild reproof. An unspoken warning.

Ravena ran after Brian as he stormed down the hall. "You foolish boy! To say what you did! It's a wonder your father didn't have you beheaded."

Even with all his distress, it struck him funny. "Be-headed? You belong in Bedlam."

"What's Bedlam?"

"A lunatic asylum."

"You're bleeding. Does it hurt?"

"You're bloody damned right it hurts."

"Why do you curse so much?"

"Why do you talk so much? Look, go back to Roger where you belong."

She stopped dead, her pretty mouth pouting, her eyes filling, for some reason she could not explain.

Ten steps further on, he stopped. Looked back at her. "What the devil is wrong with you? Gor, you're not going to cry, are you?"

"I never cry. Except when my dog died."

He nodded, and his voice was softer. "I can understand that. I think I would cry if Big Red ever died."

"Who on earth is Big Red?"

"My horse."

She brightened. "I love horses as well. Can I ride Big Red sometime?"

"Well—possibly. If he takes to you. He's a very choosy animal."

"We'll get along fine."

He stared at her thoughtfully for a time. Then he favored her with a sheepish smile. "I'm sorry I doubted you about Dan O'Connell being your cousin. He's a great man, he is. Up there with Wolfe Tone."

"Who is Wolfe Tone?"

"He led the uprising against the English back in 1798. The United Irish Rebellion. Almost pulled it off too. And he was a Protestant, what do you think of that? All Irishmen all want the same thing whether they're Catholic or Protestant. Freedom."

"We're Protestant, too."

"So am I."

Ravena hesitated. "Still, my father doesn't always agree with the English."

"Nor mine." He came back and put his hands on her shoulders. "You know, child, if you're kin of Dan O'Connell, it makes up for the Spanish blood in your veins."

Ravena pressed her lips together in a thin, grim line. "Why is it you can never say something nice without spoiling it right after with a cruel word?"

"I'm joking. I suppose the Spanish don't have the same sense of humor as the Irish."

"And you're a liar. You're English, not Irish. Your brother Roger says so. He hates the Irish."

He looked very grave, all the fun gone out of him. "Poor Roger. He *is* English, you're right. But I'm not."

"You're his brother, his twin."

"Roger is just a reflection, like when I look at myself in the mirror. It takes more than an image to be a brother. Or an Irishman."

"Well said, my boy." Old Dan O'Connell came up behind them. He put an arm around each of their shoulders.

"Young man, there's something I have to return to you."

Brian's eyes widened. "To me? What can that be, sir?"

"The apology you tendered to us. I want no part of it. You spoke the truth and in my humble opinion, you are a very courageous lad. Don't you think so, Ravena?"

She glanced from O'Connell to Brian, then let her gaze fall away.

O'Connell bent and kissed the top of her head. "Well, I must be on my way, it's getting late. Tomorrow I leave for England. I'm giving a speech in Parliament next week."

Brian's eyes lit up with fever. "Give 'em bloody hell, sir!"

The great man sighed and shook his head. His voice was humble. "No, son, it's not the right time for fire and brimstone. Too many lives depend on our getting help from England. There are some Englishmen who are good men and true. Lord Clarendon, and there are others in influence. Did you ever hear of Gladstone?"

"No. What will you say to them?"

"I'm going down on my knees and beg them to reconsider. And if I have to I'll get down on my knees in the Church of England and pray to God to sway their thick heads."

He cupped his hands in front of him and shut his eyes. He recited: "Ireland is in your hands, in your power. If you do not save her, she can't save herself. And I solemnly call on you to recollect that I predict with the sincerest conviction that one-quarter of her population will perish unless you come to her relief."

Ravena turned and fled down the hall, her eyes overflowing with tears now, and she could not bear that Brian O'Neil would be witness to her softness.

CHAPTER TWO

Daniel O'Connell's prophecy was vindicated with a vengeance over the next five years. The Poor Act at best was a stop-gap measure. The Duke and the Earl toiled hard, setting up soup kitchens and relief stations where poverty and famine were taking their biggest toll: Galway, Ulster, Tyrone.

"The poor beggars never lose their sense of humor," Edward Wilding told his wife and Ravena one day. "They've commenced to rename streets after the kind of feed we give out in different areas. Mead Road. Soup Park. Stirabout—that's *stew*—Lane. Porridge Way. That's the Irish for you."

When she repeated the anecdote to Brian and Roger while visiting the Tyrone estate the following weekend, Brian sneered.

"Your father thinks it's admirable to take one's misfortune so lightly. Well, it's not Irish to beg for English scraps like dogs at the dinner table. What your father and mine should be doing instead of playing God is to mobilize the poor beggars. Give 'em guns instead of porridge. We've got the wealth. Give 'em the wherewithal to kick all the fat English asses out of Ireland."

Roger was outraged. "You're a traitor to the Crown. If you weren't my brother, I'd report you to the Commandant at the Academy. You ought to be in chains. But being your brother won't stop me from thrashing you for using profanity in front of a lady. I've had about enough of your piggishness."

He stung Brian with a left jab, and easily ducked the other boy's roundhouse right. Roger O'Neil was the most skillful boxer in his form. The art of fisticuffs was not Brian's style. He was the free-for-all gutter brawler, no holds barred. Teeth, knees, feet, all were acceptable weapons.

He kept charging in at Roger, who danced around him like a matador taunting a bull, spearing him time and time again with his rapierlike left jab until Brian's nose was bleeding and one eye partially closed.

"You are like a bloody Irishman," Roger chided. "Strong back and a weak mind. Clumsy oafs, all of you, no style at all."

He caught Brian rushing in with an uppercut and crossed his right to the temple. Brian went down flat on his back.

Roger stood over him. "Well, have you had enough?"

Quick as a cat, Brian grabbed him by an ankle and kicked at his groin. Roger saw it coming and turned, catching the blow on his hip. But the force was sufficient to knock him down. Brian flung himself on top of his brother, and the two of them rolled over and over, kicking and punching, grunting and cursing.

Ravena kept jumping around them, shouting. "Stop it! The two of you! If you don't stop it, I'll never speak to either one of you again."

Oblivious to her cries and her threats, the brothers kept whaling away at each other. Both were bleeding from the nose and mouth now.

Gradually the tide began to swing in Brian's favor, and, at last, Roger lay exhausted on his back with Brian straddling him.

As Brian cocked his right to administer the *coup de grace*, Ravena grabbed his arm from behind.

"Stop it! Do you want to kill him?"

Brian thought about it, then dropped his fist. "Might not be a bad idea. One less Orangeman we'd have to worry about." He rolled off Roger and sat there grinning at him.

Roger leaped to his feet and brushed himself off, unleashing a tirade at his conqueror. "You filthy, cheating bastard! You don't know the meaning of fair play."

The smile vanished from Brian's face. "And I suppose you and your precious English practice fair play? Like the fair play the Limey judge bestowed on poor Bob

Kilrain last week for stealing that slimy rent-racker's watch? He sentenced him to hang."

"The dirty thief deserved it. The Irish are a nation of thieves and liars."

"Only in order to stay alive. The British have forced them into a corner. Trapped rats fight to survive, and they've been known to kill a bulldog when they're desperate enough." He grinned. "Do you grasp my meaning, brother?"

Ravena was incredulous. "Are you serious? They wouldn't hang a man for stealing a watch."

"They would and they did." Bitterness seasoned his voice. "The English, they have their own brand of humor too. When he passed sentence, the Limey judge said to Kilrain: 'You made a grab at time, egad, but you caught eternity.'"

Later that afternoon, before she left to go home, Brian whispered something into Ravena's ear. She frowned. "I don't know what you're talking about, and I don't want to know."

But that night she asked her mother casually, "Mama, what's a 'fuck'?"

The Duchess' knitting fell to the floor. But she rallied her composure. Vanessa O'Connell Wilding was a woman of breeding, but under the *grande dame* exterior, the fiery O'Connell passions burned bright and strong. She was an earthy woman, a quality her husband had discovered in the intimacy of their bed.

"Wherever did you hear that word?"

"From Brian O'Neil."

The Duchess closed her eyes. "I might have known. Your father is right. That boy is the devil incarnate. It's hard to believe they're brothers. Roger is such a fine gentleman. Ravena, I don't want you to play with Brian O'Neil any more." She put an arm about her daughter's shoulders. "About that word—I think it's time you and I had a mother-to-daughter talk."

Ravena was not shocked by the so-called "facts of life." It was a relief to have the details defined. For some time she had been aware that there were physical differences between boys and girls that were instrumental in the attraction between the sexes.

It shed light on certain experiences that had happened to her in the horseplay between herself and Brian and Roger. Hide-and-seek in the gardens or wrestling in the barn loft. Touching. It was different touching and being touched by a boy than it was with another girl. Hands brushing her budding breasts and her legs, a pleasant sensation. Brian on top of her from behind, grinding his hips against her behind with a rhythmic thrust. Making funny sounds and with his face contorted. She hadn't minded that either. Now in light of what her mother had informed her, the episode took on added significance and excitement. Yes, thinking about it, *knowing* now what Brian had been doing, she *was* excited.

But only briefly. Then she hugged herself and shuddered, rubbing the goosebumps along her forearms.

"How disgusting," she said aloud, as if to exorcise her own thoughts. "Roger's right. Brian is a beastly animal. Ugh!"

And famine and disease continued to run rampant. By the year 1852 more than a million Irish men and women and children had died while another three million were out of work, almost half the population.

That same year two million tons of wheat was shipped out of Ireland to England.

The spalpeens, migrant workers, roamed the length and breadth of Great Britain eking out meager livings so that they could bring home food for their starving families.

It was at midcentury that the mass exodus from Ireland to America was at its peak. The Irish Chautale Relief Fund had branches in Boston, Philadelphia, New York, Baltimore, St. Louis and Dubuque. Some landlords decided it was cheaper to finance tenants with the $17.50 passage money than to feed them.

Reading an account of a voyage on one of the overcrowded vessels, the Duke had to push aside his breakfast.

"Ghastly! Quite ghastly! 'Coffin ships,' that's what the *Nation* calls them," he said to the Duchess. "There's barely a square foot of empty space on the entire ship. The passengers are crowded together like cattle, wallowing in their own vomit and excrement. Five weeks of misery and starvation rations. Mind you, the water gets so polluted they have to disinfect it with gunpowder."

"I'm frightened, Edward," the Duchess said. "How long can things continue in this fashion before something gives way?"

"It's sitting on a keg of gunpowder, that's how it is. One day the fuse will burn down and the explosion will rock the whole nation, the whole British Isles. The Commonwealth itself."

Ravena, home for the summer from the Kensinggton School for Young Women in England—two "gs" to distinguish it from a second Kensington school of lesser reputation—ate silently, eyes fixed on her plate.

She had learned from Roger what dreadful things had been going on in Ireland during her absence. "There were thirty-eight thousand crimes of violence committed here last year, murder and near murder, larceny. Mostly the work of the traitorous rebel gangs. Whiteboys. Ribbonmen. Carders. Levelers. And the Molly Maguires, they're the worst of all."

"No Irishman expects justice from the English," Brian said bitterly. "The only justice he'll get is what he takes in his own hands. The thieving catchers and rental agents and scalpers, they would have been hung long ago anywhere else but in Ireland."

Brian and Roger were now attending Sandhurst in England, the official British military academy whose purpose was to train career officers for home and foreign service. Roger, as always, was in the top tenth of his class. Brian, true to form, was failing and on probation.

They were no longer a trio, Roger, Brian and Ravena. As he grew older, Brian kept himself more and more aloof from his brother and the young girl, just turned fifteen. A very mature fifteen. She had attained her full height and physical development. Tall, slender, with a lady's carriage and a wench's breasts and backside. Long-legged.

The two families, the Wildings and the O'Neils, assumed, with mutual satisfaction, that Roger and Ravena were a "match."

Ravena was not so certain about Roger. Did she love him? What was love? Did it strike one like a bolt of lightning? From what she had read in the sterile Victorian novels that graced the Wilding library, love was all chaste kisses and holding hands. None of the very intimate and somewhat embarrassing physical relationships that her mother had enlightened her about five years earlier. After the day that Brian O'Neil had asked her whether she was a "good fuck."

How would a girl find out the answer to such a question? Only one way. And the thought of doing "that" frankly terrified Ravena. Still, she was curious, contemplating the day when she finally did find out with pleasant, if nervous, anticipation.

It happened the following year.

On a day in August, Ravena had a date to go riding with Roger. That morning she bathed and perfumed her body with leisurely deliberation. Intuition whispered to her that it was going to be a special day in her life.

She put on her new riding habit. The form-fitting jacket-bodice with small basques forming a postillion in back. Double skirt draped to show the under-petticoat, shorter than the everyday skirt to reveal her riding boots. The matching habit trimmed with saddle-stitching in contrasting colors and with flat braid.

She stood before the mirror ten minutes alone adjusting the high hat.

"I can't seem to get it right," she complained to Rose, who was now Ravena's own lady's maid.

"You look just gorgeous, Miss Ravena. I think it's best tipped slightly forward, now that your hair is done up."

"Give me the scissors. I'm going to cut off the tassels, that's what's wrong."

Rose's eyes flared in alarm. "Miss, what will the Duchess say?"

Ravena winked at her in the mirror. "We'll tell her it's the latest fashion seen at the Tuileries in Paree."

She bade the Duchess good-bye in the dining room. "I told Roger we'd meet at the stables. It will save time. It's a long ride to Lough Derg. We may just stop and have lunch at a country inn."

"Do be careful, dear."

It was a warning omen that struck just the right tone. A sign. Ravena had felt a twinge of expectancy. Restless like a gray mare when the storm was hours off. High-strung. Restless. Impatient. Feeling reckless and invulnerable.

" . . . *be careful.* . . ."

At the paddock, she instructed Shane the groom: "Saddle up Apache." A pony her father had imported from the western United States two years before. Full-grown now, an enormous roan with a mind of his own.

Shane, a flat-featured mick who had once been a club fighter, was dubious. "Miss Ravena, Apache has been off his feed of late. One of his mean streaks. I think you had better—"

"I can handle him. Do as you're told, Shane," she cut him off.

He regarded her with an air of injury. It was not like the young mistress to be sharp with him.

"Yes, Miss."

She saw him riding over the crest to the north, the high crest. A half-mile off. A sea of brilliant emerald, the hills marking it like ocean swells.

She frowned as he rode closer. At one hundred yards she was certain of it. Brian, not Roger! She should have guessed before this. Roger never rode in any other attire than his formal riding habit, tight breeches, boots, crop and high hat. Brian was wearing only the breeches. The rest of it was a motley uniform: his peaked military cap and military boots; ruffled white shirt with the sleeves rolled up to show off his muscular arms.

He grinned as he dismounted. "Surprised to see me?"

"Astonished is the word. Where's Roger?"

"You're not going to believe this, but my dear brother asked me to fill in for him so he wouldn't have to break his date with you."

"You're right. I don't believe you."

"Nevertheless, I speak the truth. You see Roger's the sort who would never turn his back on duty for a frivolous ride in the country. But you know that better than I do." The mocking twist of his mouth. "Dear sister-in-law-to-be."

"Don't make plans for me, Brian," she said sullenly. "I thank you for being so chivalrous as to assume Roger's place, but you're relieved of the responsibility. Roger and I will ride another day when he has no other 'duties.' "

She hadn't intended to put a sarcastic emphasis on the word. It had just slipped out.

Brian laughed. "Don't you care to know what his duty was today?" Precisely the same flavor as her own.

"If you care to tell me."

"He's gone off with a bunch of self-appointed vigilantes after some poor peasant who stole a pig from Squire Bentley's farm. Guns, hangman's rope, the whole rotten show." His lips curled down at the prospect.

Ravena tried not to show her displeasure with Roger. Riding with the hounds to track down a human fox held far more appeal to him than riding with her.

The groom walked over with the roan on its bridle, saddled and ready to go.

"Here he is, Miss Ravena."

Her eyes darted uncertainly from the horse to Brian.

"Come on," he said. "Be a sport. You're dressed for it. So is the horse. God, he's a beauty. I don't think I've seen him before."

"It's the first time Miss will be riding him," Shane said with a meaningful glance at Brian. "He's spooky, this one."

"Good girl, you've got spirit," Brian said to her surprise. "You can tame him if anyone can, my fair lady."

In that instant she experienced an inner burst of warmth and gratitude toward Brian that she had only felt one time before: the night of the Viceroy's ball after she had fled in tears from Brian and Dan O'Connell.

That night after the ball he had discovered her crouching in a corner of the cloakroom, sobbing bitterly.

"Go away and leave me alone," she had wailed, hiding her face in her hands.

"It's all right," he said softly, almost with tenderness. "When Dan O'Connell stands up in Parliament and says what he did tonight, a lot of people will be in tears. For Ireland."

He turned and walked out of the room slowly.

Brian's voice snatched her back to the present. "Well? Do we ride?"

She gave him a quick affirmative smile. "Let's be on our way." Shane made a stirrup with his hands and gave her a boost into the expensive, silver-trimmed English ladies' saddle. She held the reins in her left hand and got a firm grip on the saddle boot with her right. Side by side, they started off at a slow trot.

The first time she had been introduced to his stallion Big Red, Ravena had inquired with mystification. "Why do you call him Big Red when he's coal black with a white star?"

Brian had grinned and patted the horse's neck. "He doesn't object, believe me. His namesake was the noblest of all the Gaelic lairds."

It came to her then. Big Red O'Neil!

"Apache's just about as big and strong as Big Red," Brian observed. "I wonder how he'd do against him in a race."

"Apache would beat him," she said confidently.

"You care to put your money where your pretty mouth is, my dear?"

"Not in this habit. If I had known we were going to race I would have filched a pair of Sean's trousers."

Her brothers Sean and Kevin were at Oxford. Sean was an undergraduate medical student. Kevin, twenty-one, was working on his doctorate. For the past two summers they had traveled abroad, and Ravena had only seen them over the Christmas holidays.

Brian's eyebrows lifted. "Do you ride in trousers?"

"Sometimes when I really want a good gallop I put trousers on under my skirt instead of pantalettes. Then when I'm a safe distance away from the house, I take off the skirt and ride like the wind."

It was a declaration, she realized with some surprise, that she never would have entrusted to Roger. It would have shaken his sense of propriety to the very foundation and devastated his image of her maidenly decorum.

"Blimey, that's rich." He laughed, reading her mind. "I give my word that my lips will be eternally sealed on the subject."

"That would be best. It would upset my mother. Not to mention *your* mother!"

Theresa de Moleyns was a petite, fragile woman with enormous eyes, which were slightly bulging from a thyroid condition, and she always seemed on the verge of hysteria, hypersensitive to the least distraction to her established daily routine. Life was a series of crises, one after the other.

Brian laughed. "Dear Mother's latest obsession is looking under the beds at night for Ribbonmen and Molly Maguires."

"Maybe she has a cause. Those two rowdy gangs have been causing a lot of trouble in the county the past month, my father says."

"Yes." Abruptly he withdrew and stared straight ahead. She studied his profile covertly, moving up and down harmoniously with the horse's body, part of the horse. Roger's dark mirror image. The same sensual, sometimes pouting mouth. The same frown lines around the identical green eyes. "Cut out of the same cloth," the expression went.

But, no, if any two brothers were not of the same material, it was Roger and Brian O'Neil who were not!

He turned his head and asked her suddenly, "Did you know there is no place in Ireland that is more than seventy miles from the sea?"

"It never occurred to me."

"Living here is sort of like being on a desert island. Yes, that's it. Lost on a desert island. Shipwrecked sailors, that's what we are."

"That would never do for me. I get seasick crossing the Channel to England."

"Did you know, your Spanish ancestor's wife took her name from Ireland? Everio, later evolved to Erin and or Eire."

Ravena shook her head and smiled. "No, I didn't. What is this you're giving me, a geography and history lesson?"

"That's a laugh, considering my scholastic abilities. But I am a student of Irish history, it's true."

"Do you know where Dublin got its name?"

"*Dubn lin*—dark pool. A fitting name it is these black days. Two hundred years under English slavery and one year more."

"Cromwell?" she asked.

"I see you know your history too. I knew at heart you were an Irish lass."

"It's part of English history as well."

"A bloody black part. He landed at Drogheda and massacred every man, woman and child in the garrison. Then the bastard knelt and praised God."

"From the way things worked out, it would seem that God is on the side of the English."

"Oh, there is no God."

And again he withdrew into brooding silence.

They arrived at Lough Derg a little after noon. A quiet lake with a surface like a tarnished silver platter, nary a ripple.

"It looks deep," Ravena said. "I'd be afraid to swim in it."

"They say it goes all the way down to purgatory."

They stopped at an inn close by the lake and left the horses with the stableboy. The innkeeper's wife was a jolly stout woman with a brogue so thick Ravena could barely understand her. She was overjoyed to see Brian, clamping his face between her pudgy hands and kissing him lustily on the nose and lips.

"Bri'n me biy, o' 's gud t' see yer. . . ." She inquired after the health of Roger and the Earl and his lady. Then, appraising Ravena boldly, she lapsed into Gaelic. Ravena was surprised when Brian answered her in kind and with an ease that matched her own command of the ancient language.

They both laughed and Mrs. Deaver slapped Brian playfully on the cheek.

"Ye got a gud biy, Miss," she told Ravena.

"What is she talking about, Brian?"

"I told her we were betrothed, and she said we could use the little attic bedroom where it's quiet and we wouldn't be disturbed."

Ravena frowned. "I don't find you as amusing as Mrs. Deaver. And just when I was getting to think we might be friends."

"I want us to be friends, Ravena." His deep green eyes reminded her of the lake.

"You haven't acted as if you even like me since first we met. You're cruel."

"You don't know me well at all," he said. It stung him, she could tell.

"I suppose not. You don't know me either. That's why we always end up fighting."

He put a hand on her arm. "I know you better than Roger does."

"You don't."

"I do, you'll see. Now let's be on our way. Mary, can you fix us up with a picnic lunch and a jug of ale?"

They took their lunch down to the lake. Ravena sat in the prow of the longboat while Brian manned the oars. He rowed out to a small island in the center of the *lough*.

"It was out here that St. Patrick had his vision of purgatory."

"In a boat?"

"No, you'll see."

He beached the boat and helped Ravena out onto the shore. She did not object when he continued to hold her hand as he led her inland to a small stone chapel standing in a clearing. There was a hill on one side of the chapel. Brian pointed to a slab of mortar that seemed to be imbedded in the hillside.

"There was a cave, still is, I guess, behind the mortar. St. Patrick had his vision here, and warned that any who entered the cave would follow it to purgatory. In the twelfth century a band of bold knights explored its depths and were never seen again. When he heard about it, Pope Alex VI ordered the cave to be filled in on St. Patrick's Day."

Ravena sniffed. "I don't believe a word of it. You're making it up."

He placed a hand on his heart. "So help me God, it's the gospel truth."

They ate the picnic lunch the innkeeper's wife had prepared for them and drank the ale from a stone jug.

"I never liked spirits," she admitted, "but this tastes like nectar."

"Sure, because we're in the great outdoors, hungry and thirsty after our long ride. Hard work and exercise sharpen the senses."

After lunch they rowed back to the mainland and bade good-bye to Mrs. Deaver.

"You tell Robert I'll be up here again next Saturday night, about that business we discussed."

Ravena caught the look that passed between them, and it puzzled her.

When they were on their way, she asked him about it. "You two are as thick as thieves, aren't you?"

The blind shot hit its mark; he regarded her warily. "What do you mean by that?"

"What business could Brian O'Neil have with an inn-keeper and his wife?"

He looked at her intently. "You said it, love. We're thieves."

She threw back her head and laughed. "I wouldn't put it past you. Wherever did you learn to speak Gaelic?"

"As a lad I used to hang around a good deal with Quigley the caretaker. It was easier for me to learn Gaelic than to understand his English. I had a natural bent for it."

A way on he asked her, "Well, do you still think your roan can beat Big Red?"

"I know he can."

"Then prove it."

"You're daft, Brian. I don't have my riding trousers, I told you that."

"What's wrong with your pantalettes? Take off your skirt."

"Don't be improper, Brian. When you talk like that, you're offensive." Two bright spots of color dappled her cheeks, but a part of her responded to the dare.

High-strung, impatient, reckless.

"... *be careful...*"

"I don't want to sound improper. What's all this non-sense about pantalettes being improper? Don't you think I've ever seen ladies' pantalettes before?"

"I'm certain you have, but they weren't the property of ladies."

He laughed. His teeth appeared whiter than Roger's in his tanned face. "Now who's being improper? Ravena, be sensible. You wear less than pantalettes when you go bathing at the beach."

She looked around nervously. "Suppose someone sees me?"

"I know a place not far from here, it's private property. No one ever goes there. There's a wide oxcart trail that runs smooth for more than a mile. What do you say? Or are you really scared that my stallion can whip your Apache?"

"You'll eat those words, O'Neil." She patted the roan's neck. "We'll show them, Apache."

He whooped. "Spoke like a true O'Connell."

She followed him across a knoll and through an arched tunnel of foliage to an immense meadow. Green rolling fields as far as the eye could see. The trail was well defined and broad, as he had claimed.

He dismounted and gave her his hand so that she could get down.

"Now turn around and promise you won't peek."

He lifted a hand solemnly. "My word as an Irish gentleman."

He turned his back, and with trembling fingers Ravena stepped out of her riding skirt and her petticoats. She felt wanton standing there in a boy's presence in her underwear. And terribly excited. She placed her skirt and petticoats behind a bush and remounted, unencumbered, as adroitly as a man.

Her cheeks were flaming. "All right, you can turn around." She stared straight ahead not daring to look at him. But she felt he was watching her.

"Well, don't stand there gaping at me like a ninny. Let's race."

Out of the corner of her eye she saw the blur of motion as he mounted Big Red. She slapped Apache's side and gave him full rein.

"Go, Apache! Go!"

The big roan hurtled forward with Ravena crouched low on its neck and her knees gripping its sides.

The stallion was back three lengths when they passed a tall oak tree at the quarter mile point. Still Brian wore a confident grin. She was quite a rider, though, he had to admit.

At the half-mile distance, the black stallion started to close the distance. Up and over a hummock, they were almost neck and neck now.

Ravena shouted into Apache's ear. "Faster, Pach! You can do it!"

They were approaching a grove of trees, and now Big

Red was out in front. Ravena was oblivious of the saplings flashing past on either side, so intent was she on exhorting her horse to catch up. She looked up at the wrong time. Didn't get more than a glimpse of the low-hanging limb before it struck her. Just enough though to trigger her reflexes. She ducked and it hit her a glancing blow on the right side of the head above the temple.

She blacked out, dimly aware of Brian's voice calling to her.

"Ravena! Oh, God! Let her be all right. Ravena, love, speak to me, please!"

His face materialized above her. Hazy. Her greatest awareness was of his hands touching her. Stroking her head, her face.

Now she was lying across his lap, cradled in his strong arms. Hard muscular biceps. It was very pleasant. Somewhat like when she was a child cuddled in her father's arms. Warm. Safe. Loving.

Loving? What an odd idea. Love was diametrically opposed to what she felt toward Brian O'Neil. Trouble was they looked so much alike, Brian and Roger. It was confusing. If she loved anyone it was Roger. *If?*

"Thank God, you're alive." He hugged her against his breast. "How do you feel?"

"Dizzy," she said in a thin voice and closed her eyes again.

"Sleeping Beauty." There was a thickness in his speech now, as if he was having difficulty formulating the words.

His breath was hot on her face, he smelled of ale. His hands stroking down her arms. Fingers unbuttoning her jacket and shirtwaist. She lay there limp in his embrace, suspended in the serene twilight between unconsciousness and consciousness. She knew what was happening, no mistake about that.

"*. . . be careful. . . .*"

"*Careful, be damned!*" Filled with glorious reckless abandon.

She gasped and stiffened when his hands cupped over her breast. Her bare breast. Sweet sensation she had never known before. Spreading out in concentric circles from the titilated nipple, through her body. His mouth came down on her mouth. His tongue slipping between her slack lips.

She was spinning around in a maelstrom, powerless to resist the powerful current that was carrying her to a forbidden destination.

She could not believe this was happening to her. No, not to her! To one of the heroines in a romantic novel. Ravena Wilding was a detached observer.

His hand slipped inside the waistband of her pantalettes. Stroking down over her quivering belly. Fingers playing and exploring the virgin forest.

And now the pleasure she had experienced when he caressed her breast was dwarfed by the overpowering ecstasy that consumed her as he ministered to her craving. She was awed by her discovery. Lust.

Gently he took one of her hands and guided it to his body. Her fingers closed around *it*. Ravena gasped and her eyes flew open. Wide and round with astonishment and more than a little trepidation.

"Heavens to Betsy! What's happened to you?"

He chuckled. "Don't play coy with me, lass. A girl your age surely knows that boys are built different than girls."

"I do indeed. After all, I have two brothers. But *this*! You must be a freak. My God! How do you walk around with it? Doesn't it get in the way?"

He threw back his head, laughing. Squeezed her until she lost her breath. "You little minx. Silly, it's not like this most of the time. Only when I'm close to you."

"Only me? Am I the only girl in the world who inspires this strange phenomenon?"

"You're a sly one, Ravena. Cannier than an English barrister."

She rather enjoyed touching him.

"Whatever, it's an alarming condition. What's to be done to relieve it?"

"Only one way to cure it." He pulled down her pantalettes. Ravena kicked them loose from her ankles and feet. They were reclining on a soft grassy knoll. Above them the sky bright blue and cloudless. The emerald hills all around them. Ravena had a sense of freedom and exhilaration such as she had never known before in her sixteen years of life.

The fact that she was about to lose her chastity didn't bother her the least. It seemed the most natural thing in the world when Brian slipped between her spread thighs and entered her ever so gently.

The first discomfort and pain was fast overshadowed by the tidal wave of passion cresting within her. She was engulfed.

She moaned and writhed beneath him, surging up to meet his thrusts with an eagerness matching his own. Emotion built and built. One peak surpassing the other. Until she could go no higher. Racing heart, ready to explode through the wall of her chest. Lungs paralyzed. All body functions deferring to the avarice of the flesh.

"My God!"

The spasms were upon her and she careened down a long slide like a leaf caught up in a freshet, tumbling down the mountainside into the sea.

Afterward she lay exhausted in his arms. Enjoying the heat of the sun on her bare limbs. Rejoicing in the blue sky and the sweet-smelling grass. The smell of him and the smell of her.

"You smell of the sea. Me too."

He stroked her hair. "That's as it should be. We are of the sea. Especially we Irish. Dark and brooding like the sea."

"I'm not dark and brooding."

"I'm not either, at this instant."

"You ought to be ashamed of yourself, Brian O'Neil. Taking advantage of me because I was helpless after that blow on the head."

He grinned. "It seemed to me that you were expending more effort a wee bit ago than you do riding Apache. For a time there I thought you were going to unsaddle me."

"You're disgusting."

"Yes, and uncouth, a bully and rowdy."

"Much more." Suddenly her eyes narrowed catlike and she inquired of him cryptically.

"Well, do you have the answer to your question?"

He looked at her dumbly. "What question would that be?"

"The question you asked of me the summer I turned eleven. The day you and Roger had the brawl."

He shook his head. "You have me, luv. I give up. I don't—" He paused as a light flash illuminated a certain corner of his mind. A grin spread over his face. "Aha, *that* day. Yes, indeed, I do remember after all."

"And the answer?"

"Darling, Ravena. . . ." There was gentle humility in his voice. "You have exceeded my most lofty expectations." He held up her hand and kissed the fingers, one by one, and then he kissed the palm.

She had never seen him look so serious before. "Brian, what's wrong?"

The question surprised him. "I must be going soft in the head," he said to himself more than to Ravena.

And now he was again the old Brian she knew. Arrogant, swaggering, impudent.

"Sure and begorra, you're a lusty wench, Ravena Wilding, and I'd like to dally with you some more, but it's getting late, and I don't want your father comin' aft' me wit' 'is sho'gun."

Ravena laughed. "You sound like Mary Deaver."

"She was a fine wench in her day too. In some ways you remind me of Mary."

"That fat tub of lard? Brian, if I had a whip I'd thrash you."

Before she knew what he intended, Brian rolled her over in the grass and gave her a resounding slap on her bare bottom.

"Lass, you could use a little more padding in spots yourself. Now, put on your pants and let's go home."

CHAPTER THREE

It was that day that Brian O'Neil made a solemn vow. It would be *he* that married Ravena Wilding, not his milksop brother Roger.

But as the poet wrote: *"The best-laid plans o' mice and men gang aft a-gley."*

Brian for more than a year now had been active in the underground revolutionary movement. He was introduced to the Young Ireland Party by a pub crony, one John Blake Dillon. The young militants, most of them from peasant stock, had been slow to accept the scion of an English peer in their midst. Out of ten men screened for membership, four were rejected as security risks. When men were tortured by the sight of their starving children, only the strongest could be expected to put honor and love of country above the mortal passion for survival. A man's own brother might be a potential informer.

Brian's chapter met weekly at Deaver's Inn in Donegal to plan next week's business and evaluate what had been accomplished the week before.

In all of the revolutionary "gangs," as the British scornfully referred to them, there was a disciplined military hierarchy.

Proper names were never used, a man's sobriquet dictated by some identifiable trademark as it were. Dillon was Lieutenant Long Nose. John Bates, Captain Ape—a hirsute man if there ever was one. Brian was Corporal Red Horse, because of his devotion to his stallion, Big Red. Deaver, the group's leader, was Major Ale. His enormous belly testimony to the prodigious quantities of the beverage he consumed.

Business that week had been good.

"We got Joe Kelly's widow two ration cards for her wee

ones. The Fitzpatricks and the Owenses didn't report the death of their babies."

Major Ale beamed at the cash and coins piled in the middle of the table in a secret cellar room. "A good take, that's for sure. Two rental agents sapped on their way back from collections. The English church in Cork, now that was a neat trick, Privates O'Brien and Mitchell. Mitchell broke into the cashbox while the priest was givin' religious instruction to O'Brien. Good work, biys."

He looked at Brian. "Corporal Red Horse here, he brung us two pistols and an English military rifle."

Brian was uncomfortably aware that all eyes in the room were turned on him, as if by prearranged signal. Deaver cleared his throat.

"Which brings us to another matter concerning yerself, Corporal Red Horse. That young lady you brung here last Monday. . . ."

"Ravena Wilding. Mary and she took to each other right off."

"Did they now?" Deaver regarded him quizzically as he puffed on his corncob pipe. "She also happens to be the daughter of the Duke of Ulster."

In his nervousness, Brian said a poor thing. "The Duke is a good man. I'd trust him as well as I trust my own father."

He winced at the laughter his statement evoked.

"That's the point, me biy. None of us would trust yer father, the Earl of Tyrone, as far as we could throw Nellie the cow."

Brian held fast to his temper, but his resentment was plain. "That isn't fair, Major. My father is highly sympathetic to the cause of Ireland. And so is the Duke of Ulster."

Deaver's eyebrow lifted. "Is that so? Then how is it that they don't give back the thousands of acres of Irish land belonging rightfully to their poor tenants?"

"It isn't that simple, Major, you know that as well as I do."

"Aye. No matter. Our purpose is not to debate the qualities of yer father or the Duke, or the lack of them. Yer one of us, Corporal, and ye have amply proven that our trust in ye is justified. Nevertheless, knowin' at me age the ways of a man and a maid much better than ye do, I must request that ye do not bring the lass here any more. And I would prefer it if ye do not see her yerself. She's a danger, ye see. No tellin' what she might wheedle out of ye for her favors."

Brian's face flamed and he leaped to his feet, fists clenched. "Nobody's telling me who I can see or can't see. That's the kind of British authoritarianism we're fighting to overthrow."

"Aye, lad . . . and in battle it's often a necessity to fight fire with fire."

"The hell with the platitudes. I love Ravena Wilding, and that's that!"

He could feel the rising hostility in the room directed at him. The whole procedure had shaken him badly. Deaver's heavy brogue was not natural like his wife's. He affected it in moments of crisis, say taking a fellow member such as himself to task for breaking the unwritten laws of the organization; a calculated light touch to take the edge off the chastisement.

Behind the pale watery blue eyes that outwardly were so harmless, Brian could see a hard determination that would brook no appeal of the major's premeditated verdict.

"Yer fully aware, Corporal Red Horse, that no one resigns from this army?"

Brian licked dry lips. "I realize that, sir."

"It would be most painful if we—" He did not finish the statement. He didn't have to. Brian could already feel the roughness of the hemp about his throat.

He jerked his head down and stared at the dirt floor. Resigned to accepting the major's decision.

"I won't see her again," he said quietly. "Not privately anyway. There will be times when I have no choice. Our families are close friends. We will be encountering each other socially."

"That is understood and acceptable to us," Deaver said, letting lapse the exaggerated brogue.

In the months and years that followed, Ravena was mystified by the change in Brian after the day they had spent together. She would cherish the memory as she cherished the precious jewels her mother had presented to her on the night of the Viceroy's grand ball, the night she had first met the twin brothers.

Every time she thought of the day and what they had done together, what they had meant to each other, tears would prickle at the backs of her eyelids. She would not permit herself to dignify his disregard for her by crying.

"Damn you, Brian! Damn you to hell!"

Eventually she came to mean it. Damn the arrogant blackguard! She would hate him with a vengeance to her dying day. All it had meant to him, that day, all that she meant to him, was another roll in the hay with an anonymous female. Ravena would have liked to feel dirty and defiled for becoming intimate with a wastrel such as Brian O'Neil, but she was incapable of lying to herself. It had been an exquisite experience, a once-in-a-lifetime experience.

A thought struck her. Was it possible to recapture the thrill, after all? Roger was Brian's brother, physically indistinguishable but for the color of their hair, identical in appearance and in all the body details of physique. She warmed to the idea of her naked body held tight against a man's hard nakedness. She was a woman, a warm and passionate woman. And Brian was not the only man in Ireland who could satisfy her desires and fulfill her. She supposed that they all performed alike sexually.

What was it she had overheard her brother Kevin say to Sean when they were discussing a certain morally loose girl from town?

"All cats are black in the dark."

Major Ale's gang represented the moderate militant point of view. It did not encourage among its members violence for violence's sake alone. True, many a rent agent, catcher, unwary dragoon or policeman took a bash from behind with a sap, but to date they had never committed murder.

In March of 1853 a raiding party infiltrated the estate of Sir Robert Dillon with the purpose of stealing Lady Dillon's valuables. Her maid Bridget was betrothed to one Bobby O'Malley, otherwise known as Sergeant Big Dick, an accurate assessment that made him the butt of a good many friendly jibes.

According to Bridget, My Lord and Lady played whist

with their neighbors, Lord and Lady George, every Friday night at the Georges' manor house. The same night that the caretaker bedded down with the kitchen maid and the footman played darts at the local pub.

"Bridget says the coast will be clear from eight P.M. until midnight. The jewels are in a wall safe in the study, but the old boy has been complaining that it was installed too loose. We can pull the bloody thing out and carry it away. We lug it back here and put an ax to it. Shouldn't be any real problem."

The real problem was that a squad of policemen lay in ambush for them, tipped off by Bridget's best friend who had once gone with Bobby O'Malley and was bitter over losing him to Bridget.

Six members of the gang were met by ten policemen when they entered the study.

"Put up your hands. You're under arrest," the police captain commanded.

They had rehearsed for this contingency. To be arrested meant the hangman's rope or a slow death in a dark lice- and rat-infested dungeon cell in the royal palace gaol.

"It's better to go down fighting," Major Ale pronounced, and no man disagreed with him.

Defying the pistols covering them, the marauders tackled the policemen, diving in low beneath the line of fire. Tom Quick took a slug in the face and was killed instantly. Another shot grazed Major Ale's head, stunning him. Brian, O'Malley, O'Toole and Mitchell downed their men and the other lawmen had to hold their fire for fear of hitting their own men.

It was a wild donneybrook with all of them rolling around on the floor, punching, kicking, biting and cursing. Ten against four, but the gangmen held their own.

Brian flattened two policemen, one with his fists and another with a poker he grabbed off the hearth.

Major Ale was up again, and he hurled a cop straight through the closed French doors. But before he could come around, another cop broke a Louis XIV chair over his noggin and he went down like a felled ox.

And when O'Toole was flattened, the remaining three decided that discretion was the better part of valor. It was a strict organization edict. If a raiding party ran into trouble, a man's first responsibility was to survive. You didn't stop to collect the wounded. Warm, functional bodies were too precious to the movement.

Leaving through the hole in the French doors that Major Ale had made with the policeman's person, Brian, O'Malley and Mitchell escaped.

The law seemed to have had enough and gave only brief chase. "We'll get them, make no mistake about it." The captain indicated Deaver and O'Toole lying unconscious on the floor. "When we're through interrogating these two, we'll have the name of every man in the gang."

Torture, until death if necessary, was standard procedure in the war against the militants. No quarter shown on either side.

The Molly Maguires, a particularly violent group, had once dismembered an English spy in their midst, finger by finger, then toe by toe, lopped off his hands and feet, put out his eyes with a hot poker and cut off his genitals.

The law of atrocity prevailed.

Major Ale was taken back to his inn and his wife and two children were dragged out of bed and locked in the barn. Police were posted at the four sides of the barn with flaming torches.

"All right, Deaver, what will it be?" the captain demanded. "Do we get the names or do we roast your family to death?"

The big man would have endured physical torture to his person without uttering a word, even if it finally killed him. But faced with threats made against his dear ones, he was lost. He gave them the names they wanted, and that night he hanged himself in his cell, not able to live with the knowledge of his treachery.

The next morning a squad of dragoons accompanied the police chief to Tyrone Castle. The dragoons were elegant and intimidating in their scarlet tunics and plumed helmets with the wicked-looking swords scabbarded at their sides.

Their lieutenant deployed them front and back and on the sides of the mansion. "Watch sharp. He may try to escape."

Then he and the captain went up the steps to the front entrance. They were admitted by Tatum, the liveried butler, and escorted into the parlor where the Earl and his wife were having their morning tea.

The two officers bowed from the waist. The captain of police addressed them.

"My lord—Lady O'Neil, I apologize for the intrusion."

The Earl stood up. "Perfectly all right, Chief Evans. It is always an honor to greet officers of the Crown in our home. Won't you sit down?"

The chief could not meet the Earl's curious gaze. "I think not, my Lord. The fact is Lieutenant Monoghan and I are here on official business." He paused. "And it's not very pleasant business, I'm afraid."

Her ladyship looked alarmed. "Oh my goodness, is it Leckie our groom again? He promised us faithfully that he would not get into any more drunken brawls."

"No, madam, I only wish it were something like that." He tugged nervously at his mustache. "It pains me to tell you this, but—but it's about your son."

He recounted the burglary attempt at the home of Sir Robert Dillon the previous evening.

"Three of the villains got away. We captured two of them last night, but out of deference to your position, we held back on serving the third warrant until this morning. I'm afraid we're here to arrest your son." He brought forth the warrant. "Brian Hugh O'Neil."

"That's preposterous!" the Earl scoffed. "My son mixed up with a rebel gang of thieves? You've been duped, Chief Evans. It's a scoundrel's lie fabricated to cast dishonor on my position and on the reputation of my son. This is an outrage!"

Lady O'Neil slumped in her chair, unable to speak.

"No, my lord, we have indisputable proof. Four signed confessions. Your son's henchmen. Is he here?"

"Yes, of course he's here." He pulled the bellcord to summon Tatum. "Tatum, will you please go upstairs and wake Mr. Brian. Tell him I want to see him at once." To Evans and Monoghan: "We'll clear this up in short order, you'll see. There has been a serious mistake, gentlemen. My son a rebel hoodlum. Impossible!"

Her Ladyship covered her eyes with a hand. She *knew*

the truth, even before Tatum came back with the declaration: "Mr. Brian is gone, sir. His bed has not been slept in."

"Good God!" The Earl sat down beside his wife and took her hand. It was icy.

Chief Evans turned to Lieutenant Monoghan. "He's had a good head start."

"Thanks to you, Captain," the dragoon reminded him coldly.

"It was irresponsible, I confess, and my error will be duly noted to my prefect. Still, under the circumstances I believe I can justify my course of action."

"Not to the army you couldn't, Chief Evans." He addressed the Earl. "My lord, I'm afraid I must trouble you for a detailed description of your son Brian."

"We can do even better than that, Lieutenant," Roger spoke from the doorway. He swaggered into the room with a jackal's smile. Slapping his riding breeches with his crop. "So my *dear* brother has finally gone and done it. Well, well, well. My mother can provide you with a tintype of my brother, but better still, take a good look at me. We're twins, and we look identical, except that Brian has black hair."

"Roger!" His mother was stricken.

"I'm sorry, Mama, but it's no secret that Brian and I despise each other." He snapped to attention out of courtesy to the dragoon's rank. "I hope to be commissioned from Sandhurst next year myself, and I intend to apply for a commission in the dragoons."

The lieutenant acknowledged the compliment. "My congratulations to you, sir. We'll be proud to have you serve with us."

"Thank you, Lieutenant." His smile widened. "And good hunting."

"We'll take leave of you, Captain," Monoghan said as they rode out of the gates of Tyrone Castle. "We must alert our garrisons in the south and east. Every port must be patrolled to prevent him from fleeing the country."

The chief, a sallow saturnine man with penetrating eyes, gazed at him thoughtfully. The dragoon was a big man, blond, blue-eyed, pompous. The heavy jaw would turn him into a caricature of an English bulldog in years ahead. He was a prototype. Career man through and through. Unquestioning. Obey orders with bulldog tenacity. Blind to issues. Uncaring.

"What's all the ruckus about one man, Lieutenant? You have thousands of missing fugitives on your lists, don't you?"

"This one is special, Captain. Brian O'Neil is not just another peasant or stonecutter. He's a member of the ruling class. Royalty at that. His family has power, reputation. What kind of image will it convey to the restless masses if a man of his high rank is permitted to roam free carrying his treasonous message to the ignorant and discontented peasants?"

"Yes, I see your point, sir. They might look upon him as the second coming of the Great Emancipator, Red Hugh O'Neil. A symbol to rally about and form a solid united revolutionary phalanx."

"Precisely. Now we must proceed with dispatch to take the fellow into custody."

"In haste. I am on my way back to town, Lieutenant, to summon every available man to duty. Brian O'Neil must be taken."

On his way down Potluck Lane, the police chief veered his mount off on a side path that led into deep wood. A half-mile further on he came to a woodcutter's hut with a straw roof. An ancient hunchback was chopping kindling on a tree stump. He arose, slow as a turtle, when the officer reined in his horse. Evans dismounted.

"Is he here?"

The old man jerked his head at the hut. "Sleeping like a baby."

"Come on." With one hand resting lightly on his holstered pistol, the captain walked to the door and pushed it open.

Brian O'Neil was shocked awake by bright sunlight pouring over him. He gasped and sat up, stunned by the sight of the police officer standing over him, behind him the leering face of the woodcutter.

The hunchback tittered. "There be he, Cap'n."

Outraged, Brian shook a fist at the old man. "You dirty bastard informer. And the Mollys said you was one of them. Trustworthy as a bishop's oath on the Bible!"

The old man was cackling now and the police chief joined in.

"You're a pair of bloody bastards!" Brian roared.

"Take it easy, lad," the police chief said. "You don't ken to what's going on. Paddy *is* with the Molly Maguires."

Brian's mouth flew open in befuddlement. "Bloody well right I don't understand. You *are* the chief of police, I know you are. Timothy Evans."

"Correct." The smug smile was pasted on his face.

"Terrible Timmy, they call you. The scourge of the revolutionary movement."

"Right again."

"Then what the hell is going on?"

"You ever hear of the *Sinn Fein?*"

The Gaelic term struck a chord of recognition. "Yes. Some talk—something about a secret organization."

"Ultra-secret. Underground. When we meet we all wear masks. The only way we can identify a fellow member is by the sign."

"What sign is that?"

The chief laughed. "Now if I was to tell you, it wouldn't be secret, would it now?"

"And *you*—" It boggled Brian's mind. "You the police chief are a member of this *Sinn Fein?*"

"I am. *Sinn Fein.* It means 'ourselves alone.' We work underground, deep underground, and we work slowly and carefully. There's a better route to freedom than banging skulls and playing highwaymen. Oh, I'm not downgrading you young hotbloods. The Mollys, the Whiteboys, the Ribbonmen, all the lot, you've served a purpose, if only in that you fire up the hopes and spirits and the imagination of the people. But the real work that has to be done has to be worked at a much higher level. Infiltrate the government at every level. Like Dan O'Connor. Did you know he's with us? Our way, the *Sinn Fein*, is the soundest way, and like that Frog wrote about the mills of the Gods, they may grind slowly, but they grind exceedingly fine. That's our method. Slow and fine. Thorough and sure. We're the wave of the future, my boy. Someday you'll be with us as well. But right now, the army is out after your blood."

"The hell with the army! I'll stay here and fight with you."

"Someday, I said. But right now you'd only be a bloody liability to us. What you're going to do is to leave the country. One, two years, that's all, until this nasty business blows over."

"And if the bloodhounds are so hot on my tail, how do I presume to leave the country? Sashay into Ulster and buy a ticket to the Continent?"

"No, you'd be nailed right off if you tried to leave Ireland by any of the conventional ways. Tonight another agent will come here with a change of clothing, dye to change the color of your hair. Fire red. That should put them off the scent. He'll have a set of merchant seaman's papers for you as well. You'll ship out on a refugee ship destined for Boston in the United States. Ordinary Seaman John Whittaker."

"I still dislike the idea of running away."

"That's selfish reasoning. There's more at stake than just your own worthless neck, lad. By your actions you have cast your family into the midst of a very ugly and dangerous scandal. The son of the Earl of Tyrone a traitor to the Crown. Your father has enemies who will only be too pleased to seize on his predicament and use it as a weapon against him."

"Aye, I see your point," Brian admitted gloomily. He remembered the night he had met Ravena at the Viceroy's ball, and the two of them had eavesdropped on the gentlemen's conversation in the private room. The inferences that Sir Robert Dillon had put forth about the Earl being descended from the great Irish patriot Red Hugh O'Neil; the veiled barbs directed at his mother's family, de Moleyns née "Mullins."

And Brian O'Neil had been one of those attempting to rob the Dillon house. Treason and grand theft. What a formidable club that could be to wield at his father from the vindictive hands of a man like Sir Robert.

"I'll do as you say," he gave in. "But I'll be back, Captain, you can depend on it."

"I do depend on it. And the *Sinn Fein,* we'll be waiting to welcome you home."

"Home." His eyes filled up. To leave this beloved land,

he never would have believed a thing like this could come to pass.

To leave Ravena, another tragic loss to him. Duty had kept him at a distance from her for the past two years. But she was always in sight. He knew she was there, no more than an hour's ride away from him. Comforted by the thought that one day he would go to her and take her in his arms and tell her, "I love you, Ravena. I always have. I always will, no matter what's happened and what you must think of me for turning away from you after what we discovered that day on the way back from Lough Derg." He rubbed a sleeve across his face.

"It was bad luck one of your boys got killed last night. It couldn't be helped."

"I realize that. What about the others? Deaver, O'Malley, O'Toole—"

"Deaver informed, then he hanged himself. He had no choice. It was that or the lives of his wife and children. Now as for those other two scoundrels, well—" Evans smiled mysteriously. "Who can tell? They just might break out of prison."

Brian held out his hand. "You're a good man, Captain. And a damned courageous one to be doing what you are. The chief of police a bloody traitor, that's a laugh."

"No, a patriot," Evans corrected him. "And there are many more like me, latched onto the Bulldog's hide like ticks and fleas. Eating away at him night and day."

They exchanged a firm handclasp and the police chief rode back to headquarters.

It was after dark when an ox-drawn cart stopped in front of the hut. The driver was a brawny man with a clean-shaven head.

"I'm Sergeant Bald Eagle," he introduced himself. "I take it you be Corporal Red Horse?"

"Aye," Brian said. "At your service, Sergeant."

He got down from the seat and walked to the back of the cart. Threw back a tarpaulin.

"Jesus!" Brian exclaimed at the sight of the dead man, lying face up on the deck, blank eyes reflecting the moonlight. "Who is it?"

The sergeant clapped him on the back and chuckled. "Why, don't you recognize him, Corporal? That's *you!*"

Shortly before noon the following day, Chief Evans and Dragoon Lieutenant Monoghan paid another visit to Tyrone Castle. Ravena Wilding and her mother, the Duchess, were present as luncheon guests of Lord and Lady O'Neil. The officers bowed to the ladies and then to the Earl.

"I regret to inform you that we are the bearers of ill tidings, my lord," Evans said in a doleful voice.

"You have captured my son?" The Earl put an arm around his wife to steady her.

The chief's gaze fell. "There is more than that, unfortunately. Your son Brian is dead. Killed in a battle with the police just before dawn this morning. He resisted arrest. There was no alternative." He shrugged helplessly.

It was heartbreaking to see the naked grief contort the face of the Earl's lady. Theresa de Moleyns O'Neil was a frail, vulnerable woman, unaccustomed to hardship or sordid realities of life on the planet.

She collapsed in hysteria and had to be carried to her room by the butler and maid, accompanied by Ravena and the Duchess.

"You are certain it was Brian?" the Earl asked.

"No doubt about it," said Evans. From his side pocket he removed a ring, a medallion, and various other trinkets and jewelry. The Earl received them glumly.

"Yes. They belong to Brian." He held up a golden medal with a four-leaf clover stamped on one face. "This good-luck piece—he bought it just the other day. Good luck, indeed." He shook his head in disillusionment.

"You will claim the body, of course," Evans said. "However, I would suggest a closed casket burial service. You see, the corpse is hideously disfigured. Burned. Your son set fire to the dwelling where he was hiding out rather than surrender."

"My God!" The Earl sat down heavily and covered his eyes with a hand.

Ravena had left Lady O'Neil with her mother and Ann, the maid, and had hurried downstairs. She stood in the doorway of the parlor, hearing the grim pronouncement of the police chief. Her heart felt like a stone in her chest. Dead. Her face betrayed no emotion.

Roger O'Neil, who was reacting to the news of his brother's grisly death with restrained satisfaction, went over to her and put an arm about her shoulders.

"We must all be brave, my darling," he said piously. "Brian and I may have had our differences, but, after all, he was my brother. It's terrible. Yet, in many ways it was inevitable. I can't count the times I've warned him to mend his ways. His volatile ways, his rebelliousness, they were bound to lead him to a bad end. May God have mercy on his soul."

Ravena closed her eyes and sagged against him.

Brian stood at the bow, a tall, broad-shouldered young merchant seaman wearing a stocking cap and a peacoat. He had flaming red hair and wore a patch over one eye. With his other eye, he watched Eire grow smaller and smaller until it was a nondescript speck on the turbulent sea. He was seized by a strange sensation, as if he had left a part of himself behind, his roots, forever with his motherland and with his beloved Ravena.

The flying scud whipped into his face, and he licked the salt from his lips and wiped a sleeve across his eyes. Then he turned his back on the two of them—his own country and his Ravena.

CHAPTER FOUR

The moment he stepped off the gangway onto the dock in Boston Harbor, Brian could feel the vitality, excitement and power of America. The New World. A fitting and descriptive christening. Like the feeling he had the first time he mounted Big Red. He and the beast were as one, and the strength of the horse flowed into him.

Wolfe Tone and all the other United Irishman had been ardent disciples of the American Revolution, their fire and zeal nourished by the colonies' Declaration of Independence from the British tyranny. But they had been too few in numbers, too close to England, and they had failed. But the matter was not closed yet. Not by a long shot.

Tingling from head to toes, Brian slung his seabag over one shoulder and marched with a purposeful stride in the direction of the Boston Common.

On the way an enormous thirst came over him, and he stopped off at a tavern, the Red Lion. It struck a sentimental note; Major Ale and all the boys, that was their headquarters in Donegal, the Red Lion Inn.

He dropped his bag on the floor and bellied up to the bar, which was crowded with seamen and traveling men at the noon hour.

"A pint of half-and-half," he told the bartender.

"Excuse me, friend," a voice beside him spoke up. "Did you just get off the boat from Ireland?"

Amused, Brian looked at the young man standing beside him at the bar: an apple-cheeked fellow with tight blonde curls and a pleasant face. His suit was dark, trousers, waistcoat and coat all of the same material. He would be a peddler, Brian guessed.

"Is it all that apparent?" he asked.

The man flushed. "I'm sorry, that was badly put. It's

58

just that I couldn't help noticing your seabag and—" He paused.

"And the brogue?" Brian teased. "You've got a bit of it yourself, you know?"

"I do, indeed. Though I've been over here for ten years." He held out his hand. "The name is Casey, Larry Casey."

Brian shook his hand. "And I'm Brian O'Neil. Glad to know you, Larry."

"Welcome to America. You'll bless God you came, I can tell you. It's a wonderful country."

"I don't doubt it, Larry. But tell me, don't you ever miss the Old Sod?"

The cherubic face darkened. "Aye. There are times—but—" He shook his head as if to cast off cobwebs. "Ireland's a slave state. No point in living at all as a slave."

"That's temporary, my boy," Brian said with such determination that Casey's eyes narrowed shrewdly. "You be one of them rebel gangs we've been hearing about?" he asked.

"I am. And that's the only reason I'm here now. I had to get out of Ireland."

"It's proud I am to know you, Brian," Casey said with admiration. "I wish I could be like you. But as my old dad used to say: 'Some of us are born to be fighters and others of us to be lovers.' I guess that's what I am."

Brian laughed. "Nothing wrong with being a lover. I've done my share of that pastime too. When did you leave Ireland? Did you say ten years?"

"Yes, it was in 'fort'-five. Before the worst of it."

"You came over with your parents?"

"No, my sister and I came with my uncle. My father could only raise passage for two of us. He and me mum were going to come the following year, but—" He broke off, and his mouth turned down at the corners. "The next we heard was in '47, from another aunt. They'd died of pneumonia."

"I'm sorry."

"Thank you. And what of your mum and dad? How are they holding up?"

Brian was too embarrassed to tell the truth, that he was the son of the Earl of Tyrone, and had always lived in a grand mansion with a surfeit of food and money, lapping up cream while thousands were perishing for lack of a penny to buy a crust of bread and a bowl of watered-down gruel.

"They're holding up," he said.

Brian and Larry finished their pints and ordered again.

"So you're a lover, my boy?" Brian said. "Anyone special you're loving?"

"Well—" Casey sounded reluctant. "It's a lengthy story and kind of mixed-up."

"Now I am interested. Keep talking. I have all the time in the world."

"When we arrived in America, my uncle settled in New York. He got us a couple of rooms near the docks. You see, he was working as a hand loading and unloading cargo. The poor devil worked like a dog, twelve, fourteen hours a day, and after three years the strain got to him. He had some kind of a spell and fell into a cargo hold, was killed instantly.

"I was only fifteen at the time and my sister was twelve, and we were in some kind of a pickle, I'll tell you. We probably would have ended up in an orphanage, if the old Jew who owned a clothing shop downstairs from where we lived hadn't come to our rescue. Solomon Levitz's his name. He gave me a job cutting cloth for men's coats and trousers and cleaning up the shop at nights. Then when his business expanded these past seven years, he promoted me to a salesman, and I've been traveling up and down the East Coast now for two years. It's a good job."

"It sounds like it. I wish I could get myself some kind of a job like that."

"Maybe you can. Solomon intends to open another shop on Broadway the end of the year, so he says. I'll recommend you to him."

Brian was grateful. "Talk about the luck of the Irish. Imagine me meeting a friend like yourself almost as soon as I walked off the boat. I'm in your gratitude, Larry." He put a hand on Casey's shoulder and squeezed.

"It's nothing at all. We Irish have to stick together." His lip curled wryly. "We 'micks.' "

"Micks?" Brian frowned.

Casey smiled sadly. "That's what they call us, the Irish. We're 'micks' to the native Americans. It's funny too. Some of 'em haven't been over here much longer than I have, yet they consider themselves pure Americans. It's best to overcome the brogue and get your citizenship. Then you'll be accepted in time."

It came as a mild shock to Brian to learn that discrimination was practiced in the land that Wolfe Tone had described as the "true birthplace of democracy," typified by those ringing declarations: "Liberty, Justice, Equality for all."

Well, the brogue would be no problem; he had affected the heavy peasant accent as part of his disguise. If he wanted to play it the safe and easy way, he could use his title—The Hon. Brian Hugh O'Neil, son of the Earl of Tyrone—as a passport into some of the most influential social and political circles in Boston and New York. But Brian preferred the challenge of making his way as a mick fresh off the boat the way Larry Casey and thousands of other poor Irish immigrants were doing.

"I'll do my best," he said. "You have the Irish way of digressing when you tell a story, Larry. You were starting to tell me about this special someone you're loving."

Casey was blushing crimson now. "Yes, she's the daughter of my employer, Solomon Levitz. Her name is Rebecca, and she's the most beautiful girl in the world."

"And you say she's a Jewess?"

"Yes, and I'm Catholic, but religion isn't important to either of us."

"And what about her father?"

"Well, he is a problem. But with patience we'll work around that one." He ordered two cigars from the bartender and gave one to Brian.

Brian grinned as he rolled the cigar around in his fingers. "Say, you are a sport. The old Jew must pay you well."

"To me father it would have been a fortune. Eight dollars a week, plus expenses."

Brian whistled in pretended awe. His own personal allowance back in Ireland had come to roughly five pounds weekly, three times what Casey was paid.

"How are you fixed for money?" he asked Brian.

"We was just paid off when we docked. I'm fine. Here, let's have another one on me?"

"I don't suppose you have lodgings?"

"No, I don't even know where to look."

"You don't have to look. You'll stay with me. I'll have the landlord set up a cot in my room."

Brian looked his new friend straight in the eye. "You know something, Larry Casey? You're too generous for your own good. Sometimes a man can drown in his own generosity. Be careful."

Two days later, Casey's business in Boston completed, the two young Irishmen boarded a train for New York City.

"The biggest and greatest city in the United States," Casey told him with pride, as if he shared in its proprietorship. They walked across town from the rail station in the direction of Solomon Levitz's clothing shop.

Compared to London and Paris, even Dublin, New York struck Brian as being crude and without style. But what it lacked in old-world values and tradition, it made up in character. Teeming with life. Crackling with excitement. Loud, boisterous, boasting.

Brian stepped off a curb and almost was struck by a careening beer wagon.

"Jesus! That was a near one."

Casey laughed. "Got to keep on your toes in New York."

"What's everyone in such a hurry about? People swarming like damned bees in a hive."

"That's it. Busy as bees. Americans are like that. England, Europe has two thousand years' headstart on us. We have to really step to catch up."

"I think America and me are going to get along just fine."

Casey clapped him on the back. "You can depend on it, Brian, me lad."

A notion that was constantly being reinforced in the weeks that followed. Levitz, the clothing merchant, welcomed him like a long-lost relation.

"Welcome to the home of the brave and the land of the free," he greeted Brian, hugging him with both arms. Then he put an arm affectionately around Casey's shoulders. "Any friend of Larry's is a friend of Sol Levitz's. Isn't that right, Becky?" He looked at his daughter.

"That's right, Papa." she said in a thin voice.

Brian had been struck with her gamin beauty when he first set eyes on her, standing in the background, with her hands folded in front of her and her eyes turned demurely downward, not daring to meet his.

Her eyes, enormous, luminous. *Dubn linn*. Dark pools of mystery. Skin as white and downy as apple blossoms. Too thin for his preference, small breasts, and childish buttocks. Hair down to her waist and black as his stallion's mane.

"Yes, sir, this *Irishe goy* is closer to me than my own son, Moishe, who ran off with a dance-hall wench to St. Louis right after my dear Sara passed on." He made a sign in the air with his hands and muttered an incantation in a language that Casey told him later was Yiddish.

"Aye, Solomon, we musn't be bitter," Casey said. "Look how me sister Kerry deserted me." He turned to Brian. "She went off with an undertaker, no less."

"A steady profession," Brian observed.

"I'd ruther starve," said Casey. He crossed to Rebecca and kissed her chastely on the forehead. "Thank the good Lord, I have this angel to take her place."

They conversed in an undertone that Levitz and Brian could not hear.

The merchant studied the two of them in grave silence for a while, affording Brian a chance to study him.

A kind and generous old man, he liked him immediately. What of it that his appearance was strange in Brian's eyes? The long gray beard and the silly little skullcap. The truth was he had never seen an orthodox Jew in his entire life until this day.

Solomon Levitz and his daughter did not resemble or behave even remotely like the caricature Jews depicted in literature and newspapers and described by his father's wealthy friends from Dublin and Ulster.

Shylocks. Blackmailers. Cunning cheats. Blackguards. Christ-killers.

"That boy Larry," he mused. "I wish he was my son. I wish—" And he took his gaze from Casey and Rebecca and shook his head ponderously. "A man cannot have everything he wants in life. Look what happened to poor Job. But enough talk already. It is time for food and drink. We celebrate Larry's safe return from Boston and God's blessing us with our new friend Brian. Becky, the neighborhood gossip, can wait until our bellies are full. That daughter of mine, she's turning into a regular *yenta*."

Whatever on earth is a *yenta*? Brian wondered. But good manners prevented him from asking for a translation.

In the succeeding six years that he lived and worked with Solomon Levitz and his daughter Rebecca, Brian O'Neil would come to know the meaning of *yenta*, *chutzpah*, *goniff*, *goyim*, *shmuck* and countless other Yiddish words and expressions destined to enrich the language of this melting-pot nation, along with their counterparts in Irish, French, Italian, Polish, German and all the other ethnic peoples' contributions to the Anglo-American tongue.

He would fast with the Levitzes at *Yom Kippur* and wear a *yumulku*. Feast with them at the *seder*, on *matzos*, *moror*, *charoses*, *Karpas*, drink the sweet ceremonial wine. The last year Solomon was alive and too weak to read the *Kiddush* and recite the long story of the Israelites' exodus from Egypt, Brian did it for him.

When he had finished the old man was nodding over his wine. He smiled sweetly at Brian and said, "I have never heard it read more beautifully, my son."

Brian squeezed his shoulder and joked. "Aw, Solomon, you didn't hear a word I said. Stop the blarney. You were asleep most of the time."

Solomon shook his shaggy head slowly, a chore for him to move at all, it seemed. "No, I wasn't sleeping. Only dreaming. I saw the angel Eliyahu ha-Navi, the angel of good news."

"And what good news did he bring you, Papa?" Rebecca asked.

"He has come to take me to the Promised Land."

She patted his hand and nodded at Brian and Larry. "I think we ought to put Papa to bed. He's had too much wine."

The next morning they found Solomon Levitz dead in

his bed, a beatific smile on his face. "*Shalom*," Brian said softly and closed the old man's eyes.

In the years he worked and lived with the Levitz family, Brian made no conscious effort to supplant Larry Casey in the affections of Solomon and his daughter. It happened nevertheless. The situation came to a head one evening about one year after Brian settled in New York. Solomon and Becky were visiting neighbors for a few hours after supper. Brian and Larry were playing cards in the three-room flat they now shared above the clothing shop. Solomon and Becky, in their recent prosperity, had purchased the building, and they shared the four-room flat on the floor above.

"Damn!" Larry threw down his hand. "You win again." A terse smile creased his face. "That's nothin' new, of course."

Brian was puzzled. "You won last night."

"So I did. But I was talking over the long haul. You've been outclassing me ever since you barged in here." He went to a cupboard and took out a bottle of Irish whisky. Drank it neat from the bottle.

"Hey, what is it with you tonight?" Brian gathered up the cards and put them into a box. "Come to think of it, you've been behaving strangely for weeks now. Anything wrong, Larry?"

Casey slammed down the bottle on the table and hitched up his suspenders. "Wrong? I'll tell you what's wrong. You're wrong, O'Neil!" He slapped his hands palms down on the table and glared at Brian.

Brian met his gaze level, and sat back in the chair, appraising Casey thoughtfully. "Come on, my friend, let's have it. No more speaking in riddles. It's an Irish affliction, running off at the mouth and saying nothing."

"You bloody son of a bitch! Don't you put on airs with me! Sometimes I wonder about you, O'Neil. Your name may be Irish, but often you make a slip, and you sound more like a bloody Limey! That's a fact."

"Weren't you the one who told me to improve my speech? Rid it of the accent?" Brian replied coolly.

Casey reddened. "Yes. I suppose I did. Still—"

"Get to the point," Brian said sharply.

"All right, I will." He took another swig from the bottle, turned a chair backwards and straddled the seat with his arms folded over the back.

"Brian, I saw it the first day I walked in here with you. The way you looked at Becky."

"It's a crime to look admiringly at a pretty girl? I wouldn't be Irish if I didn't."

"You know what I mean. Ever since you've been making up to her, as well as the old man, talking against me."

"That's a goddamned lie, Casey!" Aroused now, Brian jerked erect and reached for the bottle. "I've been doing just the opposite all this time. Whenever the two of you went out to a show or a tavern, I always said 'No thanks' when you invited me along. Two's company, three's a crowd, remember?"

Casey pounded a fist on the table. "There you go, doing it again! Getting me all mixed up, so my tongue's twisted in me mouth! So, I liked you and I wanted Becky to like you, and it was fun the three of us."

"It still is, Larry," Brian said with sincerity.

"No, it's not. It's the two of you now. I might as well be a chair for all the attention paid to me."

"Like last night at Pastor's? All right, I danced with Becky. The girl loves to dance, and you can't dance and won't learn. So whose fault is that?"

"It's not just that, it's all the time. And the way you look at each other. Calf's eyes."

"Come on, stop it, man. I've never so much as touched her hand except when we're dancing."

"But you'd like to?"

Brian rested his elbows on the table and clasped his head in his hands. "You can be an exasperating man, Casey. A thick-headed Irishman." He shook a finger at the man across the table. "All right, Larry, what do you think when you look at Rebecca? Don't deny it, man, it's as plain as the long nose on your face. You're fairly drooling over that girl. All you've got on your mind is getting her in bed, and that's as it should be. God made men and women to complement each other. To fit one into the other, to—"

"You dirty bastard! Don't talk that way about Becky. You damned lecher! I want to marry her. You! YOU!

You'd treat her like any slut on the waterfront. A quick fuck and 'So long, it's been nice to meet you.' " Casey got to his feet. All the blood had drained out of his face, and his eyes were wild and filled with hate.

"Stand up, O'Neil. The only answer to talk like that is a sound thrashing."

Brian could not repress the grin; Casey was acting ludicrous. "Calm down, lad," he tried to placate him. "I meant nothing of the sort. No offense against Becky. I myself would thrash any man who slandered that girl."

Casey picked up the bottle and sloshed whisky into Brian's face. While he was wiping a sleeve across his blinded burning eyes, Casey put a foot against the edge of the table and toppled it over on top of Brian. Chair and man went backwards.

Lying flat on his back with the table on top of him, Brian kicked hard with both feet and sent the table flying back at the other man. He bounced to his feet with blood in his eye.

"That did it, Casey. You've been asking for this for weeks." The two of them went at it with flailing arms and legs, no quarter asked or given. This was Brian's game, not the gentleman's fisticuffs they taught at military school. He was bigger and stronger than Casey, and, although Casey was game, Brian soon wore him down. He finished it off with a left to the gut and a right uppercut that sent poor Casey flying through the doorway into the kitchen. He lay there motionless.

Brian stepped over his body and picked up a pitcher of water from the sink counter. Bending, he poured the contents into Casey's face. It did the job, and Casey sat up, sputtering and shaking his soaked head.

"C'mon, enough fun and games for the night." Brian extended a hand.

Casey hesitated, finally took it, and Brian hauled him to his feet. Brian wanted earnestly to pass off the incident as nothing more than a boyish lark. A lame attempt. They were not boys, but mature men, and they both knew it.

"Feels good to blow off steam, once in a while, old cock," he said with forced gaiety.

Casey looked sheepish, avoided his eyes. "Damned fool

thing for me to blow up that way. Don't know what came over me."

"Forget it. I have already." He threw an arm across Casey's shoulders. "You know what it is, being cooped up in this flat, the two of us. By God! You and I haven't been on a real toot together in two weeks. What do you say we go down a few at Fraunces Tavern?"

"Sounds good to me."

Neither one of the men ever mentioned the conversation or the events of that night again. Yet it was another of the pivotal points in Brian's life, a fulcrum on which destiny turned about the tenuous relationship of the two men and the woman. From that night on, it was Brian who invited Casey to join him and Becky on the town. By tacit consent, she was now Brian's girl. The law of the animal pack had prevailed once again. To the victor. . . .

It gave Brian the prerogative now to court Rebecca Solomon openly. A relief to the two of them. Playing the mating game without tactile contact, depending upon eye communication alone and subtle innuendo in one's speech, became a frustrating experience if practiced indefinitely.

Although Becky never knew about the fight she had provoked between Brian and Larry, she sensed that the obstacle—Larry Casey—that had kept her and Brian acting out the role of affectionate brother and sister for almost a year had mysteriously been eliminated. Larry had abruptly decided to step aside, she deduced.

A Fourth of July picnic at Central Park turned out to be a memorable day for Brian, like the day he had spent with Ravena at Lough Derg. Some years before Solomon Levitz had organized the annual event sponsored by the Merchants' Association for the workers in the Garment District.

He and Becky won the three-legged race, and Brian won the sack race. She cheered the loudest when Brian hit a home run that won the baseball game for the Seventh Avenue Blazers.

After gorging themselves on hot dogs and beer, they strolled around the lake, holding hands. To suit the occasion Becky had made a new dress, a tunic with red, white and blue stripes, draped to show off her blue petticoat ornamented with gold stars. Her long black hair was tied at the back with a red ribbon.

"You're the prettiest girl in the whole park," he said. "In all of New York."

"Enough of your blarney, O'Neil," she said gaily.

He made some comments about her attire that made Becky curious. "You're so knowledgeable about women's clothing. Most men don't even notice what a girl's wearing."

"Well, I tell you why that is, me girl. You see my mother's a countess and my father's an Earl, and I've been around rich and elegant women all of me life. That's how I acquired me good taste."

Becky doubled up with laughter. "The son of an Earl. Would you like me to call you 'The Honorable'?"

"That would be respectful, I guess, but I was never one to put on airs. Brian will do just fine."

They left the foot path and walked through the woods until they came to a little grassy clearing.

"Nice and private, isn't it? Just the place for a feller to take his girl for some spooning."

Becky blushed. "How many girls have you brought here? Plenty, I imagine."

For an answer he led her to a shrubbery-screened corner, took her in his arms and kissed her. Her arms went around his neck and she pressed herself tight against him. He pulled her down on the grass, and his lips nibbled down the curve of her throat until he felt the pulse under his mouth. Wild beating, passionate.

She allowed him to fondle her breasts through her clothing, but no more. Bolder now, Brian slipped his hand inside the bodice of her gown. She shuddered and moaned.

"No, Brian, you mustn't."

"But I must." His other hand slipped underneath her skirt and petticoat.

She stiffened and pushed at him.

"No, please."

"I am pleasing you, I can tell, don't deny it."

"But it's sinful pleasure."

"Nothing that feels so good can be sinful."

Before she could clamp her knees shut, his hand touched her through her bloomers. Her whole body began to quake, and she was powerless to resist.

She continued to whimper while he removed her

clothes, but when he pulled her hand to touch his hot, hard male flesh, her fingers encircled him eagerly.

"Oh, my God!" she gasped. "I don't dare look."

He laughed. "It's just as good when your eyes are closed."

He fondled her until she was lubricous, and then he mounted her. She was a virgin and at first he couldn't penetrate her.

"You've got to relax, darling. Don't fight me."

"I'm trying. Does it always hurt like this?"

"Only the first time."

"I'll bet it's not your first time?"

"That's a most unladylike question."

"It goes without saying. What I'm engaged in is not exactly ladylike."

Brian laughed. She had a keen sense of humor.

"You could almost be Irish," he told her.

"Because of this we're doing?"

"No, you little twit. The way you look and talk."

"Rebecca Solomon, sure and me maither hails from County Cork," she mimicked. "All right, me boy, get on with it. Now!" She gritted her teeth.

This time he made it, and she cried out softly in pain. But quickly the pleasure of him in her overtook the pain, and she moved against him frantically.

"Oh, my God! I think I'm going to faint," she gasped as the contractions commenced.

"*La petite mort* is what the French call it. 'The little death.'"

After it was over she lay back in the grass and arched her back so that her breasts reached up at him.

"It feels so good, the sun on my naked body."

He bent over her and kissed first one pink nipple and then the other. "They taste like cherries," he murmured.

"I like that." She purred like a kitten. "Brian?"

"Yes, love?"

"Do you think we can do it again?"

"Hussy."

"I am that, and one more time won't make me any more a hussy. God! If my poor father could see me now."

He grinned wryly. "With a *goy*, no less."

"Papa loves you like a son."

"But not as a son-in-law?"

She sat up and covered her nakedness with her gown, looking suddenly vulnerable and self-conscious.

"Brian—it can never be."

"I love you, Becky, and I think you love me."

It was true. He cared for Rebecca Solomon more than any other girl in the world—here his mind held back—except for Ravena Wilding.

"I do love you, but it would kill my father if I married outside of my faith. Papa is very religious, orthodox."

"Religion," he said bitterly. "It's done more harm to the world than good."

"Brian!"

"It's true. Look what's happening in Ireland. The damned Church of England enslaving the Catholics, and Irishmen are at each other's throats as well. Your father can be brought around. He told me once the Irish and Jews have so much in common. We're both persecuted peoples. We should stick together."

Brian was resolved to talk to Solomon that very night, but before he had the chance, the old man had a stroke. And although he recovered partially, there was never any question of bringing up the matter of his marrying Becky again.

Three more years he lived before the last stroke took him after the first night of the seder in the spring of 1861, four days after General P.G.T. Beauregard ordered Confederate troops to fire on Ft. Sumter.

New York was stunned by the devastating defeat of the Union forces under General McDowell at the first Battle of Bull Run.

"They say there's nothin' standing between the Rebs and New York," Casey announced after reading the black-bordered headlines on the *Herald* one morning. "What do you say we close up the shop and go back to Boston?"

"If they take New York, Boston won't be far behind. No, I'll take my chances right here. What about you, Becky?"

She clasped his arm and smiled. "Wherever you are, that's where I will be."

Casey turned away in annoyance. He was still desperately in love with Becky and he died a little every time Brian touched her. With Solomon gone, Brian and Becky dropped all the pretense that their relationship was platonic. They had been sleeping together for three years, but the old man never had an inkling of it. Casey, however, did not have the bliss that the ignorance of the dead afforded her father. He knew what was going on, and now they were flaunting their love affair shamelessly.

Lying close together in Becky's bed one morning after making love, she said to him:

"Brian, I've been waiting for you to ask me all week."

"Ask you what?"

"Now that my father is gone—"

"Oh." She didn't have to spell it out for him. Now there was no longer any obstacle to marriage between them.

He pulled her to him, holding her cheek against his chest. "My darling. Christ! Why does life have to be so complicated and contrary? Now it's me that has to say 'no,' not for the time at least."

"You don't want to marry me any more?" she asked miserably.

"Of course I want to marry you, love, but these are not the times to be speaking of marriage. You see, darling, there's a duty I have that comes first."

"A duty to whom?"

"A duty to this country. It's treated me well these last six years, and now it's my turn to repay the debt. Freedom and Equality and Justice don't come cheaply."

Becky was distressed. "You're not going to join the Army! No, Brian! You'll be killed. What do you know about being a soldier? They have professionals to fight wars."

"The point is the professionals are hard up right now. The government is pleading for volunteers. I know they can use me. You see, I had a military education, the cavalry."

"More of your blarney. His Highness, the Lord of Killarney."

"Matter of fact, it was Tyrone, but I don't want to get into that now. I hope you understand my decision, Becky."

"I don't understand it or like it, but I don't really have any choice, do I? So I'll accept."

When he announced his decision to enlist to Casey, his friend was flabbergasted. "Join the army. I never thought of it, but you're right, Brian. We owe everything to the United States. By God! I'm with you."

Brian laid a hand on his arm. "No, Larry, it's different with you. Besides, somebody has got to help Becky manage the shop. Did you know we've been approached by the War Department with a big order for military uniforms?"

"Becky mentioned it."

"Your place is right here. That'll be your contribution, and a mighty big one it is, supplying good clothing for the men at the front. I think we'd better hire a few more men once the order is final. You know more about the business than I do," he lied.

"I guess you're right, Brian," Casey conceded. At the back of his mind a tiny spark of hope was rekindled. With Brian off to war, maybe he and Becky—he refused to let himself believe it. It would be too painful to endure, living with that forlorn hope.

Still. . . .

CHAPTER FIVE

It took almost a year for Ravena to get over Brian's reputed death by fire. Not that she would ever forget him, but she was young and healthy of body and mind, and the biggest part of her life still lay ahead of her.

In an odd way, too, Roger was a great comfort to her. He was Brian's brother, even if no love had been lost between him and Brian. He looked like Brian. It was easy if she concentrated on the notion to believe that he was Brian's reincarnation. After all if the cell had not split in the mother's womb by an act of Providence, Brian and Roger would have been one. So, therefore, Brian still lived in the body of Roger. She began to look beneath the façade that Roger presented to the world for traits that she had recognized in Brian.

Roger worshipped Ravena, and Vanessa Wilding was continually encouraging the match.

"He adores you, Ravena. He jumps to your every whim. Men like that are hard to find. Especially such eligible ones. Breeding, wealth, good looks."

"I'm not certain I love Roger, Mother."

The Duchess laughed. "Love! Child, what do you know about love? What you read in those scandalous novels you're always reading? You think that's real love?"

"I don't know, Mother." She wanted to tell her that she did know about love. The love that she and Brian had shared that day in the Donegal meadow.

"Let me tell you something, Ravena, if one party to a marriage loves as intensely as does Roger, then it can be contagious. In time you will respond to his passion."

That was it exactly. The physical appetite that Brian had awakened in Ravena did not abate with his absence. On warm spring nights she would toss restlessly on her lonely bed, dreaming of a man's lips over her lips. A man's

70

strong arms around her. A man's hands on her naked body. A man's hardness. She shuddered, moaned, could almost feel him entering her body.

"God! I can't go on like this," she told herself irritably.

She got out of bed and went downstairs in her nightgown. The house was dark and still. The only sound a hound barking in the distance. An owl's hoot. She went through the study and opened the french doors leading out to the terrace. The warm humid air was a caress. A full moon cast a phosphorescent glow over the garden.

Ravena turned her face up to it and walked slowly along the path to the pool at the far end. She felt as if she were transported back in time. Ancient Greece. The marble pool bone-white. Ghostly. The statues around her seemed to stir, take life. One of them was moving toward her.

Ravena clasped a hand to her throat and backed off. "No! I must be dreaming."

"Ravena?"

The hairs at the nape of her neck tingled.

"Go back."

"It's I, Roger."

"Roger O'Neil?"

He laughed. "How many Rogers do you know?"

And then he materialized out of the shadows, a captain of the dragoons now, resplendent in his uniform and plumed helmet.

"I've just come off special duty. The Molly Maguires struck at Sir Robert Dillon's estate again. Made off with two fine horses and some guns and ammunition. Bloody bastards! They ought to be shot on sight. That's the only thing they understand. Force!"

"They've had the best teachers in the world, haven't they?" she asked. "The English," she answered herself. It was a comment she had picked up from listening to her father and his friends hotly debate the Irish Question, as the dilemma came to be known.

This same Sir Robert Dillon had stormed out in a rage and had not spoken to the Duke of Ulster since.

"Ravena!" Roger was shocked. "You shouldn't talk like that. Not only is it treasonous, but it's highly dangerous. I wish your father would show some restraint in his public statements."

"My father can take care of himself."

"Don't be too sure about that." The remark had an ominous ring to it. "This country has practically been in a state of martial law for the past year to all intents and purposes. The Crown is getting to the point where it will not tolerate anyone lending support to these murdering rebels, material or moral. Do you know what the cheeky buggers did last week? They burned the Prime Minister in effigy after a kangaroo court in Galway convicted him of murder."

She smothered a laugh with her hand. "I wish I could have been there."

Roger gave her a long, cold appraising look. At times, he had doubts about her. Lovely as she was, as passionately as he desired her, to possess her in every meaning of the term, there were occasions when he wondered if he could afford a wife like Ravena Wilding. Not in the material sense.

Would she become a liability to his ambitions in the British Army and later, if all went well, in his political career?

"But how is it you stopped here, Roger?"

"I was riding past and I thought I heard a door open and close. Thought it best to check to see that it wasn't one of the gangs marauding about."

"Enough of this serious talk, Roger. I'm glad you're here. I couldn't sleep and I was yearning to have some company. Sit down." She patted a stone bench, one of many that ringed the pool.

For the first time he became aware of her attire. It jolted him. "Is that your—your—"

"My nightgown? Yes, of course it is."

His head reeled. "Ravena, you shouldn't be out here in a nightgown. I mean, you don't have—" He cleared his throat in mortification. "I mean—under it—"

"Nothing," she said, her laughter trilling over the still garden.

"My God! Not so loud. If I were discovered out here with you in nothing more than a nightdress, I don't know what would happen."

"You swine, I'll horsewhip you," she said in a deep imitation of her father. "Sullying my daughter's honor."

"You have a macabre sense of humor." He glanced around furtively.

"Have no fear. No one can see us or hear us way out here." She was overtaken by a sudden wild impulse. Pure madness.

"Roger, let's swim in the pool."

"Ravena! What's gotten into you?"

Nothing and no one for far too long. She felt dizzy as desire welled up inside her like a warm, sweet spring. Bending, she gripped the hem of her gown and raised it up over her thighs.

"Stop it this instant, Ravena!" he protested.

Her laughter mocked him.

As the gown reached midthigh, he whirled around and shut his eyes. He heard the *whoosh* of silk whipping the air, followed by a splash.

"It's delightful, Roger. Really, you should join me. I'm sure you're as sweaty as a horse after chasing all those bad Mollies."

"Ravena, I'm telling you for the last time. Get out of that pool and put on your nightdress."

Her answer was to fling water up at him with her hands, and teasing laughter.

"That settles it, I'm leaving."

"Roger, don't. I'm sorry."

He strode off down the path away from the pool.

"Roger!" Her voice changed. It was urgent. Alarmed. "Roger, I have a cramp. Please—help me!"

"Ravena!" He turned and ran back to the pool, casting off his helmet and tunic. He dove into the water and swam at full speed toward Ravena, thrashing about in the middle.

She appeared to be unconscious when he reached her, floating on her back with her long dark hair trailing out in the water like a fan.

As he took hold of her, his foot scraped bottom, and, to his surprise, he discovered the water was only waist deep.

"How could you—" He stopped as her eyes opened and she smiled at him like the Cheshire cat.

"Glad you changed your mind, Roger?" She held up her arms to him.

It came to him with a jolt that she was naked.

breasts and belly gleamed like alabaster in the moonlight.

"God! You—you're beautiful." Language was thick in his throat.

Her arms went around his neck as he gathered her up in his arms and waded back to the side of the pool.

"There are steps down at the far end," she guided him.

It was dark where willows grew out over the water. He carried her up the steps and put her down on the grass. She was breathing hard, and her hands were fumbling with the buttons on his shirt.

"Do I have to undress you, silly?" Her laughter was coarse and lusty. In the dark she might have passed for some wench in the village with round heels. Not Lady Ravena Wilding. He was powerless to resist her invitation. Burning with animal heat, he threw off his clothes and came down hard on top of her. Mouths locked together, they writhed around on the ground like two wild beasts in mortal combat. He was astonished and dismayed at how easily he entered her.

Ravena Wilding was not a virgin!

Her body was greedy for his. He felt as if he was being drawn down into a white-hot volcano. He had never imagined in his most licentious dreams that a woman could be a match for man in lust. She proved him wrong that night, and before the orgy was over, it was he who pleaded exhaustion.

Afterward, dressing with trembling fingers, he could not look at her. "If you ever tell anyone about this, I'll be ruined."

"*You'll* be ruined?" She laughed. "And what about me? A fallen, sullied woman. No more than a child and pure as the driven snow. Walking innocently in my garden when this brute of a dragoon, this slavering carnal brute, leaped out of the bushes, ripped off my nightgown and ravished me while I lay swooning."

"Ravena!" he pleaded in a strangled voice. "Don't say things like that, even in jest. If anyone overheard you—" He looked around with the panic of an animal being stalked. "My God! It's a wonder the whole countryside doesn't know about it. I must be out of my mind."

"Because you made love to a woman and were loved in return?"

"Ravena," he said sternly, "there is a time and a place for everything. And this was not the place nor the time. It's quite a different matter in the privacy and sanctity of the marital bed."

"I disagree." Her eyes danced merrily, reflecting moonlight. "It's the same thing, no mind where it's done. On the bed. On the grass. Or in the hayloft. You and Brian and my brothers, the four of you were doing that jig with the maids when you were dirty little boys. Don't think I didn't know what was going on, Roger O'Neil."

He clapped his hands over his ears. "I won't hear that kind of language from my bride-to-be."

It had slipped out. He stared at her, mouth agape. "I—I—that is—"

"Is it a proposal? I suppose you don't have choice after tonight. And neither do I. I'm probably pregnant. You being such a virile stud and all."

Roger fell back on the grass, arms spread wide. A posture of surrender. She bent over him, face close to his. He felt her hot, sweet breath on his cheeks.

"Do you love me, Roger?" She turned her body so that one breast hung suspended over his mouth, inviting as a ripe pear. His arms enfolded her still-nude body and he crushed her to him, burying his face in the valley between her breasts.

"I'm your slave," he murmured. "Your eternal slave. I'll never let you go."

The year 1857 marked two milestones in the life of Ravena Wilding. She became formally engaged to Roger Fitz O'Neil. And she left Ireland. It was a sad occasion, but under the circumstances, the O'Neils were fortunate to have the opportunity to leave.

Defying the admonitions of his son-in-law-to-be, Roger, the Duke of Ulster continued to deplore the plight of the starving Irish peasants, and pressed for reforms that would restore to them a measure of human dignity.

In an impassioned speech delivered at a banquet honoring Lord Clarendon, the Viceroy, Edward Wilding warned his peers:

"He who would enslave another man must become a slave himself. At present Ireland is like a running pox sore on the body of the British Empire. Given time, the infection will spread and England itself will die of the disease.

"The current condition is intolerable. There is nothing between the master and the slave. Nothing between the straw-roofed hut and the palace. There is nothing between all the luxuries of existence and the last degree of human wretchedness."

In return Lord George Halifax and Sir Robert Dillon castigated the Duke. Fumed Sir Robert: "Sir, you are a traitor to your class and to your country. A blackguard. This assembly is well aware, your Grace, that among the illustrious members of your family, you number one Daniel O'Connell, former Catholic mayor of Dublin and the first Irish Catholic member of Parliament Mr. O'Connell openly espoused rebellion and civil war against England. We must respect him, at least, for his courage and his honesty. But you, sir—"

"Just a minute!" the Duke interrupted angrily. "Are you implying, Sir Robert, that I am a traitor to England?"

Sir Robert's plump, featureless face looked as if it were a lump of half-baked bread dough, surly, with a twisted mouth and deep-set little hog's eyes. He inhaled a pinch of snuff from the back of his hand and dabbed at his nose with a lace kerchief.

"I don't have to imply anything. Your words and actions speak for themselves."

"Because I preach humanity toward my fellow man? Because I believe that it is a mortal sin to practice gluttony while my neighbor's children are crying for milk and a crust of bread? Because I believe that the good earth belongs to all men? Not to a greedy few who exploit and suppress the rest of mankind."

"Are you implying that Sir Robert is a glutton and guilty of the sin of greed as well?" someone called out from the end of the banquet table.

Laughter went around at Sir Robert's expense.

The Duke smiled. "To borrow from Sir Robert's diatribe: 'I don't have to imply anything. His actions and his appearance speak for themselves.'"

The quick laughter was silenced just as quickly as Sir Robert Dillon sprang to his feet and walked around the table to the Duke's place.

"For God's sake, Edward," said the Earl of Tyrone,

seated at his right. "Don't antagonize him any more. He's a very dangerous man, and in great favor at court."

The Duke rose and faced Sir Robert, who was beet-red and puffed up like a mad toad. He towered over the pompous little fellow.

An outcry went up from the onlookers as Sir Robert removed a leather glove from his coat pocket and slashed it across the Duke's face. Edward Wilding recoiled in surprise. More amused than hurt.

"Such melodramatics in this day and age! You should have gone onto the stage, Robert," he taunted.

"This is no joke, your Grace. My second will see you this evening to make the arrangements. The choice of weapons is yours, naturally."

The Duke was incredulous. "You can't be serious. You know perfectly well that dueling is a crime. You of all people, always the champion of law and order."

Sir Robert sneered. "There are certain laws that are enforced so that the scum of the earth will not run wild like savages, killing off each other. More's the pity they don't, in my own opinion. Those laws are not applicable to men of our rank. You know that as well as I do. I shall see you tomorrow morning dawn, on the field of honor, sir."

He did a military about-face and marched out of the hall.

By late afternoon the account of what had happened at the banquet for Lord Clarendon had spread all over Belfast. Even the lowest peasants and fishmongers could be heard passing the word. It dominated all other topics in pub and public conversation.

"I hope the Duke blows his ruddy head off."

"Aye, he's a good man, the Duke. God bless him."

In minutes a mob formed in the square, rallying for the Duke of Ulster. As the bottles were passed around, its attitude became increasingly more militant.

"Three cheers for the Duke of Ulster!"

"Hip! Hip! Hurrah!"

"Down with Queen Victoria! The Duke of Ulster ought to be King of Ireland!"

A troop of dragoons came thundering out of streets and

alleys on all sides, converging on the mob in the square, swinging clubs and the flats of swords.

Heads and noses were split. Some were trampled under the horses' hooves and suffered broken limbs. In moments the square was empty except for the dragoons and the wounded.

Captain Roger O'Neil reformed his men and surveyed the battleground grimly.

"Bloody bastards won't try that again."

His second in command, Lieutenant Bates, wore a simpering grin. He hated his captain with a vengeance. At Sandhurst, he had been a form ahead of O'Neil, but now the tables were reversed, and Roger told Bates what to do.

"He must be quite an inspiration to them, this Duke of Ulster. Protestant revolutionary, how quaint."

"The Duke of Ulster is not a revolutionary," Roger retorted coldly. "He's too soft on his tenants, a bit of a bleeding heart, but he's loyal to the Crown."

"Is he now? Hmmmm. What were they saying? 'Down with the Queen.' And, 'The Duke ought to be King.' Something like that." His eyebrows arched in feminine fashion. "Oh, I say, it never occurred to me. Aren't you engaged to marry the chap's daughter?"

"Fall in with your platoon, Lieutenant!" Roger growled.

To himself: *"Jesus! The old fool is going to get himself tried for treason if he isn't careful. Damned if I don't hope that Sir Robert hits the bull's eye tomorrow. It will spare Ravena and her family a lot of grief. It sure as hell will make me feel a lot better. The King of Ireland indeed!"*

Ravena was furious and the Duchess was distraught when the Duke informed them of what had transpired at the banquet to honor Lord Clarendon.

"I hope you blow his bloody head off, Daddy," Ravena said savagely. "The repulsive fat old toad!"

The duke was an excellent marksman with both pistol and rifle.

"The thing of it is, you can't win either way, Edward," his wife lamented. "If you kill Sir Robert, all of his conservative friends here and in England will be howling for your blood, the same way they finally broke Dan O'Connell. I always knew that family tie would haunt us some day. But why do they lay blame on you? After all, he's my kin."

"I won't hear that kind of talk, Vanessa," the Duke admonished her. "Dan O'Connell was a great patriot and statesman, and I'd be proud if his blood ran in my veins. And what kind of a thing is it to say they 'broke Dan O'Connell'? All the king's horses and all the king's men could not have broken the spirit of Dan O'Connell. It was the fire of dedication that killed old Dan. But he'd accomplished what he was born to do, and then some."

"Bravo!" sang Ravena. She hugged her father. "Daddy, I'm so proud you won't let pigs like Sir Robert Dillon and Lord Halifax tread on you. Remember the motto of the American patriots before the revolution? They designed a flag with a coiled rattlesnake on it: 'Dont tread on me!' it said."

The chimes at the front entrance echoed dimly into the drawing room.

The Duke grimaced. "I think I know who that is. Will you dear ladies please retire to some other room?"

The Duchess and Ravena went down the hall to the sewing and music room. Her mother sat down at the harpsichord and played a crisp rendition of Bach's "Turkish Rondo." She was an accomplished pianist and harpsichord-ist and often entertained guests at their dinner parties. Ravena played passably, but recognizing that she could never equal her mother's skills, she became discouraged. Vanessa Wilding could literally lose herself in music when she was performing.

Taking advantage of the Duchess's absorption, Ravena tiptoed out of the room and back down the hall. She was an unabashed keyhole spy.

As was the custom, Lord Halifax was wearing evening dress with high hat and cape. Dueling protocol was extremely formal, smacking of medieval pageantry.

Halifax was a little bantam rooster of a man with tight curly red hair, and a face which, as the Duchess described it, had the map of Ireland written all over it. Notwithstanding his Gaelic heritage, he was a fanatic Anglophile.

"There are always them what hates their own kind," Rose, the maid, had once observed to Ravena after a notorious informer had been unmasked by the Whiteboys.

"Will you take a glass of sherry, George?"

Halifax turned bright red. "*Your Grace*, this is hardly an occasion for social amenities. I am here as Sir Robert Dillon's second to finalize the arrangements for the duel tomorrow morning. The choice is yours, naturally, but I would suggest Carson's Meadow. Sir Robert is in agreement."

"That will be fine with me, *George*." Deliberately needling the lord.

Carson's Meadow was located in the midst of a royal pheasant preserve where the nobility slaked their blood lust every Sunday afternoon. It was a popular site for duels. Such contests were still common, despite the legal prohibition on them. The police could not be expected to enforce the law on the men who drafted it and who had installed them in positions of power.

"Your choice of weapons, your Grace?"

The Duke smiled thinly. "Pistols, I suppose."

Halifax nodded curtly. "Five paces."

"No, ten paces," the Duke said quickly.

The other man's eyebrows lifted. "Your Grace, I must remind you that—"

"No, I must remind *you*, Lord Halifax," the duke said sharply. "I suggest you consult the King's Club manual. I also have that option as well, as recipient of the challenge."

"As you wish." Lord Halifax bowed from the waist. "Shall we say tomorrow morning at sun-up?"

"I'll be there. Carson's Meadow."

As Lord Halifax started out of the room, the Duke called after him. "George? Can't you persuade the bloody fool to change his mind?"

Halifax turned slowly, sneering at the duke. "Not unless you are willing to issue a public apology for publication in the news tabloids."

The Duke shrugged his shoulders and sighed. "Tomorrow morning."

Ravena rushed into the room as soon as Lord Halifax was gone. She threw her arms around her father. "You put him in his place, Daddy." She giggled. "*That will be fine with me, George*," mimicking her father.

He stared at her with mock severity. "Eavesdropping

again, eh, young lady? You're not too big to spank, you know."

She slipped away from him. "You have to catch me first. Seriously, Daddy, can I come tomorrow and watch?"

"You get more outrageous every day. I don't know what I'm going to do with you. No, you may not watch the duel. How would you feel seeing your old father shot, lying in his blood on the ground?"

"Poo! That will never happen," she scoffed. "Who will be your second?"

"I thought I'd ask Edward, the Earl of Tyrone."

She smiled approvingly. "That's perfect. The two of you are such fast friends. You even have the same name."

The Duke laughed. "A paean to the Royal Family's penchant for the name. There's an old joke about one of Queen Victoria's ladies in waiting who became big with child. The old queen was so furious she vowed to hang the culprit responsible. When the girl said his name was 'Edward,' half the men at court went into hiding, including the Prince of Wales."

Ravena burst into laughter. "Oh, how Brian would have enjoyed that joke."

The laughter ceased abruptly and father and daughter stared at each other in mute understanding.

"Now, whatever made me think of Brian?" she asked.

He smiled and took her hand. "It's only right and natural for us to think of those whom we loved and who have passed on."

She looked perplexed. "What makes you think I ever loved Brian O'Neil?"

She went to him and buried her face in his chest so that he could not see the betraying gloss over her eyes.

When the Duke of Ulster and his second the Earl of Tyrone arrived at Carson's Meadow the following morning, the sun was still under the horizon. A vivid band of spectrum hues glowed over the treetops, presaging its imminent emergence.

Sir Robert Dillon and Lord Halifax were already there along with three referees, two chosen by the seconds for each side, and one appointed by the Board of the King's Club.

As they alighted from the Duke's coach, Carley the coachman called to him: "May God be with ye, yur Grace."

"Thank you, Carley. Take the horses back a ways so the shots won't spook them."

They marched to the center of the little clearing where grazing sheep kept the grass short. They exchanged curt formal greetings with Sir Robert, Lord Halifax and the referees.

Bushrod, Secretary to the King's Club, was the referee in charge. Son of a British Admiral, he had been discharged from Her Majesty's Navy after almost expiring from smallpox. His face still bore the ugly ravages of the disease.

He cleared his throat. "I realize both you gentlemen are cognizant of the rules under which this duel will be conducted." He nodded to one of his assistants who stepped forward with a teakwood box. He opened the cover and held the box up for display. Two silver-plated dueling pistols, elegantly inscribed with the Club's insignia on their butts, long barreled.

Bushrod went on: "Both pistols were tested by Messrs. Lynch and Potter and myself last night at the club firing range. Both are remarkably accurate. Whatever deviations exist, they are negligible. Do you concur, gentlemen?"

Lynch and Potter murmured assent.

"All right, your Grace, the choice is yours."

The Duke of Ulster stepped forward and selected one of the pistols at random. Sir Robert Dillon picked up the second and hefted it in his hand.

Bushrod consulted his pocketwatch and looked to the east. The upper crescent of the sun was visible above the crown of the forest.

"It is time. Gentlemen, take your places."

The Duke and Sir Robert stood at attention, back to back. The small, stout man's head only came up to the Duke's armpits.

"Beginning with my count, you will each pace off the distance in cadence. At the count of ten, you will both turn and fire at will. A single shot."

The "ten paces" count demanded by the Duke had

caused considerable controversy at the club the previous evening.

Quite a few, despite their respect for the Duke of Ulster, believed that he was a bit of a bounder insisting on ten paces rather than five.

As the Duke was an expert marksman, the increased distance, about sixty feet between the two contestants, was bound to favor the Duke. It was agreed that it would have been more sportsmanlike of him to agree to the shorter distance preferred by Sir Robert.

"One," the count commenced.

The onlookers held their breaths as the long march began. The Earl of Tyrone mopped his brow with a handkerchief. Until the last minute, his son Roger had remonstrated with him not to ally himself with the Duke in this risky venture. "If he kills Sir Robert his head will be on the chopping block for sure. And yours might just be with him. By God, I may have to resign my commission."

"Calm down, Roger," his father admonished. Edward Wilding is like a brother to me. He is going to be your father-in-law, Roger."

Roger rolled his eyes heavenward. "God! Don't remind me."

"Besides, you're being premature, aren't you? Nobody is dead as yet."

Roger had to console himself with that. And with some luck, it just could be the Duke of Ulster who would be killed.

The Earl shivered and drew his greatcoat's collar up around his face as the count reached:

"Eight.

"Nine.

"Ten!"

Sir Robert whirled around so fast, he almost toppled over.

The Duke turned leisurely, the pistol still poised in the cocked position, his forearm bent back against his upper arm. To the astonishment of the spectators, he kept it up there with the barrel of the pistol touching his shoulder and pointing up into the air.

Sir Robert spread his stocky legs in a fencing stance and thrust his arm straight out, one eye shut, the other squinting along the barrel, lining up the sights. He took a deep breath and held it. Slowly squeezed the trigger. At the "break point," a loon screamed out over Carson's Lake to the north.

The pistol fired and the recoil knocked Sir Robert's hand into the air. The shot whistled high over the Duke's head. He didn't even blink. He nodded in Sir Robert's direction and smiled as he brought down the pistol unhurriedly to the firing position. With deliberation, he braced the barrel of the pistol on his left forearm, and took careful aim.

It was to Sir Robert's credit that he prepared to meet his Maker with great courage. Throwing down the empty pistol, he drew himself up to his full height, chest out, shoulders back, and looked straight at the Duke.

A murmur went up from the Earl and the referees.

"What the devil is he doing?" Lord Halifax exclaimed.

The line of the Duke's aim appeared to describe an extreme angle with the ground. Almost as if he were aiming at Sir Robert's legs.

"I'll be damned!"

The shot rang out.

And almost at once Sir Robert yowled and leaped high into the air like a cat with a can on its tail. He hopped about on one foot, holding his other foot in his hands like a boy playing hopscotch. At last he toppled over and rolled around cursing and crying and wringing his foot. His second and the referees rushed over to him.

"By God!" Bushrod marveled. "He's been shot in the foot!"

Casually the Duke sauntered over and grinned at his fallen foe. "How are you, Sir Robert?"

Sir Robert glared at him with murder in his eyes. "You! YOU! Do you know what you've done, Wilding? You've shot off my bloody toe!"

The Duke chuckled. "What are you complaining for, Robert? That's the one with the gout, isn't it? Just think, I've saved you an expensive and painful operation."

He nodded at Lord Halifax, Sir Robert and the referees. "Gentlemen, a good morning to you." To the Earl: "Edward, it's time we had our breakfast, don't you think? I'm famished."

After the duel Sir Robert Dillon was the joke of the King's Club, of Belfast, of all of Antrim County.

A joke that would turn into tragedy which would have shattering repercussions on the Wilding family.

On a Sunday one month after the duel, Sir Robert was strolling in the park with his wife Sara when a gang of young toughs commenced heckling him.

"That's him, ol' one-foot."

"Say he shot off his big toe while huntin' for a mouse."

Hobbling over to them on his wounded foot, Sir Robert demanded that the youths leave the park. When they refused, he swung at them with his cane. In the ensuing melée, one of them grabbed the cane away from Sir Robert and bashed him over the head. He fell and struck his head on a boulder, and the youths fled. Three days later he died without regaining consciousness, of a fractured skull.

The conservative press in both England and Ireland seized on the opportunity to attack the Duke of Ulster and the fraction of wealthy landowners like him who held a sympathetic liberal view toward the poor Catholic tenants who worked the land for them.

Twisting the facts, they played up the duel between the Duke and Sir Robert Dillon as the real cause of his death.

Sir Robert was: "a loyal British subject who in defense of Queen and country demanded that Edward Wilding, Duke of Ulster, apologize and retract certain slanderous allegations he had made against the British policy toward the Irish rebels."

They further intimated that by his act in wounding Sir Robert in the duel, the Duke had lent his tacit support and encouragement to the unlawful crimes perpetrated by the hooligan gangs throughout Ireland. "That very violence had culminated in the tragic murder of Sir Robert Dillon."

The hue and uproar swelled beyond all reasonable proportions. There were hot debates in pubs and public places, even in Parliament. Radical Loyalists appealed to the Queen to strip the Duke of Ulster of his title and his land.

At the height of the crisis, Lord Clarendon invited the Duke to a private meeting at the royal mansion. It was held late at night and the Earl of Tyrone was also present at the Duke's request.

Lord Clarendon was very grave. "Edward, this situation has become intolerable and there is no indication that it will improve—" he cleared his throat— "as long as your presence here in Ireland serves as a reminder to both sides that—"

"Excuse me, my lord," the Duke interrupted. "What sides are we talking about?"

"Why to the extremists, right and left. You see, Edward, you have become a symbol, a champion to the Catholic rebels and a corresponding heretic and danger to the rich landowners and English politicians. This matter is a *cause célèbre*."

"What do you suggest I do?"

Lord Clarendon stood up and paced up and down before the fireplace in his study. "This is not easy to say, Edward. We have been friends for a long time. The Prime Minister himself has contacted me personally. The Crown sees no alternative except to make an object lesson of your situation. Unless—unless you go into voluntary exile."

"Leave Ireland?" the Duke was electrified. "Damn the Crown!" He pounded the desk with a fist. "No one is going to drive me out of my native land!"

"Might I remind you that England is your native land?" Lord Clarendon said with severity. "It is just that kind of inflammatory speech that has gotten you into this predicament. You will, of course, retain your title as well as the title to your land. You can sell it and take the profits with you wherever you decide to settle. France, Switzerland, the South of Italy, You should be very comfortable for the rest of your life."

"I'll let them hang me first!"

Clarendon threw up his hands and appealed to the Earl of Tyrone. "Can you remonstrate with him, my lord?"

"Edward, you don't have any choice," the Earl said quietly. "Remember, you have a responsibility to your sons, to Ravena and to Vanessa. If you defy this ultimatum, it is bound to effect all of them adversely for the rest of their lives."

In the end, the Duke conceded defeat. "I'll leave Ireland, if that's all that will satisfy them, then let it be so." He drew himself up to his full height. "But it will not be the continent we'll head for. Europe—it's no better than

Britain. No, I want to live in a country where a man has self-respect, dignity, room to breathe no matter what his station in life, prince or pauper. Freedom, that's what I want for me and my family."

"And where would that be?" Lord Clarendon asked.

"The United States, where else? The birthplace of freedom and democracy."

Having made his decision, the Duke went home and broke the news to the Duchess and to Ravena.

"As for Kevin and Sean, they're men in their own right. I won't influence them either way."

Both sons had graduated from Oxford and were working in England. Sean was serving his internship at King's Hospital in London, and Kevin was a professor of English literature, married with a child on the way.

"I'll write them tonight," Vanessa promised. "It will come as a shock." She shook her head. "It's not that we get to see them all that often, but at least we know they're close by, a half-day's trip away. But America—three thousand miles of ocean between us and them. We might as well be living on the moon."

Ravena put a comforting arm around her mother's shoulders. "It will all work out, and you won't be losing Kevin and Sean. Once they learn what's happened to Papa, they'll thumb their noses at bloody old England and follow us to the New World." Her eyes grew large and luminous. "New World. New. It sounds exciting. I can hardly wait to be off."

"What about Roger?" her mother asked.

"What about him? If he loves me and still wants to marry me, why he'll come with us."

The Duke was silent. *Don't be too sure, my girl.* Though he would not have revealed it to Ravena or the Duchess, he secretly hoped that Roger O'Neil would be true to his colors, Queen and country, and reject his daughter.

It almost came to that too. Roger was livid when he learned about the Wilding family's imminent departure for America.

"The damned fool has finally gone and done it," he raged.

Ravena's eyes flashed. "How dare you call my father a damned fool!"

"I'm sorry, it just slipped out. But you must admit he was asking for trouble. Has been for a long time with his radical outbursts."

"My father is not a radical. He's a moderate who believes in human rights and decency for every man, whether he's Protestant, Catholic, Irish, English, rich and poor. Black and white."

His eyebrows flared. "*Black?* I say, Ravena, now you're going too far."

Her jaw thrust out defiantly. "I don't think so, Roger."

He ridiculed the Duke's decision to go to America. "It's a contradiction, you know. There are thousands of Nigras in bondage in the United States. Freedom, indeed!"

Ravena was momentarily demeaned. "I know, that's terrible. But my father says that will change too. There are many good men fighting to abolish slavery in America. Just as there are here in Ireland."

"I refuse to listen to any more of your radical ranting."

"Roger, what we really have to talk about now is about us. What are you going to do?"

"About you? Why I thought it was settled. We're going to be married."

She was frankly surprised. "You'd give it all up, your inheritance, your commission, your beloved British Empire?"

He put his hands on her shoulders and gazed into her eyes. "Ravena, I love you more than anything else in the world. I'd follow you to the ends of the earth if I had to."

She was genuinely moved, tears came to her eyes. It was the strongest show of devotion he had ever made to her.

"And I love you, Roger. I want us to be together for always."

They embraced passionately.

What he had not told Ravena was that the Duke of Ulster's scandal had already rubbed off on him as well as his father and mother, the staunch friends and supporters of the Duke. His liaison with Ravena Wilding had put the kiss of death on his army career. His colonel had intimated as much just the week before.

"I can't put you in for any further promotions, Captain O'Neil," he had said with apology. "There are bad feelings against you at the War Office. I know it's unfair. Possibly, if you were to request a transfer to England and give it a couple of years. You know, good show of being a patriot and all that rigmarole."

Besides, he reasoned, moving to the United States would not be a permanent arrangement. His father, the Earl, was not getting any younger. He, Roger, was the sole heir to the title and the considerable inheritance. By the time the Earl was dead, all of this messy business would have blown over and he and Ravena would reign as the Earl and the Countess of Tyrone.

Lord Clarendon had been authorized to make the Duke of Ulster a generous offer for his holdings and property.

"The Duke of Essex has been looking for just such an investment here in Ireland."

The Duke accepted it, and that night, he called a meeting of all of his tenant farmers in front of the castle. He addressed them from the top of the stone steps.

"As you know, my family and I are sailing for America next week. Any man, any family, that would care to leave this land of hardship and make a fresh start in the United States, I am prepared to advance you the passage money and one extra pound to help you get started when you get to America."

He was not surprised that only a handful of men took him up on the offer. In the words of one old fellow who declined, the general attitude of the majority was eloquently expressed: "It's a hardship all right, me Lord. But it's Erin. Me dear old sod, God, how I love her, this poor wretched nation. And one day it will change, and the chains will be off of her, and then she will shine like a jewel. The Emerald Isle, as it was meant to be. God willin', I want to be around to see her then."

"Aye," a chorus went up.

The Duke dabbed at his eyes with a handkerchief. "You're right, that day will come. And you will be richer than I can ever be not being here with you all when it happens."

CHAPTER SIX

Of the servants, only Rose accompanied the Wildings across the Atlantic to their new home in America. The others elected to remain and attend to the needs of the purchaser of the estate.

The night before they sailed from Belfast, the Earl of Tyrone gave a small private dinner party for his dear friends. It was an emotional occasion, especially as the evening drew to a close.

Theresa de Moleyns O'Neil embraced the Duchess during the final farewells with tears in her eyes.

"Vanessa, my darling, it's so hard to think I will never see you again." And she turned to kiss Ravena. "And you, my daughter—to be—it breaks my heart that I will not be there to see you and Roger married. Never to see my grandchildren—" She buried her face in her hands and began to sob.

The Duchess, Ravena and Roger all rushed to comfort her. The Earl turned his back self-consciously and chewed on his cigar. He detested hysterical outbursts in women.

"You'd think we were crossing the River Styx into the land of the dead," the Duchess said as gaily as she could. "Of course you'll see us again. Next summer, perhaps." She looked at the Earl. "An ocean voyage would do you both the world of good, Edward."

"Yes, yes, yes, to be sure. A jolly good thought. We'll see."

"And you will see Ravena and me as man and wife. Along with our children." Roger hugged his betrothed with one arm and his mother with the other. "And we intend to have a baker's dozen of the little devils, right my sweet?"

Ravena smiled and said nothing, but thought: *The same old Irish axiom, rich or poor—Keep 'em barefoot and pregnant!*

Roger and Ravena said their last good-bye alone on the terrace. They kissed ardently. Roger would remain in Ireland for another month to settle his affairs and terminate his service with the dragoons. Then he would join the Wildings in Richmond, Virginia. For almost a quarter of a century, the Duke of Ulster—like so many rich and titled Englishmen—had been accruing farm property in the southern United States. Cotton was "king," so the saying went, in the South, and England was the major buyer of the virtually inexhaustible crop planted, cared for and harvested by cheap slave labor. Indeed, there was no overhead aside from the initial purchase price of a slave and the cost of feeding and housing him. English capital invested in American cotton land was even more profitable than their holdings in destitute Ireland.

A flagrant hypocrisy that even an honorable man such as the Duke of Ulster blinded himself to, considering that the British parliament had roundly condemned the slave trade and abolished it throughout the Empire in 1807.

"My heart will be with you until we meet again, my darling," Roger murmured in her ear. His hands caressed her breasts and slid down over her hips to her buttocks.

She giggled. "You can't get much of a feel with all this whalebone and crinoline I'm wearing. Would you be wanting to sneak over for a last swim in the pool tonight?"

He recoiled. "Ravena, really, this is hardly the time for—for—" He was at a loss for words.

"For what, Roger?" She was disappointed in him. In so many ways he fell short in her eyes. A normal condition, she supposed. *We are all human and imperfect.* The trouble with Roger was that he would never concede the imperfection and humanness of *Homo sapiens.* She recalled an earthy and outrageous comment Brian had offered once about his brother.

"You know, Roger refuses to admit that females piss and shit like all of us beasts."

"You know what I mean, my dear. Such a solemn occasion. It would be sacrilegious to—to—"

"I understand, Roger," she said wearily.

The voyage to Richmond, Virginia, took almost six weeks, and while it was a new and exciting experience for Ravena for the first week, she became restless and bored, and the days began to drag on interminably as the journey drew to a close.

No "coffin ship" this, but a two-masted, square-rigged brig, plying trade between the Southern states and Liverpool. All spit and polish and carrying a small and élite group of passengers.

The one thing that made the stagnant existence aboard ship tolerable was her introduction to a handsome young American Army lieutenant, who was returning from France where he had been training for six months with the French Army.

Lt. Pennel Collins was a mass of golden curls, a rakish mustache and twinkling blue eyes. His manner of speaking intrigued Ravena. Not like any English or Irish she had ever heard.

"Do all Americans speak like you?" she asked him bluntly.

He laughed. "No, ma'am. Down South—I was born in Virginia—we believe in the 'good and easy' way of life. It shows in our speech, I guess. Slow and easy, right leisurely, like we do everything else. Not like up North. Why, you wouldn't believe it, these Yankees are always scurrying about like a bunch of squirrels scrambling for nuts to hoard. Work, work, work—you'd think it was a sin to sit still once in a while and enjoy the sight of the blue sky, the green grass and—" he winked—"a pretty girl like yourself."

She laughed. "I see there's as much blarney in the United States as there is in Ireland."

"No offense, Miss. An old married man can talk like that with impunity."

Ravena's eyes lit up. "I doubt your wife would go along with that. Anyway, I am betrothed myself. My Roger, he was a captain in the dragoons."

"I'm pleased to hear it. He'll be a welcome addition to the Virginia militia. We need all the good officers we can get."

She frowned. "How's that, Lieutenant?"

His face darkened. "Nothing to alarm you, Miss Ravena. In Virginia, we like to shield our ladies from the ugly realities of life. Women were put on this green earth by God to give love and comfort and offspring to their men-folks. And in our gratitude for that wonderful gift, we have pledged ourselves to love, honor and protect the gentle sex. What is it, Miss? Are you feeling ill? There is a bit of a swell today."

"Yes, I *am* suddenly feeling a bit out of sorts. If you'll excuse me—"

And it's not from the ocean swell, you pompous ass! she mused.

At the gangway entrance she turned and said in parting: "I'm sure you and my fiancé will get along just fine."

He bowed and smiled. "It will be my pleasure, Miss Ravena."

Later she inquired of her father what Lieutenant Collins had been alluding to when he said that the state of Virginia would be needing military officers.

"Well, dear, as you've been hearing for years; the issue of slavery has been a source of hot contention between the Northern states of America and the Southern states. Up until now the rival factions have coexisted with a workable compromise. The North has not insisted on the abolition of slavery in those Southern states in which it has been a tradition since their founding. What the northern Abolitionists do object to is extending the doctrine, slave trade, into the new territories in the Louisiana Purchase and west of the Mississippi.

"Recently, however, there has been a Supreme Court decision that has inflamed the tensions between the free and the slave states. This nigger slave, Dred Scott, had been living with his master in free territory and was so declared liberated by the Abolitionists. The Court ruled that any person whose ancestors were sold as slaves had no constitutional rights, and ordered Scott returned to his master.

"It's an issue that has infuriated the hotheads on both sides because it will open the way for the extension of slavery in all those neutral Western territories.

"The Southern rebels are calling for secession from the Union, and the Abolitionists up North are demanding unconditional surrender from the South on the slavery question. There is much bad blood, and it could mean trouble in the future, possibly even war."

"The saints preserve us," exclaimed the Duchess. "And all the time I thought we'd be getting away from ugliness, violence and bloodshed when we came to America."

He patted her hand. "Oh, I think it's only a remote possibility. The Americans will find some way to resolve their differences. After all, when a nation of people have gone through a trial by fire together as they did in the Revolution against overwhelming odds, it forges a bond among them that can stand up to almost any test." Privately, he was not all that confident. Look what had happened in Ireland.

"Papa," Ravena said pensively. "This plantation where we're going to live, does it have slaves?"

"Why, of course, child. I mean, after all, who would work the farms and the cotton fields if it weren't for the slaves? The entire Southern economy is agrarian."

"Have the white Americans ever thought of working the land themselves?"

The Duke didn't like the turn this conversation was taking. "Ravena, you're only a child, you can't be expected to understand these matters."

"I am *not* a child," she said firmly. "I am a woman."

"All right, you are a young woman. Woman or not, it's out of your grasp, your understanding."

"Help me understand."

The Duke sighed. "All right. In the first place, the population in the North outnumbers the South's population by better than five to one. The North is industrial while the South is agricultural. It's how they complement each other. Naturally, the influx of immigrants into America is predominantly to the North, where the industries are that can provide them with a living. There is no job market in the South."

"Because the niggers do all the work for nothing?"

The Duke reddened. "If you want to put it that way, Ravena, you must understand, the Southern economy is totally dependent on slavery. Up North the farms are small and the returns fast and favorable. A farmer can work his farm with the help of a few paid hired hands. That's out of the question on a vast cotton plantation."

"How many slaves do *you* own, Papa?"

The Duke turned away, plainly distressed. "I'm not

certain. Oh, roughly about a hundred, give or take a few."

She stared at him, saying nothing; it made him more uncomfortable than if she had accused him outright.

Bitterly he made the acknowledgement himself. "I know what you're thinking. I find the whole concept of slavery intolerable. Detestable. Yet, for years I went along with the system and lived the life of a grand lord while my tenants—my slaves—were dying from disease and starvation."

"That's not true, Edward," his wife protested. "You were the best landlord in all of Ireland, I've heard the tenants say it. Kind, generous and understanding of their plight."

"But I made them work my land as my father had demanded of them before me. Yes, Ravena, you are quite correct. I say one thing out of one side of my mouth and quite another out of the opposite side." He shut his eyes and pinched the bridge of his nose. "Do you know, I have never seen a black man?"

"Nor have any of us" said the Duchess.

"They say that Nigras aren't human, only one step removed from an ape."

"The same as the English say about the Irish Catholics," Ravena reminded him.

"Precisely my point. We know what shameful propaganda that is because we have lived with the Irish."

"We *are* partly Irish," Ravena said with pride. "Dear Dan O'Connell."

"And now we are going to live with black men."

"And women," she added pointedly.

The Duke smiled at her. "You take pride in being a woman."

"As well as in having the Irish in me. Indeed I do."

He put an arm about each woman's shoulders. "And I am proud of what two fine women I have been blessed with. This country, this United States, we must all work to make our new homeland proud of us."

"Amen," said Ravena and hugged him hard.

That night, while Rose was brushing out Ravena's hair before bedtime, she received an education in the new democracy they would be living under.

"You will no longer address my father and mother as

'your Grace.' Their titles are no longer valid in America."

Rose lamented. "Oh, I don't believe I can do it, Miss Ravena. They'll always be the Duke and Duchess of Ulster to me."

"Then you must practice very hard at remembering it, Rose. My father says they poke fun at titles in America."

Two days after when they disembarked at Richmond, the reception committee that greeted them at dockside made Ravena eat her words.

There was Colonel Ainsley Cooper, a portly man of sixty with flowing white hair and a white vandyke beard. There was Lewis Hastings, a gangling, dark-haired man with a sallow saturnine face. There was Colonel Carter Taylor, enormous in all of his proportions, with a round Santa-Claus rosy face and beard. All three were dressed in all-white suits and broad-brimmed hats, outfits that would have been considered tasteless in Ireland or England.

They removed their hats with a sweeping flourish of their arms and bowed deferentially to the royal couple.

"Welcome to America, your Graces." The tall man was spokesman. "I am Lewis Hastings, and these here gentlemen are your neighbors on either side." Indicating the enormous man first. "Colonel Carter Taylor and Colonel Ainsley Cooper."

Lewis Hastings had been overseer of the Duke of Ulster's plantation for more than ten years. The position had been a veritable goldmine for Hastings and had enabled him to give up his former occupation as slave trader. He had supplied all of the slaves that worked the plantation, one hundred ten originally, who had multiplied to one hundred seventy, with the sixty children between infancy and eleven years of age. This venture was at a tremendous profit to himself. In addition, he always shaved twenty percent off the plantation's profits each year. His bank account now was adequate enough to buy a small plantation ten miles further up the James River from the Wilding property, a thousand acres of rich bottomland.

Every time hereafter that anyone referred to her father and mother as "Duke" and "Duchess" or "your Grace," Rose would direct a smug impudent grin at Ravena.

"Oh, yes, they do poke fun at titles in America," she'd tease.

It did seem to Ravena that more attention was accorded to rank in the United States than in the British Isles or Europe. The only difference was that the titles had a military connotation instead of a royal significance. For example, neither Colonel Cooper nor Colonel Taylor were in the military service; the titles were honorary. There was also a superabundance of "Judges" and "Governors" and "Honorables," not to mention "Senators." As many as thirty percent of "Your Eminences" had never sat on the Bench, in the State House or the Legislature.

Ravena's introduction to the homestead—which her father promptly named *Ravena* after herself—was an impressive experience. The carriage turned off the main road and passed under an archway at least a half-mile long, of cherry trees aflame with blossoms. When they reached the end of the crimson tunnel, there was the mansion, a white jewel in a setting of green velvet, two acres of manicured lawn, its grass seed imported from Bermuda, as Lewis Hastings told them with pride.

"Five pickininnies and a flock of sheep work seven days a week all year to keep it that way," he said.

The house itself, like the men's clothing, disturbed Ravena at first. A huge sprawling rectangular structure of undistinguished architecture. The façade was all windows and small balconies on the upper story. The dominant feature was the broad, covered verandah, with its roof supported by four tall white Tuscan columns. She'd never seen a colonnade like it in Europe. And like the men's clothing and so many other customs that were preciously regarded by the residents as "Southern Tradition," the house was all whitewashed brick and wood.

White. Symbol of purity. Unspoiled.

Favorite hue of attire among Southern Belles.

White. The blind color, no color at all, the achromatic part of the spectrum. Lazy, sweet euphoria of the Lotus-Eaters. The Southern aristocracy, like its European counterpart, was God's chosen people. Eternal. Nothing would ever change.

Limp, cloying, clinging like the wisteria and honeysuckle growing over the porch and balconies, intertwining with the pink crepe myrtle and the white magnolia that enlivened and lent character to the bland structure of the old homestead.

The entire staff lined up on the front lawn in front of the house to welcome the new occupants. The Duke felt as if he was back in the service reviewing troops as Hastings led him along the even ranks, identifying each black man, woman and child perfunctorily:

"Davis the coachman." An intelligent-looking man with light skin and gray steel-wool hair.

"Lenny the footman." A skinny, gangling adolescent with a perpetual grin and buck teeth.

"Gordon, the head butler." Tall, erect, distinguished, clad in black livery.

An array of underbutlers or busboys, wearing white coats over dark trousers.

"Hattie the cook." A roly-poly, jolly-looking woman, black as coal, her head bound in a checkered turban. Ravena took an instant liking to Hattie, and learned later that her feelings had been reciprocated.

"Birdy the maid. She'll be working under your maid of course." A small sprightly woman aptly named.

There were two white staff members who received personal introductions to the Wildings. Burt McCloud, the groom in charge of the stables, a tall rugged man with steel-gray eyes and a brown handlebar mustache. He spoke with a drawl that Ravena found as hard to understand as a shanty-Irish brogue, except that his words were paced slow enough to enable interpretation.

"You all have one fine stable, Mr. Wilding."

"His *Grace*," snapped Hastings.

"Beggin' yo' pawdon, sir. That is, Your Grace," McCloud amended hastily.

" 'Mister' will do perfectly fine," mumbled the flustered Duke.

The stable consisted of two carriage horses, three racers of Arabian stock, and three saddle horses. Not counting the work horses and two foals sired by the Arabians.

Horseflesh, along with courtliness, women of virtuous, if flirty charm, casualness bordering on ennui, personal honor, and an addiction to white were part of the proud Southern tradition. Three things could fire up a Southerner: an affront to his family honor, to a white woman, any white woman; and to the South. In any of these events, he could be placated with nothing less than a humble apology or satisfaction on the field of honor.

The other two white staff members were Carl Reynolds, the plantation's general manager, and his wife Dinah. Dinah, a pretty blond girl, who had the shading of a woman with octoroon blood, was not technically employed, although she was paid on occasions to lend assistance at balls and dinner parties.

Reynolds was dark and dashing, with a glint in his dark eyes brightened when he saw Ravena. She looked him straight in the eye, feeling the magnetism generating between them. Body chemistry, a term that would have shocked her parents. She'd learned it from Brian. Something about Reynolds reminded her of Brian O'Neil.

The very evening of their arrival, there was a ball at Colonel Taylor's home. Ravena and her mother wore their newest gowns purchased in Paris the spring before, the very latest fashion at the Tuileries. A princess gown that struck the eye like a dazzling field of flowers. A hoop in lieu of the heavy clumsy crinoline, molded to the upper torso to give the figure a triangular silhouette, flat in front, flaring behind. The undercorset was more flexible, the bust contained by elastic, silk ribbon and only a few supporting bones. Cut high in front and low at the back.

Ravena did a pirouette in the center of her bedroom. "How do I look, Rose?"

The maid clapped her hands. "The belle of the ball, for sure, Miss Ravena."

"Don't be too sure. These Southern belles have quite a reputation. How do you like it here, Rose?"

Rose was noncommittal. "Well, it's only been one day, Miss, so it's hard to say. Sure enough, it isn't Ireland."

"That it isn't, but you'll get used to it. How are you getting along with Birdy and the rest of the house staff?"

The girl fidgeted from one foot to the other. "I don't know about that. I mean, me being the only white servant and all. What makes me feel funny is they treat me like I was one of the ladies of the house."

"That's because you're white."

"I know. Still, I wish there was another white maid or cook for me to chum with."

"You'll make friends, don't worry. Colonel Cooper's wife has a white maid. So do several other of our neighbors, so I understand." She nudged Rose with her elbow and said slyly, "I couldn't help noticing that you had an eye for that manager, what's his name? Oh, yes, Reynolds."

Rose blushed. "What a thing to say, him being married."

Ravena sat down at her dressing table and gathered her hair at the nape of her neck. "I think the green ribbon tonight, Rose. Yes, that Reynolds is quite a figure of a man."

"Aye, and he's got a roving eye, that's for sure, Miss." She grinned at Ravena in the mirror. "Only it ain't for me."

"You are an impudent girl."

The two of them began to giggle and couldn't stop.

Colonel Taylor's plantation was similar to their own only smaller. The same unimaginative box of a house, white, with a colonnade. Jasmine, wisteria, honeysuckle.

There was no formal reception line to bedevil new arrivals, for which Ravena was grateful. Colonel Taylor introduced them to his wife, Min, almost as rotund as he was, and full of fun.

"And my son, Lieutenant Barton Taylor."

Lieutenant Taylor was in uniform, the dress uniform of a cavalryman with a red cumnerbund and sash slashing across his chest. A serious young man of twenty-five with straight brown hair slicked back and a large nose.

The colonel escorted the Duke around the ballroom, making informal introductions to key guests, who, by prearranged turn, would take the newcomers in tow and introduce them to still other members of the group made up strictly of the elite families of Richmond.

Minnie Taylor did the same for Vanessa Wilding, while their son Bart escorted Ravena around the room on his arm.

Ravena had heard Lieutenant Collins boast of the grace and beauty of Southern womanhood, but she had not expected them to be so stylish. After all, they were thousands of miles from Paris and scarcely past the pioneer stage of their development.

The dance floor was a kaleidoscope of brilliant color.

Lightning blues. Blood reds. Apple greens. Cardinals. Purples. Peacock green. Mandarins. Lapis lazuli. And even muted shades recalling old tapestries. The petticoats, pantalettes and stockings as bold as the outer garments. Stripes, polka dots, intricate embroidery, vivid in peacock blues, golden yellows and all the colors of the rainbow.

A few of the younger women were wearing gowns so *avante garde* that Ravena was green with envy. Gowns that bared their shoulders with, as the Duke put it, "no visible means of support." Breasts bunched up high and close together, their upper crescents plump and powdered.

"I must get one of those marvelous gowns," Ravena whispered to the Duchess.

"Over my dead body," the Duke muttered.

The Duchess laughed. "I notice, my dear, that you don't object to them on the women who are wearing them."

The Duke reddened and grunted. "Nonsense! Shocking sight!"

Of the scores of people she met that night, Ravena was impressed, perhaps, by a half-dozen of them at first impression.

There was Barbara Collins, the wife of the young lieutenant they had met on the ship. A pretty, petite girl with auburn hair and green eyes.

And there was Barbara's cousin Jan Seedley, a niece of Jefferson Davis, a senator from the state of Mississippi. Jan was dark, vivacious and a trifle buxom. The kind of woman whom Brian would uncouthly describe as, "built like a brick outhouse."

Mr. Davis was a tall, distinguished man with an aristocratic bearing, white-haired with a small beard. His voice was like crushed velvet.

He bowed to Ravena with a grand flourish. "Seldom have mine eyes beheld such breathtaking beauty, Miss. I am eternally grateful to you for bestowing such a privilege on me before I die."

Ravena laughed merrily. "And I thank you, sir, for making me feel so much at home. I haven't heard such blarney since leaving Ireland."

He feigned indignation. "Miss Ravena, are you impugning my honor as a southern gentleman by suggesting that I would state something that I knew to be an untruth? I tell you, the last time I set eyes on a beauty such as yours was in Savannah, Georgia. Come to think of it, she was of Irish extraction, too. Scarlett O'Hara is her name. Lovely. Reminds me very much of you, Miss Ravena. Except for the eyes. And, to tell the truth, she was a trifle skinny for my tastes."

Jan Seedley objected. "You shouldn't be comparing the Wildings with the O'Haras, Uncle Jeff. As I recall, Scarlett's father is a bricklayer, a gambler and a drunkard."

"We've had a few of those in our family past," Ravena joked.

"I dare say your mother, the Duchess, would not appreciate your humor," said Davis.

Ravena wrinkled up her nose. "My mum? Now she's no snob. Fact is, her cousin Dan O'Connell came close to being hanged by the British several times."

There was an uproar of laughter. A crowd was gathering around Ravena, and she was beginning to feel quite at home in truth now.

Her favorite at the party was Mrs. Jesse Farnsworth, a middle-aged widow with a plain, strong-featured beauty that somehow radiated an Olympian aura. She possessed the sense of natural-born aristocracy that Black Lightning, the Arabian racer in the Duke's new stable, did. Class. From the other women she learned that Jesse Farnsworth was the bellwether of Richmond's high society, the official hostess of the major city in the South.

"Her husband was a Northerner," Jan Seedley explained. "A fabulously wealthy Philadelphian. He was in some kind of secret government work. A courier of some sort. Though that's not how he came by his money. Jesse still has a lot of friends in high places in Philadelphia, New York and Washington," She lowered her voice. "My husband Nate says she's spying on the north for us. She and my Uncle Jefferson are very, *very* close, if you get my meaning."

"I do, indeed." Ravena smiled. "But what would she be spying on the government for? You talk as if the south was a separate country."

Jan's eyes narrowed wisely. "From what I hear from my uncle and other men in high places, that might be-

come a fact in the near future. The way those damned
Yankees are treating us, it's beginning to look as if the
only way to settle the argument once and for all is for the
slave states to secede from the Union and form their own
country."

Colonel Cooper came over to them. "Here, here, you
ladies musn't tax your pretty little heads with serious
business like politics."

You insufferable bastard! Ravena thought.

But she smiled sweetly and replied, "Why Colonel
Cooper, sir, I do believe you Southern gentlemen overdo
it in the way you pamper your women. We are not as
frail or empty-headed as you imagine."

He coughed self-consciously and touched a handkerchief to his lips. "Yes, ma'am, and they love every moment
of it, isn't that right, Jan?"

"It has its advantages I guess, but Ravena makes sense
too."

The portly gentleman looked dour. "Miss Ravena, I
hope you don't put too many revolutionary ideas into
these little gals of ours."

Ravena's smile was wry at life's ironic parallels, past
and present.

New ideas were anathema to the reactionaries in England and Ireland as well. His liberal thinking had cast
the Duke and his family into exile. There wasn't much
difference between the pompous oafs in this ballroom and
the ones she had met at the Viceroy's celebrations. Just
a matter of accent, and after a while her ear began to
accommodate to their way of speech.

It seemed to her that the number of men in military
uniforms was excessive. And the political repartee, which
dominated all other topics of conversation, was bellicose.
The notion of any compromise from the South's set
position with regard to the issue of extending slavery into
the western territories and the even more significant issue
of states' rights opposed to the supremacy of the federal
government was unthinkable.

"I'll be damned if some damned Yankee from Massa-
chusetts or Illinois voted into office by a bunch of so-
cialist Abolitionists tells the people of the sovereign state

of Virginia how to conduct their internal affairs," declared Colonel Taylor.

"I can tell you a few things about that crowd," Lewis Hastings said to the Duke. "Abolitionists, that's a fancy camouflage for radicals, ruffians, and outright thieves. Yes, when they aid and abet Nigras to escape from their rightful masters and take 'em up north by their infernal 'Underground Railroad,' that's the same as if I steal into your house at night and make off with your wife's jewels."

"The point is," put in Lieutenant Pennel Collins, "that the Supreme Court has ruled in our favor. The Missouri Compromise is unconstitutional, and by God, if any Yankee president refuses to abide by the decision of the Supreme Court, then he's setting himself up as an absolute monarch and we might as well have kept King George!"

"Hear! Hear!" A cry went up from the men and many of the ladies began to clap.

Ravena and the Duchess exchanged some quiet words.

"This isn't a party," the girl said. "It's a rally."

The Duchess smiled. "Yes, it is, and your Roger is going to fit into this society the way a hand slips into a silk glove."

A disturbing thought to Ravena.

"I hear you have two handsome brothers," Jan Seedley said to her near the end of the evening. "Will they be coming over to America to be with you? We have some highly eligible young ladies who'd swoon at the chance to meet a gen-u-ine Marquess."

Ravena laughed. "They'd better not get their hopes up too high. Kevin is a married man with a child on the way while Sean is married to his medical studies. He wrote that he would consider leaving England after he receives his degree and completes his internship. But that's a long way off."

"I'll bet you can't wait to see your fiancé again."

"I'm counting the days." A statement that had a hollow ring to it.

CHAPTER SEVEN

The wedding of Ravena O'Connell Wilding to Roger Fitz O'Neil, Viscount of Tyrone, was the social event of the year in Richmond, for that matter, in all of the state of Virginia.

Ravena wore her mother's wedding gown, full skirted, of white brocade over a crinoline underskirt. The tight bodice of the gown was embroidered with tiny seed pearls and trimmed with imported Spanish lace. The bridal veil cascaded from a priceless pearl tiara which had been handed down from one generation of the Wildings to the next for three centuries. It was claimed that Ann Boleyn had worn it at her marriage to Henry VIII. Virginal white did not suit her status, Ravena reflected as she contemplated herself in a full-length mirror prior to the ceremony. Well, the gown was not quite pure white. Age had mellowed it to the hue of rich cream.

Melanie Yates, sister to Barbara Collins, was her maid of honor. An ethereal pale blonde girl with an angelic face, she and Ravena had become fast friends since the Wildings had settled in Richmond. Melanie wore a pale blue taffeta gown and carried a basket of red roses.

The six bridesmaids wore gowns of goldenrod yellow, printed in festoons with wisteria blossoms, varied medleys of white, yellow and purple. Each carried a little basket of tea roses.

The bride's bouquet was composed of white roses and baby's breath with white satin ribbons streaming from the roses.

"The most elegant wedding ever celebrated in this state," proclaimed Mrs. Jesse Farnsworth, and she was quoted in the society pages of the city's journals.

Roger, as everyone expected, wore the dress blues and red sash of a cavalry captain, his rank in the Virginia militia. He looked very dashing indeed, as attested to by the sighs and fluttering eyebrows of all the assembled unwed belles.

As Vanessa Wilding had prophesied, Roger was welcomed into the men's world of Southern aristocracy as if he were a long-lost brother.

He was sponsored for a commission in the state militia by Lieutenant Pennel Collins and another friend, Major George Manson. His application was approved by a young colonel destined for immortality by the name of James Ewell Brown Stuart, known to his friends and men as Jeb.

Jeb Stuart was a cavalier in every sense of the word. Six feet tall, straight as a military epee, he seemed leonine with his flaming hair and a spiked beard and flowing mustachios to match. He dressed with the same dash that he applied to all of his endeavors in life. Flowing gray cloak lined with crimson silk. White buckskin gauntlets. His light sabre was belted over a lemon silk sash with tassels. On his gray uniform jacket, he wore a fresh rose boutonniere each day. And when roses were out of season, he tied a lover's knot of red ribbon in his lapel. His wide-brimmed cavalryman's slouch hat was turned up rakishly on the right side by a gold star and a white ostrich feather curled back on the left.

Roger was impressed by Lieutenant Col. Jeb Stuart as no man he had ever met had struck him. The two men enjoyed an immediate empathy in their fervent conviction that honor and patriotism were as sacred as the vows of a monk, and that the greatest game on God's green earth was war.

His wife, Flora, was as striking as Stuart, slender and vixenish with hair almost as red as her husband's.

Ravena found them a physically attractive couple, but she never was able to shake the feeling of "distance" between them and herself. The three of them, to be factual, Jeb, Flora and her own Roger.

Pennel Collins was best man at the wedding in June of '58, and, far into the night, he and Jeb Stuart and the groom and a rowdy, drunken bunch of cavalry officers drank toasts and sang rousing martial songs to the accompaniment of Stuart's personal minstrel Corporal Joe Sweeney's strumming banjo:

If you want to smell hell—
If you want to have fun—
If you want to catch the devil—
Jine the Cavalry. . . .

Upstairs Ravena lay alone in her marriage bed, listening to the carousers' bellowing ring through the house and fuming at her new husband's callous disregard for her feelings on this their wedding night.

When finally he did come to bed at four A.M. he toppled onto the bed in a stupor without even removing his clothes and commenced snoring like a wart hog.

Roger was humbly apologetic the next day, but Ravena refused to speak to him throughout the long journey by rail and carriage to Philadelphia where they would spend their honeymoon.

However, the first night in the hotel, she relented and allowed him to make love to her at last. Perversely, the discord between them and her denial of the consummation of their union for so many days heightened the passion, whetted their lust, when they did come together.

She closed her eyes, savoring the sensation that Roger had a score of hands or more. His fingers seemed to be all over her body at once; no square inch of burning flesh remained untouched. His lips, as well, made a circuit of her yearning body, eyes, ears, nape, shoulders, breasts, devouring her tormented nipples, teasing her navel, caressing the insides of her thighs.

Ravena moaned and arched her pelvis to meet the thrust of his tongue. Never before in her life had she experienced such ecstasy.

"Now, darling! Now! Hurry!" she panted. She opened to him as a flower opens to the hot shafts of the sun, consumed by him and in turn consuming him.

"Oh, my darling, my darling husband," she cried out at the peak of her climax. "My darling Brian!"

It shocked her as much as it shocked Roger. What had ever made her say such a terrible thing? She hadn't thought of Brian in years. Certainly he was the last person living or dead on her mind this wonderful night.

He stiffened and lifted himself up, staring down into her astonished eyes. She was frightened at the murderous rage she saw in his eyes, the unique smoldering look Roger had always reserved for his brother and no one else. The special hate.

His voice rasped. "What did you call me?"

She lied. "Roger. What else?"

"Like hell! You called me *him*! Brian!"

"That's insane. Your ears are playing tricks on you, Roger. That happens, they say, in moments of great emotional stress. Passion."

"You bitch!" He slapped her hard across the face. "You were thinking about *him*. Not me!"

"You madman!" She drew up her knee as he aimed another blow at her, digging it hard into his gut. He grunted and doubled up, affording Ravena an opportunity to slip out from under him. She rolled over and leaped out of bed, but he lunged and caught the back of her flowing nightgown.

She tugged and it ripped off in his hand. Naked she ran to the hearth in the bedroom, taking up the steel poker.

"You lay another hand on me and I'll brain you!"

The pain and fury of what she had inflicted on him blinded Roger to all else. He advanced on her relentlessly, almost warily as a fencer, a sport at which he excelled.

He feinted to grab her with his right hand, and she swung the poker at his arm. Deftly he caught her wrist with his left hand and twisted the weapon out of her grasp.

Ravena, squirming and twisting like a trapped cat, clawed his left cheek with her nails and spat on him.

Roger clubbed her on the side of her head, and the room spun wildly around. She closed her eyes and collapsed in his arms.

She was dreamily aware of being carried, floating, it seemed. Placed roughly down on the bed. He was mounting her, spreading her thighs with a knee.

"Don't! Please, Roger, not like this."

"Like this," he said grimly. He entered her forcefully this time, hurting her. She twisted and moaned, but was powerless to resist.

Moving on top of her in quickening rhythm. Muttering

to her. "This one is for Brian. Dear, dear brother Brian, may your soul rot in hell!"

His release came like white lightning. Dazzling, intense and gone by the time the echo of the bolt faded.

They made love sporadically after that night, but it was never the same for either of them. A physical act of the flesh like eating and drinking, or the act of elimination. No genuine love or passion involved. Impersonal sex.

After their return to *Ravena*, Roger was summoned to a private conference with the Duke. An intimate chat over brandy and cigars.

"Roger, my lad, welcome to the family. From this point on, the Duchess and I will think of you as our son. The way things stand now, my sons Kevin and Sean have evidenced little if any disposition to join us in America and concern themselves with the administration of this plantation. A considerable responsibility that would leave no time for them to pursue their professions of medicine or teaching. Therefore, Roger, I think it is only right and proper that you and Ravena shall inherit the land and all of the holdings, house, barns, equipment, slaves, what have you, upon my retirement or demise, whichever comes first." He smiled wryly around his cigar.

"The former, let us hope, sir," Roger said stiffly. "I must say I am overwhelmed, and eternally grateful to you. I know I speak for Ravena too."

Thinking: *"Nobody thinks or speaks for Ravena! Sweet bitch!"*

"Then it's settled, lad. I think, under the circumstances, that beginning tomorrow you should begin familiarizing yourself with the administration and technical details that make this operation a highly profitable enterprise. You and I will sit down with Carl Reynolds. By God! He's been invaluable to me and I'm sure he will serve you loyally as well."

"At your service, Your Grace."

Roger proved to be a conscientious and diligent administrator and an attentive student to the seasoned caretaker's tutoring.

"Mr. O'Neil, won't be long you'll know as much about running this outfit as I do." Reynolds laughed and shook his head. "Damn, maybe I've talked myself out of a job. Soon you won't need me."

"Not on your life, Carl," Roger said soberly. "To be honest with you, I don't have the time or the patience to devote myself full-time to this venture. You see, there's my military duties to be considered. Colonel Stuart is convinced that we are on a collision course with the Yankee Abolitionists and that it's only a matter of time before this country is plunged into a civil war. When and if that time comes, Virginia will be ready, I promise you."

Roger's military duties kept him away from home at least three nights a week and very often on Saturdays and Sundays, when Jeb and Roger drilled raw militia recruits on the banks of the James River.

Hundreds of blueblooded young dandies were rallying around the Virginia State flag from the tidewater country on their Arabian racers and strain jumpers. It was up to Jeb Stuart and Roger O'Neil and a handful of other experienced cavalrymen to make horse soldiers out of them.

Jeb Stuart was an inspired leader who revolutionized the strategy of warfare. A century ahead of his time, he armed his men with the best weapons of the day.

Jeb Stuart had only scorn for the conventional role of the cavalry established for centuries in Europe, the closed-ranks shock charge of mounted soldiers wielding heavy cavalry sabres.

"War isn't a dress parade," he lectured his troops. "We're fighting men, not showmen. The prime role of the horse is for speed and mobility.

"Hit the enemy in the nose, then kick him in the arse. And when he hits back, be gone and set to kick him on the other cheek."

He lifted the sabre. "This looks impressive in a parade, but it isn't worth a damn in modern warfare. The cavalry needs firepower as much as the infantry, and every man in my troop is going to be sharpshooter and learn to fight on foot as well as in the saddle."

He had already submitted a design to the War Department for a light sword to replace the traditional sabre that could be quickly hooked over the pommel of a saddle.

Roger O'Neil worshipped his commander and would

have ridden into the mouth of hell with him. His opportunity was not far off.

"I had an instructor at Sandhurst," he told Stuart, "who used to say that the true purpose of cavalry in warfare was to give tone to what otherwise would be simply a vulgar brawl."

The big redhead laughed. "Nicely put, Roger. I think I'd like that on my tombstone: *'Here lies Jeb Stuart. None of his battles were vulgar.'* "

On October 16, 1859, a small dinner party at the Wilding's home was interrupted by the breathless arrival of a courier with a message for Roger.

"Captain O'Neil, Colonel Stuart wants you to mobilize the troop at once. Some damned Abolitionist named John Brown has just seized the arsenal at Harper's Ferry with a band of insurgents and he's trying to instigate a slave rebellion."

"I'll be damned!" Roger leaped to his feet. "I hope you ladies and gentlemen will excuse me. You've heard what the corporal said, and I think that all of you appreciate the nature of this crisis. It could mean that war is upon us."

The news dampened the spirits of the diners and the party broke up early. After the last guest had gone, Ravena joined her parents in the drawing room for a nightcap of mulled port.

Gordon the butler, as well as the cook and kitchen staff, had adapted quickly to the family's British tastes in food and beverage. At the same time the Wildings had been introduced to some extremely appetizing Southern specialties. Two of their favorites were fried chicken and mint juleps.

"Will that be all, sir?" asked Gordon after he had served them.

"Yes, thank you, Gordon. You may retire now."

The Duke lifted his glass in a toast. "Godspeed to Roger, and may his mission be successful and may he return safely to *Ravena*."

Ravena drank with something less than enthusiasm. Her mother acutely observed her mood.

"What's wrong, dear? Are you worried about Roger?"

"Yes, Mother, I am worried about Roger. But not in

the way you're thinking. Roger and his idol Colonel Stuart rather strike me as two of the indestructible warriors out of the *Iliad*. Nothing can touch them. No, what concerns me is this passion Roger has for the Confederate cause."

"Confederate?" inquired the Duchess.

"Yes, that's a new term the Southern slave states have coined, now that there is all this popular pressure for secession from the Union," said the Duke. "A confederacy of states that renounce their allegiance to the present federal government in Washington. In fact there's been talk about establishing the Confederate capital right here in Richmond."

"But what's it all got to do with Roger?"

Her father frowned. "My dear, I'm surprised at you. This nation, this state has welcomed us to its shores after we were practically turned out of our own country. I believe we are honor bound to share in its liabilities as well as its assets. If war comes, and I fervently pray that it does not, your husband Roger—myself if they'll have me at my age—Roger and I must stand shoulder to shoulder with every other able-bodied Virginian in the staunch defense of this blessed land."

"Your father is right, Ravena," the Duchess said. "You are righteously indignant because the English won't grant the Irish people self-rule. Isn't that precisely what the North is trying to impose on the South?"

"No, Mother, it's the moral issue that's at stake in both cases, and it's the moral issue that is the same. Freedom. Equality. The English have made slaves of the Irish, just as the southern aristocracy has made slaves of the black. The North stands for freedom for all men, and so do I."

The Duchess shook her head. "Oh, Ravena, you're a headstrong girl. Roger should hear you."

The idea still possessed her after she had retired to her room. Birdy, the black maid, came into the room. Rose had been assigned to look after the Duchess exclusively when Vanessa Wilding had contracted a mild case of yellow fever the previous summer, and the arrangement had continued through the fall months.

It was no hardship to Ravena. She was fond of the pert young black woman who moved about with the quick, jerking motions of a sparrow, cocking her head to one side when speaking, her round eyes shiny and intelligent. A fetching smile, but she seldom smiled.

"I already turned down your bed, Miss Ravena. Can I help you undress?"

"I can manage, Birdy. You must be tired."

"No, ma'am, I had me a nice nap after supper. Let me help."

Ravena addressed the girl as an equal. "Birdy, what do the staff think about all this talk of secession and war? You can speak freely with me, you know that."

"You mean blacks? Mostly we're afraid."

"But you want to be free? This Mr. Lincoln who wants to be president. He says slavery is an evil and an injustice. I agree with him."

The rare, shy smile showed. "Well, that goes without saying, but you know as well as I do, Miss, that none of the plantation owners are going to let Mr. Lincoln or anyone else free their slaves. *Their* property, same as they own dogs, horses and farm animals." A hint of challenge and the smile faded. "Miss Ravena, how does your daddy feel about setting us free?"

"You have every right to ask that, Birdy, and I'm afraid I can't give you an easy answer. You see, my father is a newcomer here. He didn't buy the slaves. He inherited them. I know my father has strong pangs of conscience about your situation. He's an honorable, decent man who detests the whole notion of slavery. But he's in a quandary. If he could, he would set every one of you free tomorrow morning. But it would be unrealistic. Where would you go? What would you do? The way things are now, the authorities wouldn't permit you to go North. Besides which, they would consider my father a traitor to their society. A society that took us in as refugees and embraced us and accepted us as fellow Virginians. The Duke is highly sensitive to that stigma. 'Traitor.' He's been charged with that sin before. That's why we're here in the first place."

Birdy nodded sympathetically. "Yes. I heard all about that, Miss Ravena. Your father, he is a good man. Decent like you say. I just wish—" It trailed off wistfully.

Ravena stepped out of the last of her clothing and examined her naked body in the mirror. The ripe breasts, the flat belly, the round buttocks, the slender legs. A warm, fecund female body that had not experienced fulfillment in a long time. Forever it seemed to her. Not the honest, glorious fulfillment she had shared with Brian.

"Keep expecting to see a little bulge there pretty soon, ain'tcha, Miss Ravena?" Birdy rubbed her own belly.

Ravena felt the blood rush to her head. Such insolence would have been punished by a horsewhipping in any other household. Briefly she wanted to punish Birdy. But the anger drained out of her, realizing that it was only joy and good will toward her mistress that had prompted the maid to ask the question.

That, too, she was deprived of. A child. The one yearning that kept her coupling with Roger like a hopeful mare. Anyone would have done. Ravena wanted a child.

"Someday, maybe. . . ." Her voice trailed off. "Birdy, do you ever expect to have a child someday? Is there anyone in your life? I've seen the way Lenny looks at you."

The girl smiled self-consciously at Ravena's reference to the gangling young footman. "Yes, Lenny, he's a good boy. I think he is kind of sweet on me."

"You'd marry him?"

The climate of the conversation changed as if a frigid wind was blowing into the room. Birdy's face hardened and her voice was hostile and bitter.

"Me marry? Not in a million years. Oh, no, I've seen what sorrow it brings when two slaves marry. Even living together. It happened to me. I was only five years old when they broke up our family. My daddy to Colonel Basehart 'way up river. My maw, I don't know where they sent her. Nor my two brothers. He bought me and brung me here, that Mr. Hastings."

Ravena had never seen such sorrow stamped on a face. Even more wrenching than the grief etched on the faces of the endless impoverished Irish mourning their dead on the way to the graveyard, wailing and shouting a threnody. The "keen."

She started over to the girl to comfort her, but Birdy turned away from her, stifling a sob with the back of her hand.

"I'd best get to bed now, Miss Ravena. Got to get up early and help cook. One of her girls is got the fever."

Ravena looked after her in helpless, silent despair. All thought of sleep was gone now. She paced restlessly like a caged cat. The walls of the room were closing in on her.

"Damn it all!" She took off her nightgown and took a white silk blouse and a pair of jodhpurs out of her bureau. Ravena was one of a few daring women of the period who defied convention and rode a horse astride like a man.

A devotee of the French female novelist George Sand, Ravena had more than once threatened to appear at one of the Wilding's dinner parties in men's evening clothes with white tie and tails. The Duke, a patient, indulgent and loving parent, was adamant in denying Ravena that whim.

"Not in my house, you won't. The shock would kill your mother."

"It's not Mother you're thinking of, Father. I happen to know that she, too, agrees with much that George Sand advocates."

"That's absurd! The woman's a harlot. Worse, she pretends to be a man. She's degenerate!"

"That's how much you know about it, Father. She is a woman, and proud of it. That's the point. She's the world's foremost champion of women's equality. A man can go, do and dress as he pleases. Then why not a woman?"

The Duke groaned and clapped a hand to his head. "I've never heard anything so ridiculous. Women are not only equal to men, they have more privileges than men. They have it much better than men in every respect. They don't have to work, or go to war or—"

"Or do anything else that is constructive in life. Men have always treated women like delinquent children."

"Balderdash! I'm warning you, Ravena. My patience is at an end. You will desist from this poisonous speech in my presence. I won't have it, girl."

Ravena put a hand on his arm and said with affection, "I love you, Father, and once it was nice to be your little girl and be loved and protected. But I am no longer your little girl. I'm a woman."

"Yes, and a married woman who ought to know better. Tell me, what does Roger think of your radical feminizing?"

"It doesn't matter what Roger thinks. Father, you should really read George Sand. It might enlighten you. Women are coming out of the dark age of subjugation and subservience. They even speak freely of their affairs."

The Duke recoiled, looking so stricken she had to laugh, "Ravena!"

"I'll lend you my copy of *Un Hiver à Majorque*. It's all about her affair with Chopin."

He whirled and stormed over to the sideboard and poured himself a stiff shot of whisky.

"I'll have one too, if you don't mind, Father," she called after him gaily.

Now, with the blood racing through her veins, she felt the tension and excitement a good hunter evidences when he's being saddled up for the chase. No encumbrances for Ravena this night. She put the blouse on her bare body, relishing the sensual feel of the silk on her breasts. No lower undergarments either; pantalettes were too bulky under the tight riding breeches. She knotted a scarf around her head and grabbed her riding crop.

Burt McCloud, chief groom and trainer of the Wilding's two racers, was working late down at the stables. West Wind, a top-notch two-year-old, had pulled up lame in a race the previous Sunday, and McCloud was treating the damaged hock with the same tender, loving care as he would have administered to one of his children.

He was surprised to see Ravena. "Miss Ravena, it's kind of late." A pregnant hesitation. "Even for you."

She was amused by the intimation.

A hellion like you.

"Saddle up Ginger, please, McCloud."

Ginger was a roan who reminded her of Apache. Her favorite mount had been entrusted to the Earl of Tyrone's stables when they left Ireland.

McCloud ran a leathery hand over his long stringy face. "I dunno, Miss. Your father and Mr. O'Neil would tan my hide iffen—"

The crack of the crop against her palm brought him up short. Her eyes shone in the moonlight.

"And I'll tan your hide right now if you don't hop to it and saddle up my horse."

It was a warm Indian summer night with a hot breeze off the river.

"Go, Ginger, go!" She crouched low on the roan's neck

as they galloped across the meadow behind the house racing the clouds scudding over the sky like greyhounds. The roan's mane tickled her nose and his heaving sides were hot on her thighs through the material of her jodhpurs. Ravena's wild laughter was whipped back in the slipstream lending to it an eerie sound. A banshee wail. The Little People.

God! She was exhilarated, the depression she had felt in the bedroom dissipated now in this vital, living experience. She always felt so alive when she was riding. She and the horse one entity. A centaur.

Attuned to the universe around her. The thunder of hooves and the earth. The wind's song. The hoot of an owl. The lament of a loon. A barking dog in the distance. More distant thunder. A single gunshot. Poachers on the loose.

They plunged into a dark wood. Blind, but she and Ginger knew the route, as sure of themselves as if it were high noon.

Another shot, much closer now. Cautiously, she reined in, stroking the horse's neck. "Easy boy, slow down." She brought him back to a walk, and as they approached a bend, urged, "Whoa, boy."

Someone was approaching from the other direction, the sound of hooves quiet on the thick duff of the woods. They broke into view, the dark silhouette of a horse and rider. The intruder, aware of Ravena, reining in sharply. "Stay where you are, or you're a dead man!" A rifle came up, pointing at Ravena. She knew the voice. Laughed.

"Hold your fire, Reynolds. It's only me. Ravena O'Neil."

"Ma'am?" The muzzle dropped, but his voice was tense. "You shouldn't be out here at this hour, Mrs. O'Neil. For a second there I thought you were a poacher. I ran one of 'em off just before. Gave 'im a dose of bird shot in the butt—" He broke off. "Begging your pardon, ma'am."

Ravena laughed again. "It's all right, Reynolds. Butt, derriere, arse, all perfectly respectable terms to describe a rather important portion of the human anatomy."

He chuckled softly. "You are something, ma'am, you truly are." His informality deliberate, a liberty he would not have taken with the Duchess or any of the other maids and matrons who sat on their "butts" all day sipping lemonade and fanning themselves on the rich plantations up and down the river. This little gal had style. Like now. Riding like a man in man's gear. Not a fearful bone in her body.

And what a body. First time he had set eyes on her, his old pecker had twanged like a tuning fork!

"Maybe I'd better ride with you, Mrs. O'Neil. Can't tell one of them poachers might give it another try."

"That won't be necessary, Reynolds."

"You object to my company?"

"I don't care very much one way or the other. Suit yourself. Giddyap, boy."

He followed a quarter-length behind and at her side. Soon they broke out of the wood and looked across one of the vast cottonfields. A sea of white reaching as far as the eye could see. Silvery in the moonlight.

"A pretty sight," he mused.

"Like a cloud," she said. "I'd like to lie down on it and float away into the sky."

The horses had stopped. He looked at her thoughtfully. "That a fact, ma'am? You ever lie down in a cottonfield?" It had been a calculated risk, that question, and he held his breath and his heart thumped heavily in his chest as he waited on her reaction.

"No, I haven't," she said dryly, "but I'll wager you have done your share of lying in the cotton. And rolling in the hay as well."

His strong white teeth gleamed. He had an animal aura about him. Wolflike. Gleaming fangs. She was aware of his carnality whenever they were close. It carried in the air like musk. She knew what he was thinking now. He lusted after her. He wanted her in the desperate way a hound wants a bitch. Well, it had been a long time since her sexual appetite had been slaked. Of late her body had been wound tighter and tighter like a clock spring. It was overwound. Something had to give. And if she could use this stud, all well and good. The animal quality about him reminded her of Brian. Not that he possessed Brian's sensitivity or intelligence, but she sensed he knew how to please a woman.

"And you'd win the wager, ma'am."

She toyed with him. "How do you suppose it would

strike my husband if I were to tell him the insolent way you've been speaking to me?"

He pushed back his cap and said in his slow and easy drawl, "I dunno, ma'am. I think Mr. O'Neil would be charitable about it, considering—"

"Considering what?"

"Considering that he's been bedding down with my missus Dinah for the past two months."

That was unexpected, a sneak blow and it rocked Ravena. Not that she had any illusions about Roger's fidelity to her. Not that she gave a damn! The whores, the dance-hall girls, the sneaky little Virginia belles with saucer-innocent eyes and hot pantalettes. But this was different. Dinah Reynolds was the wife of an employee.

He knew what she was thinking. "It's a sticky wicket, ain't it, ma'am? I mean, me working for your father and him. There is a code, you know. If he was seducing a nigger wench, those Southern gentlemen friends of his, Colonel Stuart and them, they could go along with that. But Dinah. My wife—well—"

"You don't have to spell it out, Reynolds." She dismounted, put down her crop and began to unbutton her blouse. "Well, don't just sit there."

His eyes widened. "What do you mean, ma'am?"

Her eyes regarded him with smoldering amusement and contempt that heightened the heat in her loins and breasts. What more wantonly delicious act could she perform than fornicating with this hairy, sweaty, muscular, primitive, male animal?

"Why don't you want to claim your Biblical justice? Your pound of flesh?" She giggled. "I rather like that metaphor. My husband put the horns to you, and now you want to put them back on him. Isn't that it, Reynolds?"

She opened the blouse and threw back her shoulders so that her breasts pointed up at him, beckoning, gleaming like marble in the moonlight.

"Jesus! You're beautiful—" He caught the "ma'am." Silly as hell to call a woman "ma'am" when you were getting set to screw her!

Swelling with lust, he leaped from the horse and tore off his shirt and trousers. They faced each other, naked like two beasts, squaring off for combat.

She looked down at him lecherously. "You are quite a stallion, aren't you, Reynolds?"

Then his arms crushed around her and his hard body molded to her softness. Her breasts flattened against his chest so fiercely that it was hard to breathe. The maleness of him bursting against her trembling belly. His teeth bruised her lips and his breath stank of tobacco and whisky. An aphrodisiac aroma. That and the sweat.

"Fuck me, Reynolds," she gasped. "Fuck me good."

Then they were down on the soft bed of the cotton and grass. The crushed stalks and plants prickled the flesh of her back, but Ravena did not notice or care. All sensation was focused at the core of her womanhood. They worked at it industriously with the mechanical precision of two machines. Valve and piston. Bolt and sheath. Perfect rhythm, accelerating until the white hot parts could no longer endure it.

Bodies shattering.

A glorious explosion.

Tumbling down back to earth.

Her back itched now. She squirmed beneath him. "That was good, Reynolds. Very good indeed."

"Yes, ma'am, it sure was."

"Well, it's over. Get your hulk off me."

"Yes, ma'am. Ma'am, I want to thank you—"

"*Thank* me?" She laughed harshly. "You insolent bastard! How dare you!" She grabbed up the riding crop and whipped it briskly across his buttocks as he stooped to pull up his trousers.

"Yeowwww!" he howled, leaping up and down and from one foot to the other, with his trousers tangled around his ankles. Holding his smarting buttocks with his hands.

Ravena laughed until her sides ached. "What's that supposed to be, Reynolds? The mating cry of the rednecked, bare-arsed, Virginian peacock?"

CHAPTER EIGHT

The election of Abraham Lincoln as President, an avowed foe of slavery, was the last straw as far as the South was concerned. Seven southern states—South Carolina, Georgia, Louisiana, Mississippi, Florida, Alabama and Texas—seceded from the Union. A provisional government was set up at Montgomery, Alabama, and a Confederate Constitution drafted.

South Carolina demanded the return of all Federal property within the state, including Forts Moultrie and Sumter. The garrison at Moultrie moved to the more strategically situated fort at Sumter at the mouth of Charleston Harbor.

On April 12, 1861, six weeks after Lincoln took office, the Confederates opened fire on the fort and bombarded it for thirty-four hours until the post commander, Major Robert Anderson, surrendered. The Civil War had begun.

On April 17 Virginia, Arkansas, North Carolina and Tennessee proclaimed secession and the permanent capital of the Confederacy was established at Richmond.

Jan Seedley arrived at *Ravena* one morning, bursting with news. "Have you all heard? Uncle Jeff is the new president of the Confederate States. Isn't that the most exciting thing you ever heard?"

"Goddamn!" Roger exclaimed, almost as ebullient as Jan. " 'Scuse the language, ladies, but this is an occasion when a little profanity is in order." He summoned the butler. "Gordon, break out that case of French champagne my father sent last Christmas and put it on ice."

"I scarcely think it's in good taste to celebrate a funeral, Roger," the Duke said solemnly.

His son-in-law glared at him. "What the hell kind of talk is that, sir?"

"Why, we have just buried the Declaration of Independence and the Constitution, Roger."

Captain O'Neil was livid. In a strained voice he said, "With all due respect, sir, I must remind you that it is exactly that kind of treasonous talk that led to your exile from Ireland."

Before the Duke could reply, Ravena leaped up and shook a fist under her husband's nose. "How dare you talk to my father like that after all he's done for us! In his own house, too."

"Don't be upset, Ravena," the Duke said calmly. "Roger has every right to express his opinion as I have mine. And my view is that this war is a tragedy unparalleled in the history of this great country, past, present as well as in the future. If it has a future any longer. America will bear the wounds and scars of this conflict for a thousand years. Another decline and fall of the Roman Empire."

"I'm not staying around to listen to such defeatist talk. I'm going over to headquarters and see what Jeb is up to. Don't wait supper for me."

Roger was a virtual stranger in the house after that. In the first week in May he announced to the Duke, "I can no longer keep up with my responsibilities as manager of this plantation, sir, what with my pressing military duties. Day after tomorrow President Davis is personally commissioning Jeb Stuart and me as officers of the Confederate Army, and I expect we'll be going into action soon after."

The night before he left to assume his new command, Roger and Ravena dined with Flora and Jeb Stuart and the Duke and Duchess.

"Don't they look handsome in their new blue and grays?" asked Flora Stuart.

"Take good care of those uniforms," the Duke said wryly. "They may be the last ones you see for some time."

Jeb Stuart frowned. "Sir? I don't understand."

"Well, the South has no industry to speak of. I'll wager the blue-grays you're wearing now come from cloth produced in a Northern factory."

"Nonsense," Roger scoffed. "What about England and France? They've always been our friends. Best cotton customers we've got. And don't tell me that the North has the navy and will blockade the South. Hell! Between 'em the British and French Navies will blast the Union warships into kindling wood if they try and interfere with merchant ships servicing Southern ports."

"You actually believe that, Roger?" The Duke smiled thinly as he sipped his after-dinner brandy.

"Of course I believe it."

Edward Wilding sighed. "For one who has always been a staunch supporter of England and her policies, I'm surprised that you know so little about the English ethic. Both England and France have abolished slavery in their own dominions and condemned its practice universally. Although their sympathies may lie with the South, and I don't doubt they do, neither can lend open support either materially or morally to the cause for which this tragic war is being fought. The continuance and further promulgation of the institution of slavery. No, Roger, you are wrong on that score, as time will prove. In fact, the English and the French will welcome the Union blockade, for it will spare them the embarrassment of denying aid and succor to old friends. Oh, there will be a few privateers who will risk it for exorbitant profits, but such minuscule efforts will not reflect the backing of their governments."

The Duke's words were prophetic, and while both England and France paid lip service to the right of the Southern states to determine their own destiny while ignoring the slavery issue, neither one made any serious effort to run the Northern blockade and supply the Confederacy with the industrial products it needed so desperately.

On paper, as the Duke liked to point out to his son-in-law, the North "held all the aces." It had industry, it had railroads, it had the navy, it had most of the natural resources and money.

But the South had an ace of its own in its superior army. A majority of the finest officers in the United States Army, including the best generals, pledged allegiance to the South. Throughout history good soldiering had gone hand in hand with an agrarian society.

A good many of the top Union commanders had to be recalled from civilian life. Grant, MacDowell, McClellan. Ulysses S. Grant, in fact, was clerking in his father's general store, having been forced to resign from the service because of his incessant bouts of drunkenness.

The Confederate generals included such luminaries as Robert E. Lee, former Superintendent of West Point, T.J. "Stonewall" Jackson, P.G.T. Beauregard, and brilliant Jeb Stuart, the cream of the West Point officers.

The South, too, had the advantage of fighting a defensive war. Soldiers have better morale and greater incentive when they are defending their own land. The Union was the aggressor, and at the start, the green Union recruits who composed the bulk of General Irwin Mc-Dowell's invasion army marching on Richmond in July of 1861 had little stomach for the task they were assigned to. The first objective of Lincoln's High Command was to capture the Confederate capital.

On July 21, 1861, McDowell's "irregulars" clashed with Beauregard's elite troops along a small stream thirty miles south of Washington, to be forever immortalized as "Bull Run," and suffered a demoralizing defeat. They ran head-on into T.J. Jackson's men, who were "standing like a stone wall," and turned and ran for their lives. The rout was stopped at the outer defenses of the Union capital, and the fate of Washington was in doubt for some time.

And so, ironically, the Confederates, in the first major battle of the Civil War, almost accomplished the objective which the Union forces had described as their own mission. The dramatic capture of the enemy's principal headquarters.

After the Battle of Bull Run, Congress authorized augmenting the Union Cavalry's six regiments by thousands of men. No small task inasmuch as the Northern volunteers were primarily city men who had been office workers and factory laborers. Few of them had ever been astride a horse in their lives.

Men with a background of the military and horseflesh such as Brian O'Neil possessed were a precious commodity to the Union Cavalry. To his chagrin, he was commissioned a first lieutenant and assigned as an instructor with the Tenth New York Cavalry Regiment from Elmira, New York.

"Damn it, sir!" he complained to his CO. "I joined up to fight. Not to give riding lessons to city dandies."

"I know how you feel, Lieutenant," Captain Vanderbilt sympathized. "But if you can train a hundred of them to learn even a quarter of what you know about horse-soldiering, you're worth more to us than up at the front fighting the Rebs one on one. I promise you, once we whip these greenhorns into shape, you'll get your chance to swing a sabre at the enemy."

For two years after the war began the Union Cavalry stood on the defensive. And it was two years before Major Brian O'Neil saw combat.

Captain Roger O'Neil didn't have to wait nearly so long for his baptism of fire. In June, riding with Jeb Stuart at Falling Water, his troop decimated a Union outpost. Jeb was promoted to full colonel while Roger won his major's leaves.

Both were at Bull Run too, and, at the climax of the nightmarish battle, Stuart unleashed the first of his lightning-strike cavalry charges that would become a trademark. Slashing through the ranks of the Union's distinguished Zouave regiments, he turned the Union flank and rolled it up into a badly confused and panicky mob, precipitating the pell-mell rout to Washington.

Two months later Jeb Stuart received his brigadier's star and Roger was elevated to lieutenant colonel.

That night the officers' quarters reverberated with laughter and singing well into the dawn. Joe Sweeney strumming his banjo as Jeb and Roger harmonized to the strains of *Dixie Land*.

Den I wish I was in Dixie. Hoor-ray! Hoo-ray!
In Dix-ie land I'll take my stand to lib and die
* in Dixie,*
A-way, a-way, a-way, a-way down South in Dix-ie.

The Confederacy was riding high and mighty in the first two years of the war. The predicted strangulation of the South by the Union blockade was slow to materialize. Arms, ammunition and supplies poured in from Mexico and up the Mississippi. As long as Admiral Buchanan held Mobile Bay, the Union could not control the Gulf of Mexico.

Jeb Stuart's troopers contributed their share of captured booty, whirling behind the Union lines like a tornado, hit-and-running at the bewildered enemy, destroying communications, burning property and pillaging.

Twice Jeb, with Roger at his side, led the cavalry of the Army of Northern Virginia around the Army of the Potomac, commanded now by General George McClellan. McClellan had forged to Richmond's very doorstep and the fall of the Confederate capital appeared imminent in June of 1862.

With twenty-five-hundred troopers, Stuart captured hundreds of prisoners, horses and mules, so disconcerting McClellan that the northern offensive was stopped in its tracks.

In August of the same year, Stuart's Raiders struck behind General Pope's army; Pope had relieved McClellan after the debacle at Richmond.

Once again his men inflicted punishing losses on the Union forces and captured a wealth of supplies and equipment. His greatest prize was the capture of General Pope's personal baggage and official secret correspondence.

Jeb and Roger were congratulated personally by General Lee and President Davis.

"Do you realize what we have here?" Robert E. Lee exulted. He turned to Stonewall Jackson who had driven Pope's army back to the Rappahannock River. "Lincoln's ordered McClellan's troops in the west to move down and reinforce Pope. All we have to do is have Longstreet pivot to the northwest and hit Pope on the flank before Mc-Clellan is organized."

Once again the Union Army of the Potomac was sent reeling back across Bull Run and all the way back to Washington.

And once again, to the disgruntlement of many Southerners, including some general officers of the hot-blooded variety of Stuart and Roger O'Neil, Jackson did not follow up the advantage.

"Don't get me wrong, Jeb," said Roger. "Lee is a brilliant tactician, but as a field general, by God, you're worth him and Jackson put together. If that was you, there'd be gray troops patrolling the streets of Washington instead of Yankee blues."

"You know what the trouble is," Stuart said grimly. "Lee doesn't *want* to destroy the Union. He took a soldier's oath to preserve and defend the Union. All he wants is for the Union to recognize the sovereignty of Virginia and the other Confederate states."

It was an affliction that many southern and northern soldiers suffered from. The Cain-and-Abel syndrome. Brother fighting brother. Brother killing brother.

Jeb Stuart at the Seven Days' Battle was confronting his father-in-law General Philip St. George Cooke, who commanded McClellan's cavalry.

He had a sister-in-law married to the Surgeon General of the Confederate Army and another one married to a Union general.

On October 26, 1862, General McClellan, once again commanding the Army of the Potomac, launched still another invasion of Virginia. Longstreet stopped it in its tracks and Lincoln relieved McClellan and appointed General Ambrose E. Burnside to sustain the attack on Richmond. It turned out to be the most disastrous decision that Lincoln made in the entire war.

Burnside, with a fanatic determination that verged on insanity, launched a massive frontal assault against General Lee's army entrenched on the heights above Fredericksburg. Although outnumbered one hundred thirteen thousand to seventy-five thousand, the veteran Confederates won the day in the bloodiest battle ever fought up to that time in any war in history.

Six times the valiant Union infantrymen charged across the bare plain under the relentless fire of Confederate artillery and rifle companies. Long double lines of blue and national and regimental colors. Bayonets gleaming. Guidons whipping in the breeze. Six times they were driven back, leaving thousands of dead piled high against the stone wall fronting Marye's Heights.

At the height of the battle General Lee had tears in his eyes. Softly he proclaimed: "It is well that war is so terrible, or we should grow too fond of it."

When it was over, the Union counted almost thirteen thousand dead while the Confederate losses were placed at fifty-five hundred.

Fredericksburg was so shocking to the public both in

North and South who read of its grisly horrors vividly described by newspaper reporters, that it was rumored in high circles in Richmond and Washington that the two sides must reach an accord quickly or risk open mutiny by their soldiers and citizens alike.

President Lincoln confided to his advisers shortly before Christmas of 1862: "We are on the brink of destruction."

For the revelers who attended a lavish New Year's ball held at the presidential mansion in Richmond, the future looked bright indeed.

Even the Duke of Ulster had to admit that his dire predictions of Confederate collapse had been unfounded. The army had not run out of uniforms, nor weaponry, nor supplies. Morale was higher than when the war had first begun. Richmond was still a gay, exciting affluent city and everyone had plenty to eat and drink.

Oh there was inflation to be reckoned with. An egg sold for one dollar; a pound of coffee for five dollars. But life went on as serenely as ever at *Ravena* and the other plantations.

In many plantations all of the men in the family had gone off to war, leaving the women with the full responsibility of running all of the complex operations necessitated by the war. By government edict, as soon as war was declared, cotton land was to be reconverted into farm produce land. Spinning, weaving, dyeing, all of the gentle household arts were revived. Women labored in smokehouses and handed out free food to passing troops. Ravena, her mother, along with Jesse Farnsworth and other fashionable ladies of Richmond society worked five days a week as hospital volunteers caring for the wounded. Then gave or attended parties and dances at night to entertain battle veterans on leave or recuperating from wounds.

"I'm pleased to see how patriotic you've become," Roger complimented Ravena when he came home on leave that Christmas. "General Lee says that you and your mother and Mrs. Farnsworth are the most conscientious war workers in all of Richmond."

"It's not war work, Roger. It's *peace* work. Doing one's best to bring peace and comfort to those poor wounded men. Boys many of them."

"They're heroes. Not to be pitied but to be regarded with pride."

She did not reply. It would have been useless to explain to Roger that whatever patriotism might be motivating her was the patriotism of humanity. Love of one's fellow man and woman.

"No man is an island," John Donne had written. *"Every man is a part of the main . . . I am involved in mankind. . . ."*

For some reason, her thoughts turned to Ireland, and a lump formed in her throat.

"What is it?" he asked.

She forced a smile. "Nothing. Nothing at all. I'm glad you're home and safe, Roger."

"Do you mean that?"

"I wouldn't have said it if I didn't mean it."

He tried to embrace her. "I was hoping things might be better between us."

"It may be." She turned her cheek to his kiss. "Give me a little time, Roger. Don't press me."

"As you say."

Two nights later, on Christmas Eve, she went to bed with him for the first time in over a year. Her reasons were too involved, so she did not seek any self-justification for her decision. Reynolds had enlisted soon after the war began, and he was the last man she had made love to. It had been a long time. Too long for a woman of Ravena's lusty appetites. There was, too, an obligation she felt toward her husband as well. A soldier risking his life for a cause he believed in. A worthy man. A courageous soldier. Certainly he deserved whatever comfort and satisfaction she could provide for him. She his wife.

Sex was better between them than it had been at any time since that impassioned interlude in their courtship.

"Absence makes the heart grow fonder," Roger murmured into her hair.

"Abstinence makes the flesh grow hotter," Ravena thought but held her tongue.

He raised himself up on one elbow and looked down into her face. "Wouldn't it be a wonderful thing if on this night you conceived my child?"

"Positively wonderful." She was sincere.

He laughed. "Quite a Christmas present that would be."

One week later they were at the Presidential Ball in celebration of the New Year.

"A New Year, a new time for the Confederacy," President Davis offered the first of innumerable toasts in imported champagne.

One hundred miles to the north in Washington there was no champagne. Nothing to celebrate.

In the White House President Abraham Lincoln was going over the final draft of a document he would submit to the United States of America on New Year's Day.

The Emancipation Proclamation.

". . . In witness whereof, I have hereunto set my hand and caused the seal of the United States to be affixed . . .
By the President:
Abraham Lincoln"

After gazing at the myriad campfires twinkling like stars in the dark sky on that same night, correspondent Julia Ward Howe covering Burnside's rout from Fredericksburg went back into her tent and composed a spirited verse to boost Union morale:

"He has sounded forth the trumpet that shall
never call retreat . . .
He is sifting out the hearts of men before
His Judgment-seat . . .
Oh, be swift my soul to answer Him, be
jubilant! my feet!
Our God is marching on . . ."

A poem later to be immortalized as "The Battle Hymn of the Republic."

CHAPTER NINE

Like a dying star, the Confederate fortunes were burning brighter during the early months of 1863 than at any other time since the onset of war.

In May General "Fighting Joe" Hooker who had replaced the incompetent Burnside launched his campaign to take Richmond.

He was turned back at Chancellorsville when Jeb Stuart's cavalry cut in behind the Union right and cut Hooker's ninety-thousand-man force to pieces. Hooker retreated back across the Rappahannock River with seventeen thousand casualties. In a desperate effort to find a winning commander, Lincoln replaced Hooker with Major General George C. Meade.

One small, ill omen dampened the jubilance of the stunning Confederate victory. During the battle Stonewall Jackson was shot and killed by two of his own men in a tragic incident of mistaken identity.

Stuart was assigned to replace Jackson and promoted to Major General.

"They ought to be lynched for murder," Jeb complained to Robert E. Lee. "They're not soldiers, they're chicken farmers. What kind of trash are they taking in the army these days?"

"Any man with two legs, two arms and two eyes who can fire a rifle," Lee told him grimly. "Face it, Jeb, we're scraping the bottom of the barrel."

The war of attrition was swinging the tide at last.

By June of 1863 Jeb Stuart commanded a corps of twelve thousand men and twenty-four pieces of artillery. On June 5 the entire corps put on a dress parade for the benefit of the President and his cabinet and an assembly of the richest and most important members of the southern aristocracy.

The Duchess whispered to the Duke and Ravena, "In a way it's rather like the ball held by the Duchess of Richmond on the eve of Waterloo."

"That would seem to be a good omen," he said.

Four days later Stuart hurled his corps against fifteen thousand Federal cavalry on the same site and sent the Feds scattering back across the Rappahannock. The star had reached its zenith.

Three weeks later Robert E. Lee began his ill-fated invasion of Pennsylvania.

"I don't want you roaring all over the countryside this time, not knowing what you're up to, Jeb. Your main mission is to keep Hooker occupied so's he won't find out that Ewell is going for Cemetery Hill. You and I will meet at York on July 1 and force Hooker to do battle at Cashtown where we'll have the mountains behind us and on one flank."

"We'll cut 'em to pieces," Colonel O'Neil said with satisfaction.

Stuart abided by his orders until there dangled before him one of those tempting opportunities for another whirlwind foray behind the enemy's lines.

On June 26, he crossed the Potomac on Hooker's right with the intent of cutting the Union commander's line of communication with Washington and raising hell on the Union flanks and rear. It was a stunning success from the standpoint that his raiders captured 125 wagons loaded with precious food and supplies along with a thousand prisoners. The trouble was his column was handicapped by the prisoners and booty so that its progress was reduced to twenty-five miles a day instead of the projected forty miles a day required for Stuart to rendezvous with Lee in York on July 1.

General Lee's carefully laid plans went up in smoke. Not only was Stuart's cavalry support vital to the success of his offensive, but without his reconnaissance reports, Lee had no idea of the movements of Hooker and his commanders.

While Lee was waiting for Stuart, minor skirmishes at the points of the rapidly closing opposing forces quickened in tempo with the ultimate result that Lee was sucked into a major battle at Gettysburg—instead of Cashtown, where the terrain would have favored the Confederate armies.

Time and again Lee's attacks were repulsed. At the height of the Battle of Gettysburg, Confederate Major General George E. Pickett led a charge of twelve thousand four hundred infantrymen at the Union center at Seminary Ridge. The attack was repulsed at a cost of forty-five hundred Confederate casualties. By the time Jeb Stuart arrived on the scene the battle was lost, and all that his cavalry corps could provide was a diversionary action that permitted Lee to conduct an orderly retreat. The decisive battle of the Civil War had gone in favor of the Union.

In a final skirmish on the Union flanks, Stuart's troopers were repulsed by a sharp US brigade led by the youngest major general in the Union Cavalry—a slender man with shoulder-length blond hair and a drooping mustache.

"Best damned horsemanship I've ever seen from the Feds' cavalry," Stuart lauded his opposite number.

The man was Major General George A. Custer, twenty-five years old.

In the midst of the action, Stuart had observed that his always-reliable aide, Colonel Roger O'Neil, had behaved most atypically. In a clash with an enemy trooper, sabre to sabre, he had quite unexpectedly broken off the fight and had gone galloping off in another direction.

Later he had been white as a sheet and trembled from head to foot. Stuart was concerned.

"What happened to you, Roger? You look as if you've just seen a ghost."

O'Neil stared at him with glassy eyes. "By God, sir! I *did* see a ghost."

And with that cryptic reply, he walked away, leaving the general gaping in wonder.

The Battle of Gettysburg haunted Jeb Stuart for the remainder of his short life.

He was given to bouts of melancholy, and when his jester Sweeney died of pneumonia, there was no longer any music at the corps campsites.

"Nothin' to sing about, that's why the poor sonovabitch died," he told Roger one night soon after Sweeney's passing. They were sharing a bottle in Jeb's tent.

"Things are bound to get better," Roger consoled him.

Jeb stared at him with a lopsided grin, his eyes bleary from drink. "Why, you stupid Limey."

Roger bridled. "Don't ever call me a Limey. I don't care if you are a major general, I'll—"

Jeb waved him to sit down. "I'm sorry, that wasn't fair. It's just that I can't stand being patronized, Roger. You know as well as I do that the Confederacy is coming apart at the seams. Drafting fourteen-year-old boys! Shocking. And did you know that no more enlistments are being accepted for the cavalry unless the man can supply *his own horse*."

"Damn!" Roger was stunned. "Things are bad. I hadn't realized, not *that* bad."

Stuart's red hair and beard were wild and unkempt; the day before he had looked in a mirror and mused: "I'm getting to look as mad as John Brown."

He looked down into his glass, rolling it with his palms, and began to recite:

"For want of a nail, the shoe was lost.
For want of a shoe, the horse was lost.
For want of a horse the rider was lost.
For want of a rider the battle was lost.
And all for the want of a nail."

Roger frowned. "What is that all about?"

Jeb smiled wistfully. "An old rhyme. You see, there was this courier who had to deliver a vital message to his king about to do battle in the field. But his horse lost a shoe and he never got to deliver the message, and so the battle was lost."

Roger could not meet his suffering expression. "General, sir, I think I'd better be getting back to my own quarters. Lot of paperwork to finish."

"You do that, Colonel." The general slumped over the table with his head resting on his forearms.

It was at Gettysburg that Brian O'Neil saw his first major action as a colonel commanding a regiment in George A. Custer's corps.

After the battle Custer personally commended him. "Colonel O'Neil, if I had two more regiments like yours I'd have kicked Lee's ass all the way back to Richmond."

"We could have done that yesterday," Colonel O'Neil said without expression. It was the common opinion of Major General Meade's general officers that he was overly cautious, an opinion reinforced on July 5 when President Lincoln telegraphed an ultimatum to Meade: *"Do not let the enemy escape!"*

Meade hemmed and hawed for another week, and by that time Lee had reformed his demoralized troops on the south side of the Potomac, and the Confederacy gained a reprieve.

George Custer was disgusted, but there was one consolation. "We'll get another crack at 'em, that's a certainty." His quick mind leaped to another subject. "Say, Colonel, you planning to stay in the service after the war?"

Brian's thoughts were of Ireland and Ravena.

He hesitated. "Well, I'm afraid not, General. You see, I've got some commitments to honor."

Custer studied him shrewdly. "I always knew you were a man with a mission, first time I laid eyes on you. Whatever it is you'll accomplish it. You're a man with will and determination. They're almost as important as courage. When you've got all three, nothing can stop you. Yes, Colonel, it was a lucky day when I snatched you away from the old Tenth."

In the year since he had been serving under George Custer, Brian had formed an allegiance to the feisty, firebrand general very much akin to the relationship that his brother Roger had with Jeb Stuart.

It was not long after Gettysburg that one of Brian's captains told him: "It was the damnedest thing there at Cemetery Ridge. I saw this Reb, a colonel I think he was too. And the thing of it was in the heat of the fighting I thought: 'My God! What's Colonel O'Neil doing in a Confederate uniform?' Was the spitting image of you, sir."

Brian laughed. "I think maybe you'd been snorting on that white lightning we captured back in late June."

"No, sir, the resemblance was amazing."

Brian could not dismiss the incident as lightly as he pretended. Even as in infant, being one-half of a set of twins gave him an unsettling feeling. Looking at Roger was like looking into a mirror except for the color of the hair. No love lost between them but neither could deny the strong ties that bound them together. They spoke of the "silver cord" that bound mother and child for eternity. The cord that bound twins together was even more inseverable. There were times when Roger's thoughts were transmitted to him as clearly as if he had spoken them aloud. Hostile vibrations for the most part. He supposed it was a major reason why they had grown farther and farther apart as they grew up, each of them resentful of the intruder within.

The hair prickled at the base of his neck as he considered the captain's words: *The resemblance was amazing.*

Could there be still a third man on the planet with his face? It defied all coincidence. Yet to believe that the Confederate colonel was his blood twin was even more preposterous. No, in the passion and stress of battle, the captain had suffered a visual distortion. A face glimpsed briefly in a chaotic melee of men and horses; his testimony unreliable.

Brian took a deep breath and put it out of his mind. It triggered thoughts of his family though that had lain dormant for years. Ireland and home. His father and mother. Roger. Ravena. How were they faring? From what he read in the newspapers, conditions in Ireland had improved greatly in the years since he had fled. There was a rising clamor within the British Liberal Party for radical reforms in the Empire's attitude toward its poor and reluctant relation. Led by a firebrand named William Gladstone, Chancellor of the Exchequer at present and headed for bigger posts, it was predicted.

He shook his head in a sudden fit of depression. So many times he had wanted to let them know he was alive and well, but that was impossible. To do so would be a betrayal of the police chief and all the other valiant members of the underground movement who had helped him escape. Branding them with the lie of his demise. No,

Brian O'Neil must remain dead. And peace be with him!

The North had seized the initiative at Gettysburg, wrested it away from Robert E. Lee, and pursued it ruthlessly from then on.

In the West Grant's Army took Jackson, Champion's Hill, Port Hudson, tightening the noose around the South's main artery of communication, the Mississippi.

In Tennessee, Chattanooga fell, followed in rapid succession by Lookout Mountain and Missionary Ridge.

The Confederacy was staggering, but to the frustration of President Lincoln, the Union seemed incapable of administering the knockout blow. With every defeat and every backward step, the fighting spirit of the Confederate soldier became more savage and resolute.

On March 12, 1864, Ulysses S. Grant was appointed General in Chief of the Army, the highest-ranking officer in the Union Army.

One of his first acts was to dress down General Meade for his misuse of the Union Cavalry.

"God damn it, man, they've had three years to get ready and at Gettysburg they proved they *are* ready. I want this bastard Jeb Stuart stopped once and for all. He's been raising hell with us since the war started, and you tell Phil Sheridan to go get him!"

General Phil Sheridan, commander of the Cavalry Corps of the Army of the Potomac, was a bandy-legged, dour little man who liked it best when he was in the thick of the action with his enlisted men, swearing and waving his sabre.

"I'd follow Phil into hell," vowed Custer.

"And I'd be right behind you," said Brian O'Neil.

They had the chance to prove it on May 11 at Yellow Tavern.

Advancing boldly along the road to Richmond, the Yankee cavalry quite literally "dared" the Red Fox to come out and fight. Jeb Stuart accepted the challenge and moved to intercept them.

They met at Yellow Tavern on the Brook Turnpike, rolling hill country, ideal for cavalry action. Sheridan's blue horde rolled over the hills like waves breaking on the beach. Like the indomitable beach, the Confederate cavalry kept hurling them back.

Both Jeb and Phil Sheridan were in the thick of it, galloping back and forth across their lines, cursing and exhorting their men to stand fast and die before giving an inch to the "bloody rebs" and "damned Yankees."

Later in the afternoon, Custer's persistent hammering on Lomax's brigade, which held the key position on Stuart's left, began to pay off. Lomax began to buckle.

"We've got 'em now!" Custer shouted. "Charge!"

Brian O'Neil's regiment broke through the ranks of horsemen in gray and pressed Lomax's flank back three hundred yards. Soldiers and horses milling around in swirling clouds of dust that made it difficult to tell friend from foe at times.

Colonel Roger O'Neil rallied a troop of disorganized Confederate cavalrymen and reformed them on a hill, threatening Custer's flank. Under heavy enfilading fire, Colonel Brian O'Neil drew back momentarily.

Jeb Stuart rode out ahead of Roger, firing after the retreating Yankees with his pistol. A good many men on both sides had had their horses shot out from under them and were fighting on foot. Colonel Brian O'Neil dismounted to organize a group of ragtag bluecoats. They met the oncoming rebels with volley after volley of shots from their new repeating Spencer rifles. The Confederates went down like wheat before the scythe.

An anonymous sergeant cast aside his empty Spencer, difficult to reload under pressure, and drew his pistol.

He drew a bead on the red-bearded man leading the charge and fired at point-blank range as Stuart's horse sent him flying. The slug went straight through Jeb's liver.

As they were carrying him back to the rear, Jeb Stuart was put through the further agony of seeing his once-proud and unbeatable corps crumbling center, right, and left as Sheridan's spearheads pierced the gray line at a score of points, chopping it up piecemeal and dispatching each group methodically.

"No, no, go back and do your duty!" he implored Roger. "I'd rather see you dead than whipped."

Roger's eyes glistened with tears as he took the hand of

his beloved commander and said in a voice choked with grief:

"But we are whipped, Jeb. There were just too many of them."

He turned and looked toward a distant hill where a cordon of Yankees tightened around a hill where a little band of dismounted Confederates were making a last-ditch stand.

Unexpectedly, anger ignited inside Roger like a flash of lightning. Intense murderous anger and hatred. He shook his fist in the direction of the bluecoats.

"You lousy, bloody bastard!" he shouted.

One of the litter bearers addressed him: "Who are you talking to, Colonel?"

Roger looked dazed, and it was gone as suddenly as it had come over him, the white-hot sensation. "I–I– to no one in particular, Corporal. Carry on."

Over at that same hill, Colonel Brian O'Neil was wiping out the last survivors of this hornet's nest. When it was done, the battle was over. The field was Sheridan's.

The general rode up and down the line, thanking his men and congratulating his generals Merrit, Wilson, Gregg and Custer. All of them in their twenties. Sheridan himself only thirty-two. A triumph for youth that day at Yellow Tavern.

Sheridan shook hands with Custer. "Good work, George. It was your men who got there first." To Colonel O'Neil. "And you were magnificent, Colonel, the way you turned back that charge." His face darkened. "Did you know that one of your men shot Jeb Stuart?"

Brian was stunned. "No. By God! There was so much going on I didn't know."

Sheridan removed his hat and gazed after the rolling dust that marked the retreat of the Confederate Cavalry Corps.

"I hope he makes it. He's a hell of a cavalryman. I'd like to get a chance to fight him again some day."

There would be no more days of glory for Jeb Stuart. Before he lapsed into unconsciousness, he whispered to Colonel O'Neil.

"Roger—the rose in my lapel. . . . Take it to Flora and tell her I love her."

After his death, luminaries from both South and North paid tribute to Jeb Stuart. One of the highest came from a tough old cavalryman, Union General John Sedgwick: *"He was the greatest cavalry officer ever foaled."*

CHAPTER TEN

On May 15, Custer called Colonel O'Neil into his tent. "I've got some news for you, Brian."

"Good or bad?"

"Depends on how you view it. I'm not happy about it."

"I suspect I won't be either. Am I being transferred?"

"You are."

Brian bridled. "But it's not fair. For more than two years the army kept me bound to a cadre training snotnose kids how to ride a horse. And now when I finally get into the action, they pull me back again."

"I know how you feel." Custer was sympathetic. "But there's nothing to be done about it. This came straight from the top, General Halleck, the Chief of Staff, by special courier." He waved a paper in the air. "You're to report directly to General Halleck at the War Department as soon as possible. There's a horse saddled and ready for you at the compound. I'll have an orderly pack your gear and we'll send it on to you."

Brian was curious as well as angry. "What the hell is the big hurry?"

Custer shrugged. "I don't honestly know. It's all very mysterious. These orders merely state that you have been assigned to General Halleck's staff for an indeterminate period."

"Damn! A bloody desk job, is that what I'm in for?"

Custer stood up and held out his hand. "Colonel O'Neil, if that's what Halleck has in mind for you, then the Union deserves to lose the war. You're the best Goddamned natural cavalryman I ever rode with."

"Thank you, sir."

"Brian, you're no longer under my command. I'm speaking as a friend now. I can't help feeling that they wouldn't waste a man like you behind a desk without some

145

very special reason. Maybe it'll turn out better than either of us imagines. You'd better get moving. Sergeant Munson, the courier, is waiting for you by the paddock."

They shook hands, and as Brian was leaving the tent, the general called after him. "Don't you worry, Brian, someday we'll meet again. I won't rest until you're back with me again."

"Thank you—George."

Brian and Sergeant Munson rode into the capital after dark. His quarters at the post officers' barracks were ready for him.

"I'm to be your orderly, sir," Munson informed him. "Is there anything I can do for you?"

"Yes, my luggage won't be arriving until tomorrow. Do you think you could dig me up a clean uniform and a bottle of whisky? I want a bath and a snort before I face General Halleck tonight."

The nature of his mission to Washington was as much of a mystery to Munson as it was to Brian.

"All I was told, sir, was to bring you to General Halleck's office at the war department at nine o'clock tonight."

Brian grimaced. "Old boy is really burning the midnight oil, eh?"

"Nobody sleeps in Washington anymore, Colonel. Even the President paces most of the dark hours, so it's said. I suppose he's worried about the election."

Brian was surprised. "Abe's worried? I should think he'd be a shoo-in the way the war is going for us now."

"There's a lot of folks don't like the way he's run this war, sir. Particularly they didn't like him drafting men into the army. No, he's got a stiff fight ahead of him next November."

"I'm sorry to hear that," Brian mused. "Well, I think I'll have that bath now, Sergeant."

Promptly at nine o'clock Brian O'Neil presented himself at the War Department offices. He was ushered into General Halleck's spare unpretentious office, and was mildly surprised to find two civilians chatting with the Chief of Staff.

A short, squat man with a balding head and wearing

rimless spectacles. But it was the woman who captured Brian's practiced eye. A patrician-looking woman with a cameo profile. Rich auburn hair that cast off glints from the lamp lights. Ageless beauty. He judged her to be in her forties; it made no difference. She was ageless.

General Halleck introduced them. "Colonel O'Neil, this is Mrs. Jesse Farnsworth of Richmond and Mr. Allan Pinkerton of New York."

Brian bowed to the lady, shook hands with the man.

"Please sit down, Colonel." The general indicated a chair in front of the desk between Mrs. Farnsworth and Mr. Pinkerton.

When Brian was comfortable, Halleck explained the nature of his urgent summons. "You may have heard of Mr. Pinkerton. He is the founder of the Pinkerton National Detective Agency. His agents broke the famous Adams Express robbery case back in '60."

"Yes, I vaguely recall reading about that."

"Mr. Pinkerton also uncovered the plot to assassinate Mr. Lincoln one year later."

Brian's eyebrows lifted respectfully. "That's amazing, sir. Just how did you manage that?"

Pinkerton's smile was modestly thin. "Merely a matter of keeping our eyes to the keyhole and our ears to the ground, Colonel."

Brian and Mrs. Farnsworth laughed.

Halleck elaborated. "Mr. Pinkerton is also the originator —this is top secret, Colonel—of the United States Bureau of Secret Service. Its functions are to protect the president's life and to gather information about the enemy's military and political plans. An intelligence agency is what it is."

"Spy work," Brian said.

Pinkerton smiled. "A rose by any other name. Yes, Colonel O'Neil, we have a more sophisticated network of spies within the Confederacy than has ever been possible in any other war in history."

Brian looked wry. "Begging your pardon, Mr. Pinkerton, but as a native-born Irishman I know a bit about under-cover work myself. There was a saying going around that for every British soldier in Ireland there was an Irishman spying on him."

They all laughed and Pinkerton commented. "I rather like your terminology, Colonel. 'Undercover work,' yes, that is precisely what it is. Undercover. Yes."

Brian looked at Mrs. Farnsworth. "Am I to understand, ma'am, that *you* are affiliated with Mr. Pinkerton's agency?"

"Mrs. Farnsworth is one of our top agents," Pinkerton said with pride. "In fact," he smiled, "she is a double-agent. That is, the Confederates believe she is spying on us for them."

Brian stared at the lady with admiration. "That must be a dangerous game, ma'am. A real juggling act."

"It's had its moments," she admitted. "The secret is to steep yourself in the role. Play-acting, as it were. When I am in Richmond, I *am* the fervent champion of states rights, slavery and the Confederacy."

Brian studied her quizzically. "After a while, it must be difficult to separate the roles from the real you?"

She met his gaze unblinkingly. "Not in my case. You see, my late husband, John Farnsworth, was killed by Southern extremists for standing up at a public forum and speaking out against slavery and the dissolution of the Union."

"How is it, then, that they trust you?"

Her eyes slid away from his. "I denounced him publicly and refused to attend his funeral. It nearly broke my heart, but it has been an investment that has paid off." Her inner bitterness surfaced. "John's murder has been avenged time and time again, and I won't rest satisfied until the real murderer—the Confederacy—has been trampled in the dust."

He had never witnessed such open ruthlessness in a woman. He looked to Halleck. "This is all very fascinating, General Halleck. But what does it have to do with me?"

"We'll come to that now, Colonel." The general opened a folder on his desk blotter and lifted out the top sheet. He passed it across the desk to Brian. "Take a look at this, Colonel O'Neil. This dossier contains the service records, copies of the records secured by Mrs. Farnsworth, of an officer of the Confederate Army."

The sheet Halleck had passed to him was an enlistment form. His eyes scanned it briefly. One glance was all it took. He stared at it stunned and disbelieving:

Roger Fitz O'Neil.

"It's impossible, there must be some mistake."

"There's no mistake, Colonel," Mrs. Farnsworth declared. "Colonel Roger O'Neil of the Confederate Cavalry Corps. When you walked into the room before, I was flabbergasted, even though I knew you were his twin from the records. Except for the hair coloring, the two of you are identical peas in a pod."

Pinkerton explained. "You had no idea your brother was in America?"

"No inkling. It's been nine years since I've had any contact with my family. I'm sorry, but I can't elaborate on that condition. It's highly personal."

"It's of no concern to us," said Pinkerton.

"How is it that you know my brother? When did he come to the United States? Why did he leave Ireland?"

The detective held up his hands. "One at a time, Colonel O'Neil. I can appreciate that this must come as a profound shock to you."

"Yes." In retrospect he could not attest that he was all that shocked. After Gettysburg, when his captain had told him about the Confederate officer who had his face, he had felt an uneasy premonition. Twice he and Roger had been in battle with scant yards between them. Twice he'd felt the vibrations, the supernatural feeling that he was being stalked by some one or some thing unknown and evil. He shuddered.

Mrs. Farnsworth related how the Duke of Ulster and his family had been compelled to go into exile because of his unpopular political views.

"They settled in Richmond, Virginia."

Brian sat up rigid in the chair, his heart hammering in his chest. "The Wildings are here, in America. Ravena—"

"Yes, of course, their daughter Ravena accompanied them." She appraised him knowledgeably. "And so did your brother Roger. In fact he's married to Ravena."

Now he felt the true shock. It struck him like a physical blow, leaving him paralyzed, mute. His nose and mouth and fingers were numb, his cheeks the consistency of wax.

"Are you all right, Colonel?" General Halleck asked with concern.

He regained his composure and masked his desolation

behind a brittle smile. "Yes. Yes, sir, I'm all right. It's just that catching up with nine years in one's past so quickly can be overwhelming. You say you are well acquainted with my brother and the Wilding family, Mrs. Farnsworth?"

"We are very close. Edward and Vanessa, Ravena and Roger, I'm extremely fond of them. Ravena in particular. There's much more to her than a pretty face. She has intelligence, character, courage."

Ironically, Brian took pride in her praise of Ravena. His brother's wife she might be, but she would always be his one true love.

"Aye, ma'am, she hasn't changed, then." To Halleck. "But you still haven't told me why you relieved me in the field and recalled me to Washington."

General Halleck chewed the end of a cigar and spit it onto the hearth to one side of his desk. "Colonel O'Neil, the War Department wants you to perform an espionage mission for the government. You'll be working with Mrs. Farnsworth and Mr. Pinkerton."

"What kind of a mission, sir?"

The other two men exchanged pregnant glances, and Mrs. Farnsworth was regarding him with a cryptic half-smile.

Halleck cleared his throat and lit the cigar with a wooden match. "We want you to change places with your brother Roger, Colonel. Assume his identity for the purpose of infiltrating the inner sanctum of the Confederate government. You see, after the Battle of Yellow Tavern, Colonel Roger O'Neil was assigned to new duty as Special Military Consultant to President Jefferson Davis. He is privy to the top-secret military and political stratagems of the Confederacy."

Brian stood up, too high-keyed to remain still. He put the heel of a hand to his forehead and walked around Mrs. Farnsworth to stand before the fireplace.

"Forgive me. My head, it's spinning. You expect me to impersonate my brother Roger? That's sheer madness."

"You're twins, and you look exactly alike, but for the hair, which we can remedy," Pinkerton smiled.

"The hair?"

Mrs. Farnsworth smiled. "My hairdresser has worked

far greater miracles than that. A simple dye job. The texture is no different."

"Still—" He threw up his hands. "No, I'm sorry, it's out of the question. I cannot do it. I'm a soldier, not a spy." He glanced at Mrs. Farnsworth. "Nor can I act worth a damn."

She was worthy of the challenge. "Then I will teach you. I'll tutor you on every aspect of the life of the Wilding family and of Roger and Ravena's life since they arrived in Virginia."

"I've got a terrible memory."

Her eyes were bright. "You remember Ravena?" It was a calculated statement and it hit the target.

His face warmed and he changed the subject. "General Halleck, assuming I were to accept this assignment, what kind of information would I be seeking?"

"Very specific information, Colonel. Incidentally, the assignment is not yours to accept or to reject. It is a direct and binding order from the Commander in Chief, President Lincoln. The success of your mission could well determine whether or not the President is elected or defeated in the elections next November."

Brian was awed by the import of the statement. And for the first time, he experienced the spark kindling within him when confronted by a demanding and intriguing challenge.

General Halleck indicated that Brian should follow him to the military situation map hanging on the wall by the door. Brian inspected it cursorily. It designated the southern portions of Louisiana, Alabama and Mississippi bordering on the Gulf of Mexico.

"Grant and Banks shut down the Mississippi River effectively last year, but as long as the Confederate Navy is free to operate out of the Bay of Mobile, our embargo and blockade of the Gulf of Mexico is incomplete. The British and French can still ship supplies from Mexico across the Gulf to Mobile."

The general put a finger on the triangular body of water wedged into Alabama like an arrowhead.

"The Confederate Navy is holed up inside Mobile Bay like a pack of wolves in a lair. Now, Admiral Farragut has got them outnumbered, we do know that, but he can't entice them into a showdown battle, and he can't launch a direct assault on the harbor; at this point it would be suicidal because we don't have enough intelligence information on the Bay's defenses or the size of Admiral Buchanan's defending forces. We do have a report, unconfirmed, that the Confederates have a secret weapon under wraps down in Mobile. The biggest and most heavily armed ironclad in either the Northern or Southern navies, the *Tennessee*. They say it's over two hundred feet long and sports batteries of six- and seven-inch guns. If it's true, one of these days she's capable of storming out of the bay and raising hell with Farragut's fleet. It is imperative that we make the first strike, Colonel, but we can't gamble with what amounts to the major part of the Union Navy. Your mission will be to get all the information you can about the defenses guarding Mobile Bay and about the size and firepower of Buchanan's Navy, and especially the vital intelligence concerning the *Tennessee*. Do you have any other questions, Colonel?"

Brian turned away from the map and looked at Mrs. Farnsworth. "When does school start, ma'am?"

She smiled. "Nine o'clock tomorrow morning, bright and early."

"I'll be there."

General Halleck extended his hand. "I thank you, Colonel O'Neil, not only in my own name but in the name of President Lincoln and the people of these United States. I am confident that this undertaking will prove to be another brilliant chapter on a service record that is already outstanding. Your country is proud of you, Colonel."

"Thank you, sir." But a part of Brian O'Neil dwelt still in the country where the grass was emerald green year 'round and the breeze was warm and sweet off the sea and chill in the late afternoon with the clouds scudding over the sun like a pack of hunting wolfhounds.

My country.

Someday Ireland would be proud of him too, he vowed.

For five days Brian sat with Jesse Farnsworth in her room in the Washington Manor Inn, reconstructing the lives of Ravena and Roger since their arrival in America six years earlier.

Jesse shot question after question at him after each session with the rapidity of a Gatling gun. "Do you remember that stunning New Year's party back in '63?"

"Of course. That was the night that Nate Seedley got drunk and slurped champagne out of Melanie Yates's slipper."

"Who was the best man at your wedding?"

"Pennel Collins. I wanted to ask Jeb Stuart, but Ravena said it would be an affront to Pennel. After all, he was the first to sponsor me with Jeb."

"What was the biggest scandal in Richmond just before Fort Sumter?"

He grinned. "The rumor that Jeff Davis was having an affair with a certain *femme fatale*, one Mrs. Jesse Farnsworth."

They both burst into laughter. Jesse stood up and walked to her bureau. On a tray were several bottles of whisky, courtesy of General Halleck.

"I think it's time we took a break for a nip, Brian."

"Aye, I'll go for that. How did I do today, Jess?"

"Letter perfect." She poured bourbon into two glasses and brought them back to the couch. Brian accepted one and held it high.

"To Admiral Farragut. May he be victorious at Mobile Bay and end this damned stupid war soon."

"Amen to that."

They sipped in solemn silence, each lost in his and her own reveries. Brian admired her profile: Strong-featured, noble with sensual lips, auburn hair piled in a beehive coiffure high on her oval head. His gaze wandered downward to her full breasts, straining against the material of her crimson dressing gown. Modest in the sense that it was buttoned high at her throat, the mother-of-pearl buttons fastening it snugly all the way down to her ankles. But the tight cut and the texture of the material were something else again. He was sure she wore nothing underneath, the way it clung to her voluptuous form.

She cut her eyes at him and caught him in the act. "I

wish you wouldn't look at me that way, Brian. I feel positively naked."

He flashed white teeth in a face tanned leathery by constant exposure to sun and wind. "I wish you were."

She tried to look severe without success. "That's no way to speak to a lady old enough to be your mother."

He hooted. "Old enough to be my mother. That's very funny, Jess. You can't be more than four or five years older than me."

She was pleased. "Enough of your blarney, O'Neil. I'm forty-five. Thanks just the same."

"Age," he scoffed. "What the hell difference does it make? Marks on a calendar. So many revolutions of the earth." He moved across the couch near her. "I'm a man and you're a woman. Simple equation." He ran his arm across the back of the couch and caressed the nape of her neck with his fingers. She shivered, and her eyes met his. Dark and smoldering. Not like Ravena's eyes, the deep-purple blue of the *lough*, filled with promise and mystery.

"It has been a long time for me," she said candidly.

"Me too."

His other hand went to her buttons and began to unfasten them from the throat down.

She smiled. "It's a big job, dear. I think I'd better help you." And she did.

At last he opened the dressing gown gently and inspected her lush body without any self-consciousness. A large woman, well proportioned. Breasts like firm melons. Loins a man could revel in without the distracting grind of pelvis and hip bones. He liked meat on a woman. Not fat. Comfortable.

"You look at me the way you'd size up a piece of horse-flesh," she accused him playfully.

"My second favorite pastime," he said.

"Well, don't just sit there, lad. Take off your clothes. Don't you know it's impolite to keep a lady waiting?"

She watched him undress with undisguised pleasure. "God! If only we had met when I was ten years younger! You have the qualities that bring out the slut in a female."

They lay down on the couch, pressed tight from breast to thigh. He kissed her. Long and deep. Gentle at first, the two of them savoring the slow glow of the flesh. Restless now. Stirring against each other with increasing ardor. His hand slipped between her thighs and she sighed.

"No need for that, love. I've been ready since the first night we met in Halleck's office."

He chuckled. "And we've been wasting five days playing school when we could have been playing adult games."

"Hurry!"

When it was over they slept for a while in each other's arms. He woke first, got up softly, and went to the bureau to pour himself another drink.

When Jesse awoke he was sitting in a chair by the window, dressed, with a glass in one hand and a cigar in the other. His expression was dark and brooding.

She rose and put on her robe. Got up and walked over to him. Dropped a hand on his shoulder. He looked up at her and his smile was forced.

"You're quite a woman, Jesse Farnsworth."

"And you're quite a man, Brian O'Neil. What were you thinking just now?"

"Nothing, nothing at all."

"About Ravena?"

He was truly startled; she was a clairvoyant witch. "What makes you say that?"

"Because I can read your mind. You're feeling guilty because you made love to me and she's only one hundred miles away instead of the three thousand you've always believed."

He pulled her down in his lap and kissed her lightly. "You are daft, woman. Why would I be thinking that about Ravena? She's my brother's wife."

"But you're the brother she really loves. And you love her."

"How do you know that?"

"Ravena confided in me once. We're very close, as I told you. It was a time when she and Roger were having it very bad. He was whoring around, and she was seriously think- ing of leaving him."

"Is that a fact?" He tried hard not to show how grateful he was to hear what she was telling him.

"Ravena told me how it was between you and her back in Ireland."

"She told you—" He bit his tongue.

"Everything."

"I won't deny that I love her. I always have. How could she bring herself to marry a cur like my brother?"

"Because she thought you were dead."

"I had no choice." He told her about the friends in the underground who had helped him escape with a new identity. "There would have been reprisals against them. Possibly even against my family. Does Ravena ever hear from them?"

"Yes, last Christmas. Your mother had a touch of the fever, but she'd recovered. Ravena said the Earl wrote that conditions have improved twofold since the days of the famine."

"They'd have to. When you're at the bottom of the barrel, there isn't any direction to go except up."

She got off his lap. "Well, my lad, it's about time to go back to work."

"Yes, Jess. One thing more. This charade, will Ravena be in on it?"

She looked at him levelly. "That will be up to you to decide. Ravena is an extremely intelligent and sensitive woman. She's been his wife for more than five years. It won't be easy to deceive her."

He rubbed his chin fretfully. "I suppose not. Still—"

"You'd prefer she didn't know in the event you are unsuccessful in the impersonation?"

"That's the rub. If she knew it was me, not Roger, they'd jail her as an accomplice. And her crime would be even more serious than mine. The wife of a Southern colonel betraying the cause of the Confederacy."

"Treason. I live with that ax over my head every day. Since the war began."

"Yes. God! You are a courageous woman, Jesse. One thing I don't understand. How is it you have *carte blanche* to travel back and forth across the lines any time you damned well please?"

She smiled. "I've always had high friends both in Richmond and in Washington. Both sides know that, and when war broke out they put me to use for their mutual advantage. In a war between civilized parties, it's imperative

to keep a line of communication open, a courier who can
be the mouthpiece through which they can bargain. I can't
tell you how many legitimate missions I have conducted,
particularly in the first two years of war. Offers from
Washington. Counteroffers from Richmond. There was
one occasion when I was positive that a compromise would
be reached. That hope faded after Lincoln issued the
Emancipation Proclamation. From that point on the only
solution could be unconditional surrender." She gazed off
into the distance.

"You sound as if you have reservations about Abe's
decision?"

"Yes, I do. It was the final ultimatum. It left no room
any longer for Richmond to sue for an honorable armistice." She shrugged her shoulders. "But I am a patriot.
The Union must be preserved. But I will always love the
South, my native Virginia." She looked at him with sudden
insight. "I imagine you must have kindred feelings about
your brother? You don't actually hate Roger, do you?"

It caught him off balance. "No. I don't suppose I do.
It's Roger who hates me, always has."

"Because you favor Ireland's partition from the British
Empire, and he's an ardent Loyalist? Brother against
brother, don't you see the parallel?"

"I never thought of it that way before, but you're right.
In a way I feel like a swine doing a thing like this to
Roger. From what you've told me, he's fought a bloody
good war for his adopted country. I'm glad the English
don't have him on their side."

"That he has."

His brow furrowed. "Jesse. Are Ravena and Roger
sleeping together?"

"I can't say for sure. I know they were estranged for a
long time. Then after the war began, things improved
between them. He wasn't around except when he was on
leave. Not grating on her nerves every day the way it had
been. From things she said, I had the feeling they were
sleeping together infrequently. Now that he's stationed
permanently in Richmond—" She let it hang.

"Back to work." Brian stood up and rubbed his hands
together. "I'd like to work on Roger's voice some more.

He's bound to have picked up Southern characteristics of speech, same way I've adopted Northern nuances."

"Don't worry. You're going to be splendid. The perfect impersonation."

Brian poured himself another drink.

CHAPTER ELEVEN

On the following Sunday, a rainy day in mid-June, Mrs. Jesse Farnsworth departed Washington in her coach-and-four. Her oversized steamer trunk rode in the boot, securely anchored by heavy rope.

"Be very careful with it," she cautioned the driver. "I'm bringing back some extremely fragile crystal and porcelain figurines as gifts for my friends, the Duke and Duchess of Ulster."

At four-thirty the driver reined in the team in front of the Cock and Bull Inn where Mrs. Farnsworth would spend the night. It required the efforts of the driver and two bus boys to carry the bulky trunk up to her room.

"She must have a load of bricks in the damned thing," one boy gasped to the other as they heaved, shoved and grunted their way up the narrow staircase. Mrs. Farnsworth appreciated their efforts gratefully, and rewarded each with a silver dollar.

As soon as they left, she bolted the door and hurried to open the trunk. Brian O'Neil came crawling out on all fours, blinking like a mole emerging from its hole.

"Christ! I feel as if I've been buried alive." He attempted to get to his feet and toppled over on the floor. Groaning from the agony of his cramped muscles, he lay there spread-eagled.

Jesse Farnsworth could not suppress her laughter. "Forgive me, love, but you do look ludicrous."

"The hell with you, wench. I'd like to see you trussed up in that infernal box for ten hours."

"It was only nine."

"I don't know if I can go it another day, Jess. There must be a better way."

"There isn't any other way that's safe, Brian," she said firmly. "You beat Jeb Stuart. You can manage this."

159

Wincing, he finally got to his feet and staggered over to the bed and collapsed again. Jesse joined him there, still giggling.

Brian pulled her down and rolled on top of her. "I'll wipe that smirk off your face, madam."

His hand sneaked underneath her skirt and crinoline. Jesse closed her eyes and put her arms around his neck, arching her back like a cat. The smirk was replaced by a rather feline smile. She was fairly purring by the time he mounted her.

That evening the innkeeper commented to his wife on the hearty appetite for food and drink that his distinguished guest evidenced.

"Can't recall Mrs. Farnsworth being such a hog before. What she put away tonight would do two grave-diggers."

The following morning the boys and driver struggled with the trunk again and stowed it away in the boot.

"Be sure those ropes are tight," she nagged at them, and, once again, bestowed a lavish tip on each. The team of four responded to the crack of the whip and thundered down the road in a cloud of dust.

Twice that morning they were stopped; first by a patrol of Union soldiers and later by a Confederate cavalry squad.

Both parties treated the lady with the utmost respect, declining her smiling offer. "Would you care to inspect my luggage?" she asked.

That would have been an unforgivable breach of etiquette. Mrs. Jesse Farnsworth carried personal letters of identification from President Abraham Lincoln and Confederate President Jefferson Davis!

The last leg of the journey was uneventful, and, at five o'clock that afternoon the carriage pulled up before the fashionable Farnsworth residence in midtown Richmond within walking distance of the capitol building. Her Negro footman and butler helped the driver unload the trunk and the three of them carried it up to her bedroom.

"That will be all, Samuel," she told the butler. "I'm tired and I want to bathe and then I'll take a nap."

"Do you want me to send Ruby up?" he asked. Ruby doubled as her personal maid and as assistant to the cook. Most of the wealthy residents of Richmond had cut down their staffs drastically so that more laborers could work in the fields.

"No, thank you, Samuel. I can manage fine. The Wildings and Colonel and Mrs. O'Neil are having supper with us tonight. She'll be of more assistance to Carrie in the kitchen."

"Will President Davis be here as well, madam?" Samuel spoke with an ear-catching West-Indian lilt.

"I spoke with him just before I went to Washington and he promised to be here if he could, but said we should not count on him. Nevertheless, it won't hurt to make two extra place settings. Thank you, Samuel."

She bolted the door quietly behind him and opened the trunk. Brian had fared better on the second leg of his torturous trip.

"Proves you can get used to anything," he muttered, massaging the knots out of his arms and legs. "One more day and I'd have come to enjoy the bugger." He winked at Jesse. "How would you feel about making love in the trunk, old girl?"

She laughed. "You are positively perverted, Brian. And don't call me 'old girl.'"

"Sorry, love." He put his arms around her.

"Not now, you sex maniac. I must bathe. We're having guests."

"So I heard. You didn't mention that Ravena would be here tonight. It's so—" He could not find the words to describe his feelings. His arms dropped to his sides, his desire for Jesse ebbing fast.

She gave him a knowing look. "You're experiencing a small pang of conscience, aren't you?"

"Don't be silly," he objected too vigorously. "I don't have anything to feel guilty about."

"No, you don't." She placed her hands on his shoulders and her serious brown eyes contemplated him gravely. "What you and I have had together has nothing to do with your love for Ravena. Nor, for that matter, with the deep feeling I had for John Farnsworth. We have enjoyed a diversion and an extremely exciting one I must confess. But it was something apart from love. Just so we both understand that and don't burden ourselves with any ridiculous recriminations. You're a man and I'm a woman and the two of us are caught up in the chaos of this terrible war. We have given each other some comfort and solace. And I think we both deserved every wonderful moment of our encounters."

He smiled and put a hand to her cheek. "You do have a way with words, woman. Are you sure you don't have any Irish in you? You make me feel absolutely noble bedding down with you. You are one hell of a woman, Jesse Farnsworth."

"And you're quite a man yourself." She stood on her tiptoes and kissed him chastely on the chin. "Now I must take my bath."

"Jesse, what about the servants? It's one thing to hide out for one night in an inn, but how do we keep it from the butler and the maid? I can't go on holing up in the trunk every time I hear footsteps in the hall."

"Oh, you'll be quite comfortable here. And safe." She walked to a closet and opened the door. It was a spacious walk-in compartment with racks of gowns on both sides. Jesse went to the far end and put her hand on a hanger fixed to the rear wall, turned it. To Brian's amazement, the wall swung like a door into a secret room about ten feet square. It contained a cot, a desk and chair and a chamberpot.

"I'll be damned!" Brian whistled appreciatively. "We had a room like this back in the castle."

"John's idea when the house was first built. He hid runaway slaves here while they were awaiting transportation North via the Underground."

"This will be fine." He went inside and sat down on the cot.

Jesse fetched a match and lit the oil lamp on the desk. "No window, of course, but there's good ventilation." She pointed to a grille in the ceiling. "Anyway, you don't have to stay in here unless one of the servants is upstairs. The maids make the bed and clean the room every morning."

"Don't worry. I have sharp ears." He stretched out on the cot. "I think I'll have forty winks myself."

Dinner was spare and so was conversation. Not at all like the gay, animated parties of the year before characterized by babbling voices all talking at once and happy laughter. Richmond, the showcase of Southern gentility and graciousness, had maintained its façade of casual ease and indomitability until the bitter end.

Roger O'Neil still spoke hollowly of "ultimate Confederate victory—a stalemate at the very least."

"Stop pretending, Roger," Ravena said wearily. "The South has its back to the wall, and you know it."

The President and Mrs. Davis who had dropped in after dinner for coffee and pecan pie still mouthed platitudes and whistled in the dark.

"If the Union is going to win it will have to do so before the elections. The North is sick of Mr. Lincoln, and once he's been voted out of office, the new President will scrap that damned Emancipation Proclamation and sue for a truce." The President lit a cigar with hands that trembled.

It pained Ravena to look at him. The war had taken a heavy toll of the man. He was a pale caricature of the tall, proud man she had met at the Taylor plantation the first night they had arrived in Richmond, bursting with confidence and exuberance.

He coughed and went on talking as the others listened with attentive respect. "General Early is set to press across the Potomac and march clear to Washington. We've checked Grant at Petersburg, and Sherman's stalled before Atlanta. Yes, sir, Mr. Lincoln has shot his wad and he hasn't got time to fix another charge."

Jesse sat with her hands folded in her lap, staring into her coffee cup. The President leaned over and patted her shoulder.

"Don't look so glum, my dear lady. Things are going to get better, mark my words."

She smiled weakly. "I hope you're right, Mr. President."

After the guests were gone, she described the evening to Brian in the bedroom.

"The President assumed I was depressed because I did not share his optimism when the truth is I'm worried he might be right. If Mr. Lincoln can't come up with a big victory before the election, General McClellan stands an excellent chance of beating him. The people regard Mac as a second Napoleon."

"Then we must get Mr. Lincoln his victory, at the Bay of Mobile." He filled their glasses a second time with sherry. "How much longer?"

"Next weekend. President Davis wants me to undertake another mission up North. I'm to meet with McClellan and sound him out about his terms for an armistice. Roger will brief me on Friday night. I've asked him here to the house."

"And?"

She stood up and walked to her bureau. Came back with a vial containing three white tablets. She opened the bottle and poured them into her hand.

"These, in his wine or bourbon. The Surgeon General claims one of these will render a man unconscious for eight hours. Then we truss him up and it's into your secret room. After you exchange clothes with him."

Brian had shucked his uniform before the journey from Washington for a pair of denim trousers and a wool work shirt.

Brian held up his glass. "I think it would be fitting to toast my dear brother. After all, if it weren't for Roger none of this would have been possible."

"A generous sentiment."

They drank solemnly.

"How is she?" he asked.

She smiled. "I thought you'd get around to that. Ravena looked lovely, as always."

"So many years." he mused. "It's hard to believe that she's—" He frowned. "How old is she? Let's see, I'm twenty-nine so that makes her twenty-seven."

Jesse laughed. "She'd have a fit if she knew you tattled about her age."

He paced back and forth. "God! I only hope I can pull it off. What do you think she'll do if she sees through me?"

"It won't matter. It's you she loves, not Roger."

"You can't be sure. Things may have changed between them. How did they behave toward one another tonight?"

"Cool. Distant. Your brother can be insufferable, and now that he's on the president's staff and home every night I imagine he's getting on her nerves again."

"We'll see."

"Brian, I don't like to pry. But certainly you must have known other women after Ravena?"

He grinned. "Not much you don't like to pry. I don't mind. Yes, there have been a lot of women." He winked.

"And a few 'ladies' such as yourself. There was a girl when I first came to New York. Rebecca. I worked for her father in his clothing shop. A Jewish family, but they took me in as if I was their own flesh and blood."

Jesse's smile was sly. "You and Rebecca were like brother and sister?"

"Not quite. I would have married her, but she wouldn't have me. Even after her father died. She was very religious. Oh, I think she was on the verge of giving in, but then the war came and I enlisted."

"Do you ever hear from her?"

"At first. We exchanged two and three letters a week." He looked rueful. "Then her last letter came. It seems she was going to marry the other apprentice in the shop, Larry Casey. Aw, he was better for her anyway. Larry really loved Becky."

"Yet you would have married her?"

"I used to believe so, but I don't think it ever would have come off when we got down to the wire. I would have found some excuse, even if the war hadn't started."

She yawned. "I've had an exhausting day. I think I'll retire, if you don't mind. Care to keep me company?"

He frowned. "I don't think that would be advisable, do you? Suppose the maid should come in and find us *flagrante delicto*?"

"Is that the only reason?" she asked wisely.

"Why, of course."

"Then be off to your cell, Brian. Sleep well, and pleasant dreams."

She was omniscient. His dreams were of Ravena. The two of them young and riding madly over the fields of Donegal. She in her pantalettes. And then they were on the grass, the two of them. Eager naked bodies straining against each other. Consumed by love. Yes, that was love. Becky, Jesse, all the others, assuaging the lust and the loneliness, but not true love.

For the remainder of that week Brian lived in a twilight zone. The caged existence of the beast in the zoo. And like an animal he spent most of his time sleeping, ten, twelve, sometimes fourteen hours at a stretch. His meals were meager, whatever Jesse could smuggle upstairs without arousing the suspicion of the servants. In the evenings after she retired to her room, he would come out of his "hole," as he called it, and they would talk and drink wine or bourbon. He and she did not make love again.

Finally it arrived, fateful Friday. Roger was due to arrive at eight o'clock in the evening. Jesse wore her burgundy taffeta gown with the small bustle that was becoming more chic than the bulky crinoline. Her auburn hair was piled high on her head and she dabbed rouge on her cheeks.

"Gilding the lily," Brian teased her.

"Do I look all right?"

"Like a queen. No, I take that back. Every queen I've ever seen is an old frump, compared to you, my lovely."

"More of your blarney."

Before she went down, he kissed her. "Good luck. I'll be chewing my fingernails down to the knuckles waiting."

"Be patient." She left and closed the bedroom door behind her.

Colonel Roger O'Neil arrived punctually at eight and was showed in to the parlor by Samuel. He looked very dashing in his gray cavalryman's uniform, and she told him so.

His handsome face creased. "I feel like an ass wearing it. A man in this uniform should be at the front, not behind a desk in the President's mansion."

"You've done more than your share in this war, Roger, you and Jeb. It would only be a matter of time before you were wounded or killed too. Besides, you are invaluable to Mr. Davis. He told me so when I visited him on Wednesday."

"Just the same, I don't care much for the position."

"Has a decision been reached on the precise wording of the statement to General McClellan?"

"Yes, the Cabinet approved the final draft this afternoon." He took an envelope out of an inside pocket and handed it to her. "It's short, only three pages, but it states the position of the Confederate government thoroughly. In the event that General McClellan is elected to the Presidency, the eleven states of the Confederacy would be willing to accept a compromise satisfactory to both parties providing for the reunification of these states with the Union. Our proposal is this: McClellan, upon his election, would withdraw the Emancipation Proclamation; in return, the eleven Confederate states would agree to the terms of the original Missouri Compromise; that is, we would not promulgate slavery in the territories. And, in return, the Northern Abolitionists would cease and desist in their spurious efforts to generate a revolution among the Southern slaves. That's the gist of it, Jesse. You'd better read it carefully and commit it to memory, then burn it. We can't risk a document so volatile falling into the wrong hands."

"I understand. Don't worry, I was blessed with a photographic memory. Although, at times, it has been anything but a blessing. I can't forget a good many things that would be better off forgotten."

She placed the envelope down on the table beside the couch. "I'm going to have a little sherry. Will you join me?"

"Delighted. Shall I do the honors?" He started to get up.

She detained him with a hand on his arm. "No, my dear Colonel, I won't have one of our weary war heroes waiting on me. You stay put and light up a cigar."

She went over to the server against one wall and picked up a decanter of sherry that she and Brian had doctored earlier in her room. She noted that the white powder from the pill they had ground up finely had dissolved. She filled his wine glass from this decanter and stoppered it.

"On second thought, I think I'll have port tonight," she said casually, and filled another glass with the darker grape.

She brought them over to the couch on a small silver tray. "Sir."

He accepted the sherry and waited until she was seated before offering a toast: "To the success of your mission."

A glint of irony shone in her eyes. "Yes, to the success of my mission."

They sipped the wine. Roger frowned and rolled the beverage around in his mouth and under his tongue, tasting it.

Jesse put a hand to her throat. "Is anything wrong, Roger?"

"No, not at all, it has a distinctive bouquet but I can't identify it."

"John brought it back from France in '55. Our last trip abroad."

"Unique, very unique." He swallowed it and took another sip.

"How is Ravena?"

"Same as always. She's been working hard at the hospital this week."

"It's such rewarding work. I only wish I had more time to devote to it."

"Your time could not be better spent," he assured her. "Mr. Davis dotes on you, Jesse."

She was grave. "I don't like the way the President looks these days. So wan, so tired."

"Yes. The Confederacy is his life. As it goes so he goes. Well, let us hope that after the elections, both the President and the Confederacy will have a turn for the better."

"I certainly hope so. Roger, I realize this is a very delicate subject and I would not mention it to anyone but you. We're both so close to Mr. Davis, dear Jefferson. His mind seems so vague, I mean the way he rambles on, not making sense a good deal of the time."

He sighed. "I know, all of us who are around him cannot help but notice. The poor man is under such a strain and he can't sleep. It's got to take a toll."

"Do you know what he said to me on Wednesday? That he has it on good authority that Maine is considering seceding from the Union and joining Canada."

"That isn't as crazy as it sounds, Jesse. Maine, New York, Pennsylvania, our agents say there's a lot of discontent with Mr. Lincoln. That's why this meeting with General McClellan is so vital."

"Yes, I can see that it is," she said grimly. Covertly she watched him for some sign that the drug was taking effect. Her heart skipped.

Roger was perspiring heavily although the night was not all that warm. He smiled. "That sherry really packs a punch, Jesse."

"Let me pour you another." She reached for the empty glass on the tray.

"No, I think not. Wouldn't be surprised if I'm coming down with another bout of yellow fever."

"Oh dear." She feigned distress. "I'll fetch you some iced water."

"Thank you, no. I'd better go home and take some of the quinine the doctor prescribed. That and a good night's sleep will fix me up."

He got up laboriously and swayed from side to side.

"Good God! It's never come on so suddenly before." His face was ashen and his eyes could not focus properly. His voice was tremulous. "Jesse! I think I'm going to pass out!" His knees gave way and he collapsed in a heap at the side of the couch.

Jesse contemplated him for a while with a thin smile of satisfaction, then she pulled the bell cord for Samuel.

When the butler saw Roger lying there unconscious, his eyes widened in alarm. "What happened to Colonel O'Neil?"

"It's his fever, Samuel. He has these spells periodically. Please, help me get him up to the bedroom. It will pass quickly and he'll be fine after a time."

"Are you sure we shouldn't go for the doctor, ma'am?"

"Quite sure. Here, give me a hand with him."

"No, you won't, Mrs. Farnsworth. He's a big man. I'll get one of the boys to help me."

Not long after Roger was stretched out on Jesse's bed. He looked like a dead man.

Samuel was still concerned. "I don't like his color, ma'am. You think maybe Barney ought to drive over to the Wilding place in the carriage and get Mrs. O'Neil?"

"I tell you what, Samuel, I don't want to worry her or the Wildings unnecessarily. Why don't we wait for a while, and then if he doesn't improve, we'll send for the doctor and for Mrs. O'Neil. Now you go downstairs and brew us a pot of fresh coffee. Colonel O'Neil always likes black coffee after one of his bouts."

"Yes, ma'am."

When he left the room, Jesse slid the bolt quietly and ran to the closet. She opened the door into the secret room.

"The deed is done. Come on."

On his last day in Washington Brian had been visited by Monsieur Calais, a make-up man who was a member of a repertory group playing at the Booth Theater.

"Monsieur Calais once kept the ladies of the French Court looking beautiful."

"Well you really have your work cut out for you on this job. *monsieur*," Brian said dryly.

Directed by Jesse Farnsworth, the Frenchman cut and dyed Brian's hair to conform to the tonsorial appearance of his brother Roger.

"A little shorter at the base of the neck, Pierre," she instructed. "That's fine. Now about the curls around the ears—"

Before it was over she almost drove Brian and poor Monsieur Calais crazy.

"I'm sorry, but it has to be perfect," she told them.

And now as Brian stood over the unconscious man on the bed, he realized just how perfect her judgments had been.

"I always knew we looked alike," he said in awe. "But never so much as now." He turned and looked in her vanity mirror. Ran a hand through his blonde hair. "It's incredible."

She appraised him from all angles. "Roger's a bit grayer at the temples, but with such light hair nobody is likely to notice." She took hold of one of Roger's cavalry boots and tugged. "Don't stand there gawking, Brian. Help me get him undressed."

In short order, Brian was wearing Roger's Confederate uniform, and Roger was dressed in the nondescript work clothes.

Jesse went to the closet and took down a hat box. Inside were a pair of handcuffs and leg irons. "Compliments of Allan Pinkerton," she said.

They locked on the cuffs and irons and carried Roger into the secret room and laid him on the cot. Brian was solemn.

"Poor bloody bastard," he sympathized. "That trip was bad enough, in any case. I'd hate to make it trussed up like that."

"It won't be as bad as you imagine. This time we'll drive straight through to Washington. Arrangements have been made for my carriage to change horses at the Cock-and-Bull. Besides, Roger will be unconscious for most of the way. I'll give him another dose of the drug before we leave tomorrow morning."

"How will you manage to get him into the trunk by yourself? He's quite a large package."

She smiled. "Oh, I'll manage with Samuel's assistance."

"Samuel?" Brian was shocked and concerned. "Isn't that a bit risky?"

"My dear Brian, Samuel has been with me for twenty years. John and I helped five of his children and nephews escape to Illinois. Samuel would lay down his life for me, and I'd trust him as much as I'd trust Allan Pinkerton, or General Halleck or Honest Abe himself."

"What will happen to Roger when you get to your destination?"

"He will be detained naturally. In a private home secured by a dozen of Pinkerton's top agents. He'll be accorded every courtesy and comfort due to an officer of his rank. He'll be just fine."

"And after the war?"

"He'll be released with the other Confederate prisoners of war. Now, don't you think it's time you went home— Roger?"

"Jesus!"

Through all of the sessions with Jesse and all of the other preparations he had avoided thinking of this moment when, finally, the charade would begin in earnest.

"My mind is an absolute blank," he told her. "Everything you've instructed me is gone."

Jesse laughed. "You've got a case of stage fright. Don't worry, once you're on stage, you'll give a splendid performance."

"It had better be good," he said. "If I muff my lines, there won't be a second chance." She brushed off the lapels of his tunic and patted his cheek. He bent and kissed her quickly on the lips.

"Good luck, Roger."

They went downstairs where Samuel was making work for himself in the hall, scrubbing away industriously with a brush and water at a minuscule spot on the carpeting. He got to his feet and contemplated Brian warily.

"You're feeling better, Colonel O'Neil?"

"Much better, thank you, Samuel."

"I made the coffee you asked for, ma'am."

"I'm afraid it's getting too late," Brian said. "I really must be leaving."

"I'll have the coffee, Samuel," Jesse said. "Bring me up a cup to my room. There's something I must talk to you about."

"Yes, ma'am. Good night, Colonel, and get home safely."

"That I will. Good night."

When the door shut behind him, he felt rather the way he had on the night that he set foot on the ship that would carry him away from Ireland. On his own and alone.

He hailed a carriage at the corner and gave the driver instructions. "I want to go to *Ravena*."

"Yes, sir." Jesse had told him that the plantation was well known and prestigious throughout Virginia.

"I want to go to Ravena."

Symbolic statement.

His heart beat faster in anticipation. He rubbed his hands together with relish. Jesse had been right as usual. The fear had left him abruptly. He was warming to the game ahead.

He let himself in the door with Roger's key. The butler came down the hall from the kitchen—he knew the layout of the house as well as if he had been born in it—and greeted him.

"Good evening, Colonel. Have a pleasant evening?"

"Excellent, Gordon. Where is Mrs. O'Neil?"

"In the sewing room, sir." He took Brian's cape and hat. "Can I bring you a drink?"

"Thanks, the usual."

He went through the parlor and down a second side hall that led back to the library and music and sewing room. He paused a moment before he came abreast of the open door and took a deep breath.

This is it, old cock!

Whistling Roger's favorite tune, "Dixie," he swaggered into the room. Skirting the clavichord that dominated the center of the spacious room, he walked to where Ravena was sitting in a rocker in the bay window that overlooked the garden. The room was well lit with lamps in wall brackets. She was embroidering a Confederate flag on a tablecloth that was to be auctioned off at a patriotic auction the following week.

The experience of seeing her for the first time in so many years was more traumatic than he had reckoned on. All he could do was to stare at her mutely. It was a visual feast for him. He devoured her hair, her violet eyes, her chin, her nose, her mouth. He could still taste the nectar sweetness of her lips. Fuller in the hips and bosom than the seventeen-year old girl he had left. Her figure was divine. A rush of emotion engulfed him, and, for an instant, he came perilously close to unmasking himself. He had all he could do not to take her in his arms and tell her:

"My darling, I love you, and I have always loved you. Forgive me for deserting you the way I did."

She looked up at him quizzically. "Roger, what is it? Are you feeling ill?"

He brushed a hand across his forehead. "It's nothing. I had a dizzy spell at Jesse's place. Must be a touch of the fever again."

"You should have the doctor examine you. Dr. Sloan mentioned it to me when I was at the hospital yesterday. He said I should remind you."

"No time for that nonsense in times like these," he said brusquely. Then seized by an irresistible impulse he bent over and kissed her on top of her raven-sheened head.

"You're looking well this evening, my dear."

She looked up at him in astonishment. "Whatever on earth brought that on?"

Jesse had warned him that Roger detested public displays of affection.

He laughed shakily. "Like to keep you on your toes, my dear. Hate to be predictable."

"Well, fancy that. I never—" She put down her embroidery work on the table and regarded him curiously.

Roger had always taken scrupulous pride in his predictability.

"Jeb and I fit together like a right and left hand. We know exactly what each of us will do next."

* * *

"Roger, have you been drinking?"

"Just a little sherry with Jesse."

"Is she looking forward to her trip tomorrow?"

"She's anxious to get on with it, I suppose. But it's not the kind of journey one makes for enjoyment."

"No, of course not."

He sat down in the easy chair opposite her and crossed his legs. He began to get the feel of it after a while, and, after Gordon brought him in a bourbon and branch water, he and Ravena made small talk about his day, her own day and about mutual acquaintances.

He sensed a coolness setting in when she introduced the topic of Samantha Wade. He recognized it vaguely as one of the names on the list Jesse had prepared for him. Yet it did not register as a significant character in Roger's life.

"Samantha tells me the two of you had a marvelous time in the country last Sunday. I thought you were going to the racetrack."

He felt flushed. This was a development he had not counted on. He took a wild stab at replying to it as a defensive husband might well do.

"Didn't I mention it to you? Bart Taylor and I ran into Melanie and Samantha at the track. Afterward we took them for a spin before we took them home."

Ravena was filled with disgust. Roger usually was more inventive than this in covering up his chronic peccadilloes with other women. Not that she gave a damn any longer. The marriage had been a masquerade from the beginning. She didn't love Roger. Never had. The man Ravena loved was dead. In their infrequent encounters she used Roger as much as he used her. One thing, though, she refused to grant him sexual favors when he was in the throes of an affair. And from Samantha's smugness she was convinced that their dirty little business was at its hot peak.

No, it was not his infidelity that bothered Ravena. There was something else. A strangeness about him that had not been apparent when he left the house to visit Jesse. Or was it she who was behaving strangely? No, she was not. The way he had just lit the cigar. The way he was holding his glass cupped in his palm. The way he crossed his legs wide with his boot resting on his knee. They were different. He was different somehow.

It disturbed her out of all proportion, and she began to worry: *"Am I losing my mind?"*

He consulted his pocket watch, a gift from Jeb Stuart. "Well, it's about time I turned in."

"Yes, I think I'll finish this in daylight." She put aside the tablecloth in a cedar chest built into the bay window.

The butler met them in the hall. "Will there be anything else, Colonel and Madam?"

"No, thank you, Gordon," Brian said. "The bourbon hit the spot."

Both Gordon and Ravena stared at him. She caught the butler's eye and he dropped his gaze quickly.

"Good night then." He spun on his heel and walked down the hall.

Climbing the stairs Ravena lagged a few steps in back of him. Studying him, wondering. Mystified. She knew that Gordon was thinking the same thing that came to her mind.

It was the only time in all the years she had known Roger that she had ever heard him say "thank you" or "please" to a servant. Roger O'Neil was a petty, arrogant tyrant.

It was inconceivable that he should turn about in the space of a few hours. He had been his reliable surly self when he walked out the door. Now he was treating the servants with civility. And, wonder of wonders, he had kissed her impulsively. And on the hair no less! Not her insufferably fastidious Roger! Maybe the fever had affected his mind.

Even though the change was an improvement, Ravena didn't like it. This Roger made her uneasy and uncomfortable. There was no doubt in her mind that there was a motive to his seeming madness. She would have to maintain her guard vigilantly until she found out what he was up to.

At the top of the stairs, she faced him and announced. "Roger, I think it would be better if you sleep in your own room for a time. You know perfectly well what I mean. Good night."

He looked after her without saying a word as she walked to her room and went inside. Truthfully, he was relieved. Looking like another man was one thing. Making love in his unique style was quite another. Her rejection was a reprieve. It pleased him for another reason as well. She was no longer enamored of Roger, if she ever had been.

Brian walked to the room across from hers and went in. He was satisfied with his first-act performance in spite of his repeated slips. Tomorrow he would do better.

CHAPTER TWELVE

And improve he did. By the Fourth of July he was so immersed in the role he was playing that at times he *was* Roger! He had even mastered the surly arrogance of his brother.

He seemed more natural to Ravena now, although there was about him an aura of "strangeness" that troubled her for an elusive reason that she could not put into words.

"Gut instinct" was what Brian had called the intangible vibrations that emanated from one human being to another foretelling future knowledge.

These days, whenever she thought of her dear departed Brian, she would be overcome with a sensation of suffocation. It was terrifying. An eerie sensation that his spirit was hovering over her, weighing her down with the heavy, dank lifeless air of the tomb.

In his official capacity as military adviser to Jefferson Davis, the part came even easier than that of Ravena's husband. Brian was a brilliant cavalry tactician, as was Roger. The Confederate President and his cabinet were totally oblivious that he was impersonating his brother.

There were a few awkward moments. In late June when they were debating the strategy of General Johnston's defense against Sherman's offensive at Kennesaw Mountain, Brian's immediate instinct was to sabotage the Confederate effort. Without thinking, he proposed:

"A heavy cavalry assault on Sherman's right flank."

Major George Manson, his aide, stared at him with disbelief: "But, sir, Sherman has the natural defenses of the mountains on his right. Just last month we were discussing this same possibility and you were unanimous in your opinion that the cavalry should strike the left flank of an attacking force at Kennesaw Mountain."

He recovered brilliantly, frowning at the major. "Well,

that's what I just said, George. Hit Sherman's left flank."

The others present chuckled in good humor at what they considered a slip of the tongue by a man who would not tolerate the slightest misstep in his subordinates.

"Major Manson is correct, Colonel," President Davis chided him lightly. "You did say the right flank."

Brian looked around the table openmouthed, purposefully exaggerating his mortification. "How stupid of me. Forgive me. I'm sorry, George."

"Perfectly natural, sir. We all make mistakes." His smile said: *"Even you!"*

As it turned out the Confederates under Johnston soundly trounced Sherman at Kennesaw Mountain. The Union suffered three thousand casualties as opposed to a meager six hundred for the Confederates. It was a short-lived victory; two weeks later Johnston was forced to evacuate the position. But it did provide the South with a lift in morale to get it through the Fourth of July.

On the night of the Fourth, Brian stood out on a capitol building balcony with Confederate Secretary of State Judah P. Benjamin watching the display of fireworks over Richmond Harbor. Benjamin, considered by many, in the North as well as the South, as one of the most politically sophisticated men in the diplomatic service before the war, had an interesting observation to offer.

"It's ironic, isn't it, Colonel O'Neil? At this moment, in Washington, they're watching a similar celebration over the Potomac River. Both of our nations paying tribute to a better time when we stood shoulder to shoulder against England determined to win our independence. Our finest hour. We were truly all brother Americans. The United States of America." He shook his head sadly. "Now less than ninety years later, here we are tearing at each other's jugular veins like mad dogs. The world is a strange place indeed."

"Aye, sir," Brian agreed. "I've heard similar sentiments expressed about the troubles between England and Ireland."

"Yes. I understand there's a young hellion by the name of Parnell who is giving the Crown even more headaches than the Mollies and all the other gangs put together, including the Young Ireland Party."

Brian held his tongue. Undoubtedly Benjamin was only too familiar with Roger's fiercely loyalist views with regard to the Irish question.

"How is that lovely wife of yours, Colonel?"

"Doing very well, sir. Keeping busy with her volunteer work."

An orderly came out onto the balcony and informed them: "Gentlemen, the President requests your presence in his office now."

They joined the conference which included the Secretary of the Army and the Secretary of the Navy.

President Davis addressed the assembly:

"Gentlemen, I have received word from Admiral Buchanan at Mobile Bay that the Union fleet has been joined in the Gulf of Mexico by four monitors and six additional gunboats. It is obvious that Admiral Farragut is girding to do battle. Mr. Secretary, the map, if you will."

The Secretary of the Navy walked to a rolled-up wall chart and pulled it open. Brian's heart accelerated as he recognized the distinctive configuration of Mobile Bay on the situation map.

The President went on: "As you know we've been able to stalemate the North in the Gulf because of the strategic location of the Bay of Mobile and its complex defenses."

Brian tuned out the President's words, concentrating all of his faculties on memorizing the notations and the symbolic military vocabulary penned in on the chart.

The open water across the face of the triangular bay was dominated by the forts on each side of the bay, Fort Morgan and Fort Gaines. That was common knowledge.

What was not known to Union intelligence was the location of the rows of concrete pilings and explosive torpedoes sunk and anchored to the bottom of the bay beneath the waterline, designed to tear or blow out the bottom of any unsuspecting enemy warship that attempted to venture inside the bay.

Brian did all he could to contain his heady exultation as he marked the only safe route into Mobile Bay. A narrow channel that ran parallel to the shoreline and directly under the guns of Fort Morgan. It would be a perilous course for Farragut, but considerably less so, once he knew precisely the key to the bay's hidden defenses. Brian's mission was all but accomplished.

"Mr. Davis," a minister inquired, "why is it that Admiral Buchanan has permitted this build-up of Union firepower under his very nose? I mean, was not containment of Farragut's fleet our purpose in constructing the mightiest warship in the world, the two-hundred-and-ten-foot iron-clad, *Tennessee*? As I understand it, with her six-inch armor, she's virtually indestructible. Why hasn't she challenged Farragut's fleet to do battle before this?"

"Ahhh, yes, indeed. Why not?" President Davis mopped his face with a handkerchief. And with a trace of sarcasm deferred to the Secretary of the Navy. "Be my guest, sir."

The secretary looked most uncomfortable. "Gentlemen, in answer to the question, let me take it part by part. Yes, the *Tennessee* was designed with the purpose of routing Farragut's fleet clear out of our Gulf. Yes, with her six-inch armor she is virtually indestructible, barring ten consecutive lucky hits on the afterside of the casemate. That's where her tiller chains are. And now I must reveal to you for the first time a highly embarrassing secret insofar as the Confederate Navy is concerned. Unfortunately, when the *Tennessee* was built in the Mobile yards, they gave her so much draught that she cannot steam across the bar in normal tides to get at the enemy. We've been able to conceal that tragic mistake so far by sheer bluff. The *Tennessee* fakes an attack out of the bay and lets go a few salvos at the enemy fleet. Then when Farragut withdraws, we pretend to scorn his puny vessels, and she steams back to her berth. What we're waiting for is the first good fall storm in the Gulf to raise the water level sufficiently so that she can get out of the bay."

Brian's brain reeled at the incredibility of it. The *Tennessee* was a prisoner within her own lair! He had it all now. All the essential details to insure Farragut's success. And then his ear picked up the clincher.

"At low tide she even has trouble maneuvering inside the bay. Like a hippo in a mudhole."

A rumble of discontent, indignation and alarm went up from the listeners.

"Damn fool Navy!"

"The architect ought to be hanged for treason."

"It's a damned lucky thing that Washington doesn't know about this fiasco!"

Brian bit his lip to stifle the smile.

After he left the capitol building, Brian and President Davis rode in the executive carriage to Jesse Farnsworth's home, where a lavish party was in progress. Mrs. Davis and Mrs. O'Neil had been escorted to the affair by Colonel and Mrs. Taylor and Colonel and Mrs. Cooper.

Brian had spoken to Jesse only twice since her return from Washington, D.C. Her mission to General McClellan had fallen on interested ears but uncommitted mouths. Encouraging enough to lift Southern spirits anyway.

Roger O'Neil had undergone his unwilling journey and reached his destination intact. From his cell in the secret confinement site, he had shaken his fist at Jesse through the bars and literally frothed at the mouth with rage.

"You'll hang for this treason!" he'd vowed.

He was in the dark about the true nature of the treason she had committed, and knew nothing of his brother Brian's part in the conspiracy.

That night when Jesse greeted him, he smiled at her with a cunning glint in his eyes. When he bussed her cheek, he whispered:

"I've got it. Mobile Bay."

"We'll talk as soon as possible," she whispered back and went on to greet the next guest in line.

Brian saw Ravena on the dance floor with Captain Pennel Collins. He dodged deftly through the other dancers and tapped Collins on the shoulder.

"Mind if I steal her from you, old man?" he said with a smile.

"Colonel O'Neil, good to see you. Of course." He bowed to Ravena. "Thank you for the pleasure, lovely lady."

She nodded and smiled. The smile wiped off when Brian took her in his arms. "Samantha is here," she said impersonally.

He laughed. "Samantha who? Never heard of her."

She looked up at him sharply. "You are in a fine mood tonight. Something must have gone well at the capitol?"

He disciplined himself not to display too much ebullience. "Oh, well, we're still basking in the warmth of Johnston's victory at Kennesaw Mountain."

"Is that all? Father says it's the last gasp of a dying man."

The Duke was correct, Brian believed, but he put on Roger's petulant frown. "Your father had best keep his mouth shut. These are no times to be spouting such defeatist talk in the capital. Somebody might take it into their heads to burn down the old plantation."

"Do you mind if we sit down?" she asked icily.

"If you wish. Think I'll get myself a drink. Can I fetch you anything?"

"Thank you, no. I'm going up to the powder room."

He mixed with the revelers, shaking hands and exchanging bracing words of cheer about Johnston's victory. At last he spied Jesse speaking with the President and Major Manson. He walked past her and caught her eye. Then he slipped out of the ballroom and walked down the hall to her study.

He poured himself a drink from a decanter on the server and lit a cigar. She came in minutes later and closed the door behind her.

"You've got it?"

She came over to him and he took her hands in his. "Everything Farragut needs to penetrate the defenses of Mobile Bay and blow Buchanan's fleet out of the water."

"What about the *Tennessee*?"

"She's invincible the same way Achilles was, and she's got an Achilles heel. She's got too much draught to sail across the sand bar at the mouth of the bay at normal tides. And at low tide she drags her butt so she can't maneuver. Farragut has got to strike as quickly as possible." He removed an envelope from an inside pocket. "It's all in here. How soon do you think you can get it to Washington?"

She grinned like the Cheshire cat. "It will be on the President's desk by tomorrow afternoon. We have a *veddy*, *veddy* British journalist with us tonight. He's covering the war for the *London Times*: Archibald Brougham."

"What about him?"

"He's a Pinkerton agent."

Brian relaxed. "That is convenient. Look, I'd better get back to the party. Here." He handed her the secret report.

"Good work, Brian."

At the door, he hesitated. "What happens now that my job is done?"

"You'll continue to furnish whatever information you can to Washington via me. The war isn't over yet."

"No, it isn't. There's still much to be reckoned with." And it was not just the war he was thinking about. There was the triangle consisting of Roger, Ravena and himself.

As if reading his thoughts, Jesse cautioned. "Don't rush things, Brian. There's plenty of time for you and Ravena."

"Is there?" He turned and left the room.

It was a highly successful party in spite of the state of the Confederacy. Ravena felt that everyone talked too loudly, laughed too loudly and behaved too exuberantly. The same hysterical gaiety that prevailed at the French Court in Poe's *The Masque of the Red Death*. At midnight she asked him to take her home.

"I have a splitting headache, Roger."

"I'm sorry. Of course."

They bade farewell to close friends, paid their respects to the hostess and departed in the Wildings' carriage. They said very little until the carriage was approaching *Ravena*. Then he asked her:

"Do you really have a headache?"

"Yes, it was all that noise and smoke and mindless chatter. It grated on my nerves like fingernails scraping along a blackboard."

Impulsively he said, "Do you know what would cure your headache? A brisk canter over the fields."

"At this time of night?"

"Remember how you used to sneak out of the house back in Ireland? We'd ride for an hour or two." He paused. Just in time. He'd come close to saying: *"And make love in the meadow."*

It was obvious from her consternation that Ravena made the connection in her own mind. She turned and looked at him. "Roger, you and I never rode together at night. It was—" Now it was her turn to rein back. *"It was Brian I came out to be with."*

"Did I say 'night'?" he parried it blandly. "Of course you and I rode in the day time."

"But you said *sneak out*. I didn't have to sneak out in broad daylight."

He touched a hand to his head. "Guess I'm a bit light in the head myself. You know how the fever comes over me without warning. I do believe I could do with a midnight ride myself. What about it, Ravena? Will you keep me company?"

She stared at him in bewilderment. The idea of her husband, Colonel Roger O'Neil, doing anything as impulsive and unconventional as riding a horse in the dark of night was preposterous.

"I—I really don't think—"

"Come on, be a sport."

A shock ran through her whole body like the time she'd been standing near a tree in the Bois de Boulogne in Paris when it was struck by lightning during a rain storm.

"Come on, be a sport."

Words spoken by a ghost. The occasion when she and Brian had gone riding to Lough Derg. She hadn't wanted to go with him. He'd coaxed:

"Come on, be a sport."

"What's wrong, my dear?" he asked. "Why are you looking at me so strangely?"

She wagged her head slowly from side to side. All of the will had deserted her. She was a puppet activated by some mysterious external force.

"All right, Roger, I'll go with you." Mechanical voice, her eyes staring fixedly like a doll's.

Dimly aware too of a familiar sensation stirring inside of her. A fluttering. A keen sense of anticipation and anxiety. The sense that something momentous was about to happen to her. That she was approaching another one of the pivotal high points in the life's journey from birth to infinity. The identical feeling she had experienced that same day long ago.

"Come on, be a sport."

She clutched her throat as the carriage rolled up the long circular drive and stopped before the wide white-washed steps of *Ravena*.

"Will that be all, Colonel, sir?" the darky coachman inquired.

"Yes, Davis, Mrs. O'Neil and I will be riding as soon as we change. Will you saddle up Black Lightning and Ginger?"

"Yes, sir." He stared at them as they walked up the steps, muttering to himself. "They done gone crazy, that's what. Damn fools!"

Since McCloud had gone off to war, most of the burden of the Duke's stables fell on the coachman. He drove around to the barn and put the carriage horses back in their stalls. Then he walked to Black Lightning's stall.

"You ain't gonna like this, horse, but your bedtime is over."

Davis was tightening the cinch on Ginger when Ravena and Brian arrived at the stable. She wore a loose white blouse and black velvet trousers custom made by George Sand's personal couturier. Brian's eyebrows arched high when he saw her. How like Ravena to scorn the traditional women's riding habit! He remembered her girlhood ruse of snitching a pair of her brother's trousers to don when she was out of the house. He remembered her lace pantalettes the day they had ridden out to the lough.

Jesus! But you are beautiful!

The desire to take her in his arms was almost uncontrollable. He turned away quickly.

"Let's go."

Ravena was nonplussed at his appearance as well. She had never seen Roger ride unless he was in uniform or impeccably groomed in his neat riding habit and boots.

"Why so informal tonight, Roger?" she asked.

He played it cagey. "Oh, one has to kick over the traces once in a while. Besides it's so late, no one will be likely to see us."

She accepted the explanation, but she was still leery. What was happening to Roger O'Neil, the staid, conventional, meticulous Roger that she had known for seventeen years? That Roger wouldn't have been caught in a dirty work shirt and gardening trousers even in the middle of the night.

Brian swung onto Black Lightning and Davis assisted Ravena onto Ginger. The roan reminded her of her own dear Apache. Seeing Roger astride the big black Arabian gave her another jolt. Except for the absence of a star on its forehead, the horse was remarkably like Brian's Big Red!

Gooseflesh tingled on her forearms and thighs. It was eerie. Almost supernatural. Once she and Brian had joked about reincarnation. He said he wanted to come back into the world as the steed of a beautiful lady.

"I'd like the feel of her riding me every day."

"Are you shivering?" he asked as they rode along the cowpath that led back through the woods to the fields in the north meadow.

"Some one is walking on my grave."

He cut his eyes at her. "I haven't heard that one in a long time."

"It was something your brother Brian liked to say."

"I believe you're right."

"What's so funny?" she demanded as he laughed softly.

"We are. You and I. The whole damned ridiculous human race. This damned absurd war, isn't that proof enough?"

She looked at him with growing disbelief. Roger O'Neil would never say anything so radical. Could it possibly be that the spirit of Brian O'Neil was trying to reach out to her through the flesh and bones of his brother? Her mind reeled.

"You're daft, lass!"

It came with the heritage. Gaelic superstition. Ghosts, goblins, devils, the Little People.

A stretch of rolling green lay ahead of them beyond the cotton crop.

"I'll race you," he dared.

She wanted to get away from him far more than she wanted to race. Now she was terrified. She put the whip to the horse's flank and Ginger shot away from Black Lightning. His laughter trailed off in the slipstream. Then he was in hot pursuit.

"Go, Lightning! Go!"

"Faster, Ginger! Faster!"

It had happened before. Another time. Another place. Reliving that wonderful day when she had been deflowered by Brian. So why was she so frightened? Because the man on her heels was not her husband Roger; he was a phantom, a ghost!

Ravena glanced over her shoulder and saw the bigger stallion was closing the distance fast. Now he was abreast of her, edging Black Lightning over so that his leg nudged hers.

She screamed and struck at him with her crop. He caught her hand and his teeth glowed in the bright moonlight.

"Leave me alone! Please leave me alone."

Unexpectedly he leaned across her and one powerful arm whipped around her waist. A game he'd played with Custer's crack horse soldiers. The next thing she knew, he had pulled her off the roan and thrown her across the stallion's neck.

Ravena fainted from sheer terror.

Not totally unconscious. Aware of what was going on but powerless to resist. He reined in Black Lightning and dismounted. He carried her gently to a grassy knoll and placed her down. Kneeling beside her he began to unbutton the buttons down the front of her blouse. He removed every shred of her clothing and she lay there petrified. She watched mutely as he began to undress himself.

Finally she found her voice and reason. "We can't. We mustn't."

He laughed. "And why not? It's just like the first time, remember?"

She nodded. "How could I ever forget—" She swallowed hard and said it. "You're Brian's ghost, and somehow you've taken over Roger's body."

"The walking dead," he intoned in a sonorous voice from the grave.

She began to quake and whimper as he swung one leg across her body.

He took her hand and brought it to his penis. Reflexively her fingers closed around him.

"Does it feel like a phantom to you, lass?"

"Ohhhh—" She let out a moan, and then the fear was eclipsed by emotion so much more powerful that it engulfed her from her scalp to the tips of her tingling toes. Consumed in the flash-fire of her desire.

Her body accepted him hungrily. Greedily. Her arms locked around his neck. Her heels dug fiercely into his hard buttocks. She wanted all of him.

When it was over, they lay together, still joined, basking in the aftermath of ecstasy. She was the first to speak.

"If only you could capture the beauty of an experience and put it in a bottle the way you can with a scent. And when you want to smell the roses or the lilacs or the magnolia, you unstop it and it's with you once more."

He laughed. "That would be quite a trick. Instant sex!"

"There!" she exclaimed and sat up. "Roger would cut out his tongue before he would use that word in front of a lady."

"Roger is a horse's ass!" He glanced over at the two horses, grazing in the high grass. "My apologies to the two fine beasts," he said gravely.

"How did you manage it, Brian?" she demanded.

"Manage what?"

"Taking possession of Roger's body?"

"Holy mother of God!" He roared with laughter, grasping his aching sides. "You don't actually believe that malarkey, do you? Oh my God, you surely have your share of the dark Irish in your blood." He grasped her shoulders and shook her gently. "I'm real, Ravena. I'm Brian. Not Roger. Brian, lass. Say it."

"Brian—" She whispered and put a hand to his cheek, filled with awe. "If you are—Brian—you can't be Brian. Brian was killed. They found his body."

"They found a corpse burned beyond recognition. It had to be done that way. You know the law was onto me for being a member of the underground resistance movement. I would have gone to prison, maybe worse, and brought disgrace down on my father. This way, the name of O'Neil would be absolved by my demise. I'm sorry I put all of you through the ordeal, but there wasn't any other way."

She shook her head in befuddlement. "Then where is Roger?"

"I'll start at the beginning, the night I boarded the ship at Belfast." And he ended by recounting how Jesse Farnsworth had drugged Roger and he had commenced the great impersonation.

"I knew I couldn't fool you forever, darling."

"I guess you really didn't fool me. Not altogether. I knew you weren't the Roger I knew. Your strangeness puzzled me. Frightened me at times. Like tonight."

He laughed and slapped her bare bottom. "You thought you were making love to a ghost. That would shake up a woman a bit, I imagine." He started to get up. "We'd better put on some clothes before we catch our deaths of cold. You that is. Naturally, a ghost can't catch cold. I'm already dead."

His back was to her as he bent over to pick up his trousers. Grinning impishly, Ravena planted a foot on his vulnerable bottom and shoved as hard as she could. He went sprawling on his face, knocking the wind out of his lungs.

When he was able to breathe again, he looked up at Ravena standing over him and gasped, "Now what did you do a thing like that for?"

She stuck out her tongue. "Because you're a sneaky, conniving, fraudulent mick of an Irishman."

His hand whipped out and he caught her ankle and yanked. She fell beside him in the grass.

"And you are a bitchy little Irish doxie."

Nose to nose their eyes aglow, her breasts brushing his hairy chest, her breaths quickening. She reached down between them and found him.

Ravena giggled wickedly. "I see you have the same thought on your mind too?"

He sighed and took her in his arms. "Scandalous wench."

CHAPTER THIRTEEN

The next month was glorious for Ravena. She had never been happier in all of her life. And it showed.

"You are positively radiant, dear," Vanessa Wilding said to her daughter at breakfast one morning after Brian had gone to the capitol building and her father was out watching his two racers practicing.

It was curious that, even at the lowest ebb of the war, the Southern aristocracy never lost interest in the sport they claimed as the "Confederate National Pastime."

"Thank you, Mother. I feel wonderful."

The two women smiled in secret feminine empathy.

"Could it be that you're pregnant? Your father always said I was more beautiful in the early months after you children were conceived. An inner glow."

"I'm not sure, Mother, but it is possible."

The Duchess arched her eyebrows. "I would say it is distinctly possible. I'm so pleased that you and Roger are getting along so well these days. It shows in him as well. Why, he's been like a different man since his return from active duty. Oh, maybe not that long but he has changed radically."

Ravena suppressed the urge to laugh. "Yes, I think he's finally outgrown his belated adolescence."

"A child would do you both a world of good. Having a baby makes both a man and woman more responsible. Childless couples tend to grow selfish and think only of satisfying their own individual gratifications."

"That is a point, Mother. Well, I hope you're right. I'd adore having a baby."

The Duchess came around the table and bent to kiss Ravena's cheek. Tears glistened in her eyes.

"And I'd adore being a grandmother."

"But you are. What about Kevin's boy?"

The older woman sighed. "Yes, but I've never had a chance to hold the little lad. That's what being a grandmother is all about."

Ravena laughed. "Yes, hugging, squeezing, kissing. Oh, if it is true what a spoiled little brat you'll make of him, or her."

"I guarantee it."

It was the end of the first week in August when Major Manson came running into Colonel O'Neil's office, his voice hoarse with emotion.

"Farragut attacked Mobile Bay this morning at dawn. The President has called an emergency meeting, come on."

"That's impossible! There must be a mistake!" Brian displayed the proper degree of shock and incredulity.

By the time they reached the Cabinet Room, all of the members were seated. Brian felt a pang of remorse when he saw the haggard face of Jefferson Davis. He sat at the head of the long table, head bowed, a hand shielding his eyes. Secretary of State Benjamin made the dire announcement. "Gentlemen, it is with deep sorrow that I advise you that Admiral Buchanan's fleet has been defeated at the Bay of Mobile. Admiral Buchanan was wounded in the action and he is now a prisoner of the enemy."

Exclamations of shock, dismay, grief sounded a dirge around the table.

"Fort Morgan and Fort Gaines are under siege, and it is only a matter of time before they too will be in the hands of the Yankees."

The Secretary of the Army pounded the table with both fists. "By God! How? How did Farragut do it?"

"With seven sloops of war, ten gunboats and four monitors. Obviously they knew the exact locations of the pilings and the torpedoes at the mouth of the bay. Farragut steamed right up the channel under Fort Morgan's guns."

"What about the *Tennessee*?"

"Evidently Farragut was also aware of the dilemma of the *Tennessee*, and he attacked at low tide when she was mired at anchor. His warships kept ramming her while one of the monitors took up a position by the casemate and kept pounding round after round of eleven-inch shells at her vulnerable spot until the armor plate finally collapsed and the tiller chains were shot away."

Brian sprang to his feet mouthing outraged indignation. "How in hell did Farragut come into possession of such vital information? It was highly classified. Top secret."

Benjamin shrugged and spread his hands, palms up in resignation. "Top secret. Colonel O'Neil, as an army veteran, you know better than most of us that if more than one person knows a thing, it ceases to become a secret. The Yankee spy system is probably the best in the world." He sighed ruefully. 'Yankee ingenuity,' I believe that is the term. I don't have to elaborate on the far-reaching ramifications of the loss of Mobile Bay. Mobile City is sealed off, and the Union Fleet is in indisputed control of the Gulf of Mexico."

It was not easy for Brian to conceal his elation. *"Mr. Lincoln, you have the victory you so dearly needed before the election!"*

Ravena did not altogether share his elation when he broke the news to her that night.

"I can't help feeling guilty, Brian. You are a Union spy and I'm a traitor to my homeland. Don't rationalize it, we've been Virginians for six years. This land and its people have been good to us, Brian. All of our dear friends, the Coopers, the Taylors, the Collinses, Melanie, Jan, and here I am betraying their friendship and graciousness with treachery."

Brian took her hands and looked into her eyes solemnly. "I understand and I love you more for acknowledging that you feel guilty. You're a decent human being, and it's a dirty business, war. General Sherman had it right: 'War is hell.' And it's one of the worst wars that we're involved in right now. You know, I'm a soldier, not a spy. It doesn't set well with me, stabbing good men like Davis and Benjamin and Roger's brother officers in their backs the way I've had to do. But my allegiance is sworn to the Union, and when my commander in chief, President Lincoln, gives me a direct order, I obey it to the best of my ability and my personal feelings have nothing to do with it."

She was staring at him strangely and with some uncertainty. "You know something, Brian, your speech might almost have been given by Roger."

"Why not? Whatever his faults are my brother is a man

of honor, and I believe he would defend his principles to the death."

Ravena knew he was right, and yet she felt let down. "You don't mind if we don't make love tonight, Brian. I'm suddenly exhausted."

"I understand." He kissed her forehead.

It was pitch dark when Brian was awakened by an urgent knocking on the bedroom door. Gordon's voice was excited.

"Colonel O'Neil, Mrs. Farnsworth is here to see you."

Brian sat up and fumbled for the matches on his bed table. He lit the oil lamp and sat on the edge of the bed collecting his fuzzy senses.

"Colonel O'Neil, sir!"

"Yes, yes, I'm coming, Gordon."

Ravena was awake now. "What on earth is going on? What time is it?"

He consulted his watch. "Three-fifteen. Jesse Farnsworth is here."

"At this hour? Jesse must be losing her mind."

"I think not," he said with a note of doom.

He put on his robe and Ravena followed suit. "Wait for me."

Jesse was waiting for them in the study, a glass of sherry in her hand. Her expression corroborated his note of doom.

"Shut the door," she said.

"What's happened, Jesse?" he asked.

"The worst thing that could possibly happen. Your brother Roger has escaped."

"My God!" Ravena turned pale and grabbed hold of Brian's arm.

"How did he manage it?" Brian asked calmly. He put an arm around Ravena.

Jesse's smile was ironic. "The same way we got hold of him. The officer second in command of the detachment guarding him was a Confederate agent."

Brian laughed without humor. "Tit for tat, we can't fault that, can we?" He could be dispassionate about it. All part of the game. The police chief who had bamboozled the British. He in turn had tricked Jefferson Davis and the Confederacy. Now it was Roger's turn. He could imagine what his brother was feeling right now.

Vengeance be mine, sweet vengeance!

"He's gotten clean away," Jesse was saying. "I received word from Allan Pinkerton no more than an hour ago. They're certain he's on his way back to Richmond."

"What are we to do?" Ravena asked. Her anxiety was growing with every word Jesse uttered.

"Not 'we,' darling," he said quietly. "What am I going to do. You can bring it off, Ravena. Claim you were taken in just like the rest of them. Roger will believe you. Everyone will."

She drew herself up tall and the upward thrust of her nose and chin recalled the stubborn determination of old Dan O'Connell defying all others in the British Parliament.

"Not on your life, Brian O'Neil. You're not getting away from me again."

"Ravena, be reasonable. I'm a fugitive. At least I will be when Roger gets back here. I've got to run and run fast."

"Then I'll run with you."

"If they catch us, we'll both be shot for treason."

"He's right, Ravena," Jesse said. "Washington, through the Pinkertons, is making plans for Brian's safe passage from Richmond."

"Safe passage?" He frowned.

"Exactly. Aboard a ship. There's a clipper due to sail Tuesday afternoon from Portsmouth bound for San Francisco. That's two days off. You'll be aboard. A garbage scow will transport you down the James tonight. You'll get there after dark tomorrow."

"Does her skipper know who I am?"

"He will by the time you report to him. I imagine he's being contacted right now. The state is teeming with Pinkerton agents."

"Can he be trusted?"

Jesse smiled. "He's the nephew of President Lincoln's Secretary of State, Mr. Seward."

Ravena was skeptical. "Why does he have to go to San Francisco? Why don't we make a run for it North?"

"Because by tomorrow morning, the entire Southern army and navy will be looking for Brian. That's what they'll all be expecting, that he's trying to get back to the Union lines or to Washington by sea. On the other hand, a clipper ship under English registry, sailing for San Francisco won't arouse any suspicion. Look, we don't have time to stand here talking about it. Pack up a few possessions and we'll be off. My carriage is outside and I'll drive you down to the docks. When you arrive in Portsmouth, go to a house of ill repute called the Blind Pig. The madam is another Pinkerton agent. You'd be astonished at the amount of information her girls have gathered from the Southern soldiers and sailors who frequent it."

Brian shook his head wonderingly at Allan Pinkerton's resourcefulness.

Ravena took his arm and said stoutly, "That settles it. I won't hear of Brian spending the night in a brothel without me."

Jesse and Brian laughed, despite the gravity of the situation.

"I don't believe you'll get away from her, my lad," Jesse said. She was thoughtful for a moment. "You know it just might work out quite well. Captain Swift was married in London just before the *West Wind* sailed. His bride is accompanying him, and you could fit in nicely as her companion and maid."

Ravena clapped her hands in childish glee. "Oh, that does appeal to me, Jesse. A lady's maid." She affected Rose's brogue: "Yes, mum. No, mum, 'tain't nothin' wrong wi' me at all, mum. . . . Oh, I can do it, Brian. Please! Don't make me stay here!"

"If Jesse say it's safe for you, then you'll come."

The clock in the hall chimed the quarter hour.

"Hurry, you two," Jesse urged. "It's almost four o'clock!"

"We'll be ready at four," Brian promised. He took Ravena's elbow and pushed her ahead of him into the hall.

Gordon was waiting for them at the stairs, clutching his nightrobe around him. He was confused and apprehensive.

"Colonel O'Neil, is there anything wrong, and can I do anything to help?"

Brian gripped the butler's thin shoulder. "I won't lie to you, Gordon. There's a good deal wrong, but I don't have time to tell you about it now. Mrs. O'Neil and I will be leaving here as soon as we can dress. Don't worry, everything is going to be all right. The best thing you can do to help us is to give me your word that when you're questioned tomorrow, tell the authorities that you were asleep all night, and that you don't know when we left or why we left or where we are going. Do you understand?"

"Yes, sir."

Brian took his right hand in both of his hands and squeezed it. "Good-bye, Gordon. God willing, we'll meet again."

"And when we do, you'll be a free man, Gordon," Ravena put in. She reached up, cupped Gordon's face in her hands and kissed him on the cheek. "I'll miss you, Gordon. You're one of the dearest men I know. And I'm proud to have known you."

The butler's eyes filled up and his voice was thick. "God bless you, Miss Ravena. You too, Colonel." He whirled and hurried down the hall toward the rear of the house.

Ravena dressed in the drabbest gown she owned, a wool town garment adorned by a mantelet and a bonnet that shadowed her face. She threw a cashmere shawl over her shoulders.

Brian's dress was equally nondescript, an ancient suit of Roger's that had hung in the closet since Roger's arrival in Virginia.

When they were ready to leave, Ravena told him: "I must say goodbye to Father and Mother." She anticipated what he was going to say and shook her head. "No, I don't think you should see them just now. Someday. Brian, go down and wait with Jesse. Please. I'll be just a minute."

"As you wish." He squeezed her hand and walked down the hall carrying their two small bags.

The Duke and Duchess listened in stunned silence as Ravena explained in as few words as possible why she and Brian were leaving Richmond.

"Incredible!" Edward Wilding kept shaking his head. "Brian O'Neil come back from the dead."

"He's very much alive," Ravena said with a lightness she did not truly feel. At any moment the whole world might cave in on her and Brian. "Don't worry, Mother, we'll be fine. I'll get word to you as soon as we get to San Francisco. By telegraph."

Seated on the edge of her bed, Vanessa Wilding was in a state of shock.

"What are we to tell Roger? The authorities?"

"You won't tell them anything. Behave as if you had no inkling of what was going on. In fact, I think it might be advisable for you to denounce Brian and me. Act as if you are outraged for poor, dear Roger. You're going to have to live with this, you know, and it won't be easy to live down your daughter's treason. Look, ducks, I really have to run."

She embraced the two of them ardently and hurried to the door.

"Good luck, my darling," the Duke said hoarsely as she left. He sat down on the bed and took his wife in his arms. They sat there clutching at each other like two orphans of the storm.

The coach rattled and bumped over the cobblestones to the tempo of the *clomp-clomp-clomp* of the horses' hooves, setting up a cacophony that echoed up and down the narrow street.

As the coach rumbled on, a patch of light materialized like the opening of a tunnel. The hatch in the roof opened and the driver called down:

"Mrs. Farnsworth, the harbor is just up ahead."

"Please stop at the next corner," she instructed him. "I believe from there we turn left and proceed to the third quay."

On critical missions like this one, reliable Samuel doubled as coachman.

The interior of the coach was illuminated by candles set in brackets on the walls. The side curtains were tightly drawn; this fueled the imaginations of the sprinkling of early-morning risers and late-night straggler pedestrians as dawn broke over Richmond Harbor. They noted that the coach was more ornate than vehicles generally seen on the waterfront, and they speculated that the circumspect occupants were undoubtedly a dashing clipper captain being spirited back to his ship by his wealthy and prominent mistress. Not an idle fancy, for although the age of sail was drawing to a close, the clipper captain had been regarded as an idol and hero the world 'round for more than two decades.

The coach creaked to a stop and the hatch opened again. "We're here, ma'am," Samuel informed them.

Jesse reached across and put a hand on each of their arms. "The end of the line for me. Madam is expecting you. Good-bye and good luck."

"What will you do?" Brian asked. "Roger knows you're a spy."

"I'll go underground. I may well slip back to Washington by the same way you got here and Roger was whisked away."

Brian and Ravena each kissed her on the cheek.

"I don't know what we would have done without you, Jesse. Then again, I don't know what the Union would have done without you."

"Bah! Humbug! I love the excitement."

"Take care, Jesse. It's dangerous work you're mixed up in."

She laughed. "Don't fret. Nothing is going to happen to this li'l ol' Southern belle. Now, be off with you. Have a good voyage and bring me back a souvenir from San Francisco."

They descended from the coach and walked out on the quay where four vessels were moored. A man came forward to meet them, carrying a lantern.

"You be Colonel O'Neil?" he asked.

"And Mrs. O'Neil."

The old man removed his cap. "Ma'am, we weren't expecting no lady. My scow ain't exactly the *Empress of India*."

"No," Ravena said brightly. "But just think how much more quaint it is. I've never sailed on a garbage scow."

"It's an experience you'll never forget, ma'am," he said crustily.

His was an understatement, but at least the trip was uneventful. They docked at Portsmouth the following midnight and were taken by coach to the Blind Pig. Above the narrow doorway hung a weatherbeaten sign featuring a caricature of a fat hog, up on its hind legs, tapping its way along like a blind man with a cane. A seaman's bandana was tied over its eyes. Brian opened the door and let her precede him into the establishment managed with a tyrant's hand by one Della Spasky. They were overwhelmed by their first sight of Della. An enormous blonde woman in her mid-fifties who, as Brian described her, had "bazooms like observation balloons and an arse like a cavalry horse!"

She turned out to be a soft-hearted woman with the proverbial heart of gold. "Or as my father would say of her, 'a diamond in the rough,'" Ravena later opined when she and Brian were settled in their dingy, roach-infested room.

"You're gonna be right comfortable in here," Della assured them. "It's the best bed in the house. Only my best customers get to use it."

Ravena contemplated it with a jaundiced eye.

"You're as generous as you are beautiful, Della me lass." Brian turned on the Irish charm.

Della stood with her hands on her wide hips, grinning at him and showing blackened teeth. "You're buttering me up, boy, and I love every bloody lie of what you say." She nudged Ravena in the ribs with an elbow. "I usually don't take on customers any more. You might say I am in retirement. But in your boyfriend's case, I just might make an exception. I'll bet he knows how to treat a gal right, eh honey?"

"Bloody well right he do, Della," Ravena played Brian's game. "'Tain't often a simple 'ousemaid like me gits to latch onto such a fine gentleman."

Della winked. "Well, good night, you two. Sure I can't get you some vittles or a bottle of hooch? You name it."

"No thanks, we want to grab some sleep before it's time to go."

Della winked. "I'll bet you want to grab some sleep, oh, sure," she said lecherously. "Well, don't do anything I wouldn't do. I'll rap on the door when the messenger gits here."

"Good *night*!" they said in chorus and then fell back on the bed, laughing as quietly as they could.

"Quite a girl, Della," he said.

Ravena put her arms around him. "It's a lucky thing for you that you relented and let me come along, or that Amazon would have raped you."

Brian was awakened by a rough hand shaking his shoulder. He opened his eyes and shuddered. A face like Della Spasky's was a hell of a sight to greet a man first thing in the morning.

"Visitor to see you." She leered at Ravena, still asleep, the rumpled coverlet exposing one of her bare breasts. "Guess you two didn't get much sleep, eh?"

Brian pulled the cover over her and sat up.

"Where is he?"

Della's huge bulk moved aside, revealing a small, wizened hunchback standing behind her. He gave Brian a toothless smile and doffed his filthy cap.

"Bob the beggar at yer service, sir," he said in a heavy cockney accent. He held out a large package wrapped in brown oiled paper and tied with a cord. "Compliments of Mr. Pinkerton."

"I'll leave you gentlemen to talk business," Della said and withdrew.

The hunchback dropped the accent now. "Colonel O'Neil, inside this package you'll find papers of identification for you and your wife—"

"She's not my wife," Brian said with a grin.

The hunchback grinned back. "Your lovely lady, then. There's a second mate's uniform for you; the lady will have to make do with what she has. Once you're aboard the ship, the captain will fix you up with additional duds. You'd better hurry. The *West Wind* is due to sail at three P.M. And you're to be aboard by noon. It's eleven now."

"Plenty of time. If you'll wait outside, I'll wake the lady and we'll be ready in ten minutes."

"I think not." He laughed. "There's a little job you must attend to first. You'll find a razor in the package, a bogus mustache, and an eye patch. Orders are for you to shave off your hair. Bald as a billiard ball, you'll be. There's spirit gum to fix on the mustache, and the eye patch is the final touch. Not even your mother would recognize you."

Brian protested. "Shave off my hair? Nonsense! I'm not one of Pinkerton's agents!"

The little man's voice hardened. "O'Neil, you want to get out of this city alive, you'd better follow instructions. The streets out there are teeming with soldiers and police looking for you. Their orders are to shoot on sight."

"I see." Brian rubbed the stubble on his chin. His mouth was awry. "I suspect you are right, my friend. What about her? They must be looking for her as well as me?"

The hunchback's brow puckered like crepe paper.

"Hmmm. Not so good. You see, the original plans did not include Mrs. O'Neil. Wait a minute, I think I've got something—one of Della's wigs."

"The madam?"

"Yes, she's bald as you're going to be, Colonel. Some disease years ago. Yes, a blonde wig will do very nicely. Then we can fix her up with one of the girls' dresses, so she looks the part of a real tart. I'll see to that right off. You better get started." He turned and limped out of the room.

Ravena's eyes flew open the instant the door closed behind her. Brian laughed.

"You weren't asleep?"

"Of course not. I really didn't care to be formally introduced to the gentleman under the present circumstances. In bed, naked, with a man who isn't my husband. A gentlewoman of my station. It's too mortifying."

Brian threw back his head and roared with laughter. "Excellent background for the role you're about to play."

Her mouth turned down at the corners. "I know. Imagine—Now I've been demoted from lady's maid to whore."

He got out of bed. "You have all the right qualifications. Now to get to work."

He opened the parcel and put on the one-piece union suit, that was the standard undergarment of seafaring men. Next came the maritime officer's blue trousers. Then he gathered up the straight razor, soap and shears, and went over to the washstand in one corner of the room.

By the time Della Spasky walked into the room, he had sheared off most of his hair and was soaping his scalp for the razor.

"Here you are, dearie." She tossed a bundle of clothing on the bed along with a fuzzy blonde wig. "Mind, a girl of the streets don't wear no crinoline, so you best leave your own duds here. Hurry it up, you ain't got much time." She left.

A quarter of an hour later Brian and Ravena were ready for inspection.

He whistled in admiration. "Gad! If I were a tar looking for a little cuddle, I'd sure enough proposition you."

She wore a white satin blouse with a low square-cut neckline that exposed half of her breasts, and a tight red skirt that reached halfway down her calf. A slit on the right side exposed her leg up to midthigh when she walked.

"Don't be so smug, love. If a bloke that looked like you propositioned me, I'd turn 'im down. Gor, you're ugly!" Her voice went with her appearance.

He looked at himself in the mirror and grimaced. "Can't say I blame you. I look like Blackbeard the pirate."

Ravena stuffed her own clothing into her bag with the exception of the bulky crinoline. The Pinkerton agency had provided Brian with a seaman's canvas bag with his name and rank stenciled on it: *Second Mate Paul Dexter*.

He slung it over his shoulder and said, "All right, wench, let's get on with it."

They went downstairs where Beggar Bob and Della Spasky were waiting in the parlor, where her girls got acquainted with the house's clients. A few of the seedy whores were loitering in the background, whispering and tittering.

"Shut yer fuckin' traps!" Della bellowed and they slunk off like beaten dogs. She grinned at Ravena. "Excuse the language, ma'am. But now that yer one of us, you best get used to the lingo of the trade."

"I've heard even worse, Mrs. Spasky," Ravena said airily.

Della cackled and slapped her enormous thigh. "Yer all right, dearie."

The hunchback walked around them, inspecting them from head to foot and from all sides. Finally he gave his approval.

"Fine. Just fine. Like I said, you'd fool your own mothers."

"I should hope Mama wouldn't recognize me in this monstrosity," Ravena said gaily.

"One more thing," Beggar Bob said. "Della and I have decided that you should go to the ship separately. Della will go with Mrs. O'Neil. One of her girls always accompanies her when she does her daily marketing. I'll tell you how to find the ship. It's in Slip Eleven. No more than a ten-minute walk from here. Della, I guess you two better get started."

Ravena's heart was racing so fast she couldn't distinguish one beat from the other as she and Della stepped out into the street. "Street" was a misnomer, she thought. It was little more than a wide alleyway, jammed with people at this hour of the morning. The odors on this hot August day were overpowering. The myriad stenches of sweat, human excrement, animal manure and rotten garbage as well as other malodorous stinks.

She fixed her gaze straight ahead as they passed a pair of policemen scanning the faces in the crowd. A rivulet of cold sweat wriggled down the hollow of her back, and she shivered.

Della spoke to her out of the corner of her mouth. "Relax, dearie. Yer stiff as a board. You might as well scream out loud: 'I'm guilty as hell!' You may not be so lucky next time we meet the law."

Before they had traveled the length of the block Della exchanged greetings with a score of pedestrians and tradesmen. The huge jolly madam was a waterfront showpiece, with the law as well as the inhabitants.

They turned the corner and ran into two soldiers, military police. The corporal's face lit up.

"By Jesus! It's been a long time, Della, honey."

"Billy boy, I thought you'd forgotten all about us," she replied in an injured tone. "Little Janie has been crying her eyes out over you, Billy."

He cackled. "You tell Janie I'll be in tonight, sure as shoot. Soon as we get off this special duty." He took out a daguerreotype from his jacket pocket and held it out to her. "You seen either one of these people, by chance?"

Ravena's heart stopped beating, and a lesser woman would have collapsed out of sheer terror. She summoned the iron within.

"Pull yourself together, wench!" Brian would have scolded.

She craned her neck and peered over Della's gross arm at the picture of herself and Roger taken at their wedding. In her best Cajun drawl she said:

"Lan' sakes, boy-y-y-s, what would a pa'r of swells like them be doin' down ha'r?"

"She's right, Billy." Della handed back the photo. "What they do anyway?"

"Damned if we know. Orders are to pick 'em up, that's all."

Della patted Ravena's arm. "I think my new gal here, li'l Bonnie Belle has taken a fancy to you. Aintcha, Bonnie?"

Ravena fluttered her eyelids at the gangly towheaded corporal. "I'd sure like it fine if you was to honor me, suh."

He feasted his eyes on the luscious fruits bulging over the bodice of the blouse. "I can see that yer my kind of gal, Bonnie Belle. I'll do my best to see you tonight, honey chile."

Ravena waved over her shoulder as Della dragged her on. "Don' you forget, you all."

Della chuckled delightedly when they were out of ear-shot. "That was marvelous, dearie. Get in the spirit of it, and you'll be jus' fine."

There were no further overt incidents until they arrived at the gangplank leading from the dock to the immense clipper ship, *West Wind.* A uniformed guard armed with a rifle was posted there, as there was at the gangplank of every other ship on the dock.

Della and Ravena approached the sentry boldly. "Let me handle this," the fat madam muttered.

She beamed at the soldier. "Well, good mornin' to you, Sergeant."

He touched his cap. "Mornin', ma'am—ladies." His gaze was riveted to Ravena. She tilted her head coquettishly to one side and winked at him.

"Hi thar, *Sarg*-ent."

He reddened and swayed from one foot to the other. "I'm only a private, ma'am."

"You ought to be a sergeant." Della tittered, gave him a playful slap on the arm. "Haven't I seen you at my place?"

"Don't believe so, ma'am. What is your place?"

She and Ravena went into girlish peals of laughter and Della shoved Ravena, almost knocking her off her feet.

"You hear that, hon? This nice boy doesn't know Della —Della—Della Spasky—Della's place. This here is one of my girls."

His face lit up. "*That* Della! Yessiree, I've heard the boys speak of your place," he coughed. "Ma'am."

Della punched him on the arm. "*Mad*-am, not ma'am. Son, you kind of fancy my little gal here, Bonnie Belle?"

He cast a shy glance at Ravena, eyes drawn to the slit at the side of her skirt. "She's a purty thing all right."

"You come down to Della's place soon as you get off duty, and little Belle will treat you real nice. Now if you'll excuse us, son, we have some business to transact on board." She winked. "It's gonna be a long voyage and Belle wants to give the boys something to remember that will keep 'em warm when they're sailing 'round the Horn."

"Yes, ma'am." He giggled as Ravena followed Della up the gangplank.

CHAPTER FOURTEEN

Brian's walk to the ship was uneventful. He was just another blue uniform in a section of the city teeming with seamen.

As he walked out onto the quay where the *West Wind* was being loaded, his gaze traveled from her sharp, arching head over her slim bow along her convex sides down to her light, round graceful stern.

"Clean as a barracuda," he murmured.

The *West Wind* was an "extreme" clipper, the largest of her class. She measured two hundred twenty feet from stem to stern, torty teet in breadth and her hold went down twenty-four feet.

Aloft she was a staggering size. Her lower masts were iron-banded, her short masts taut and tapered. From her lower to skysail yards, her spars were long and graceful. Within the next few hours, he reflected, those towering latticeworks of arms and fingers would be stretching a cloud of canvas skyward to the wind.

The term "clipper" was coined in 1835. As a boy, Brian had read everything he could lay his hands on about these magnificent queens of the seven seas. To serve aboard a clipper was the highest honor that could fall to a sailor. The clipper was designed for speed rather than cargo space, heavily sparred to spread more canvas than any other ship afloat. Speed meant money for clipper owners, a decisive factor in the international competition for sea commerce.

The *West Wind* had a long sharp bow, and her run was clean but full and short. Her greatest breadth was amidships, and her hull was deeper at the bow than at the stern.

Brian had never heard of her skipper Jason Swift, but it went without saying that he had to be a special man. There was an axiom in seafaring circles that it had taken a hundred years to build the clipper ship and a generation of hell to develop the men to sail it. A special breed from the lowest deckhand to the master. Tough, reckless, aggressive, they feared nothing, death included, except the skipper. A clipper captain had to be able to dominate the meanest, biggest brute among his crew. Typically he was a strong, silent, withdrawn man, a stern and merciless master. He was often worshipped by his men, but seldom loved. He had to be a driver, a daredevil for speed who spared nothing to strengthen the rig and extend the canvas, a bull-dog who would hang on grimly until the spars began to go and the head knees cracked.

Brian showed his papers to the soldier guarding the gang-plank and marched aboard with his seaman's swagger. He was greeted at the top by a tall slender officer with black hair, a mustache and steel-gray eyes.

"Mr. Dexter, I presume?"

Brian blinked, the name not registering immediately. "Oh, me. Yes, I'm Paul Dexter."

"I'm Dick Carson, the First."

"Pleased to be serving under you, Mr. Carson."

They shook hands.

"Captain Swift wants you to report soon as you're settled in. Come along, I'll show you where your quarters are. I hear you lost your last ship because you came down with the fever?"

"Yup, been stranded here in Portsmouth since early July."

"Glad to get you, Dexter. We're short-handed. Been without a second since we left Liverpool."

Brian followed Carson down a long gangway aft to his cabin. It was small, but comfortably appointed, and the mattress, on the wall bunk was clean and firm.

"You've got interesting company right across the hall. A Miss Belle. Supposed to be a maid and companion for the captain's wife, but there's something fishy about the whole thing. She looks like a tenderloin whore to me. Don't abide with women on ships, including the skipper's lady."

Brian stared him straight in the eye. "Neither do I. It's bad luck."

Carson jerked his head. "Now for the captain."

The captain's cabin was large but unpretentious. It was

divided into two sections, a small bedroom with a double bed, and a sitting room and office with a secretary desk.

Jason Swift was a big rawboned man with hawklike features and curly blond hair. His eyes were a deep ocean blue. A ship's officer at nineteen, he had won an enviable reputation for his courage and seamanship. Now at twenty-nine he held the distinction of being the youngest member of the small élite society of "Clipper Captains."

Swift rose from his desk and returned Brian's salute. His tanned, leathery face made him appear older than his years.

"Second Mate Paul Dexter reporting for duty, sir."

"Welcome aboard, Mr. Dexter." He accepted the credentials his new mate handed over and nodded to the first. "You may carry on with your duties, Mr. Carson."

The captain glanced perfunctorily at Brian's papers and handed them back. "Everything seems to be in order, Mr. Dexter." His eyes twinkled. "Do you know anything at all about seamanship?"

"A fair amount, actually. I've done some sailing for sport and then I did put in a hitch as a seaman working my way over from Ireland to America. I know how to use a sextant and make nautical observations. I can work up time from the chronometer and can keep a reckoning of position on the charts. The rudiments."

"That's excellent, Mr. Dexter. We're a lean crew aboard the *West Wind*, so maybe you can work off your passage. Every hand counts."

"I'll be glad to lend a hand, whatever you say, Captain. Our destination is San Francisco, I understand?"

Swift sat down and motioned for Brian to sit on the leather couch. He put a cold pipe between his teeth.

"San Francisco may be your destination, but it's only the first leg of the voyage for us. The *West Wind* is bound for the Hawaiian Islands, then on to China, London and back to New York. We'll be at sea for seventeen months altogether. But it's only five months to California."

Brian whistled in awe. "Compared with seventeen months it's not bad, but it's still a long time. It only took five weeks from Ireland to the States. It's a good thing you have your wife with you. She'd forget what you looked like in seventeen months."

Swift laughed. "I wouldn't have accepted the command

if the owners hadn't agreed to allow Mary to accompany me. I'm delighted to have Mrs. O'Neil with us, too. She'll be good company for Mary. The last I heard of them they were jabbering away about gussets and drapes and God knows what else feminine frippery. A beautiful woman, Colonel O'Neil." He caught himself. "Damn careless of me, *Mr.* Dexter."

"That's all right. I have trouble remembering myself. What about Carson? Does he know who I really am?"

"Not yet, he doesn't. Once we're at sea, I don't give a damn if he finds out." He took a bottle of whisky out of a drawer and poured a few fingers into two water glasses. "The Secretary of State speaks highly of your exploits, Mr. Dexter. Perhaps you'd fill in some of the more exciting details while we're at sea."

"I'd be more than happy to oblige." He smiled. "We'll certainly have plenty of time."

The captain handed him a glass and they drank a toast to a fast and profitable voyage.

There was a knock on the door. "Come in," Swift said.

It was the first mate. "Captain, there's a Confederate major on the dock who wants to bring a search party aboard. What should I tell him?"

"Tell him to go to hell! No, I'll tell him myself." He cast a long, guarded look at Brian. "Come along, Mr. Dexter."

Brian experienced a shock as he saw his reflection in a mirror over the couch. Getting accustomed to his new looks would take time and doing. A one-eyed, bald-headed rogue. All that was missing was an earring in his right ear!

The captain led the way on dock. At the head of the gangplank a dozen or more of the *West Wind*'s crew had lined up in silent confrontation with a detail of soldiers on the dock. They pulled back as the captain called down:

"Can we be of service, Major?"

"Yes, sir. I'm requesting permission to bring my men aboard and search your ship."

"Search my ship! I'll be damned!" Swift feigned astonishment. "Permission denied, Major. I've never heard anything so outrageous in my life. I dare say you are not acquainted with maritime regulations governing international immunity of a neutral party from the combatants in a state of war. I must remind you that if you set foot on board this ship you are in direct violation of British territory, and I promise you, sir, the repercussions will cost you your commission."

Brian had never heard a more masterful example of circuitous double-talk in his life. He had all he could do to keep a straight face.

The major could only gape at Swift with his jaw sagging. The captain did an about-face and marched off with Brian at his heels. Carson looked after them thoughtfully, then turned his attention to the belittled major on the dock. Slowly he walked down the gangplank.

"Sorry, we can't oblige, Major. The old man was spawned by the devil and born out of storm and the sea. What you looking for anyway?"

"Spies. Union spies." He produced one of the fuzzy daguerreotypes of Ravena's and Roger's wedding. "Ever seen these two?"

The mate shook his head. "Never set eyes on them. What would they be doing aboard a clipper ship bound around the Horn?"

"Trying to escape, that's what they're up to. We've got Richmond bottled up, so this is the only way out. By ship. You carrying any passengers?"

"No. That is no one that looks like that woman. There is a Miss Belle, but she's a blonde floozy." He frowned in concentration. "Let me see that picture again."

He studied it narrowly, rubbing his jaw. "I wonder? Hmmmm. Can't say for certain, but it's possible."

"What's possible?"

"That under all the powder and paint this Miss Belle might be hiding this gorgeous filly. A blonde wig is easy enough to get."

"But you said she's traveling alone. She wouldn't go off and leave her lover behind."

"Then she's not your woman. Miss Belle is definitely alone."

The major shrugged. "Too bad. You might have made yourself some money if she was Ravena O'Neil, the woman we want. There's ten thousand dollars reward money on each of their heads. Well, let's be off, men." He threw a salute at Carson and the soldiers marched off, with the exception of the gangplank guard.

At five minutes after three that afternoon, the *West Wind* eased out of her slip and sailed slowly out of Portsmouth Harbor into Chesapeake Bay.

Midway between Hampton Roads and Fisherman's Island, a Confederate Navy cutter drew alongside and her captain addressed Captain Swift through a megaphone. "Heave to! We're putting a boarding party on your ship!"

Swift took the megaphone from his bosun. "Permission denied! I gave my reasons to the army. Evidently the major did not understand. The *West Wind* constitutes British territory. Any action you take to violate that territory would be considered a hostile and provocative act by my government."

The Confederate captain conferred with an aide and when he addressed Swift again his voice was uncertain.

"Sir, we have direct orders from President Davis. This is a very serious matter. We have strong reasons to suspect that you are harboring two traitors to the Confederate government."

"That's hogwash!" Swift called back. "You relay my respects to the president but inform him that I have my orders from Queen Victoria and that the British Navy is prepared to back them up." He pointed across the water to Hampton Roads, where a British man-o'-war rode at anchor, looking very formidable indeed.

Before the Confederate captain could reply to that, Captain Swift bawled at his crew straddling the yards and hanging in the rigging: "Make sail for a race!"

He turned to the first and second mates flanking him on the quarterdeck. "Take over, Mr. Carson. Mr. Dexter, you will accompany me to the bridge."

Carson took the bull horn and commanded. "All hands aloft!"

The men went scampering up the shrouds and spars like monkeys. With the wind aft, the majestic clipper drew quickly away from the Confederate cutter while her crew flung jibes and jeers at the Southern sailors. The cutter passed quickly out of sight as the *West Wind* plunged into a squall and was shut in thick with rain and flying scud.

"You stick close to me, O'Neil," Captain Swift advised him as they climbed the steps to the bridge. "I've assigned you to the middle watch. You won't run into many problems midnight 'til daybreak unless we're struck by a bad storm. This is the season, but hopefully our luck will hold out."

Before the supper meal, Captain Swift invited Brian and Ravena to his cabin for a social visit with him and his wife, Mary.

Mary Swift was a pretty blonde girl of twenty-three. Brian was astounded that a woman so youthful could be so knowledgeable about ships and seamanship.

When Brian commented on it, Swift chuckled. "I'll let you in on a secret, Colonel O'Neil. This little slip of a thing has the ability to bring the *West Wind* safely into San Francisco without any help from me."

"I have no doubt about it, Captain," Ravena said a bit testily. "Though I would have to disagree with you that Mary is 'a little slip of a thing.' She's a mature woman and a highly intelligent human being."

Captain Swift looked nonplussed and Brian laughed. "I should have warned you, Captain, that Mrs. O'Neil is a very independent lady with a mind of her own."

"Yes, I can see that," Swift said with some uneasiness, puffing on his pipe. He had enormous admiration for Ravena. Rid of her tart's togs and the hideous wig, she was a breathtaking beauty. It was a pleasure for him to gaze upon the two of them—his beloved wife and this royal beauty. One a golden angel, the other dark and a fiery Jezebel, from what he could make out. Those violet eyes of hers—*a man could drown in such eyes*, he thought.

Ravena and Mary had become fast friends within a few hours.

"But we must drop this pretense that you're my maid, Ravena. The truth of it is that I look like your maid."

The four of them laughed in good humor. They were safe at sea, and there was no need to maintain the pretense any longer, as Captain Swift pointed out.

"There is no possible way that you can be apprehended or detained at this stage of the game. We won't see port again until we arrive in San Francisco, so your problems are over." He lifted his glass in a toast. "To your good health and future happiness—Mrs. O'Neil—Colonel O'Neil."

The appearance of Ravena that evening at the captain's

table came as a rude shock to First Mate Carson. He could only stare at her, as Captain Swift introduced her in her true identity.

"Mr. Carson, may I present her Grace the Viscountess O'Neil."

Ravena chided him. "My mother, the Duchess, is 'her Grace,' Captain Swift. I really can't lay claim to but one title, sir, 'Viscountess,' and even that carries no weight in America."

"You forget, madam, that we are on British territory," the captain said slyly.

Ravena's riposte was wicked. "True, but Captain, that is one title I can do without: *Madam!* I can't help but think of dear Della Spasky."

They all laughed, with the exception of Carson, who was still struggling to cope with his shock and surprise. His tongue felt thick in his mouth. "You mean to say—that is —you—*not* Miss Belle?"

"One and the same," she answered brightly. "Don't look so stricken, Mr. Carson. It was a necessary ruse."

The parts of the puzzle were falling into place now for Carson. "Then you are the couple the Confederates were seeking?" He looked from one to the other. Ravena, a lady of quality, royal blood. Brian, minus his eye patch and bogus mustache, no longer the fierce salt he had first appeared to be. The two of them sitting there so smug and self-confident seemed to mock him.

With a little bit of luck, with a little more ingenuity on his part, Carson might have come up with a method to foil their escape and collect the reward.

"There's ten thousand dollars reward money on each of their heads."

"What is it, Mr. Carson?" the captain asked. "You look so pale."

"It's nothing, nothing at all, sir." He lifted his glass of wine. "May I propose a toast to Colonel and Mrs. O'Neil? Congratulations on your daring escape and may this voyage be a source of celebration for you and for all of us."

"Hear! Hear! Well said, Carson."

From the moment Brian had met Carson he had certain feelings of reserve about the man. To his surprise and chagrin Dick Carson proved to be an entertaining social companion and raconteur. Both Ravena and Mary were enthralled by his account of the stormy courtship of his grandparents.

"One of the best skippers to sail out of Liverpool, the old boy was. Didn't marry until his fiftieth year when he became wildly impassioned of a Spanish noblewoman in Barcelona. A bit of a pirate he was, old Bull Carson. Do you know he had the lady kidnapped by his crewmen and spirited her onto his ship? Oh, what a voyage that was, I heard tell. She was a fierce Latin wildcat, and near scratched him to pieces."

He smiled at the ladies, especially at Ravena, in a way that Brian thought was just beneath the threshold of insolence.

"But when they docked at Liverpool, she followed him down the gangplank like a pet kitten. And when her influential family made a direct appeal to the King for his head on a spike, she threatened to kill herself. Now there was a man for you."

Ravena was intrigued. "There's a similar thing in my family line, isn't there, Brian? My great-great grandmother married a Spanish naval officer washed ashore when his ship was sunk in the Irish Sea."

His dark eyes flashed at her. "Then we share the same hot Spanish blood, my dear lady."

Brian moved to get to his feet, fed up with this upstart, but Ravena's hand came down on his knee firmly under the table.

She gave Carson an icy smile and said. "Not really. Didn't you say that your grandmother followed him down the gangplank like a kitten? He'd have had the same wild-cat he started out with upon his return to England, if I had been she."

Carson's face flushed, and he rose in place and excused himself. "It's time I was on deck and see if it's cleared enough to take some celestial sightings."

"I don't like Mr. Carson," Brian said when he was gone.

Mary Swift laughed. "Could it be that you're jealous, Colonel O'Neil? Just a wee bit?"

"Not in the least, Mrs. Swift. It's just that I don't trust him."

Captain Swift snorted. "Nor I. He's a competent First, so long as I keep my eye on him."

"I think he's rather charming," Ravena teased. "A trifle pushy, but his type is easily put in place."

"Just see that you keep him there," Brian said.

"See, Ravena," Mary said mischievously. "The colonel is jealous."

Out on deck Carson went up to the poopdeck. It had been raining on and off all through the afternoon, but now the stars were showing through the scudding clouds and the barometer was rising.

"How goes it, Benson?" Carson inquired.

"Steady as she goes, sir. Wind's due south."

"Good. Hold your course."

Carson took his sightings with the sextant at the stern, planting his feet against the roll of the slim clipper.

Sam Bonny, the bosun's mate, came up behind him. Bonny was a new hand they had taken on at Portsmouth, a Virginia lad born and bred.

"Evening, Mr. Carson. Looks like we're in for a spell of good weather."

"That it does." Carson lowered the sextant and looked at the bosun's mate. "What do you think of our passengers?"

"Passenger. You mean Miss Belle?"

"No, I mean Mrs. Roger O'Neil and her brother-in-law, the Honorable—no, make that 'dishonorable'—Colonel Brian O'Neil. The two of 'em are Northern spies, the pair the Confederate military were looking for before we shipped out."

"Who's Colonel O'Neil?"

Carson's mouth turned down at the corners scornfully. "Our brand-new second mate, Dexter. The captain was in on the whole thing. He's no more a second mate than I am the Queen of England. What do you think of that, Bonny? How does a good Southern boy like you feel about helping a couple of Union spies escape?"

Bonny was not a particularly bright man and he'd been at sea since he was fourteen. Now at twenty-eight, his allegiance to the Confederacy was vague.

"Well, I dunno, sir. I never give it any thought. It's hard to think of them two as spies."

"Well, it's true anyway. Hell, Bonny, don't you have any sense of patriotism? I'm from Pennsylvania myself, but I don't like the idea of being a party to this kind of treachery."

"Yeah, I suppose you're right, Mr. Carson. Yeah." Carson was fanning the spark of righteous indignation. "The captain had no right to trick them Confederate soldiers and sailors the way he did."

"What's even worse, Bonny, if the captain had done his duty and turned them in, we all would have got a share of the reward money."

"Reward money?"

"Ten thousand dollars apiece. Twenty thousand dollars, can you picture all that money, Bonny?"

The bosun's mate shook his head, befuddled by the picture it conjured up. He'd never seen more than seventy-five dollars at one time in his life when he was paid off at the end of a voyage.

"How would you like to get that money after all, just you and me?" Carson looked around to make certain they could not be overheard by the helmsman.

"How can we manage that, Mr. Carson?"

"If the *West Wind* was to put in at Tierra Del Fuego, Rio Grande, and if we could get O'Neil and the woman ashore, it would be easy. The South did a lot of trading with the island of Tierra Del Fuego before the war and the people there are sympathetic to the Confederate cause. I know, I was there last voyage. We could get the authorities to arrest them and hold them for extradition."

Bonny was getting more bewildered. "Extradition, what's that, sir?"

"Never mind, Bonny. I'll explain it to you when we're ready to move."

"But I didn't think we were goin' to put in at any port before San Francisco."

"Well, that's the present plan, Bonny." Carson's expression was sardonic. "But plans can be changed, mate. Plans can be changed."

Below decks Brian escorted Ravena back to her cabin after supper. "I've got the midnight watch," he told her. "Think I'll grab some sleep."

She put her arms around his neck and pressed herself

against him. She pinched her lower lip with her teeth; her eyes were narrow and slanted, lending her a foxy expression.

"Are you sure you want to sleep?" Her voice was sultry.

His body answered the question. She felt him beginning to harden against the swell of her belly.

"You vixen," he said. "A Viscountess shouldn't take advantage of a gentleman this way."

She pulled him back into her cabin and shut the door. Her fingers went to work on the buttons of his uniform. Her breath was hot in his ear as she whispered.

"If you're so tired, my darling, just lie back and let me do the work."

She pushed him down on the cot and began to undress him. He lay there naked, with his hands folded behind his head, watching Ravena remove her clothing. The thrill never slackened for him seeing her lovely body slowly and tantalizingly unveiled for his pleasure.

When she was naked she kneeled on the cot and swung one leg over him. Her breasts dangled over him like beckoning fruits as she settled down on him. Brian reached up and cupped them in his big hands. Raised his head and kissed the nipples.

Ravena moaned and came down full upon him until he filled her.

He awoke with a start. The candles in their wall brackets were a good inch shorter than when he and Ravena had commenced making love. He rolled away from her and sat up. His watch was on the table beside the narrow cot. It said twenty minutes before midnight.

"Jesus! I'll have to hurry."

"What's wrong, darling?" she called to him, still half asleep.

"If I'm late for duty and the captain throws me in irons, it's all your blame."

She laughed softly. "Not if you tell him why you were late. From what I've observed, Jason and Mary enjoy the pastime as much as we do."

"No doubt you came right out and asked her: 'And how is the captain in bed?' Did you now?"

"No, it isn't necessary. You can tell by the way they look at each other. Aren't you going to kiss me before you go?"

"To be sure."

She was lying on her stomach with her plump buttocks exposed, and Brian bent down and kissed one pink cheek and then the other.

Ravena purred and arched her back. "Oh, I wish you didn't have to go."

"Sex maniac, that's what you are. By God! The part was right for you, all right. Bonnie Belle."

Brian stepped out of the gangway onto the deck and breathed in deeply of the brisk, clean air. The sky was dazzling with stars now. He made a full round of the ship and then climbed up to the poop deck to take over from Carson the First.

"I'll spell you now, Mr. Carson."

"You can't be serious, *Colonel* O'Neil." The sarcasm was undisguised.

"Captain's orders. He wants me to earn my passage."

"The man must be daft." Carson laughed scornfully and said to the helmsman, "Can you imagine? First he brings his wife aboard. Then he takes on two stowaways. And now he puts his ship in the hands of an army officer."

Brian bristled. "I wouldn't take on a responsibility unless I was capable, Mr. Carson. You know the *West Wind* is short-handed, and I intend to do what I can to make things easier for you and the captain. If I run into something I can't handle, you can be sure I'll call you."

At twelve-thirty the helmsman struck the small bell on the binnacle with a hammer. The tinkling was all but obscured by the wind and the slap of the waves against the hull. But the lookout up forward had ears that could hear the grass grow, and, an instant after, the flat loud *gong* of the big ship's bell carried back to them.

Carson squinted up at the sails. "The wind is falling off. Haul two points to westward. We'll catch a sidewind," he ordered the helmsman.

"But Mr. Carson," the man protested. "The captain said—"

"The captain's off duty," Carson cut him off. "I'm the officer of the bridge. Take her two points west."

Brian looked at the first mate with disbelief. The masts and spars were creaking and the sails were taut balloons.

Carson's laugh was brittle. "It won't last, Mr. Dexter—slip of the old tongue—Colonel O'Neil. Take my word for it. When you've been at sea as long as me you feel it in your bones. The wind won't hold much longer."

Brian had neither the authority nor the experience to dispute his judgment.

"Good night," snapped Carson, and stalked away.

At six A.M. Captain Swift stormed onto the bridge, his face a picture of wrath. "What the hell is going on here?" he demanded. "Who countermanded my orders? Was it you, sir?" he asked Brian.

"No, sir," the helmsman said while Brian hesitated, uncertain how to handle the situation with tact. "It was Mr. Carson's orders."

The captain paled and his fists balled like cudgels. "We'll see about that. Put her back on the original course, helmsman. Colonel O'Neil, I want you to come with me."

Captain Swift confronted the first mate in his cabin, wakening him up unceremoniously. "Are you daft, Mr. Carson? The *West Wind* has spent the better part of the night zigzagging."

Carson, brown and muscular in a union suit, swung his feet off the bunk to the deck. He stifled a yawn.

"Beggin' your pardon, Captain. But your orders were to hold a steady course as long as the wind held out. My considered opinion was—and still is—that the wind was about to slacken off abruptly the way it so often does off Hatteras after a storm."

"Well, your considered opinion proved to be wrong," Swift said with sarcasm. "The wind never abated all night."

"That's hard to prove, sir. Our position this morning is not the same as it would have been if we had maintained our original course. I submit that as your second in command, I did what I presumed you yourself would have done under the circumstances."

The captain was relentless. "Your presumption is as erroneous as your considered opinion."

Carson scratched his head, blinked his eyes and favored the captain with a lopsided smile. "Well, sir, if I had your natural talent for reading the wind and the sea and all of nature's phenomena, I'd be a master instead of a mate."

Brian repressed a smile. He had to admit Carson's gift of gab was worthy of an Irishman.

It registered on Swift as well. He could read the wavering resolution in his eyes. The captain knew full well that many a master he had served with had made the same mistake as his mate. Seamanship was more than sextants and charts and compasses and rote skills that you learned from books. The vital ingredient was instinct, the same instinct that sent the salmon in the Columbia River swimming back upstream every spring to their spawning grounds.

"All right, Mr. Carson, no great harm has been done. I'm sorry we disturbed your sleep."

"Time I was rising anyway, sir."

Alone again, Carson took out a bottle of rum from the seabag underneath the bunk and uncorked it. He took a long swig, capped the bottle and mused:

"A small score, to be sure, but a promising beginning."

CHAPTER FIFTEEN

A series of misfortunes plagued the *West Wind* the first three weeks at sea and cut into her running time. The spanker boom broke loose one dark night, and, before it was discovered the sail was ripped and slatting in the wind.

A fire broke out in the paint locker.

Shroud lines and stays loosened mysteriously in the night.

One afternoon Brian took the noon sight and went back to his desk to calculate latitude and longitude on the chart.

"Jesus Christ, I must be losing my touch," he exclaimed.

Ravena looked up from sewing a button on his jacket. "What's wrong?"

"By my reckoning, we're twenty-three degrees off-course. That's impossible, certainly."

He went back on deck and took a second set of readings. Repeated his calculations on the chart. He looked up mystified.

"I still get the same error. Twenty-three degrees. I'd better see the captain. Is that jacket finished?"

Captain Swift was more amused than bothered by Brian's agitation. He clapped a hand on his shoulder. "All the bad luck we've been having, it's shaken your confidence. I know that feeling well. Come on, we'll find out where you've erred, Colonel."

Captain went topside and recorded a meticulous set of sextant sightings, then he went back to his office and plotted the position of the clipper on the chart. The small smile faded, giving way to confusion and then grim foreboding.

"You were right, Colonel O'Neil. Your figures were letter-perfect. We must get to the bottom of this mystery at once." He took a pocket compass from a drawer of his desk. "Will you kindly round up Mr. Carson, Bosun Prince, and the bosun's mate and have them meet with me on the bridge as soon as possible?"

Within the quarter-hour they were all assembled around the wheel observing Captain Swift checking the binnacle compass with his pocket compass.

"You will note, gentlemen, that the ship's compass is about two points off. South, southwest."

"Your own compass may be in error, sir," Carson suggested.

"That is so." He addressed the bosun. "Prince, do you have your compass handy?"

"Yes, sir." The burly bosun handed over his pocket compass to Swift.

The captain compared its heading with the ship's compass and with his own. The variation of the ship's compass was confirmed.

"She's two points off, all right. Mr. Prince, will you and your mate kindly remove the compass from the binnacle?"

As they lifted the big compass out of its housing, a sliver of metal clattered to the deck boards. It lay there glittering malevolently in the bright sunlight.

"It's a broken knife blade." Brian stooped and picked it up, held it out for inspection in the palm of his hand.

They were all silent as Captain Swift took it from him and slowly moved it toward the ship's compass resting on the deck. The needle swung obediently in its direction.

"Exactly two degrees," Swift said grimly. And a string of oaths such as the skipper had never used since bringing his wife aboard assaulted the eardrums of the crew on deck the entire length of the ship. The explosive tirade even brought Mary Swift and Ravena out of their cabins.

He seized the helmsman's shirt and shook him savagely. "What do you know about this, Flint?"

"Nothin', sir, so help me God!" the man said in abject terror. "I never seen it before, honest."

"Whom did you relieve this morning on the middle watch?"

"Benson it was, sir. Charley Benson."

Captain Swift ordered the bosun. "Mr. Prince, go down

and pull Benson out of his bunk and have him report here immediately!"

Bonny the bosun's mate spoke up. "Funny thing about Benson. I came topside 'bout three bells to check that cussed spanker boom. Benson asks me to spell him at the wheel for a few minutes so's he can relieve hisself—"

"That's when he got the knife blade," Swift cut in. "Don't get Benson, Bosun. We'll go below and surprise him. The other part of this blade may still be on the ship, no doubt in Benson's bunk or seabag. If not we'll search the whole ship. This is sabotage, clear and simple."

First Mate Carson had moved around so that he was leaning back against the poopdeck railing, hands braced on the top bar.

"That's hard to believe, Captain," he said casually. "Why would anyone want to sabotage the *West Wind*?"

"A question that I intend to find the answer to, Mr. Carson. Come along."

At the foot of the ladder, Brian saw Ravena standing off to one side near the railing with Mary Swift. He caught her eye but did not speak. The occasion was too grave for idle conversation, and the two women sensed it.

One thing bothered Brian. Her eyes were following Carson rather than on him.

It was obvious to Brian the instant the captain put the question to Benson that the middle-watch helmsman was innocent of sabotaging the ship's compass with the magnetized knife blade.

"I swear on me dear mother's life, sir, that it's as much of a mystery to me as it is to you," he pleaded. "Lord, what's anybody on this ship got to gain by such trickery? We finish this run behind schedule and every man jack of us loses his bonus money!"

His logic was irrefutable.

"Thank you, Benson," said Captain Swift, and half-heartedly to the others: "Let us go on with the search."

They went through the motions, sifting through sea bags, foot lockers and closets to no avail.

"Whoever done it, Cap'n, must of thrown it overboard by now," the bosun said finally.

"He's right, sir," Brian agreed.

Captain Swift shook his head wearily. "I suppose that's

it. You are dismissed, gentlemen." He walked back to his cabin, shoulders slumped.

Later in the day while Brian was sleeping, Ravena paid a visit to First Mate Carson's cabin.

"Come in," he answered her knock promptly.

He was sitting on his bunk, stripped to the waist, a bottle in one hand and a cigar in the other. His eyes widened when he saw her.

"Well, well, well, this is a pleasure, Mrs. O'Neil. Do come in and shut the door." He stood up and bowed.

"The door will remain open, Mr. Carson."

"As you wish." He walked toward her, swaying unsteadily, and she realized that he was drunk. His eyes were bloodshot and she could smell the brandy on his breath from three feet away.

"Got lonesome, little lady?" he said with a simpering grin. "What happened, did you wear the big chief out? 'Scuse me, I mean the *cunnel*."

She stepped forward and slapped him across the face as hard as she could. "You insolent pig!"

He staggered to one side and fell against the bunk. "Jesus!" He lost his balance and sat down hard.

Ravena walked over to him and stood with her hands on her hips. "I saw you do it, Mr. Carson. Throw the knife overboard."

The shock of it sobered him. His eyes cleared and the slur was gone from his voice. "You're seeing things, Mrs. O'Neil. I think you need this more than I do." He held out the bottle to her.

She slapped it out of his hand and it shattered on the deck. Eyes blazing with fury he grabbed for her. Ravena eluded him, stooped and picked up the neck of the broken bottle. There was a good three inches of jagged glass protruding from it. She held it at face level, so that if Carson tried to get off the bunk he'd run into it head-on.

"You infernal bitch!" he hissed. "You ought to be keelhauled!"

"You'll be the one who'll be keelhauled when the captain finds out it was you who altered the compass."

"You're out of your mind!" His eyes narrowed cunningly. "How is it you've come to me instead of Captain Swift?"

"Because I can't prove it, and you know it. Still I'm curious. Why did you do it, Mr. Carson?"

He slumped. "I told you. I didn't do anything. It's all in your imagination. Or maybe I picked up a bent spike absently and tossed it overboard. I don't recall."

The clipper lurched unexpectedly and she pitched forward, hands outstretched. Carson ducked and grabbed the wrist above the hand holding the broken bottle. Ravena cried out with pain as he twisted her wrist brutally. The weapon fell out of her hand to the floor. His other arm snaked around her waist and he pulled her down on the bunk. She battled him savagely, but he was too strong for her. His mouth came down on her mouth, and he slipped one hand underneath her skirt.

With her free hand she raked him across the cheek. He reared up, bellowing like a stuck bull.

"Goddamned bitch!" He backhanded her hard, and her head snapped back against the wall. Stunned, she could only protest feebly as he lifted her skirt above her hips.

The sight inflamed him: her slim white thighs and full bottom encased in the brief pink silk chemise that had recently been introduced to the bolder Richmond belles from Paris.

Ravena found her voice as he began to unbutton his trousers. Her scream was enough to wake the dead, as Brian later told her.

Carson was kneeling on the bed with his trousers bunched up about his ankles when Brian came bursting into the cabin.

The sight that greeted him filled him with murderous rage.

"You slimy bastard!"

He grabbed the first mate by the shoulder, pulled him off the bunk and spun him around. He drove a knee into Carson's groin. The First screamed and doubled over. Brian's knee drove up again into his face. That finished him off, but Brian did not let him fall. Grabbing him by the hair, he pulled his head up and smashed an overhand right cross into his already smashed face. Carson went down rigid as a pole and lay insensible on the deck.

He took Ravena by the hand. "Come on, let's get out of

here. I can't stand the stink." He bent over and spit in the First's face before they left the cabin.

Back in her cabin he asked her, "What the hell did you go there for in the first place?"

She told him how she had seen Carson drop the knife overboard from the poopdeck that morning. He listened gravely, but had to concur with her. "It's your word against his. The captain would be powerless to act. At least, *we* know that Carson is our saboteur. The thing of it is though, *why*?"

That night the first mate was absent at mess.

"I spoke to him before," Brian said innocently, "and he told me he was feeling under the weather. Took a bad fall, he said."

Captain Swift frowned. "Carson has been drinking too heavily. I never would have signed him on if I'd known about his problem."

"It's my guess, Mr. Carson has a lot of problems," Brian commented with a glance at Ravena.

The luck of the *West Wind* took a turn for the better for the next four weeks. Captain Swift took advantage of fine weather and a strong breeze to drive the clipper at record speed. In one stretch of thirty-one hours they made over three hundred miles close-hauled, carrying skysails. In that month Swift didn't reef her skysails once, and, for eighteen consecutive days she carried skysails and royal staysails.

As they were approaching Cape Horn at the southern tip of South America, First Mate Carson became surly and morose.

"This is our last chance," he told the bosun's mate. "We're only a day's run from Rio Grande. The old man has got to be persuaded to make port there before we run the Horn for repairs."

"He'd never fall for that, Mr. Carson. He knows this ship better than any man aboard. There's nothing wrong with this old lady that can't be repaired at sea."

"I've got a thought. Tonight, dump some drums of pitch overboard. Then tomorrow—"

The next morning Bonny reported to the bosun, "Mr. Prince, we're awful low on caulking, and the seams fore an' portside are leaking right bad. See if you can convince the skipper to put in for a half-day at Rio Grande so we can take on some more pitch."

When Prince relayed the request to the captain, Jason Swift consulted the ship's manifest. He exploded.

"Damn it, Prince! What have you been doing with the pitch, feeding it to the fish?" He slammed the papers down on his desk. "By even the most extravagant estimates we should have a dozen more drums than you say we have. Are you sure that Bonny's count is accurate?"

"Aye, sir, I counted 'em myself."

Captain Swift considered the problem a few minutes then made one of his typically incisive decisions.

"It's out of the question, Bosun. We've just managed to make up the time we lost the first two weeks, and I'm not giving it back to Davy Jones. No, the crew will have to make do with what we have in the way of caulking. The *West Wind* is a thoroughbred, and she won't let a few sprung seams stop her. Double the pump crew if necessary, but there'll be no more dragging of our heels on this run!"

Carson was furious when Bonny reported the captain's refusal to put in at the island of Tierra Del Fuego.

Desperate, he made the rounds of the ship expressing his hostility to the crew.

"The old man's daft. He's determined to send the *West Wind* to the bottom, and all of us will go with him! They get like that after a while, these clipper skippers, they think they're gods. The strain gets to them. Christ! I've seen it happen time and time again."

A few of the crewmen responded immediately to the first mate's propaganda campaign.

Seaman Abel Hare expressed the majority opinion that: "Nay, Mr. Carson, the master knows what he's doing. No better man ever commanded a clipper."

But, as the day wore on and Carson's dire predictions were echoed by the bosun's mate, one by one they began to waver.

"That spanker's bound to go again the least bad weather we run into. Blimey! Then there's the two cracked spars aft! They'll snap like match sticks in a blow. And without proper caulking we can put every man aboard on the pumps and she won't stay afloat after those seams begin to spring when the seas at the Horn batter 'em. We'll sink sure as my name is Jim Bonny."

By five o'clock that afternoon, Carson had enlisted a committee of twenty-five crewmen to petition the captain to put in at Rio Grande.

Led by the first mate, they gathered at the ladder leading up to the poopdeck while Carson went up to confront Captain Swift on the bridge.

Swift heard him out in silence as he presented a list of reasons why the *West Wind* should make port at Rio Grande before rounding Cape Horn.

When Carson was finished the captain denounced him and the other petitioners as "mutinous rabble."

"How dare you make demands to me, the master of this vessel! You're all old hands, you know what this demonstration constitutes. You are challenging the authority of the captain. That's mutiny plain and simple! If I do put in at Rio Grande it will be solely for the purpose of clapping the lot of you in irons!"

That took the wind out of the demonstrators' sails, and the mob at the foot of the ladder scattered and slunk off their separate ways.

Carson was crimson with rage and frustration. Even Bonny was cringing away like a dog with its tail between its legs.

"Damn it, man! You have no right to gamble with the lives of the crewmen. And what about your wife and Mrs. O'Neil? To subject women to this danger, it's rotten, it is."

Swift towered over him like a wrathful god, his eyes boring into the first mate like cold steel.

"Mr. Carson," he said in a dangerously quiet voice, "I'm relieving you from duty as of now. Please leave the bridge at once."

Carson's voice quivered with suppressed fury. "You can't do this to me, Captain. I'm the only officer you have." He looked scornfully at Brian. "Except for *Mister* Dexter here."

Captain Swift came at him menacingly. "If you're not off this deck in ten seconds, I'll have you put in irons."

Carson backed off, arms held up in front of him as if to

ward off a blow. "All right, I'm going, but you're going to regret this, I promise you."

"Yellow bastards!" he shouted to the crewmen on his way across the main deck. "Serves you right if we all go down with that madman. Bonny, I want to see you in my cabin. *Now!*"

He slammed the cabin door behind them and sat down on his bunk. Hauled the bottle out of his bag and took a long swallow.

"Do you know what you are, Bonny? You are as the Germans say: 'A *schweinhund!*' A pig-dog, the lowest form of life."

The bosun's mate wrung his hands and whined. "I'm sorry, Mr. Carson, but the skipper wasn't fooling. If he was to accuse us of mutiny, we'd all swing from the yard-arm when we got back to New York."

"He was bluffing, you fool. Never mind, what's done is done." He handed the bottle to Bonny. "Here, take a swig of this and stop trembling like a girl about to lose her virginity."

The bosun's mate grabbed at it eagerly. Carson knelt down by a small chest at the end of the bunk and opened the padlock with a key from the ring on his belt. He swung up the cover and rummaged through the contents until he found the bottle. He held it up to Bonny.

"Jimson weed, I got it in Mexico."

"What's it for?"

Carson's smile was sinister. "It's for the captain. Come on."

They climbed a ladder at the end of the passageway to the main level. Carson looked down the corridor.

"Coast is clear." He led the way to the captain's cabin and knocked. There was no response.

"All right, you watch. If anyone comes along, you detain 'em. Any way you can. Throw a fit, break a leg."

He opened the door and went into the room. Hurried over to the desk and unstopped the captain's water bottle. Quickly he emptied the contents of the bottle into the water and swished it around until the white powder dissolved.

The bosun's mate breathed a sigh of relief when he

reappeared. Carson winked and shut the door. "I think we both need another drink. To celebrate."

Entering the Straits of La Maire the *West Wind* ran into heavy squalls and an ugly sea. The ship was rolling badly by three P.M. and Captain Swift ordered:

"Colonel O'Neil, I want the fore and main top-gallant sails furled."

"Yes, sir." Brian left the bridge to relay the order.

Before he went back to the bridge, he went in to see Ravena. His slicker and sou'wester shed water all over the cabin floor.

"Darling, you look like a drowned rat."

She staggered as the ship lurched sharply to starboard. Brian caught her by the arm.

"Better get your sea legs in order, you're going to need them."

"It's bad, isn't it?"

"Not as bad as it's going to be. Stay inside. I don't want you washed overboard."

She put her arms about his neck and hugged him tight.

"You'll get your gown soaked."

"I don't give a damn about the gown. It's you I'm concerned about. Suppose you get washed overboard."

He smiled. "Don't worry about me. I'm very careful. They've strung lines from one end of the ship to the other so the danger is minimal as long as you take your time and hold on." His expression turned grave. "What I'm worried about is the captain. He's white as a ghost and he's sweating and shaking."

"He must be coming down with fever."

"And a fine time for him to get sick. Maybe Carson was right. Maybe we should have turned in at Rio Grande. I'd better get back to the bridge."

He kissed her and pinched her bottom. "It certainly is a boon to mankind that you ladies have abandoned those damned crinolines and bustles."

She gave him an equally bold pinch in return and winked. "Actually, the 'ladies' haven't abandoned them."

"No matter." He kissed her again and departed.

The trip back to the stern was a tortuous one. It reminded Brian of being aboard one of the western mustangs they had been assigned to break at cavalry school. Black thunderheads rolled across the sky like tumbleweed, and the fog was fast closing in on the itching clipper. The tips of the mast were already obscured, and before dusk a fine, driving mixture of sleet and snow slashed across the ship, biting into the flesh like sand and singing a dirge against the taut canvas.

"The Horn is running true to form," the helmsman said through chattering teeth.

"Aye. It looks bad, but I figure we'll outrun the worst of it by nightfall." Suddenly conscious that the helmsman and Brian were staring at his trembling hands, Swift jammed them into the pockets of his slicker.

Brian was truly concerned about the captain's welfare now. He was burning with fever, his pupils were dilated and his speech was beginning to slur.

The *West Wind* canted to port and he would have fallen if Brian hadn't caught him.

"Captain Swift, you'd better go below and lie down for a while. Flint and I can handle things up here."

Swift rubbed a hand across his face. "Yes, perhaps you're right. I don't feel well. I think it must be a touch of food poisoning. That fish last night."

Brian called to one of the crewmen. "Jenkins, help the skipper down to his cabin. He's not feeling too good."

During the night the wind swung around to the southeast and increased in intensity. After twelve hours on the bridge with only short respites below, Brian had to leave his post and put the ship under the command of Bosun Prince. Exhausted, he collapsed on his bunk while Ravena brought him a pot of hot tea from the galley.

He smiled ruefully at her as she poured it into a tin cup. "You're beautiful even wearing a slicker and a sou'wester. I'd like to make love to you, but I'm weak as a baby."

"And you'll be treated like a baby," she said, throwing off the wet storm gear. She sat down on the side of the bunk and cradled his head against her breasts.

"Ah, that feels good," he sighed.

She held the cup while he sipped at it. "Taste good?"

"Like nectar." He squeezed her thigh. "Mother's milk."

There was mischief in her eyes. "Before this year is out it could be flowing. No, it'll be next April."

"What?"

"Mother's milk."

Brian was thoroughly baffled. "What about mother's milk? You've lost me, dear."

She hugged him hard. "Just that I am going to be a mother."

He sat up, ramrod stiff. "Don't be joking about a thing like that, Ravena."

"I am perfectly serious. You are about to become a father."

"I don't believe it!"

"It's hard for me to believe too, but it is true nevertheless. So many years I've been waiting for this. Roger and I were barren together."

"You are sure that—" he couldn't say it.

She laughed. "That it's your child? Absolutely certain. It's been months since Roger and I—" She broke off as there came an urgent knocking on the cabin door.

Ravena got up and opened the door. Mary Swift stood in the gangway, distraught and trembling.

"It's Jason. He's much worse. In a delirium."

"Come inside, my dear, and have a cup of tea."

Ravena took her arm and led her into the cabin.

Mary began to cry softly. "I'm afraid he's going to die. He keeps babbling about white whales and sharks swimming about the room, Wild apparitions. Now he's in a coma again."

"My God! Brian, what shall we do?"

Adrenalin revived Brian's strength. He got off the bunk. "I'm afraid there's only one thing to do. I can't sail this ship by myself. I'm going to take it on my responsibility to restore Carson to duty. And then we're going to put about and go back to Rio Grande. The captain has got to have medical attention."

He went to the first mate's cabin and told him of his decision. He was surprised that Carson was so gracious about his victory.

"You're doing the right thing, O'Neil," he said. "I told you the old man was cracking up, but nobody would believe me. Well, it's not too late anyway. And we'll make it safely back to port." He picked up his foul-weather gear. "I'll take over on the bridge right now. You better get some rest, friend. You look like you're ready to crack up yourself."

"Thanks. I'll grab a few hours' sleep. Call me if you need me."

The instant his head hit the pillow, Brian was asleep. It seemed only moments later when a hand was shaking his shoulder and a voice was calling his name.

"Brian! Brian! Wake up!"

He came back to consciousness like a swimmer surfacing from the deep sea. Ravena's face was blurred as he opened his eyes. It was a strain to bring her into focus.

"How long have I been asleep?"

"Six hours. The captain wants to see you."

"He's conscious?"

"Yes, Mary says he's passed the crisis. His fever has broken and he's quite lucid."

Brian reached for his trousers on the chair beside the bunk and swung his legs to the floor. Minutes later he and Ravena were standing beside Jason Swift's bed. Mary was wiping his brow and head with a cloth soaked in alcohol. He still looked wan and haggard, but the abnormal brightness was gone from his eyes. His voice was weak but rational.

"How do you feel, sir?" Brian asked.

"Like a cat that's had kittens. A lot's gone out of me. But I'll live." He smiled weakly. "Though there were times last night when I had my doubts. Now what's this I hear about the *West Wind* turning back to Rio Grande?"

"It's true, Captain. You need medical attention. And I don't believe that Carson and I can take her around the Horn without you."

"You've got me. I'm fine now. Weak but my mind is clear, and I can sail this clipper from my bed. You can be my eyes, my ears, my hands and my spokesman—the link between me and the crew and the ship. No, don't say it. You're only the second mate and I'm the skipper. Now get topside and put this ship back on course. Is that clear, Mister?"

Brian shook his head and smiled in resignation. "Yes, *sir*!"

Carson was talking with the helmsman, Benson and with the bosun's mate when Brian appeared on the bridge.

"You feeling better, O'Neil?" Carson asked.

"I'm fine, and the captain is coming around too."

The First tensed. "He is, is he? He still needs a doctor."

"I tend to agree, but he does not. And he is the captain." He spoke to Benson. "Helmsman, put her hard astarboard. We're going around."

The helmsman looked in confusion from Brian to Carson and back to Carson.

Carson shouted. "Keep her steady on course. I'm relieving the captain from duty on grounds of his incompetency."

"Hard astarboard, Benson," Brian said firmly. "That's a direct order from Captain Swift. And if any man aboard refuses to obey the order, he'll stand trial for mutiny and I'll testify *for* the captain."

"You damned fool!" Carson raged. "We'll be wrecked for sure. This storm is building into a hurricane, can't you see?"

Brian had to concede that the weather and the sea were worsening. He hunched down deeper into the high collar of the mackinaw under his slicker to ward off the sting of the snow and sleet driven by gale-force winds.

"Look," he said, "the captain wants to see you himself, Mr. Carson. And the bosun and the bosun's mate. There's more to his decision to go on than simple stubbornness. You'd better hear him out."

Fifteen minutes later they were all gathered around Captain Swift's bed. The master listened patiently as Carson made an impassioned plea to return to Rio Grande: "You're all alike, you clipper men. You'd risk every life aboard, including your own wife's rather than admit that the sea has beaten you for once. You've got a block of keelwood for a heart."

Although Swift's voice was weak, it still had the ring of authority: "All right, Carson, you've had your say. Now hear this! You told me once that if you were the seaman that I was, you'd be a skipper instead of First Mate. That was an understatement, Mister. You're a yellow-bellied traitor not fit to command a ferry boat!" He thrust out an arm at the bosun and the bosun's mate. "But *you* men! I never thought I'd live to see the day a clipper sailor turned tail for port at the first sign of a blow!"

"You don't know what it's like out there, skipper," Prince

said falteringly. "It's the worst I've seen all the times I been 'round the Horn."

"All the more reason you shouldn't listen to Carson. If you do, your bones will be rotting at the bottom along with bones of all the other cowards who ran from the Horn in a blow like this one."

"What are you talking about?" Carson sneered. "You see he's still daffy."

"You blind fool!" Swift said with scorn. "The *West Wind* won't be running away from the hurricane if she heads back to Tierra. She'll be running *with* it! The wind will pulverize her on the rocks in the straits!"

The clipper canted sickeningly to starboard, flinging anything that was not pegged down pell-mell around the cabin. They all had to cling for dear life to the captain's bed.

"She's a killer, that's for sure," Swift said. "And she's overtaking us fast. If we get hit with the full impact of her with the stern to the winds, these quartering seas will tear the ship apart. She'll broach and though she's a courageous, sturdy old girl, she won't last long sailing broadside."

"Don't listen to him," Carson whined.

"You listen to him and you're dead men. Maybe fifteen minutes, a half hour at the most, and the helmsman won't be able to hold her. He might as well toss the wheel overboard for all the good it will do. The water is piling up along her as fast as she can run. Soon there won't be any drag on the rudder at all."

"The captain's right," the bosun said with sudden insight. "If her nose is into the wind, maybe we can tack west-southwest and punch through the hurricane."

"Now you're talking like a clipper sailor, Prince," the captain said. His voice was fast regaining its vitality.

Brian and Carson and the helmsman lashed themselves to the binnacle with heavy rope to keep from being swept over the side by the mountainous waves breaking steadily over the bridge. The deck was a bucking skating pond. The clipper was steering badly and yawing constantly under the battering-ram of sea and wind as it strained, literally, foot by foot, to gain another mile of westing.

The first mate was on the bridge at Brian's request. "I need the benefit of his experience," he told the captain, "where a split-second decision has to be made and I don't have time to consult with you."

"I guess you're right," admitted the skipper with doubt. "But can we trust him?"

"Whatever his motives were for sabotaging this ship, they have to be superseded by the common concern of all of us aboard right now. Carson is fighting to save his own neck."

Wind and sea continued to increase until they reached hurricane proportion. Icy waves exploded against the hull of the clipper and cascaded across her decks, leaving a film of building ice in their wakes. Crewmen slipped and skidded at their posts waist-deep in frigid water, yanking at straining wheels and pulling in chorus on frost-crusted lines that tore the skin from their hands. Going aloft on spars that were sheathed in frost and ice was a dauntless invitation to a horrible freezing death, but not a man faltered. They were going to drive the *West Wind* around the Cape or be whipped from the flailing masts before they gave up.

Carson ordered the ship rounded-to on the port tack after having run to the west-southwest for two hours.

"We're getting deeper into it, sir," the helmsman warned.

"It just looks that way, Benson," the First assured him. "We're running across the storm's face."

The bosun's mate came up from the deckhouse. "The barometer is bad. Twenty-nine-point-ten."

The officers nodded silently. To speak was an effort now. To breathe. The flying spray choked a man every time he opened his mouth.

One wave, higher than any of the others, raced toward the clipper, a solid wall of water.

"We're falling off to starboard!" Bonny screamed. "She'll take us broadside!"

"Hard left rudder!" Brian shouted.

"I can't hold her!" the helmsman said. "We're broaching!"

In fascination Brian saw the forecastle go spinning across the water like a top. The loft masts heeled over until they were almost parallel with the boiling water. Then the wave hit and it seemed to him that the ship had been swallowed up by the ocean. There was a sickening cant to port. A tremor ran down the full length of the *West Wind* and the creaking and groaning of her timbers sounded like mortal cries of pain.

She bobbed to the surface like a cork, floundered to right herself. Shook herself like something alive to shed the water from her ballooning sails. Through the blinding scud Brian saw Carson and Benson both battling the wheel. He dragged himself over to them, hand-over-hand on his anchoring rope.

"Got to give her more rudder!" the First said through gritted teeth. With Brian's strength added to the effort they managed to bring her around ever so slowly.

The wind pressure was terrific; now it was impossible to communicate except by hand signals. The sky was as black as night, and, through the murk Brian could see the yard-arms slashing through the foaming crests, on each side. The ice-laden spars whipped and buckled under rigid canvas like puny saplings.

In mid-afternoon, Brian went below to report to Captain Swift.

"He's worse again," Ravena told him as she swabbed his brow with alcohol. Mary was curled up on a chair in the corner in a dead sleep.

"Poor thing, she hasn't been off her feet in twenty-four hours." Ravena was near collapse herself.

"Is that you, Colonel?" the skipper whispered without opening his eyes.

"Yes, sir, how are you feeling?"

"Fever's back, and I can't see." He pulled feebly at the ropes binding him to the bed against the wild pitching and tossing of the ship. "I feel like a trussed-up pig. All they need to do is stick an apple in my mouth."

Brian laughed. "Well at least you haven't lost your sense of humor."

"Hell, Colonel, I'm going to pull through. And so will the *West Wind*!"

"Damned right you will," Brian said with more confidence than he felt.

"How's the wind?"

"Hurricane force and shifting to the south-southwest. The barometer started up a tenth, then depressed."

"Wind's shifting, is it?" A hint of a smile creased his white face. "That's a good sign. That and the erratic barometer. She'll break soon. Keep her head west-northwest."

Brian nodded and turned to go topside once more. Ravena walked to the door with him.

"Will we make it?"

He cupped her chin in his hand. "We will. There's no way I'm going to lose you again."

He kissed her lightly and dragged his protesting legs up the companionway to the deck.

An hour later the glass read twenty-nine-twenty.

At four bells, six P.M., the storm showed promising signs of abating.

At eight bells, eight P.M., the barometer had shot up to twenty-nine-eighty-three, and the wind was moderating. Overhead the black clouds began to dissipate and a full moon burst through.

The men on the bridge were laughing and shouting congratulations back and forth, drunk with exultation at their magnificent triumph over the giant forces of nature.

"Well, we made it, O'Neil," the First said with a grin.

"Thanks to that old bulldog down there," Brian said with a nod at the deckhouse. And with sarcasm, "The one with the block of keelwood for a heart."

Carson looked sheepish. "About that, O'Neil—about a lot of things, I—"

"Stow it," Brian told him. "Whatever past mistakes any of us have made, we've all paid our dues over the past twelve hours. I'm going down to see the old man."

He could see the strength flowing back into the *West Wind*'s skipper, and his voice rang stronger than it had in days:

"Enough talk, Second. You skedaddle back on deck and tell the bosun to get the men cracking. Prepare to make sail! All of it! Topgallants, royals, and staysails, fore, main and mizzen!"

"Aye-aye, sir!" Brian snapped to attention and gave his captain a smart salute.

Brian took Ravena's hands before he left. "Next stop, San Francisco. Our troubles are over, darling."

Once around Cape Horn, the *West Wind* streaked up the west coast of South America in fine weather and before favorable winds. In the days that followed the clipper's crew drove themselves and the ship hard for Jason Swift. The captain continued to improve under the care of his wife Mary and Ravena.

"Two prettiest nurses in the world," he joked with Brian one day while taking the hot tropic sun in a deck chair.

Brian watched the women standing at the rail in animated conversation. Their long hair flowed back in the clipper's brisk slipstream, Ravena's as dark as Mary's was fair.

"They look like two ships' figureheads," Brian said.

"Ah, yes, you Irish always come up with the poetic phrase." He became serious. "Brian, just what are your plans after you reach San Francisco? It's not exactly the place for a refined woman like Ravena to set up housekeeping. It's a hotbed of gambling, vice and violence, including murder."

Brian frowned. "Yes, it's been troubling me, Jason. Especially with Ravena pregnant."

"Yes, Mary is terribly worried about her. Look, why don't the two of you stay aboard the *West Wind*? Ravena and Mary get along so well, and you've been an indispensable aid to me. You can come all the way back to New York with us."

"That's kind of you, Jason, but what about the baby? It can't be born at sea."

Swift rubbed his chin. "Yes, I keep forgetting about the baby."

"Another thing. We can't go back East after what's happened. There's no way we can be married because of my brother. He won't rest until one of us is dead. I know my own flesh and blood. He'll follow Ravena and me to the ends of the earth."

Swift's tanned brow was furrowed in concentration. Abruptly his face lit up. "I've got the answer! You'll come with us as far as Hawaii. An old friend of mine, George Deal, runs a sugar plantation, and I'll wager he could use a bright fellow like you, Brian. There's a critical shortage of administrative help throughout the Islands."

"Which of the Islands is his plantation on?"

"Maui, I believe."

"It is rather like the end of the earth," Brian said a bit wistfully, thinking of his own native Eire. You couldn't get much further apart than Ireland and Hawaii, he supposed.

"What do you say?"

"It's a good thought, Jason, and I appreciate all you've done for us. I'll talk to Ravena about it."

"I think it's a wonderful idea," she said when he broached it. "Do you know, I used to read everything in father's library that had to do with the Hawaiian Islands? It always impressed me as being a fairy-tale land."

He kissed the top of her head and smiled fondly. "You can be such a child at times."

She sniffed. "Child, indeed. Do you know I'll be almost twenty-eight when my baby is born?"

"You'll always be ten to me, the first time I laid eyes on you at the Viceroy's ball."

She put her arms around him and pulled him down beside her on the bunk. "Your blarney is showing again, darling."

"It's the truth, love."

"No matter, I love it. Keep telling me how young I am." Her eyes glowed and she took on her peculiar foxy aspect around the mouth. "Right now though, I want to be treated like a woman."

Brian was concerned. "How much longer are we to keep at it?" he asked. "I mean, could it hurt the baby?"

Ravena giggled. "I haven't heard any complaints from him as yet. When I do, I'll let you know."

He caressed her bottom and shook his head. "Oh, you are a wench, Ravena O'Neil." He chuckled. "At least you are an honest woman in the sense that I have given you my name, even if it was by proxy."

They laughed softly together and then they made love.

On a soggy, chill afternoon in January 1865, the *West Wind* sailed proudly into San Francisco harbor, breasting the sagging tide, her studding sails crumpling one by one as the light canvas was being taken in and furled.

Brian and Ravena stood at the rail with their arms around each other's waists.

"I'm so excited, Brian, aren't you?"

"Apprehensive is the word."

"Oh, maybe a little, but that's what life is all about, my darling. New experiences. Plunging into the unknown. Like the day in the meadow in Donegal when first you made love to me. What a new experience! Life is something like a book, Brian. You come to the end of one chapter and you turn the page to begin a new chapter."

He hugged her close. "Oh, me darlin', what a romantic nature you have." He glanced down at her belly, just beginning to burgeon. "How is he today?"

"He's fine. What makes you so sure it's a 'he'?"

"Paternal instinct."

"He or she, it's my very best love."

"Oh?"

"Outside of you, only more sacred because he or she *is* our love. Our fused loves for each other."

"Aye, that's a fact."

A whistle blew on the dock as they eased into the berth and the mooring party yelled and waved, awaiting the lines to be cast ashore.

"What's new with the war?" Brian yelled to the dock boss.

"Just about over. The Rebs are beaten on all fronts."

"Was Mr. Lincoln reelected?"

"Sure he was. Good old Honest Abe."

Brian O'Neil said a small prayer of gratitude to God and to St. Patrick.

"My patron saint," he said aloud.

"Who?"

"Abraham Lincoln," he said. "Did you know he was Irish, dear?"

"I only wish he was. Too bad there isn't one like him in Britain. An Englishman with the courage to set the Irish peasants free."

"In time, darling. In time."

Jason Swift and Mary came up in back of them. "Ready to go ashore, Colonel O'Neil?"

"Ready for anything, Captain Swift."

CHAPTER SIXTEEN

The *West Wind* sailed into Lahaina harbor the second week in February. Brian and Ravena were spellbound by the lush, dazzling beauty of the Hawaiian Islands. The swaying palm trees. Snow capped peaks towering out of jungles as green as the fields on the Emerald Isle. Dazzling blossoms of every imaginable color. It was a sparkling jewel in a setting of crystal clear blue water and even bluer sky.

"It's the most beautiful sight I've ever laid eyes on," Brian declared.

"More beautiful than Ireland?" Ravena teased.

"That's different. Beauty's in the heart as well as in the eye. But this—this spectacle is an assault on the senses. You get the feeling that if you gazed on it too long, you'd go blind."

"A lovely spot for the baby to be born. Thank you so much, Jason and Mary, for letting us come with you." She placed both hands over her belly, its girth increased considerably since leaving San Francisco.

"I wish you were coming all the way with us," Mary said. "I'll miss you."

"And I you, dear Mary."

Jason Swift pointed to the south. "There's Hawaii, the largest of the Islands. "Maui, here, is second largest. To the West we have Oahu, Kauai, Molokai, Niihau, Lanai and Kahoolawe. It's been less than one hundred years since the white man first set eyes on this Pacific Paradise. Captain James Cook in 1778."

"I read his journals," Ravena said. "He was enraptured by the beauty of the Hawaiian people, men and women. They reminded him of bronzed gods."

"Yes, and with a beauty of generosity and spirit to match their physical appearance," Swift said. "They wel-

242

comed the whites to share their rich and lovely land. Missionaries, farmers, merchants."

"What do they farm?" Brian asked. "Pineapples and coconuts?"

Swift smiled. "That's the common notion, and it's partially true. But the main crop of the Islands is sugar. The plantations keep multiplying and still they can't keep pace with the world demand for cane."

That same afternoon they were received as house guests by George Deal, owner of one of Maui's largest sugar plantations. His rambling white house was reminiscent of *Ravena* and it gave the expectant mother a twinge of homesickness.

Deal was a portly, balding man of sixty with a faint Scottish brogue. Hearing him speak made her even more homesick for the land of her birth. The Scots and the Irish had close ties.

Deal served them tea and cakes and then took them on a tour of the cane fields.

"It's mighty thankful I am to have you with me, Colonel O'Neil," he told Brian. "You'll get the hang of things within a week."

"I hope so. Let's not be formal. I'm Brian and you're George."

"I fancy that, Brian."

The tour of the plantation turned out to be a shock to Ravena. "You've got all Orientals as workers," she commented to Deal.

"Mostly, ma'am, except for the *lunas*, the superintendents. They're whites from all over the world. The Chinese laborers are imported from the mainland. My men come from Kwantung province. They sign up because they all have the idea of making it rich in the Islands and then going home to become big men in their villages." He snorted. "A few of them do make it back to China, not rich, but comfortable enough. It takes years at twelve dollars a month. And they're great gamblers—dominoes and Fan Tan, that's cards. My best worker, Lum Wong, managed to save a thousand dollars in seven years with me. Then one day off he lost it at Fan Tan in Lahaina."

"How awful," Ravena said. "The poor man."

Her heart went out to the laborers—small, stooped and

painfully thin for the most part, toiling in the fields under the blistering sun. Each group was supervised by a *luna*, a Caucasian dressed in white trousers and shirt topped off by a pith helmet. As they passed one section, the *luna* began to strike one of the Chinese across his bare shoulders and back with a bamboo stick studded with nails.

"Somebody stop him! Stop it, you brute!" She rushed at him and would have beaten him with her fists if Brian had not caught her.

"Easy, lass. Easy."

The incident embarrassed Deal. Red-faced, he stepped up to the *luna* and put a restraining hand on his arm. "Colt, I've cautioned you about losing your temper with the men."

Don Colt was a big man, even bigger than Brian who measured six feet, two inches. The ugliest man Ravena had ever seen, with the cruel, twisted expression of an enraged gorilla.

He answered Deal sullenly. "Aw, George, he's the laziest coolie of the lot, you know that. I've warned him six times today already."

Deal spoke in Chinese to the cringing little yellow man on the ground. His tone was friendly and cajoling.

The laborer responded excitedly and gestured at Colt. The big man roared and grabbed him by the long pigtail that hung straight down the back. He picked him up as he would a cat by the tail.

"You lying Chinaman! You know what I'm gonna do? I'm gonna tie up your *queue*!"

The Chinaman's reaction to that was far more distressed than he had evidenced at the beating. He screeched and he howled and tears ran down his cheeks.

"All *right*, Colt, that will be enough," Deal said, angry now. "Let him go." To the Chinaman, "Nobody is going to tie up your *queue*."

The matter settled, they proceeded on their way. "I must apologize for this unpleasantness, my dear ladies. Colt is a hothead, though, in all fairness, some of the beggars deserve to be whipped. They're a lazy, irresponsible lot, and they do as little as possible for their pay."

"Well, it's little enough pay," Ravena sniffed. She was reminded of the time she had come upon Carl Reynolds beating a field worker with his crop. She had grabbed it away from him and lashed out at him with it.

George Deal was staring at her, and when he replied his resentment was scarcely contained. "Well, ma'am, it was their choice to come here and work for that sum. Not the same as with your black slaves, after all."

"I'm not so sure that our black slaves aren't better off than these poor wretches. On our cotton plantation the slaves ate well, slept in clean, comfortable quarters, and nobody laid a hand on any of them." But again, she remembered Reynolds' treatment of the slave.

"Your father is not exactly a typical slave owner, Ravena," Brian chided her gently.

"Well—" She bit her lip, knowing that he was right.

The sight of the small, overcrowded barracks where the field workers lived made her ill. Instead of beds, they slept on straw mats, one almost on top of the other, with blocks of wood at the head of each mat.

"What on earth are they?" Ravena asked.

"Pillows. The Chinks prefer 'em to soft headrests," Deal told her.

"How primitive."

She was relieved when the tour was finished and they returned to the big house. A Chinese servant in a white jacket served them cool drinks on the terrace—the most delicious beverage that Ravena had ever tasted.

"Nectar of the gods," she raved. "What is it, Mr. Deal?"

"A native concoction. Pineapple juice, coconut juice, passionfruit and rum, of course."

It was a paradise. She felt like a pagan goddess on Mt. Olympus or Nirvana. The breeze blowing in off the sea smelled as good as the drink tasted. Scents that would make the most exquisite perfumes of Paris go begging!

"Brian, I'm going to love it here."

Deal looked relieved. "I'm pleased to hear you say it, Mrs. O'Neil. From some of your reactions, I wasn't certain you wanted your husband doing this kind of job."

"It will be different with Brian. He'll gain the men's respect without thrashing them."

"Then it's settled, Brian. You'll sign on with us?"

"Aye."

"Good. First thing tomorrow morning we'll ride over

the whole tract and I'll give you some pointers. Mainly your job will be to take some of the administrative load off my shoulders. You'll check with each field section three times a day and report back to me. And then there's the books."

"I can help with them, Mr. Deal. I've a good head for numbers," Ravena offered.

"Thank you, ma'am. Tonight you'll be sleeping here with me. By tomorrow we'll have the small bungalow cleaned and painted up for you to move in."

Captain Swift consulted his watch. "I think it's time you and I were getting back to the ship, Mary."

Deal and Brian and Ravena walked out to the waiting carriage.

"We'll stop by tomorrow and see your new home," Mary told Ravena.

"When do you sail?" Brian asked Swift.

"As soon as we load a few tons of George's cane into her holds. Oh, by Friday at the latest."

They bade the Swifts good bye, waving as the sulky pulled away.

"I'll miss them," she said. "And the *West Wind* as well."

"It's good to miss things," Deal said. "It shows how happy you were with them. I think of Glasgow often myself. Sometimes I'll wake at night and the smell of the glue and the fresh-cut wood from the shipyards is so powerful in my nostrils that I almost believe I'm back there."

The three of them stood there silently for a while, lost in nostalgia.

That night lying in the big fourposter bed with the canopy over it, Ravena luxuriated in the feel of a soft mattress under her body for the first time since they had fled Richmond.

"I wish there was some other work you could do here," she told Brian.

He lay back with his hands folded under his neck and yawned. "Such as joining the Hawaiian Army?"

"Be serious."

"I am serious. Being the son of the Earl of Tyrone and a cavalry officer all of my life hardly qualifies me as a candidate for success in the business world."

"You worked in that clothing shop in New York before the war."

He sighed. "I'm almost thirty years old, Ravena. Past the age of a shop clerk. Besides, ninety per cent of the population here wear little more than loincloths and those cloth tents the women call *muu-muus*."

"Just the same, I feel so sorry for those poor Chinese laborers. Paid slaves, that's all they are. It was true what I told George Deal. Our slaves are better off at *Ravena*."

"Don't be too hasty to judge. You know all the *lunas* aren't like that brute Colt."

"I despise the man." She rolled on her side and propped her head up on the heel of one hand. "I've been wanting to ask you. Why was that Chinaman so upset when Colt threatened to cut off his braid?"

Brian laughed. "Not cut off. He said he'd tie it up. In China the *queue* is a symbol of masculinity. A man with his *queue* tied up is held in contempt by his peers. It's rather like the curse of impotence in the Caucasian world."

Slyly she ran her hand down over his bare chest and belly. "Something you've never had to concern yourself with, my wild stallion."

He grabbed her hand. "My sweet, it's torturing me is what you're doing. We must be continent for the remainder of your pregnancy. You're too far gone."

Purring like a kitten, she disengaged her hand from his. "As the Irish say: 'There's more ways than one to skin a cat.' I want to please you, Brian."

She thrilled as much to the feel of his body under her hands as he did to the feel of hers.

"Lie still, my darling and let me love you," she whispered. She ran her hands over his hard biceps; her fingers combed the glossy hair on his muscular chest. Stroked across his sinewy belly. Closed around the hard shaft of his manhood.

"Oh, my darling," he moaned. His fingers were tangled in her long, thick hair.

Ravena edged down on the bed until her hair fanned out across his belly and loins. She bent her head down toward his body, her lips parted to receive him.

* * *

The following day they moved their meager belongings into the freshly painted bungalow that would be their home for the next two years. The home where their daughter Sabrina was born. A home overflowing with love, happiness and contentment.

The first time she cradled the newborn infant to her breast, Ravena found the inspiration for her name.

"Ravena and Brian created you, my love. Sabrina— somehow it has the sound of the two of them. Brian, Ravena, Sabrina. We're truly bonded together forever now, Brian." She took his hand and kissed it. He bent over the bed and kissed her softly on the lips and then he kissed the baby's cheek.

It awed him. "I've never felt anything so soft in my life. My God! She's so small and fragile."

Ravena laughed. "Don't let her frighten you, Daddy. She's tougher than you imagine."

It was true, he discovered. By the time she was eighteen months old, Sabrina would pull at his trousers and implore him to play her favorite game. He'd sweep her off her feet with a loud *whoop* and toss her high into the air, catching her in a bear hug on the way down.

"Be careful. She's so small and fragile," Ravena would tease from the front porch.

Like all states of true bliss, their situation was leavened by moments of sadness. General Robert E. Lee's surrender to General Ulysses S. Grant at Appomattox.

"It's so unfair that the North put Mr. Davis in prison like a common criminal," Ravena complained. "He's a true gentleman, and a crusader for what he believed in. No greater patriot."

"But a patriot for the losing cause," Brian explained to her. "Like the Irish. They're in for a bad time of it, I'm afraid, the South. The North will get its pound of flesh, you'll see."

The news that President Lincoln had been assassinated was startling and shocking, even if it did arrive three months after the fact.

"I'm glad we're not living in the United States anymore," Ravena said. "I think the war and its aftermath will destroy the country. Every ship that comes in from America has some new terrible story to tell of chaos and violence and bloodshed. It sounds like the war is still going on as strongly as ever."

The fact of the matter was that sailors ashore on leave catered to the insatiable hunger for news from home of American expatriates on the Islands. Eager to please, they frequently embellished the truth.

One grizzled captain of a copra freighter told them: "It's pure anarchy down South these times. You wouldn't believe it. Niggers living in the houses of their former masters and the masters now working for the slaves. Their daughters in bondage to satisfy the lust of the big black bucks— you must excuse me, ma'am, but it had to be said."

Such tales had Ravena close to distraction at times. "My poor mother and father, they might be dead for all we know. All my dear friends. The Seedleys. The Tates. Barby and Pennel. Colonel Cooper and his family. What's become of them, Brian?"

"My guess is your parents and friends, none of their social class, has suffered too much at the hands of the Yankees. Besides, there's no use worrying about it, anymore than it is for me to dwell on my family back in Tyrone."

In the Spring of 1867 Brian had an opportunity to buy a small taro plantation on the other side of Maui.

"Whatever on earth is a taro?" Ravena wanted to know when he told her about his plan.

"Taro is to the native Hawaiians what potatoes are to the Irish. The fruit of the plant is called *corm* and it looks something like a potato. One drawback is the *corms* take a full twelve months to mature. But it's an advantage in the sense that between planting and harvesting, there'll be ample time for me to keep up with my chores here."

"Oh, I know what *corm* is, of course. They boil it, steam it and pound it into mash."

"And mixed with water and served as *poi*."

Although it was practically the Hawaiian national dish, Ravena had never acquired a taste for *poi* any more than she had for Irish potatoes!

When Deal learned of Brian's new acquisition he was delighted. "You're on your way now, my boy. Congratulations!"

And as a generous gesture he released the strongest and

best worker on the plantation from his contract so that he could work for Brian.

"Lum Wong is a gem," Deal said. "And he knows all there is to know about growing *taro*. You'll need a gang boss who knows what he's doing."

Brian was overwhelmed. "I can't let you do it, George. I know how you feel about Lum Wong."

George waved a hand. "No, Brian, actually I'm glad to get rid of him. No, I mean 'it. There's bad blood between Lum and Colt, and it's bound to come out in the open someday. He'll be better off with you."

Lum was a prize acquisition.

Another addition to the family was Anise Wong, a sixteen-year-old native girl who was Sabrina's nursemaid. Susie, as she was nicknamed, was a pretty half-caste, the product of three blood lines, Hawaiian, Chinese and Norwegian.

And, of course there was Sabrina's dog, Donegal, Donny for short, who claimed even more blood lines than Susie. A brown-blackish mutt with legs and ears much too long, a gay tail and a pair of the most loving, loyal, soulful brown eyes that Ravena had ever gazed into.

At night Brian and Ravena would lie side by side in the big bed in their new home on the taro plantation. No mansion or castle such as the O'Neils and the Wildings had inhabited in Ireland. No palatial *Ravena*. Not even in the class of George Deal's rambling home.

"Only the most beautiful place I've ever lived in," Ravena extolled.

Brian would smile at her hyperbole. It was a fair-to-middling structure. Plain but sound of construction. The beauty Ravena saw was the beauty within. The beauty of their relationship, their love of each other and of Sabrina.

It was the same every night at bedtime. Sabrina sighing and mumbling in her early slumber. Donny snuffling and scratching as he settled himself for the night under the child's bed. The rise and fall of Ravena's bosom in the moonlight spilling in the open window. The exotic aroma of the Islands wafting into the room on the ocean winds. The pounding of the surf on shore in the distance.

Her hand resting snugly and confidently in his big brown paw, callused from working in the fields alongside his laborers. The Chinese workers adored Brian. No boss had ever been like him before.

Then the quiet pressure of her fingers against his palm. The unspoken message that said:

"I want you."

Paradise. For all eternity. Nothing would ever spoil it.

BOOK TWO
1874

PROLOGUE

I reflect with bitter irony on the naïveté and idyllic lines with which I closed my first book: "Paradise. For all eternity. Nothing would ever spoil it."

Brian and Ravena, as innocent as Adam and Eve in the Garden.

Children really. Children clinging to childish dreams and unrealities. Believing the phantasmagorias implanted in our minds by the promises made in the novels we so much revered:

"And so they lived happily ever after."

Fictions.

Deceits.

Fairy tales.

All of them supplying the inspiration that compelled me to begin this second book. I hereby submit this solemn vow:

I will not deceive myself or my readers by pretending that there is permanence in either the happinesses or the sorrows described in these pages.

I think the reader will recognize that the author's style, philosophy, her general view of life has matured considerably—as has the woman herself.

> (signed) Ravena Wilding O'Neil
> July 7, 1881

CHAPTER ONE

On Sabrina's ninth birthday, Brian declared a holiday for all of his Chinese laborers and provided a *luau* the like of which had never been equalled on the island of Maui. Whole pigs and sides of beef were slow cooked over fiery coals in pits covered with palm leaves. Two days they roasted. A Hawaiian band came over from Oahu to entertain the more than one hundred guests.

One of the guests was an Irish sea captain laying over on his way to China to pick up a cargo of tea.

"She's the spittin' image of her maither," he said in a rich brogue that stirred memories in Brian that he had imagined were all but dead.

"She is that," he agreed. A lump formed in his throat as he looked at mother and daughter trying to learn the *hula* from the buxom girl singer who had accompanied the band on its assignment. Sabrina *was* the same little girl he had seen for the first time at the Viceroy's ball.

"How are things in dear old Erin these days?" he asked the captain.

"Aye, the best they've ever been in this century. Young Charlie Parnell, he's not afraid to stand up to the British. And they say he's sure to land a seat in Parliament next year. Then there's the new British prime minister, William Gladstone. What a fine gentleman he is. He's forced bills through that are gonna give the Irish tenant farmers rights."

"Security of tenure," Brian said.

"Aye, I'm not a man for big words. And he's introduced other bills to give the farmers a piece of the land they're workin'. What's more, Gladstone is for Irish Home Rule."

"We finally found us a Lincoln," Brian said with irony.

"How's that, Mr. O'Neil?"

"A man who cannot tolerate the human outrage of slavery."

"Aye, I see what you mean."

"Do you ever get to Tyrone?"

"I was born there. Let's see, I was in Omagh last December."

Brian's heart accelerated. "Do you know the O'Neils?"

"Lots of O'Neils, I do."

"The Earl of Tyrone."

Captain Casey laughed. "To be sure, the Earl is always havin' us over for tea and crumpets. Now yer not gonna be tellin' me that yer one of them O'Neils?"

Brian smiled. "No, I'm not goin' to feed you any blarney like that, Cap'n. But I do recommend the pork. Please help yourself."

He went into the house and poured himself a scotch in the study. He sat down behind his big desk and swiveled around in his chair to face the big window that overlooked the Pacific.

"Clear across two oceans," he mused. "And I can still hear 'em keening for the dead."

"You've been speaking to Captain Casey," Ravena's voice said from just behind him.

He smiled and reached for her hand. "Aye, and it seems you have as well."

"He mentioned you had asked him about the Earl of Tyrone. He says your parents are alive and well, if a wee bit poorer thanks to Mr. Gladstone."

"Aye, and great things are happening over there. God, I wish I could be there."

"I know. So do I."

They were quiet, each preoccupied with his and her own thoughts. The same thought, really.

At last she said, "You know, Brian, we could do it. The authorities have long forgotten you. As Captain Casey says, there are lots of O'Neils."

He shook his head. "No, it would never work. They'd find out who I am, and then it would heat up all over again. My parents have outlived their grief over my demise. Let them have their peace. Besides, what about all we've built here in the Islands? Just throw away Sabrina's future legacy for a selfish whim? No, my darling, here's one sleeping dog that is going to lie very still indeed."

He pulled her down on his lap and kissed her. Fondled her breasts. Ran a finger up the inside of her thighs. She shivered with pleasure.

"How is it I never get tired of having you do that?"

He kissed the pulsating vein in her throat. "And I never get tired of doing it. Love."

Unexpectedly she shivered again, this time not with delight, and hugged him fiercely.

"What's wrong?" he asked.

"I don't know. It came over me suddenly like a dark cloud passing over the sun. A premonition."

He joshed her. "We Irish are prone to such happenings. And if we are right one time in a hundred we claim second sight. It's all this reminiscing that's getting to you, love. Now put the past out of your head and let's go back to our party."

George Deal had been ailing with gout and arthritis for the past few years and Brian found himself saddled with more and more of his duties at the sugar plantation. He would have been lost but for Lum Wong. The year before Sabrina's birthday party, Lum and Susie had been married. Now that Sabrina was growing up, the girl was personal maid and housekeeper for Ravena.

Life on Maui was idyllic, and Ravena's premonition seemed preposterous. Then came The Day. The Day was how she would always think of it. A day etched on her mind with fire like a cattle brand.

Brian and Lum had ridden over to Deal's place early that morning. When they arrived, Brian told Lum:

"You might as well start checking the north field. I'll go in and let George know we're here, and then I'll catch up with you."

He went inside and exchanged amenities with Deal. His gout was worse. The arthritis was better.

Brian went out and mounted his horse and rode in the direction of the north field. Breaking out of the trees, he spotted the commotion in the middle of the field. Angry shouting. The laborers milling about like uneasy cattle.

Brian put the crop to his horse. "Giddyyap, General!"

As he drew near he saw that the protagonists were Lum

and Don Colt. Colt was slashing away at Lum's head with his bamboo nail-studded pole. Lum kept lunging at him, half-blinded by the blood streaming down from a gash over one eye. Finally he managed to grab the pole-wielding hand, and he wrenched the weapon out of the *luna*'s grasp.

Then, as Brian leaped off his horse to intervene, Lum broke the pole over Colt's head. The big man went down as if he had been axed. He lay there stunned for a while, glaring at Lum. Struggled up on one elbow.

"You dirty Chink! Hitting a white man, you could get ten years for what you did."

It was true. Racial prejudice on the Islands was aided and abetted by the law. Justice for whites was one thing. Justice for coloreds, yellow or dark-skinned people, was quite another thing.

"Come on now, Colt, you asked for it." Brian tried to smooth his ruffled feathers.

"You stay out of this, O'Neil."

"You had no right to strike Lum."

"I'll strike Lum and any other goddamned Chink I feel like." He started to get up. "This bastard ain't gonna get another chance to hit a white man again."

On his knees, his hand moved toward the revolver holstered at his side, standard gear for *lunas*.

"Don't do it, Colt!" Brian warned, and he put his hand on his own revolver.

Colt ignored him. "Yellow scum!" he snarled at Lum and drew his revolver.

Agile as a panther, Lum rolled to his left and hit the ground. The shot missed him by a wide margin. Before he could squeeze off the second shot, Brian fired. He was trying for an arm or shoulder shot, but Colt half-turned, and the slug hit him dead in the heart.

He hurried over to the fallen man, but knew it was no use even before he felt for a pulse. Colt had been killed instantly.

"Christ!" he muttered. He knelt down on one knee, the smoking gun still in his hand. For the first time he was aware of the crowd forming around them. Laborers from Colt's section and curious workers from an adjacent field.

Their *luna*, Louis Lasseur, a Frenchman, pushed through the milling, chattering Chinamen.

"*Mon dieu!*" he exclaimed. "What happened, O'Neil?"

"He was beating my man, Lum," Brian said thoughtlessly.

Lasseur stared at him with disbelief. "And you shot him for *that*?"

"No, of course not. Lum took the stick away from Colt and then he went daft and tried to kill Lum."

The shock and disbelief only intensified in the Frenchman's expression. You might as well try to explain to a *luna* that you had killed a man because he kicked your dog, so little regard did the whites have for their Chinese slaves.

Brian stood up. "I'll go back to the house and call the police. Lum, you continue with the inspection."

George Deal was sympathetic but angry with Brian. "For God's sake, man! Couldn't you have stopped him some other way?"

"You don't think I would have shot him had there been any other way, George?"

"I suppose not." His expression grew graver. "You should have let him do it, Brian."

"Kill Lum? I don't believe this is you talking, George."

"Damn it, Brian! Maybe he was only bluffing. Maybe he would have shot in the air to scare Lum. I don't believe you realize how serious this is. A white man killing another white man over a tiff about a Chinaman."

"I don't see it at all," Brian said coldly.

"There's something else you don't know that makes it worse," Deal advised him. "Don Colt was the nephew of the Islands' Chief Commissioner. You might say the apple of his eye."

"Rotten apple," Brian said, but the information didn't make him feel any better.

The police interrogated Brian for almost an hour, and their attitude was less than reassuring. Captain Schultz and Sergeant Barker kept regarding him throughout the interview the way they would look at an ape in a cage. A curiosity. Uncivilized. Dangerous when aroused.

When the session was over, Captain Schultz informed him dispassionately: "I'm sorry, Mr. O'Neil, but we are putting you under arrest. You'll have to come back to Oahu with us."

"I'll go with you," Deal said. "Ben Newton is the best barrister in Hawaii. We'll arrange for bail."

"You're not up to that trip, George," Brian tried to dissuade him, but Deal was adamant.

"I'm fine, and I'm going to Oahu with you."

"How long will I be gone?" Brian asked. "I'd like to notify my wife."

"Don't worry Ravena with this mess before it's necessary. Send back a message with Lum that some unexpected business has come up and that you have to go to Oahu to handle it for me. You may be detained for one or two days."

"That's good thinking, George. I'll tell Lum at once." His lips curled with sarcasm at the police officers. "I suppose you want to come with me to make sure I won't escape."

"Not at all," said Captain Schultz with a sneer. "Not much place you can run to, now is there, Mr. O'Neil?"

As things worked out Brian was released on twenty-five-hundred-dollars bail pending a preliminary hearing at which time the presiding magistrate would determine the nature of the charges against Brian in consideration of the report of a coroner's jury.

Now he was faced with the ordeal of telling Ravena the truth. She took the bad news well, as she always accepted adversity.

"I loathed the man," she said, "but I'm sorry he's dead. But what's done is done, and no sense stewing over it. What's going to happen to you? I mean you didn't intend to kill Colt, it was an accident."

"That's the truth, but it's only my word, and the word of a murderer doesn't carry much weight with the officials here. Frankly, Ben Newton was not optimistic."

"But you're not a murderer."

He put his hands on her shoulders. "But I am, my darling. Murder is murder, accidental or otherwise. And remember, Colt was the favorite nephew of the Chief Commissioner."

"That is bad." Ravena put a hand to her throat and sat down.

"As you said, we are not going to stew over it any further. We'll put it out of our minds now until the hearing. What's for supper? I'm famished."

One week later a courier presented himself at the house with a summons for Brian to appear at court in Honolulu the following afternoon at one P.M. A boat would pick him up at Lahaina early in the morning.

"What's the worst they can do to me?" he philosophized. "Unpremeditated homicide or some such charge. It was an accident and they'll believe it. I may get off with a fine and a reprimand. I understand we plantation owners have an unofficial diplomatic status with the courts."

Ravena's hand flew to her mouth. "I almost forgot. My premonition! And you telling me it was my Irish superstitious nature! Oh, Brian, darling, I'm frightened."

"Nothing to be frightened about." He nuzzled her neck and nipped her ear. "Come to bed and I'll give you something that will make you forget all about it."

Her eyes narrowed and she bit her underlip. "I believe I'd like that kind of comfort, Colonel O'Neil."

"Colonel indeed! Would you care to see me fine sword?"

"I can't wait. I've always been partial to military men."

Upstairs they checked on Sabrina. She was fast asleep, and Donny's tail thumped the floor as Brian stooped to pat him.

"Good lad, Donny. Guard my princess well, and you'll get the thigh bone tomorrow night after supper."

"You won't be here tomorrow night," Ravena reminded him.

"Well, the next night then."

They retired to their bedroom and shut the door. There was an intensity about their lovemaking that night which left Ravena with a disquieting feeling.

"It's almost as if you were leaving me and maybe never returning, Brian," she tried to describe it to him. "I can't get enough of you." She buried her face in his chest.

"I never can get enough of you." His hands stroked her breasts, her belly and her buttocks. She adored him with her hands and her lips.

Three times she climaxed that night, and then fell into an exhausted swoon.

She awoke with a start and the terrifying sensation that she was falling. She gasped aloud and felt for Brian in the bed beside her. His place was empty.

"Brian, where are you?" she gasped.

She reached for the discarded nightgown on the chair beside the bed and pulled it over her head. Barefooted she ran out of the room and down the curving stairs.

A lamp was burning dimly in the foyer. Gazing down the dark hall she saw the sliver of light under the library door.

She put a hand to her breastbone where her heart was beating a thunderous tattoo. Steadying herself she walked to the library and knocked.

"Come in," Brian's voice called to her.

She opened the door and the blood drained out of her face when she saw George Deal sitting opposite Brian in front of the hearth. They both held glasses, deep brown with whiskey. The stricken look on George's face was more eloquent than words.

"I didn't want to wake you," Brian said. "You were sleeping so soundly."

She ignored him. "What's happened, George?"

He took a deep breath. "It's bad, Ravena. Very bad, I'm afraid."

"It seems the commissioner is determined to have my head on a pole," Brian said. "They've managed to persuade—bribe is more like it—three of George's *lunas* to swear that there was bad blood between Colt and myself and that I threatened him on another occasion. Not to mention the allegation that it was I who drew my gun first."

"That's ridiculous! What about all the witnesses who were there?"

"Coolie laborers," Deal said wearily. "Not very dependable, my dear. You see those poor devils will be working under those same lying bastards for months, years. They won't dispute what the *lunas* tell the court."

"This is monstrous! What are we to do?"

Brian stood up and embraced her. "Only one thing to do, darling. It looks like O'Neil is on the run again."

"Captain Casey's ship is due to leave Lahaina at dawn tomorrow morning," Deal explained. "I had him up to the house earlier in the evening, and he's willing to smuggle Brian out of the Islands."

"If it's the only way he can stay out of prison, then it

must be." Her jaw hardened. "Only this time Sabrina and me will be with you."

"Ravena, darling, use your head. This isn't a pleasure voyage. We don't get to stand at the rail and wave good-bye to the well-wishers on the dock. It may not even work with me alone, but it would be impossible with excess baggage."

"Is that what we are, me and your daughter, excess baggage?" she sniffed. Tears glistened in her eyes.

He hugged her fiercely and kissed her forehead. "My sweet, you know what I meant. I worship the ground the two of you walk on. And one day you'll be walking on Ireland's ground, you and Sabrina. By God! I do believe there is a manifest destiny to our lives. I would have died here on Maui, a fat, lazy contented old codger with a mind filled with nothing more than *poi*. This was meant to be, Ravena. My fate lies elsewhere than here. Our fate."

"Now who's speaking like a superstitious washer-woman?" She forced a brave smile. "We don't have much time. I'll pack you some things."

"I still have my seaman's bag and some duds I've kept as souvenirs." Brian said. "They'll do fine."

George Deal stood up painfully and limped to the door. "I'll be waiting outside for you in the carriage, Brian. Good night, Ravena. I'll see you tomorrow after he's safely on his way."

Brian and Ravena looked at each other in silence. Then she said. "You'll be wanting to say good-bye to Sabrina?"

"I will."

The child had no inkling of the trouble he was in.

They went upstairs together, hand in hand, and woke the girl. She yawned and stretched.

"It's so dark." she complained.

"Yes, and you can go right back to sleep, baby," he told her. "But your daddy has to go off on a trip again, and I wanted to give you a hug and a kiss before I leave."

"When will you come home?"

"I'm not sure, sweet. It may be a long time before we see each other again. But I promise you that as soon as it's possible I'll send for you and your mother to join me."

She threw her arms around his neck and gave him a big hug. "I'll miss you, Daddy."

"Aye, and I'll miss the two of you."

He kissed the smooth brow so much like Ravena's. The perfect nose, the strong chin. The violet eyes. She was so very much like Ravena. A miniature.

"Now sleep tight, my darling, and dream of the day when we see each other again. Pray God, it won't be too long."

He eased her down gently onto her pillow and pulled the sheet up over her. He got down and spoke to the faithful Donny.

"Laddy, you're the man of the house now. Take care of my two girls."

The dog got up on its haunches and licked his face, tail wagging furiously. He stroked its head and stood up.

"Time to go. George is waiting."

He kissed her at the front door. Not with passion but with tenderness. Almost a chaste kiss.

"I'll come out with you," she said.

"No, it's bad luck to watch someone you love leaving on a journey. Go back to bed, my love."

"I couldn't sleep. I may never sleep again."

"Pretend I'm going over to George's for the day."

"That will take some pretending." She fought back the tears.

"Take care of yourself, you hear."

"You're the one needs taking care of. That goddamned Colt! May he rot in hell!"

"I told you it was all meant to be. Written in the stars."

"Superstitious mick! Be off with you now."

He went out the door and down the path and never once looked back.

CHAPTER TWO

Brian stood at the rail and watched the Hawaiian Islands recede behind the ship until Maui was no more than a green dot on the horizon. Then there was nothing but the unbroken circle of blue water and the sky above all about the ship.

"Good-byes aren't easy," said Captain Casey.

"I've had my share of them. Ireland. The States. By the way, Captain, what do you know about the policy of extradition as it affects the States and Hawaii?"

"Colt was an American citizen, and his uncle the Commissioner has the influence to make matters hot for you, my boy. If you can get safely through customs you'll be all right. That's where they'll be waiting to nab you. What you need is to find a new identity. As a matter of fact, I think I can help you. One of my crew died on the way over from Ceylon. Name was Barry Larkin. The dysentery. I have all of his papers and belongings in the safe. No kin. You're welcome to it all."

Brian put a hand on the little man's shoulder. Casey was sandy-haired, freckled and toothless. His favorite pastime was gumming a cold pipe.

"You're a good friend, Captain Casey. I've been lucky to find good friends all of my life, or I wouldn't be alive to speak of it. So Barry Larkin it will be."

Brian was standing the middle watch one night about a week out of Maui and chatting with the helmsman, Ransom Dolan.

"This is my last hitch," Dolan told him.

"What's your plans?"

"Gold."

"I thought that rush was back in '49."

Dolan shook his head. "This strike is up in Dakota. The Black Hills."

266

Brian smiled. "By the time you get there, it will be all over. The whole damned Black Hills will be staked out."

"Not so. The government has been keeping out prospectors. That's Injun land, and a treaty will have to be negotiated."

"Interesting."

"You want to come in? My buddy, Drew Mason, and I are looking for another partner." He winked. "Specially one who can shoot like you."

"I'll consider it. How much will it cost me? I had to leave quickly, and all I had was a thousand dollars in cash give or take at the house."

"That's just about right. We're putting in twelve-hundred. But we'll let you owe the rest until we make our strike."

Brian laughed. "I always knew there was a pot of gold at the end of the rainbow."

The *Nelly Bligh* sailed into San Francisco Harbor at dawn in October of 1875. Before he left the ship, Captain Casey turned over the papers of Barry Larkin.

"You can have his seabag as well. It's got his name stenciled on it."

"I don't know how to thank you for all you've done, Captain."

"It's always a privilege to help out a brother Irishman. Your wife says you were with the Sinn Fein?"

"Aye. Have they come out in the open, now that the English are easing up on the people?"

"They're bolder, but the English still refuse to acknowledge their existence as a bona fide political group to bargain with. So you're off to seek your fortune with Dolan?"

"I've nothing better to do. Besides, I want to stay out of the mainstream for a while."

"It would be best, and the law wouldn't think of looking for you in Dakota." He held out his hand. "Well, good luck to you."

Brian shook the hand warmly. "Thank you, Captain. Would you do me one last favor? Next time you stop over at Maui, would you let my wife and daughter know that I made it here safely?"

"That goes without asking. Don't you worry. Maybe after you strike it rich, she can join you here."

"Not for a time, I'm afraid. Maybe when Sabrina gets to be a little older. I don't want to uproot the child right now."

"You'd get a fine price for your plantation. They could live in comfort."

"It's a thought. They could buy a place in southern California. I hear there's good farmland in the valley."

"The finest in the States."

"You might sound her out about it when you see her. She can talk it over with George Deal. We had no time to make long-range plans."

"How will I be able to get in touch with you?"

"Leave a letter for me at the Merchant Seaman's Society in Frisco. I'll check in when we get back from the Black Hills."

If you ever do get back, the captain mused to himself.

All hell had broken loose in the Dakotas and Wyoming. Stirred up by huge newspaper headlines proclaiming the richest gold deposits since King Solomon's mines, prospectors from all parts of the country stampeded into the Black Hills, trampling on all the treaties and agreements between the Sioux Nation and the United States which protected the Indian's claim to the area. The government protested, but not too strenuously, and the rush was on.

The outraged Sioux left their reservations and joined with the Cheyennes to make war on the usurpers. It was into this powderkeg that Brian O'Neil, Ransom Dolan and Drew Mason came in the spring of 1876 with a pack train of ten mules laden with equipment to prospect for gold.

Deadwood City in Deadwood Gulch was the wickedest and bawdiest and bloodiest settlement in the gold strike area.

"It's plain how it got its name," said Brian as they passed the local cemetery on the edge of town, Boot Hill. The corpses of men killed in the past 24 hours were, indeed, stacked up like cordwood for burial.

Deadwood had literally sprung up overnight, complete with saloons, whorehouses, gambling houses, and a government assay office. Most of its inhabitants lived in the suburbs in hastily erected shacks, and Brian and his two partners picked a site near a stream and commenced to build their dwelling.

Most of the heavy labor fell to Brian and Ransom. Drew was a cadaverous young man with a hacking cough and limited endurance. The chores like cooking and doing the wash fell to him, and he was content.

It took them three days to complete the two-room, relatively sound structure, and, as soon as it was done, Ransom announced:

"I'm going into town to get drunk and screwed in that order."

Brian grinned. "Better reverse the order. Or you might not be up to the last."

Ransom winked. "Don't you be worrying about this boy. Want to come along?"

"I could use a drink, but I'll pass up the girls."

The truth was that every time he looked at a woman he'd be reminded of Ravena. Once in Frisco he had been walking down a street when he saw a woman ahead of him who was her replica from the rear. For an instant he'd had the crazy notion that it *was* Ravena, and his heart had gone wild. Giddy, he'd rushed up to her side and said:

"Pardon, ma'am."

The face she'd turned to him would turn milk sour! Gulping, he'd asked for a fictitious street, and fled from her grating voice:

"No, honey, but my street number is—"

He and Ransom washed up in the creek and headed for town. Drew declined, preferring to take a nap.

The Deadwood Bar was their first stop. They had to step over a corpse lying under the swinging doors.

"Wild Bill Hickok done 'im in," someone in the throng commented. Two white-aproned barmen arrived soon after to dispatch the unfortunate gun fighter to the alley next door until the burial squad came to pick him up.

The bar was packed four deep, and the tables, what few of them there were, were occupied by card players. Serious grim men who chewed anxiously on cigars and drank whiskey from the bottles scattered about the tables.

There were a dozen dance-hall girls circulating among the patrons. They wore low-cut spangled gowns with breasts bunched high and together by whalebone bodices. Short skirts that showed their legs encased in mesh stockings high on their thighs.

"Hot damn!" breathed Ransom as one plump girl bent over in front of them to pick up a handkerchief, showing off her black lace panties. "God! How I could use some of that!"

Brian laughed. "Patience, my lad. The night is young." He patted the girl on the backside and said, "Could you bring two thirsty wanderers a bottle and glasses, my lovely minx?"

She turned and sized him up brazenly, hands on hips. Her face had more paint on it than did the Indians he had seen along their journey.

"Hello, handsome, would you like to have me serve it upstairs in a private room? I can tell Madam to put you on the list. Only about an hour's wait."

"That's a long time to wait for a drink. Thank you, but we'll take it now." He spotted two crates over in a corner, and pointed. "Right over there."

Ransom interceded. "But you can put our names on the list, and bring us another bottle later upstairs."

When she had left, Brian clapped his friend on the shoulder. "You're the horniest bastard I've ever run into."

"Horny? Damn it all, O'Neil, when I was at sea, I'd get a pieec of ass maybe one, two times a year. And now I've been living with you two plug-uglies for the past six months."

A shot rang out above the din of raucous voices and laughter, followed by two more shots in rapid succession. Across the room at the bar, the mob parted and departed, leaving the field to two cowboys, one bareheaded, one wearing a high, pointed stetson hat that resembled a sombrero. He sagged against the bar and his head fell forward. The hat slid down over his face and then to the floor. He followed it, very slowly, as if his legs were melting out from under him.

The victor blew the smoke out of the end of the muzzle of his six-gun and replaced it in its holster.

The white-aproned house men—Deadwood Pallbearers —were on the scene briskly. Each took hold of a foot and dragged the deceased out of the barroom. The patrons made a mad rush back to the bar. And through it all the piano player never missed a beat.

"Jesus! What a rough place," Ransom said in awe.

Brian let his hand rest on the butt of the six-shooter holstered at his gun belt and wondered, should the occasion arise, how he would comport himself in a showdown with an experienced gunfighter like this fellow. Moments before he had shot down a human being in cold blood and now he was laughing and squeezing the behind of a sequined wench.

"I think we better take some target practice with these revolvers," he said to Ransom.

After that they spent an hour every afternoon shooting at tin cans perched on rocks near the creek. Ransom and Drew were flabbergasted by Brian's skill with a gun. The big Colt six-shooter was a newer and more sophisticated model of the one he had carried in the Union cavalry, but after firing a few dozen rounds he felt as confident using it as he had firing his trusty military sidearm. The "quick draw," as the miners and cowhands called it—the technique of the fast, violent gun battles that resolved altercations of every sort in the lawless Western territories—was something he was determined to master. He and Ransom would draw on each other with empty revolvers after shooting practice.

Prospecting for gold, however, was not the exciting adventure that Ransom had touted it to be. Nor was it the profitable enterprise he had promised. Long, dreary, backbreaking hours of drudgery from sunup to sundown, panning for the precious metal in the streams and rivers that abounded in the region.

"Up to our asses in water twelve hours a day," Brian grumbled as he sifted the sludge accrued in his mesh pan, eye aching from the strain of searching for one or two grains of yellow amidst the mud and gravel.

The third week they constructed a sluice trough to channel the water more efficiently, and were rewarded by acquiring two sizable nuggets of pure gold.

It prompted a celebration that night which culminated in two memorable and significant events in Brian's life.

One of the girls, Sue Holt, had taken a fancy to Brian,

an affection that was further stimulated by his refusal to go to bed with her.

"What's wrong with me?" she'd demand. "I'm not good enough for you?"

He laughed one night and told her. "The truth of it is you're too good for me."

"Don't make fun of me, Brian O'Neil. You'll be sorry one of these days!" She flounced off in a huff.

This night was no different, she kept at him at the bar while Ransom and Drew were watching a no-limit game of five-card stud.

"I tell you what, Brian. There'll be no charge."

"I never accept charity."

"Then I'll pay you!"

"That would be unfair to the other customers."

"Damn right!" said a voice behind him. "What's so great about this bum anyway, Susie?"

He looked back at the lank-haired cowhand who had killed the man the first night they were in the saloon. His pale eyes cold as ice chips, a sneer on his thin, mean mouth. His whole posture was an unspoken challenge. Body taut, shoulders hunched slightly forward, the muscles in his forearms and biceps straining tautly at the material of his dark shirt. Gun hand poised, one thumb hooked over his gun belt.

"You know somethin', Sue girl?" he drawled. "Maybe he's one of them preacher fellers, come to clean up Deadwood and save all our souls?"

"I'd give up on yours, Fernwood. It's beyond redemption." Brian confronted him with amusement, relaxed and dispassionate.

Fernwood's scowl intensified. "Don't you get funny with me, city boy! It sticks out all over you. All them fancy words you throw around. Preening like you was some fine gentleman and treating everyone as if they smelled bad."

Brian smiled and picked up his whiskey glass. "It's funny you should bring it up, but do you ever take a bath, Fernwood?"

"You know what you are, O'Neil?" Fernwood erupted in rage. "I bet the reason you won't go upstairs with Sue is because you cain't get it up with girls! You're probably stickin' it up that little fag's ass hole!" He thrust an arm in Drew Mason's direction.

Brian's expression never changed. Solemnly he held up his glass to the light, inpecting it. Then he took a sip of the amber brew. And with unhurried deliberation, he sloshed the remainder into the other man's eyes.

Roaring in pain and anger, Fernwood clasped his hands over his stinging eyes. Brian measured him with his left arm, drew back his right fist and hit him on the point of the jaw.

Fernwood ricocheted off the bar and fell to the floor on his hands and knees. The exodus from the bar was precipitous. And this time the maestro stopped playing the piano. Silence settled over the room like a shroud.

Word of Brian's marksmanship had spread around town, via some of the miners who had witnessed him practicing out by the creek.

The saloon's patrons had seen Fernwood finish off a half-dozen men since his coming to Deadwood. But this imminent showdown held infinite promise. Voices murmured in low tones around the room as men placed wagers on the outcome.

Fernwood glanced up balefully at Brian, and slowly levered himself to his feet. The instant his hands cleared the floor, his right struck like a rattler at his Colt.

"His move was a blur, hand and gun too fast to see clearly," a nearby spectator later described the action. "But O'Neil you couldn't see at all."

He shot from the hip and the bullet hit Fernwood clean between the eyes before he could bring up the muzzle of his six-gun. The impact hurled him flat on his back and the last reflex of his trigger finger pumped a shot into the ceiling.

It was later discovered that the stray slug almost castrated one of the customers in the room above!

Brian was a little embarrassed as Ransom and Drew and a throng of well-wishers mobbed him all demanding first honor of standing him a drink.

Madam Mahoney, the hostess and proprietor of the Deadwood Bar, climbed onto the bar and held up her hands for silence.

"Quiet! Shut up, you bums! Nobody buys drinks here

tonight! It's on the house!" She bent over and pinched Brian's cheek. "You did us a big favor, O'Neil, the whole town owes you a debt. That Fernwood was bad for business, made the customers nervous. Another thing, any girl you yen for is on the house too, all night."

"Thanks, Dolly, I appreciate it." Brian was blushing now. His eyes went to Susie. "Tell you what, Sue, you got a date."

The poor girl squealed and fainted.

As one of her coworkers cracked: "Like a virgin about to lose her cherry. I don't believe it!"

As the happy patrons lined up for their free drinks, a big burly man in a deerskin jacket decorated with fancy beading and embroidering walked up to Brian.

"I'm Sam Schaffer," he introduced himself. "Just got into town tonight. I'm boss of a big outfit prospecting up by the Grand River."

"Good mining country?" Brian asked as they shook hands.

"The richest. Trouble is we're rubbing shoulders with that Injun reservation due north over the border. They're on the war path, that's why I came back to Deadwood. I'm looking to expand my outfit, take on reinforcements, you could say. We could sure use a fast gun like yours. What do you say? You'll be cut in as equal partners."

"That sounds fine to me," He looked to Drew and Ransom. "What about you boys?"

"Count us in!" Ransom was delighted, and Drew did a little jig to the tune of an Irish song played by the honky-tonk piano.

"How bad is the Indian situation?" Brian asked Schaffer. He liked the man right off. Big, rawboned with dark curly hair and a homely face that was engaging when he laughed.

He was not laughing now. "Couldn't be much worse. The US Cavalry is mobilizing for full-scale war.

"Custer's Seventh Cavalry Regiment is alerted for action at Fort Abe Lincoln, across the river from Bismarck."

"George Custer?" The very name made him tingle from head to toes.

"Yeah, and there's Crook's regiment policing the Rose-bud. And John Gibbon and General Alfred Terry, he's in command of the whole shebang."

Brian's head was spinning.

George Custer!

John Gibbon!

Al Terry!

Georgie Crook!

A wave of nostalgia swept over him. He felt as if he was on his way home to a family reunion. He was seized by an overpowering urge to see George Custer again. Reminisce.

"When will we be leaving?" he asked impatiently.

"First thing tomorrow morning. I didn't expect to round up men so fast. How are you men fixed for equipment and mules?"

They talked about the details for another hour or so, during which little Sue kept hovering around their table, making suggestive motions to Brian.

Finally everything was settled and Brian stood up. "If you gentlemen will excuse me, I have some other business to take care of."

Brian was tender with Susie, and when it was over, she cried. He tried to make light of it, not to shame her.

"I've never had that effect on a woman before. Was it all that bad?"

"No, that's just it," she bawled. "It was wonderful for me. Just the way I used to dream it would be when I met a man I loved and he loved me—before—before—" She choked on her tears.

"It's all right. It's all right." He cuddled her like a child and stroked her hair, speaking gently to her. "You'll meet that man someday."

"I won't! What man would ever love me . . . want me as his wife?"

"There's plenty would. I would too, if I didn't have a wife already," he lied.

She sat up and wiped her eyes with a handkerchief. "You really would?"

"I told you so."

She seemed better now. "What's your wife like?"

He closed his eyes. "I can see her as plainly as if she was in the room. She's about five feet and maybe five inches, with the blackest hair in the world. Her eyes—ah yes, her eyes—they're—" And suddenly the tears began to roll down his cheeks.

Susie smiled and kissed his hand. "How much you must love her. Lucky girl."

The following morning Brian, Ransom and Drew pulled up stakes and headed north. Sam Schaffer was riding on ahead on his horse. The mule team moved too slowly for his taste, but he had given Brian explicit directions how to find his campsite. It was at the junction of the Grand and Missouri Rivers.

Along the way they repeatedly encountered bands of Indians watching them from distant hilltops. The red men did not evidence any overt hostility, yet there was a quality of menace about them.

"Christ! I'll be glad when we get to Schaffer's outfit," Ransom said. "I get the feeling this bushy head of hair is gonna end up on some Injun's belt." He rubbed his scalp.

It took them all that day and part of the next to reach their destination. On the last leg of the trip they had the most dangerous brush with Indians. A band of at least forty, in full war paint and battle dress. The leader wore a head piece that sported ram's horns. The other braves had a single feather in their hair which was long and braided.

"They look like Sioux to me," Brian muttered as the Indians came galloping down a dry streambed about a half mile away.

Ransom went for his rifle tied to one of the mules, but Brian called him back. "No use antagonizing them. There's too many to fight. All we can do is try to make them understand that we're friends."

Luckily a confrontation was avoided when the Indians spied a contingent of US cavalrymen riding toward the mule train from the opposite direction. The leader threw up his hand and shouted, and the formation executed a smart half-right maneuver and galloped away to the north. Brian looked after them with admiration.

"Goddamn, they are some horsemen."

They hailed the approaching cavalrymen. "You fellers always come across the hill just in the nick of time," Ransom shouted gleefully.

"Not all the time, unhappily," said the lieutenant in charge. "We just came from a prospector's camp. All dead, six of 'em with their scalps taken."

"Not Sam Schaffer's bunch?" Brian asked fearfully.

"No, Sam's got a bigger outfit, and they're armed to the teeth."

Brian grinned in relief. "They're going to be bigger. We're joining up with Sam."

"That's fine," the lieutenant said. "We'll ride along with you just in case that bunch of Sioux are lying in ambush for you some place."

"I figured they were Sioux. Fine horsemen."

"General Crook says the Sioux are the finest light cavalry in the world. Were you cavalry?"

"During the war. What outfit are you with?"

"The Seventh. Colonel George A. Custer commanding."

Brian felt the old excitement that had constantly pervaded him when he rode with Custer. The man's dynamism was infectious, even at a distance. To be this close to him as he was now, speaking with one of Custer's officers, was a thrill.

"How is the old bastard?" he asked, laughingly.

The lieutenant's eyebrows raised in surprise. "Sir?"

"I was one of Custer's battalion commanders in the war. Gettysburg, Yellow Tavern, you name it, Lieutenant." He held out his hand. "I'm Brian O'Neil."

"I'll be damned!" He gaped at Brian wonderingly. "So you're *that* O'Neil? I don't believe it. The old man is always talking about you. Colonel O'Neil, the best horse-soldier in the US Cavalry, he says. This is a great honor, Colonel."

Brian laughed. "Past tense, I'm a civilian now." He accepted the lieutenant's enthusiastic handshake.

"Colonel Custer tried tracking you down through the War Department after it was over, but you seemed to have vanished into thin air."

"Something like that. It's a long story. Well, how is he, still the same old martinet?"

"He runs a tight regiment, that's for sure. I'm glad I'm with him now that we're getting into another war."

"That's exactly how I felt. War is a hell of a risk in any case, but there's less risk when you're fighting alongside troopers that George Custer made."

A sergeant came up and cleared his throat. "Remember me, Colonel O'Neil?"

Brian examined the slim, dark-haired man with bushy

eyebrows and a hooked nose. "Hell, sure I remember you. Pettibone, Lieutenant Pettibone."

"Busted back to sergeant after the war. How are you, sir?"

"Right now, I couldn't feel better. I can't wait to see George."

"We've got a couple of spare horses with us," Lieutenant Levi said. "When we get to Sam Schaffer's outfit, why don't you come back to the camp with us? You can spend the night with the regiment, and ride back to your campsite tomorrow. That way you and the general can chew the fat and down a few and talk over old times."

Brian grinned from ear to ear. "Jesus! That sounds like a fine idea, Lieutenant. Come on, let's get started. I can hardly wait to see his face."

They reached Schaffer's camp at three P.M. and pitched tents and watered the mules.

"Drew and I will unload the gear," Ransom told him. "You better get moving and see your old C.O. Tell him to shoot a few of them Sioux for me."

"And don't let Custer shanghai you," Schaffer warned him. "I hear they need cavalrymen real bad right now. Right, Lieutenant?"

"It's the truth," was the thoughtful reply. He looked Brian up and down. "I'll bet you're in as good shape now as when you were in the service, Colonel?"

Brian pretended to be indignant. "Oh, no, you don't, Lieutenant Levi! I did my time. And stop calling me *Colonel!*"

Field headquarters for the Seventh Cavalry Regiment was the dumpy army supply steamer, *Far West*, moored on the north bank of the Yellowstone River, across from the mouth of Reno Creek. The rhythmic slapping of water against her port side and the seesaw creak of her timbers chafing the high clay bank had the sentry at the foot of the gangway nodding drowsily.

He snapped to attention as two horsemen came galloping along the bank from the main camp. He recognized Lieutenant Levi, but the big man in rough miner's togs was a stranger to him. Broad shouldered with dark good looks and strong chiseled features, his face tanned as bronze as an Indian's.

They dismounted and the sentry snapped to attention and saluted.

Levi returned it. "Wilson, at ease. Anybody with the general?"

"Yes, sir, it's a big staff meeting. Colonel Custer, General Terry, Colonel Gibbon, Major Brisbin, Major Reno, I guess that's about it."

The lieutenant grinned at Brian. "All the big brass, they sound familiar?"

"Hell, yes, just about the best damned cavalry leaders in the US Army."

"Come on." Levi started up the gangplank but the sentry stopped him. "Sorry, sir, but Colonel Custer gave me firm orders that the meeting was not to be disturbed by anybody short of Chief Crazy Horse riding into camp."

Levi patted his shoulder. "I think this gentleman ranks right up there with the chief. Colonel O'Neil, one of Colonel Custer's dearest friends."

The man looked uncertain, then shrugged. "I guess it's all right. Go on up."

The cavalry officers were gathered around a small table in the main cabin, poring over a situation map. So absorbed were they in drafting battle strategy that none of them looked up when Levi and Brian entered the cabin.

The lieutenant coughed several times before he caught anyone's attention.

"Excuse me, Colonel Custer, but there's someone here who wants to see you."

Colonel Custer whirled around, pale blue eyes blazing, his yellow hair and drooping mustache practically standing on end.

"Goddamn it, man, how dare you interrupt this meeting! I'll have that sentry horsewhipped! And who the hell are you?" he pounced on Brian.

Brian grinned impishly. "Glad to see your disposition hasn't improved any, Colonel."

"You insolent cur!" He advanced threateningly, then stopped short, an expression of utter amazement and disbelief spreading over his face. His voice was faint.

"Nooooo. It can't be! I must be dreaming. Brian? Brian O'Neil, tell me I'm not going crazy, it *is* you!"

Brian laughed. "It is me, myself, in the flesh. How've you been, George?"

The two men closed and threw their arms around each other, whooping like overgrown boys. First Brian lifted Custer off the deck and then Custer lifted Brian off his feet, going around and around until they crashed into the table.

Now the other officers got into the act, mobbing Brian and slapping his arms and shoulders.

"The old mick himself, by God!"

"Brian the bastard!"

"Jesus, you're a mess, O'Neil! George, I think he rates ten demerits, don't you?"

Lieutenant Levi withdrew discreetly from the cabin and disembarked from the *Far West*.

"How'd the general take it, sir?" asked the sentry.

Levi clapped him on the shoulder. "He says he's going to have you horsewhipped for disobeying orders."

Wilson looked after him, speechless, as he mounted his horse and rode off.

It was more than an hour later before the cavalry commanders resumed their staff meeting. And two bottles of whiskey later, passed around the table, while Brian related all that had happened to him since he had been relieved from duty in Custer's regiment and summoned to Washington for a special undercover mission for the War Department.

"By God, Brian!" Custer said with heavy-handed humor so common to horse soldiers. "I always knew you'd end up running from the law for murder."

Brian's grin was feeble. "It's no joking matter, George. That damned accident has cost me almost everything."

General Terry stroked his beard. "It's been almost two years, O'Neil. I'll wager the whole thing has blown over. Damn it, man! You don't think the United States is going to persecute one of its greatest war heroes over the accidental death of some asinine sugar-cane farmer. Bosh!"

"Al is right, Brian. But hell, my friend, you've held the floor long enough."

"I sure as hell have. You start an Irishman talking and you can't shut him up."

Custer put an arm around his shoulders and steered him around the table to the right side of the map. "You can stand a refresher course in cavalry tactics, old man. Look sharp and listen, maybe you'll learn a thing or two."

General Terry took up where he had left off before Brian's intrusion. He traced an ellipse with his index finger around an area encompassing the headwaters of the Little Big Horn River and Rosebud Creek.

"Major Reno's scout has established that the Cheyennes and Sioux are gathering at a big camp somewhere in this vicinity."

"Prime hunting grounds there," Colonel Gibbon commented."

Terry looked at Custer. "What do you think, George?"

Custer was laconic. "I think you can never predict what the Injuns are up to, sir."

"I damn well know they haven't slipped back east into the badlands," Major Reno said. Reno was a handsome man with thick black hair, patrician features and the sensitive eyes of a doe.

"How can you be so sure, Marcus?"

"We uncovered a dozen separate trails, and every one of 'em was heading west. That village we spotted on the Rosebud was prepared to move at any moment."

Custer's smile was mocking. "Yes, that village. I still think you made a mistake letting them off the hook, Marcus."

Reno flushed and his voice rose an octave. "My orders were to make a scout, not a fight."

"That's right, Marcus. Never fight without a special order."

Major Brisbin interceded. "Stop riding him, George. Major Reno was perfectly right not to attack that village." He turned the needle back on Custer. "We all realize, George, that you feel it's beneath your dignity to obey an order but—"

"All right, gentlemen," General Terry said impatiently. "Enough of this bantering. Let's get on with the business at hand." He put his finger on the map at a point a few inches below the squirming red line that represented the Rosebud Creek. "General Crook's column is moving in from the south. We will move in from the north. Assuming that the main body of the Indians is on the Little Big Horn, the two columns will close on them like the jaws of a trap."

He described a sweeping arc on the chart with his hand. "Colonel Gibbon, your command will move up the right bank of the Yellowstone to the mouth of the Big Horn. You will cross the river and follow the Big Horn upstream to the fork of the Little Big Horn. At this point your movements will depend on the reaction of the enemy."

He addressed Custer. "George, your regiment will follow the main trail that Major Reno discovered on his scout. You will proceed up the Rosebud to the headwaters of the Tongue River, then turn toward the Little Big Horn. Keep a constant scout on your left flank in case the Indians try to slip around you and attack from the southeast."

Custer frowned. "General Terry, suppose the Indians are camped further downstream on the Little Big Horn than we suspect?"

Major Reno took it as a personal affront. "I think it's obvious, George, that the main body of Indians is headed for the hunting grounds at the headwaters of the Little Big Horn."

"The odds favor it, Marcus, but we cannot be positive about anything. In any case, George, I have too much respect for your resourcefulness and tactical ability to impose an arbitrary battle plan on you. Fight your own fight." He smiled, but Brian detected the sarcasm in his voice. "You always do anyway."

Custer accorded him a short bow. "I appreciate your confidence, sir."

General Terry took out his pocket watch and squinted at it. "Gentlemen, this meeting is adjourned. I have a report to finish before the special courier from Washington goes back tonight. We'll have a late mess tonight. Brian, you'll join us, of course."

"Thank you, General."

The men put on their gun belts and cavalry gloves and campaign hats. They shook hands with Brian and filed out of the cabin.

When they were alone, Custer poured two drinks for Brian and himself.

"So they broke you back to Colonel," Brian joked.

Custer showed two rows of perfect white teeth. "I'm damned lucky they didn't break me back to buckass private."

"You never were one to win friends among your peers. Did I detect a faint animosity between you and Major Reno?"

Custer snorted and downed his whiskey neat. "Reno!" Scathing contempt. "He's got a yellow streak running up his back wider than the Big Horn River. But he's a harmless pipsqueak. The bastard who's out for my scalp is the President."

"President Grant?" Brian was impressed. "When you look to make enemies, you really aim high."

"Last year I testified before a Congressional committee investigating Indian affairs. I laid the blame precisely where it belonged. Grant's brother. The man's an incompetent boob, and half the mess we're in today is his fault. Putting him in charge of a sensitive project like Indian affairs is the most flagrant case of nepotism I've ever run across. Anyway, Grant and General Sherman lowered the boom on me. If our old buddy Phil Sheridan hadn't stood behind me, I'd have been cashiered. This assignment, it's do or die for me, Brian. Jesus, I could use a man like you."

Brian chuckled and shook his head. "I'm getting too old to be riding all over the country playing games with Indians."

Custer was grave. "Playing games, is that what you think it is? Let me tell you something, Brian, I've been fighting these red bastards for ten years, and there are times I'd rather be up against Jeb Stuart. The Sioux—" Undisguised admiration. "God, they're born in the saddle. The finest horse soldiers in the world."

"So I've heard."

"Brian, I need you. I really do."

"George, it's absurd. I was discharged from the service."

"It doesn't matter. I have the authority to enlist civilian scouts with an unofficial rank and pay of a second lieutenant."

"Me a scout?"

"You were one of the best."

"That was in the East, country I knew. Hell! I don't know any more about this desolate territory than I do about the moon."

"Nonsense. One intense cramming session with the maps; I'll brief you myself. In two or three days you'll know as much about this place as I do. Besides, you know it as well as I do, ninety-percent of it is gut instinct and the ten percent book soldiering, hell, that's just icing on the cake."

Brian was annoyed at himself for the strong enticement Custer's proposition exerted on him.

"It's out of the question," he snapped.

Custer's eyes were bright; he grabbed Brian by both arms. "You want to do it, don't try to fool me, Brian. It's written all over your Irish pan."

"Even if I do, it's out of my hands. I've got responsibilities to my friends, and Sam Schaffer. Besides, every cent I have in the world is tied up in that prospecting gear and the mules."

"All the more reason to make this last ride with the Seventh. That's what this job is all about, clearing out the hostile Indians who are waging war against the miners. Hell, Sam Schaffer and his boys spend more time fighting Indians than they do hunting for gold. When it's over you can go back to your outfit and do some serious prospecting."

Brian grinned ruefully. "You never take 'no' for an answer, do you?"

"No, and you never run away from a good fight."

Brian threw up his hands. "You win. All right, just this one time. But don't think you're going to talk me into staying in the goddamned cavalry."

Custer laughed and put a hand over his heart. "My word of honor."

Brian shoved out his hand and they sealed the bargain with a firm handclasp.

There was a knock on the door and a young captain poked his head into the cabin.

"George, are you busy?"

"No, come on in, Tom. Brian, I don't believe you've ever met my younger brother, have you? Tom, this is the fabulous Brian O'Neil you've heard so much about."

There was a strong resemblance between the two brothers, Brian noted.

Tom Custer approached Brian, his manner one of undisguised veneration. "I know, it's all over camp. Colonel O'Neil, I can't tell you what an honor this is."

"Oh, Jesus!" Custer groaned. "Cut that crap out. You sound like an academy plebe meeting the super for the first time. You'll be giving this old muleskinner a swelled head."

They entertained Tom for a while with anecdotes about their service together in the war, then Custer asked his brother. "Now what did you want to see me about, Tom?"

"I was just talking to Major Brisbin. He says that you refused to take Low and his Gatling guns with the column."

"That's right, I did. They'd only slow us down with those old condemned mules it takes to lug them around. Let 'em go with Gibbon and his infantrymen."

"Brisbin also said he offered you Gibbon's four troops of cavalry. Why in hell did you turn them down?"

Custer slammed his hand down on the table. "Brisbin and his fucking grandstand plays! Gibbon's cavalry has been on the march since nine o'clock this morning. If they have to double time it back here and start out again on a forced march day after tomorrow, half of 'em will drop by the wayside before we've gone twenty-five miles."

Tom winked at Brian. "Was he always like this, Colonel? Has an answer for everything?"

Brian laughed. "And his answers were almost always right."

"Almost. One of the biggest words in the language. Like 'if.' "

Custer snorted. "Maybe you should have been a philosopher instead of a soldier. Look, one thing I know without any qualification. The Seventh can take care of itself. It doesn't need any help from Gibbon's drag-ass troopers!"

"The Seventh. You even say it with religious fervor. As if it was your own precious creation and property."

"The Seventh is mine, Tom. I created it from scratch. I personally hand-picked every man in the regiment. I drilled 'em and drove 'em and forged 'em into the best goddamned cavalrymen in the United States Army. I love them. Sure, I know they hate my guts. But they've never let me down and they never will. Me, the regiment or themselves."

He took a cigar out of his pocket and bit off the end savagely. "Hell! I guess I've been wrong a few times. Like Reno. Marcus is a competent officer, no denying it, but that's not enough for the Seventh, mere competence. He's a thoroughbred that's too highly strung. He spooks under pressure."

Tom smiled and shook his head. "You're an arrogant bastard, George."

Custer's intense blue eyes bored into his brother. "I could have you court-martialed for calling me that. But I won't because it's true. I am an arrogant bastard, and I'm proud of it. I'd rather be a bastard who gets the job done than an idiot like Brisbin, or an old woman like Gibbon or a coward like—" He cut it off abruptly and averted his eyes from Tom's penetrating stare. "Hell, it's late. Let's get over to the mess."

Tom would not let go of it. "Than a coward like me, is that what you were going to say, George? My brother takes a dim view of my military faculties, I'm afraid, Colonel O'Neil."

"That's not true!" Custer was clearly on the defensive. "I said let's go and eat." He picked up his gun belt and his hat and gloves.

That night the *Far West* was an oasis of light in the heart of a wasteland whose pitted desolation was as absolute as the pockmarked craters of the moon. A group of officers stood at the starboard rail with their arms flung over each other's shoulders singing the regimental marching song, "Gary Owen."

> *"Instead of spa we'll drink down ale,*
> *And pay the reck'ning on the nail;*
> *No man for debt shall go to jail*
> *From Gary Owen in glory."*

Colonel George Custer was in the act of inscribing a neat number 10 at the top of the blank sheet of writing paper on the desk when a sudden draft sent the tongue of the flame curling over the candle's lip.

Brian had opened the cabin door. "Am I disturbing you?"

"Not at all. I was just writing a letter to Elizabeth. Page ten, I think I'll break off for the night."

Brian whistled. "Page ten. By God, I don't believe I've written ten pages in me whole life."

"Stop acting the part of the thick Irish peatcutter."

Brian's smile was sad. "Ten pages. After all this time the flame hasn't dimmed, has it, George?"

"Flame?"

"Between you and Elizabeth."

Custer's head dropped. "It's brighter if anything. Ahhh, that's the only part of this life that I don't care for. It keeps me away from Elizabeth." His expression was worried. "I suppose that's my weakness, my Achilles heel. The constant yearning to be with Elizabeth. You think I'm weak on that score, don't you, Brian?"

"You've never been more wrong in your life, George. There's a woman I feel the same way for. And it seems, too, that fate is always coming between us, keeping us apart."

They sat in silent communion for several minutes. Then Custer sighed and stood up. "All right, you shavetail, suppose we get started with the briefing." He walked over to the table and lit the oil lamp on it. "Spread out the maps if you will, Brian. Would you care for a drink?"

"Not right now. I want to keep a clear head."

Unexpectedly there was a loud crash against the cabin door; it flew open and Major Reno staggered into the room.

"Ooops, 'scuse me," he mumbled. "Did'n' mean to interrupt anythin'."

"Well you did," Custer said coldly. "Apology accepted, now please get out."

"Tha's unkind, Colonel. The boys an' I thought you might join us for a chorus of 'The Girl I Left Behind.'" He was making a great effort to compose his slurred speech. His eye fell on the unfinished letter on the desk. "See you've been writin' to the li'l gal you left behind, George."

"You're drunk, Marcus!" Custer's voice cracked like a whip. "Go to your tent and lie down! And that's an order. One more word out of you and I'll have you thrown in the guardhouse!"

"Yes, *sir!*" Reno came to attention and saluted, almost toppling over in the process. He did a ludicrous about-face that almost sent Brian into outright hilarity, but Brian contained it.

At the door, Reno looked back and asked. "Does Elizabeth know you're a bigamist, George?"

"Get the hell out of here!" Custer shouted. He started for Reno but Brian held him by the arm.

"Easy. He doesn't know what he's saying."

"It's true, O'Neil," Reno went on. "He's not only married to his wife. He's also married to the Seventh Cavalry. Good night, one and all."

He stepped out onto the deck and closed the door heavily behind him.

CHAPTER THREE

It was six months to the day after Brian fled Maui that he came down the road on horseback. Ravena and Sabrina were sitting on the swinging hammock on the front verandah drinking iced coconut milk. From a distance Ravena had the wild notion that it was Brian come home. She sprang to her feet, her heart beating like a frightened bird's.

Sabrina thought so too. "It's Daddy!" she shouted in glee and ran down the path to the road.

"No! Come back here at once!" Ravena screamed.

The child stopped, looked back, her mouth agape. Her mother had never used that tone of voice with her before.

"*Come here*, Sabrina!"

"What's wrong, Mama?" She started back. "Why are you angry? What did I do?"

"I'm sorry, I shouldn't have yelled at you." She went down the steps and put her arm around her daughter. Together they watched the horseman approach. At a distance of one hundred yards he removed his wide-brimmed tropical hat and wiped an arm across his sweaty brow.

"His hair!" Sabrina exclaimed. "Daddy's changed the color of his hair! It's blond!"

"No, darling." It took a monumental effort to keep her voice steady. To keep from running inside the house and locking the door against him. "It's not Daddy. It's your Uncle Roger."

"Uncle Roger? You never spoke of him before."

"No, there seemed no point in talking about him. He lived halfway around the world, and we never expected to see him again. We didn't even know whether he was dead or alive."

She hugged the child close to her and braced herself, bit

her lip. But her shoulders were back, her head held high and her eyes unblinking.

He dismounted, tied the horse's tether to the fence post and came slowly up the walk. A smile spread ever so slowly across his face. He stopped a yard away and bowed graciously, sweeping the hat across his body.

"You're as beautiful as ever, Ravena." And to the girl. "And you, my dear, are every bit as beautiful as your mother. Sabrina, isn't it?"

"Yes, sir." So faint the words were barely audible. Gaping at him, her eyes as round as saucers.

"How did you know her name, Roger?" She held her daughter even more desperately. "Or that we were here?"

His manner was as casual as if he were a neighbor from down the road, pausing for a chat. "Oh, it wasn't easy. In the beginning, that is. Once we found the first piece, then the rest of the pieces all fell into place rather easily. Actually, I borrowed a note from my brother's book. We in Richmond had just about given up on you, but we never forgot you. Even after more than a decade your name is topical at parties, Ravena. Two years ago I got the idea of hiring the Pinkerton Detective Agency to track you down." The smile was bitter now. "They did such an excellent job for Abe Lincoln, I decided finding you would be a simple assignment.

"It took time. Pinkerton was able to locate that sea captain and his wife. They were not very communicative, but then a seaman came forward to claim his thirty pieces of silver. After that, there was no problem. Brian has done rather well for himself, hasn't he?" He looked around admiringly. "He's made quite a name for himself in the Hawaiian Islands. In more than one respect." The sarcasm made her wince. He shook his head. "That temper of his, it had to destroy him in the end."

"That man's death was an accident."

"Yes, my dear brother is accident-prone, or was, I'm afraid."

Her hand flew to her throat and her lungs were paralyzed. "Was?" It was all she could say.

He stroked Sabrina's long hair. "My dear, I'd like to speak to your mother alone for a spell."

She found her tongue. "Yes, dear, go in the kitchen and ask Susie to give you some milk and cookies."

The girl ran up the steps and into the house. "Roger, come up and sit down."

Unsteadily she climbed the stairs and collapsed onto the hammock. He sat down opposite her in a wicker chair.

"What's happened to Brian?"

He sighed and said with uncharacteristic charity, "I'm sorry to have to be the one to tell you. I know it will be even harder coming from me. Brian is dead."

She felt absolutely nothing. Only numbness. "I don't believe you. Brian's not dead."

He was totally dispassionate. "You don't think I'd be here if he was alive. I'd be tracking him down wherever he was to strangle him with my bare hands."

It made sense. What Brian always said would be foremost in Roger's vengeful mind.

"Here, read this, it's the Pinkerton report." He took an envelope from his pocket and removed a sheaf of papers from it, handed them to her.

Her hands were steady, but inside she was dead. She skimmed the early part of the report; she and Brian had lived through it together. The *West Wind*. Maui.

She came to it on the second page.

"On October 15, 1875, one Barry Larkin was killed in a barroom brawl in the Barleycorn Café on the San Francisco waterfront. Larkin was ostensibly a merchant seaman on the cargo ship, *Nelly Bligh*, according to his identifications. But when the authorities interrogated the ship's skipper Captain Liam Casey, it was learned that the real identity of the dead man was one Brian O'Neil, a fugitive wanted for murder."

She stopped reading and handed the report back to him.

"I'm sorry," he said. "I truly am. I wanted to get to him first."

"Yes, I believe you," she said dully. "It's just like you." Her eyes were suspicious. "But why are you here, Roger? You could have sent the report by mail."

"No, there's more to it than that. I want you to come back to Richmond with me."

Her laughter was a dirge. "You can't be serious."

"I am serious."

"It's out of the question."

"Think of the child. It's been fine up until now, this primitive life. But she's getting to be a young lady. Doesn't she deserve some of the advantages of your own up-bringing?"

"There are fine schools in Hawaii." But she was wavering.

And he pounced on the sensitive spot. "And your mother and father, how they've pined after you, Ravena. He's been ill with pneumonia and his heart is weakening. What time is left to him, seeing you could bring him happiness and contentment in his last days. And seeing the child would be bliss to the both of them."

That persuaded her. "All right, I'll go back with you. But the child is Brian's, you do understand?"

"Naturally, but she'll pass as mine."

"No, they must know the truth."

"And have your darling Sabrina branded as a bastard for the rest of her life?"

"You win again, Roger. She'll learn to call you Father in time."

"I'll be her father. I give you my word I'll treat her as if she were my own. I'll make her love me, you'll see."

Tears welled up briefly in her eyes, and she covered her face with her hands.

"Brian. . . ." she whispered.

"There's a cruise ship heading back to the States from Honolulu on Thursday."

"There's too much to be done. I must sell the plantation."

"I spoke with Brian's solicitor yesterday in Oahu. Mr. Newton will make the necessary arrangements. In fact he has another client who is looking for another investment, and he's sure there'll be no problem about price."

His arrogance outraged her. "You had a hell of a nerve, Roger O'Neil, poking your long nose into my business!"

"I apologize. I thought it best to make inquiries before I saw you. Now I think it's time you broke the bad news to Sabrina."

"Yes. I prefer to talk to her alone."

She stood up and walked into the house, her legs and feet leaden.

Sabrina accepted the news of her father's death with healthy fatalism that children of her age cultivate. She cried bitterly for the remainder of the day closeted in her room.

The following day she was moody and quiet, but ate supper after fasting for the three previous meals.

And the day after that she was romping on the lawn with Donny and Roger. She was fascinated by his resemblance to Brian, and Ravena could tell he was winning her over.

By the time Thursday arrived, she had conditioned herself to addressing him with the formal title of "Father."

Ravena did not resent it. He was right about one thing. Sabrina needed a home, family and friends, and what ten-year-old should be deprived of a doting granny and grandpa?

There were tearful farewells with Susie and Lum. Ravena invited them back to the Richmond plantation, but they loved Hawaii too dearly. Against Roger's wishes, Donny, the faithful mutt, accompanied them. But he conceded the point grudgingly when Sabrina vowed she would never call him "Father" again if he left Donny behind.

The trip back to Richmond seemed endless. The long voyage to San Francisco and then cross-country on the Union Pacific Railroad.

They enjoyed the most lavish accommodations that money could buy, but the cramped staterooms on the train gave Ravena claustrophobia.

"It must be that after living all these years in so much freedom, water and sky as far as the eye can see, I feel like I'm in chains," she said to her daughter.

"I think it's fun, Mama." Sabrina was awed by the spatial grandeur of the country they sped across. Snow-capped peaks that seemed to touch the sky. Bottomless gorges. Oceans of high grass that undulated in the wind like waves. Stone spires that looked like church steeples, carved out of gigantic rocks by glaciers, wind and water. Great herds of grazing buffalo and wild stallions that outraced the locomotive.

At dusk on the second day of their circuitous journey that would take them first to Chicago, then to New York and, lastly, south again to Richmond, the Union Pacific's

Overland Flyer stopped at Wilcox, Wyoming to pick up passengers.

The station master paid scant attention to the roughly dressed man sporting a handlebar mustache and a ten-gallon stetson who swung onto the blind end of the baggage car as the train pulled out of the station.

Nor did the passengers in the first coach pay heed to the fashionably dressed gentleman with the bowler hat who sat down in the last seat at the back of the car.

A half-hour later as the train approached a railroad bridge, the engineer cut the throttle.

"Red warning lanterns along the right-of-way," he said to his fireman. "Somethin' must be wrong."

The big locomotive ground to a halt as he applied the brakes, her wheels spewing sparks up from the steel rails.

Intent on what was up ahead, neither man in the cab observed the dark silhouette climbing over the tender. Catlike, he dropped behind them. Two six-guns covered the engineer and fireman.

"Just do as you're told and you won't get hurt," he snapped.

Back in the first coach, the fashionable gent in the long coat with velvet lapels leaped to his feet and threatened the passengers with a brace of Colts.

"This is a hold-up, folks. Don't panic and don't try to be a hero, anyone. There's a gang of my friends boarding this train right now."

Inside their compartment, Ravena and her daughter were preparing to go to the dining car, oblivious of what was going on outside.

"Maybe the engine broke down," Sabrina suggested.

"Oh, I don't think it's anything that serious," her mother assured her. "More likely we hit a cow or some animal. Roger says that's quite common. That's why they call that plowlike thing at the front of the locomotive a 'cow-catcher.' I think I'll ask the conductor what—"

Before she could finish, the door to the compartment was flung open and two men stepped into the room. Both wore bowler hats and carried pistols.

Sabrina ducked behind her mother and screamed. Ravena was uncowed.

"What's the meaning of this?" she demanded.

"It's a train robbery, ma'am," said the clean-shaven man pleasantly.

"Get out of here!"

"Glad to oblige, as soon as you turn over your money and jewels."

There was the sound of footsteps running down the corridor outside. Displaying an air of professionalism that required no instructions, each man moved quickly to either side of the open doorway and flattened himself against the wall.

Roger appeared in the doorway. "Ravena, are you all right? Quickly, lock yourself in the lavatory!" Before she could warn him, he came into the compartment. The man in the long greatcoat stepped up behind him and slashed the butt of the pistol across the base of his neck. He went down on his face, unconscious.

Ravena was outraged. "You cowardly brute!" She slapped him across the face as hard as she could. He staggered back, shocked and angry.

"You bitch!" he croaked. "I ought to—" He raised the gun again as if to strike her, but the clean-shaven man stepped between them.

"Take it easy, Kid. The little lady has real spunk. I like that." He smiled showing perfect white teeth and a dimple in one cheek. He was really quite good-looking, she thought, not the type one would expect to be an outlaw. His piercing blue eyes looked her up and down brazenly. "I take that back," he drawled. "You ain't so 'little' at that, not in the right places."

The impudence earned him a slap in the face even more telling than the one she'd inflicted on his partner.

"You said it, Butch," the man with the mustache jeered. "The little lady has real spunk."

He rubbed his smarting cheek and glared at her, no longer amused. "He's right, ma'am, we don't have no more time for fun and games. Hand over your valuables."

"Please, Mama, do as he says!" Sabrina rushed to her mother and buried her face in her bosom. She was close to hysteria, so Ravena gave in.

"Take what you want," she snapped. "The jewel box is on the shelf over the bunk." She was heartsick. The box contained five of the most precious possessions she had in the world. Not in mere monetary value; all the money in the world could not have persuaded her to part with them. The earrings, bracelet and necklace that her mother had presented to her the night of the Viceroy's ball, so long, long ago. And a matching necklace and ring that Brian had given to her for her birthday, two years before—small emeralds on a golden chain, and a perfect solitaire ring.

"Whenever you look at 'em, you'll think of the Emerald Isle," he had told her.

She fought back the tears as the one called Butch ransacked the box.

He whistled in admiration as he held up the emerald necklace to the lamp light. "Get a load of this baby, kid. Christ! I'll bet it's worth four, five thousand."

Tight-lipped, she said: "Seven thousand, and that was a bargain from a merchant from Macao. You have cheap taste, Mr.—"

"Cassidy, ma'am, but my friends call me Butch."

"Then I'll call you Mr. Cassidy. I don't suppose there's a sentimental side of your nature that I can appeal to? The value those items have to me, the true value, it can't be expressed in numbers. My dead husband whom I loved dearly gave me the emeralds to me as a birthday gift." She waited hopefully.

He put the jewels back in the ivory case, grimaced, rubbed the back of his neck. "I tell you, ma'am—er—Mrs.—?"

"O'Neil."

"Mrs. O'Neil, now, I tell you, in my business, you just can't afford to get sentimental. I mean, you take this train robbery we're pulling off, a job like this takes time. You don't sit around the fire one night and say: 'Hey, boys, let's go find us a train to rob.' It requires weeks of planning and practice runs. So, if every time a pretty lady worked on your soft side, you gave her her way, why, we'd end up penniless at the end of the year."

He had an infectious grin and a slow, easy way of speaking that reminded her a little of Brian's manner. Given different circumstances, Ravena would have liked him.

"You're destroying a part of me when you walk out of here with them, Mr. Cassidy."

There was a sincere note of contriteness in his voice. "That won't be easy to live with. I do have a conscience, in spite of what you might think. But—"

"Come on, Butch!" his partner said with annoyance. "We don't have time to stand here palavering."

"Right you are." He slipped the jewel case into the broad slit pocket of his mackinaw. "Good-bye, Mrs. O'Neil, it's been a pleasure meeting you." He tipped his bowler.

Ravena led Sabrina over to her bunk. "There, there, darling, it's going to be all right. You lie down."

"My head hurts, Mama."

"I'll put a cold compress on it."

She wet two towels from the water pitcher and applied one to the child's forehead. Then she stooped beside Roger and applied the wet towel to the egg-sized lump at the nape of his neck. She was concerned about him, so still was he, like death. She took his hand and felt for a pulse. It was thin, but he was alive.

Outside the car there was loud shouting and commotion. Horses stomping. Intermittent shots. From time to time the train would lurch.

The explanation, which Ravena had no way of knowing, was that the Cassidy gang was uncoupling the Adams express car from the rest of the train, the last car except for the caboose. Then Butch Cassidy went up to the locomotive and instructed the engineer.

"When I give you the signal, two shots in the air, you can be on your way."

He went back to where the Sundance Kid was setting the charges to blow off the armored door of the express car.

"Somethin' I got to attend to," he said.

He climbed the steps into the sleeping car where Ravena's compartment was and walked along the narrow corridor. The door was closed, and he knocked politely.

Ravena opened it and stared at him in surprise. "What do you want?"

"Thought you might lend a hand to the women in the coach up front. There's a young gal giving birth; I guess the shock brought on her labor."

"You are the scum of the earth, Mr. Cassidy," she said scathingly. "Terrifying innocent women and children."

He hung his head. "I'm not denying it. But will you help out, Mrs. O'Neil?"

She looked back. Sabrina was asleep. Roger had come around and was lying on her bunk. "I don't see how I can refuse. I'm a human being, not an animal like you. Wait, I'll put on a coat."

She went to the closet at the side of Sabrina's bed and put it on. Then she stooped and placed her cheek against the girl's forehead. She was cooler. In her sleep she mumbled, "Mama. I just dreamed about Donny. Is he all right?"

"Yes, darling, he's fine. I went up there a few hours ago and fed and watered him. The baggage man is very nice and he loves dogs as much as we do. He even allows Donny to get out of his cage and run around the baggage car when the train is in motion. Now you go back to sleep. There's an errand Mother must attend to."

She followed Cassidy along the corridor to the front of the car. When they reached the foyer he turned to face her.

"You're a very beautiful woman, Mrs. O'Neil."

"And you are the most unspeakable man I have ever had the misfortune to meet. Now where is this girl in labor?"

He grinned sheepishly. "Ain't no girl in labor. That was just an excuse to talk to you in private."

"I've had enough of this." She turned to go back to her compartment.

He took hold of her arm. "Mrs. O'Neil, hear me out. This jewelry of yours, I've been thinking—"

"Thinking? How novel for you."

"What you said about how much it means to you. Well, like I said, I've been thinking. It would be a shame to separate you from something you cherish so much."

She stared at him in amazement. "Well, there is a trace of humanity underneath all those layers of crudeness, uncouthness and amorality after all." She extended her hand. "Please give it to me."

His eyes crinkled at the corners in amusement. "No, I don't think you understand. I'm not *giving* them back to you. I'm *taking* you along with them."

"You son of a bitch!" she hissed and flung herself at him like a wildcat. Nails raked his cheeks. A knee drove up into his groin. He barely managed to wrap his arms around her, pinning her arms to her sides. But her feet hammered at his shins and knees.

"Jesus!" he hollered. "Hey, Logan and Curry, lend a hand. Hurry it up before I git killed!"

Ultimately Ravena was subdued and tied up with a lariat. "Toss her over my horse," Butch ordered his men. And he went to help Sundance at the express car.

"Charges all set?"

"Ready to blow. But what did you have to go and do a stupid thing like that for?"

"The woman? Why, I told you, outside of being the most beautiful woman I ever seen, she's a real spitfire. I like spunk in my women."

The Sundance Kid snorted. "That one ain't never gonna be your woman. Not the way she reacts to you, Butch. You look like you been in a sleeping bag with a bobcat."

Butch grinned. "Shucks, wait 'til she gets to know me better. Come on, let's blow 'er."

The dynamite was detonated and the steel door of the express car caved in. The blast had knocked the express guard unconscious, and he was trussed up. Then the safe door was blown off. And what a lovely sight it was that greeted their greedy eyes! Row upon row of neatly stacked currency, all in small denominations.

"Goddamn! We sure hit the jackpot this time!" the Kid exulted.

"In more ways than one." Butch glanced at Ravena lying across his mount's back, the way the Indians carried off women abducted from hostile tribes.

He unholstered his six-gun and fired two shots in the air. The engineer acknowledged the sign with a blast from the locomotive's whistle and the train creaked and groaned as the cars strained against the couplings. Slowly it moved forward.

They watched it until it was across the bridge, then Butch fired two more shots into the air. The gang members posted on the approach to the span put the match to the fuses and ran back to join the others. A few minutes later, the bridge disappeared in flashes of fire and smoke.

When the air had cleared there was no bridge. The distinctive touch of the Cassidy gang. Now they could ransack the safe and the other valuables in the express car at their leisure without the risk that gun-toting passengers and crew aboard the train would form a posse in order to ambush them or trail them back to their hideout.

CHAPTER FOUR

The Seventh Cavalry marched away from the camp site on the Yellowstone at noon, June 22, 1876, to the clear, high bugle notes of "Boots and Saddles."

From a high ridge overlooking the river General Terry, Colonel Gibbon and Major Brisbin reviewed the regiment.

Troop F passed by, guidons whipping sharply in the breeze; the "Bandbox Division" never had a boot unpolished or a button or buckle unpolished.

Troop E—the Gray Horse Division—passed, the legs of its gray ponies flashing like spokes in a wheel.

Astride a sorrel stallion, Brian rode up to the top of the bluff to join Terry's group. Like all the other officers in the regiment he wore the nonregulation uniform dictated by Custer. Floppy, wide-brimmed hat, a deerskin jacket trimmed with leather fringe over a flashy sailor's shirt; only the breeches and boots identified him as a cavalry officer.

Major Brisbin bristled. "I see you're following the party line."

"Sir?"

"Those godawful clothes."

The general made light of it. "Don't let him push you around, Brian. Out in this country it's an ideal uniform. I thought George was coming up to say good-bye."

"He sends his apologies. We're behind schedule as it is. He asked me to thank Colonel Gibbon for the lend of his Crow scouts. And my thanks for Mitch Bouyer. He's one of the best guides in the army."

"The best," Gibbon said.

Brian shook hands all around and saluted General Terry.

"Good luck," Terry said. "And see to it that George doesn't run too wild."

Brian laughed. "That's a little like trying to put the wind in a bottle."

They rode all morning and through the afternoon, with the Crow Indians scouting far out on the flanks of the regiment and Brian and Mitch Bouyer heading the point.

They camped at sunset after an uneventful day during which not any Indians, nor even the trace of any Indians, had been spotted.

The next day was better. Late in the morning the Seventh came upon the remnants of an Indian camp. Custer dismounted and stooped to pick up the shin bone of a buffalo chewed clean by the vultures and bleached white from the sun.

"This camp must have been the bunch that Major Reno let get away," he said, careful to keep any trace of sarcasm out of his voice.

Brian studied Reno covertly. If looks could kill—

The column covered thirty miles that day and made camp at five o'clock. That night Custer held an officers' briefing.

"From now on there'll be no more bugle calls in camp. We're so close to those Injuns I can smell 'em. Have the sentries wake their companies at oh-three-hundred hours. We march at oh-five-hundred."

The trail was hot now. On the morning of June 24, the Crow scouts reported excitedly that there were "many Sioux up ahead."

Custer was elated. "O'Neil, Reno, Wallace and Bouyer. We'll ride on ahead of the column with two companies."

For the next three hours they passed numerous small campsites that had been hastily evacuated according to the Crows.

At one o'clock they came upon the wooden skeleton of a sun-dance lodge. The chief Crow scout examined it thoroughly, mumbling to himself all the while and, finally, announced:

"Uncapa Sioux. They hold big war council here. Many chiefs."

A little way on they met another lead scout who reported the discovery of a fresh camp at the forks of the Rosebud.

FLOWERS OF FIRE 303

"Where are they now?" Custer asked. "Following the trail south to the Tongue River?"

"No, they cross over to the Little Big Horn," was the reply.

Custer nodded with satisfaction. "That means they're only about thirty miles ahead of us. A good day's march."

"One thing worries me, sir," Brian said. When Mitch and I scouted the valley before, we saw evidence of an exceptionally large camp. The entire valley floor is scratched up from ridge poles. There must have been thousands of them."

"Thousands?" Custer was concerned for the first time. He asked Reno, "Marcus, how big would you say that camp you found was?"

"Four hundred lodges at the very most."

Custer scanned the barren mountain ridges all around them, stark, silent and ominous. "That could mean the tribes are moving up from the south."

"Crook must have flushed 'em up from the Rosebud."

"Yes, where is Crook?" Major Reno posed the uneasy question. "If he's in hot pursuit, the scouts would have seen some sign of his advance patrols by now."

Brian had a grim thought. "And that could mean that the Sioux beat Crook at the Rosebud?"

It was a flash of omniscience. Eight days earlier the Sioux under the brilliant leadership of Chief Crazy Horse had inflicted a devastating defeat on General Crook's column and sent it reeling back to Goose Creek.

Custer scoffed at the idea. "Goddamn it, man, Crook is the best Indian fighter in the US Army. He's a genius. Thinks like an Indian. Unbeatable."

"Unbeatable," Brian repeated flatly. "That's what they said about Jeb Stuart."

Custer laughed and slapped him on the back. "Now you're beginning to sound like Reno. Come on, let's ride up and have a look at that camp the Crows found."

The Seventh made camp that night at the forks of the Rosebud. The last of the scouts straggled in after dark and reported that the trail of the Indians led across the divide.

"Big village on west bank," the interpreter translated. "Many times one hundred." He held up ten fingers and flexed them three times. "That many hundred. Maybe more."

"That would seem to indicate that the main force of Sioux is a good sixty miles farther downstream than General Terry's intelligence reports state."

"It's mere speculation," Major Reno reminded him. "Our orders specify that the regiment is to proceed south until we make contact with the Indians."

Custer cast him a withering look. "Nonexistent Indians who have already gotten a big jump on us. What you're really suggesting, Major, is that we put as much distance as we can between all those Indians across the river and ourselves! My God, man! Where would that leave poor Gibbon? Tomorrow, if he's on schedule, his six companies of infantry and four troops of cavalry will be on a collision course with that camp!"

"Your effrontery is becoming unbearable, Colonel," Reno said stiffly. "I intend to file a complaint with General Terry as soon as we get back."

"Oh, shit!" Custer said in disgust. "You know what you can do with your complaint, Major. Shove it up your ass!"

Later when they were in the tent they shared, Brian brought up a point as tactfully as he could. "You know, George, Reno has a point."

Custer's short fuse exploded. "Jesus! You too, Brian? Look, why don't you and Marcus hightail it back to Fort Lincoln?"

"You'd better slow down, George," Brian said evenly. "You're as tight as a porcupine's arse . . . All I am suggesting is this: You're worried about Gibbon walking into that bee hive. All right, suppose Gibbon and Crook don't keep the rendezvous with the Seventh. That leaves us up the creek without a paddle."

Custer stood up and began to pace restlessly, running his fingers through his thick yellow hair.

"Hell, Brian, for all we know we could be tilting at windmills. First we've got to establish beyond any doubt that there are all that many Indians on the Little Big Horn. The Crows may be friendly, but they are not above tweaking our noses from time to time. I want to see for myself. And, if the reports, are true, we'll send a call for reinforcements back to Terry and sit tight until they arrive."

"Sounds like the sensible thing to do. Let's have a snort before supper."

Custer grinned. "That is the best suggestion anyone has made to me all day. But only one. We're going to have to keep our heads clear, because we're breaking camp at midnight."

"Midnight?"

"Yup, when the sun rises tomorrow, we'll be ready. If we have to fight the red bastards, I want to pick the time and the place. Not git hoisted on my own petard like Lee did at Gettysburg."

After supper Custer sent Lieutenant Varnum and guide Charlie Reynolds with twelve Crows up to Crow's Nest, a high peak on the divide between Rosebud Creek and the Little Big Horn.

"Come daybreak, you'll be in fine lookout position to scout the valley of the Little Big Horn."

Soon after they left, the regiment broke camp and headed east up Davis Creek under cover of darkness. At dawn the column broke for breakfast, and Custer, his brother Tom, and Brian rode up to Crow's Nest to see what the scouts had to report.

The Crows were in a state of tense excitement. The interpreter Bloody Knife told them: "Red Star see thousands of ponies, many campfires in the night."

Tom Custer mopped his brow with a red bandana. "Even allowing for exaggeration that means it's a damned big powwow."

"Big enough so that our best bet is to sit tight until Gibbon gets here," Brian said.

"I have to agree," Custer said reluctantly. "Unless—" He turned back to Bloody Knife. "Do they know about us?"

"Red Star say six Sioux scouts were on that ridge." He pointed to high ground back in the direction of the regiment. "They ride fast back to river."

"Damn! The cat's out of the bag for sure." He slapped his thigh with his campaign hat, beating up a cloud of red dust. "Bloody Knife, you know the Sioux. What will they do now that they know we are here?"

The Crow went into consultation with his fellow scouts. An animated conversation punctuated with elaborate gesticulations of the hands, a part of their language. At last Bloody Knife answered Custer's question.

"Best thing you attack first and fast."

"He's out of his mind!" Tom Custer said. "I say we get the hell out of here and pull back the regiment."

Custer said dryly, "My brother speaks with the heart of a squaw, Bloody Knife. But when we meet the Sioux he will fight like a man."

Bloody Knife laughed and repeated it to the other Crows. They all appreciated the joke and Bloody Knife told them:

"No time to be afraid when Sioux come. Too busy shooting."

"That's the spirit." Custer grabbed his shoulder. "You're a good man, Bloody Knife."

Tom Custer was furious. "George, you're a damned fool! And go ahead and court martial me, I don't care. Brian, can't you reason with the man?"

"What do you think, Brian?"

"I think what Bloody Knife is trying to say is that if we run away the Sioux will think we're cowards, and that will put the taste of blood in their mouths. But if we make a show of force, a bluff, they'll have more respect for us."

"Precisely!" Custer said triumphantly. "If we take the offensive, it will give them pause for thought. Long enough for us to pull back with dignity and buy time for Gibbon's column to get here."

"There's an old Gaelic saying," Brian told them.

" 'Tender handed stroke a nettle, it will sting you
    for your pains,
Treat it like a man of mettle, it as soft as silk
    remains.' "

"Well put, old man. It's decided then. We attack."

They rejoined the regiment about a mile below the divide, and Custer called a meeting of all his officers.

"If we don't attack the Sioux camp, the probabilities are that they will attack us." He looked around at hummocks and ravines all around them. "This terrain is ideal for Indian warfare, but it's deadly for cavalry. As I've said before, if we're going to fight, I want to choose the time and the place."

"But why should the Indians attack us?" Lieutenant DeRudio of Company A asked.

"They know we're here, a threat to their camp, and the last thing they want is to be forced to defend a fixed position. As most of you know, the Sioux are strong on attack and weak on defense. All right. Our strategy will be to compel them to fight in the open by attacking their camp. On the flatlands in the valley one regiment can demoralize an Indian army three times its size."

It was a convincing argument to these seasoned Indian fighters and the majority voiced their approval.

"Good!" Custer said with satisfaction. "Well let's get on with it before they make their move."

The Seventh Cavalry Regiment crossed the divide shortly after noon. Captain Benteen with Troops D, H and K went off on a left oblique to scout the valley above the village to find out if any Indians were moving to the south, Major Reno with Troops A, G and M followed the south bank of a small creek. Custer rode parallel with Reno's force on the north bank with Troops C, E, F and I. Captain McDougal and a hundred thirty men recruited from all the troops brought up the rear with the pack train.

Benteen pursued his southwest course for about four miles. At this point his advance scouts reported that there was no sign of Indians moving south in the valley of the Little Big Horn, so, following Custer's orders, he headed back to rejoin the command.

When Custer and Reno reached the fork in Sundance Creek, they encountered the Crow scouts and the guides gathered around a lone tepee with a dead Sioux brave inside. One of the scouts put a torch to it, and, minutes later, it was a blazing cone with a column of black smoke funneling out of the top.

As Custer pondered his next move, a guide named Gerard came galloping down from a high ridge to the west.

"Big dust clouds in the valley, Colonel! They're getting ready to move out."

"Damn!" He slapped his scabbard. "They're going to get the jump on us!" He looked back down the trail for some sign of Benteen. "We'd really be in a tight spot if they attacked us here with Benteen and the pack train way back in the rear. Brian, you play poker."

Brian grinned. "I did, until that game right after the battle of Yellow Tavern when you cleaned me out."

"Bluffed you out."

"That's right. I folded with aces and tens, and all you held was a pair of deuces."

"That's what I'm going to do now. Play 'em like I had 'em. Major Reno, take your men down to the river double time. Cross at the ford and move down the valley. I'll lay back until you make contact, then we'll hit 'em with everything we've got on the flank. Make 'em think we've got a whole division backing us up." He placed a hand on Brian's shoulder. "O'Neil, it's been a long time since you and I fought together. I'm grateful to have you with me."

"Thanks, George. I hope when it's over, I still have me fine head of hair."

Captain Keogh and Adjutant Cook accompanied Major Reno and his hundred-and-ten-man force as far as the river. From the high ground on the east bank they traced its progress down the valley. Their function was to act as liaison between the two commands.

Custer, meanwhile, set off on a northeast route designed to bring his troops to the river opposite the south end of the Indian village in conjunction with Reno's approach on the north.

The first hint of disaster came when Cook rushed down from his observation post to inform Custer: "It's not going to work, Colonel! They're all set for Reno. And Red Star was not exaggerating. There's thousands of them!"

"Too late to turn back now," Custer said. "Let's go, men!" He put the spurs to his mount Vic and led the command at full gallop to the bluffs overlooking the Little Big Horn. Here they had their first look at the Indian camp, a sprawling cluster of tepees and wickiups stretching for miles down the valley.

"My God!" Brian said softly. "There must be fifteen thousand of them."

Custer pointed with his rifle. "There's Reno."

A half-mile off, the pathetically small column was advancing in a skirmish line. To the amazement of everyone but Custer, the Indians elected to go on the defensive. Despite their overwhelming superiority, they kept galloping around in circles and backing off while they sniped away at the cavalrymen with old muzzle-loaders and clouds of arrows. Stirring up a screen of dust around themselves.

"Watch it, Marcus!" Tom Custer shouted. "Look, some of them are cutting in behind Reno."

That did not alarm Custer. "If Reno wants to withdraw, he'll breach that ragtag line easily."

Brian thrust out an arm. "There's his real danger, George." He was pointing to a long ravine that was at right angles to the valley and out of Reno's field of vision. Poised in this ravine were at least three hundred Sioux waiting to ambush the troopers as soon as they came abreast of the position.

Then unexpectedly, Reno—almost as if he knew the danger that lay in wait for him—as he neared the ravine swung his skirmish line ninety degrees, so that it was parallel to the river, and deployed his men in a patch of timber along the bank.

"Brilliant maneuver." Custer let out his breath in relief and slouched in the saddle. "Marcus, my boy, I'll make a soldier out of you yet."

Adjutant Cook scratched his horse's neck. "What do we do now, Colonel? Recall Reno? Send down a troop to cover their crossing and fall back on Benteen and the pack train?"

"It wouldn't work, Charlie. We'd be sitting ducks for all those Indians out in the open. No, Reno's in a good defensive position. They won't rush him again, not until nightfall. He's kicking the shit out of them." He raised his binoculars and scanned the trail behind them. "We've got to keep them busy until Benteen gets here with the pack train. Create a diversion to take the pressure off Reno."

"Why don't we attack at the other end of the village?" Tom Custer suggested.

"What do you think, Brian?"

"I don't like it. The terrain favors them. Like Gettysburg."

"I agree. Still, we could make a few feints and pull back.

Keep them off-balance. It always worries an Indian when he doesn't know what's going on. Then we fall back to a good defensive position where we can rally the regiment."

Brian had been scrutinizing the terrain all around them through the glasses. "How about that valley over there?"

"Looks promising. Let's go have a closer look." He turned to Sergeant Kanipe. "Sergeant, take a message back to Captain MacDougal. Tell him to bring the pack train straight across country downstream as fast as he can instead of following the trail."

They resumed the march downstream for about a mile and one half. Custer halted the column in a ravine and he and Brian rode up to the summit of two twin ridges followed by Cook, Keogh and Tom Custer.

Brian pointed out the valley. Even without binoculars it was obvious that the terrain was ideal for cavalry tactics. The floor of the valley was level, and about two miles into it a long high ridge was etched against the blue sky.

"We could hold out there indefinitely, don't you agree, George?"

"Damn it! I've never seen a better defensive position. Look at those long, unbroken slopes. With their creeping, crawling offense, we'd slaughter them. They'll get it worse than Pickett did."

From their vantage point, the lower limit of the Indian village was visible. Custer pointed out a ford at the northern end of the village.

"We'll bluff an attack across the ford, then fall back to the high ridge and wait for Benteen and Reno. Tom, send a messenger to Major Reno. Tell him as soon as he hears the firing down here, to fall back across the river and join us at the ridge."

Custer's five troops rode down a curving ravine that led into Medicine Trail, a triangular drainage basin whose increments of soil and gravel had formed a ford across the Little Big Horn. The coulee was defined by two steep ravines running east and northeast from the apex at the ford: South Medicine Trail and North Medicine Trail.

Upon entering the coulee, the troops started down North Medicine Trail at a gallop in the direction of the river. They had covered a mile when two horsemen appeared on a ridge to the west. Custer halted the column and turned his glasses on them.

"Mitch Bouyer and Curley! I wonder what's up?" He hailed them with a pistol shot.

It took the two guides ten minutes to reach them.

"Major Reno is in bad trouble," Bouyer announced.

"His troubles will be over soon. Just as soon as we fake our attack down at this end of the village."

Bouyer squirted a stream of tobacco juice at a lizard crossing in front of his horse. "No, General, it's worse than before. He'd have been all right if he'd sat tight, but he must have got itchy britches. He ordered a retreat across the river. Then all hell broke loose. The Injuns really lit into them and it turned into a stampede."

"Oh, Jesus Christ!" Custer pounded the pommel of his saddle in frustration. "Just when I thought he was shaping up, too. Oh, shit! Reno. Reno, Major Reno," he agonized like a father grieving for a wayward son.

Bouyer added some pertinent details. "I figure they lost about forty men so far. They're trying to regroup on the high ground east of the river."

"Well, that changes our plans," Custer said. "Now we've got to put on more of a show than a mere feint at the village. An attack that will get them off Reno's back at that end."

He addressed Lieutenant Algernon Smith, commanding officer of Troop E. "Lieutenant, you will continue down the ravine toward the ford. The rest of us will take North Medicine Trail and we'll link up at the bottom."

He called to a messenger: "Martin, take a message back to Captain Benteen. Tell him we've found a big village and to hurry downstream as fast as he can with the ammunition packs. I don't give a damn about the rest of the train."

Captain Cook detained Martin. "Wait a minute, son. Better let me write you out an official order." He took out his notebook and scribbled a brief order on a blank page:

Benteen—come on quick—Big Village—Be quick—Bring packs.

He neglected to include one word:

Ammunition!

As the Gray Horse Troop made ready to descend South

Medicine Trail, Custer told Lieutenant Smith. "When the bugler sounds retreat, break off the fight and withdraw to the ridge."

The two forces split up and thundered down the twin trails.

As Custer had anticipated, the Indians swarmed down to the north end of the village to meet what they believed was a major attack. They rushed across the ford and up the two ravines into the withering fire of the cavalrymen's repeating rifles.

Relentlessly the men of the Seventh drove them back towards the ford. The fight lasted fifteen minutes. Long enough, Custer reasoned, for Major Reno to have made good his escape and to reform his troops. Operation Decoy had been accomplished.

"Sound the retreat," he ordered the bugler.

The Indians were thoroughly bewildered when the bugle notes cut through the noises of battle, and the cavalrymen broke off the battle and rode up the sides of the coulee and away to the north. It had to be some kind of a trick. They stared after the receding horsemen thoughtfully as Custer's troops galloped on to the ridge where the regiment would make its final stand.

As Custer had predicted, the Indians mauling Reno's command broke off their attacks when the heavy firing commenced at the north end of the village. The survivors of Troops A, G and M limped up a high hill east of the river to lick their wounds.

A short time later Captain Benteen arrived with his three troops. Appraised of what had transpired, he asked Reno: "Well, what are we waiting for, Major? Let's start downstream and join the rest of the regiment.

Major Reno was sullen, his handsome face streaked with gunpowder and dirt. "I'm not going anywhere. Not without ammunition. My men are just about out."

It rang a bell in Benteen's mind. He took out the note Custer had dispatched to him and read it again: "Be quick—Bring packs."

It was suddenly clear to him. "He didn't mean the entire train. God knows MacDougal is doing his best to move that train. The Colonel meant the ammunition packs." He whirled to Lieutenant Hare. "Take two fast horses and ride back to the pack train. Load the ammo on 'em and get back here on the double!"

Benteen then instructed Captain Weir: "You ride ahead and tell Custer the rest of the regiment will follow as soon as the ammo arrives."

But too much time had elapsed. Too many quirks of fate had intervened with the well-laid plans of George A. Custer.

When Captain Weir reached the high point overlooking the two Medicine Trails, the valley between him and the long ridge three miles to the north where Custer and his men were holed up was overflowing with Indians.

Heartsick, he turned his horse back to rejoin Benteen and Reno.

"Our only hope now is Gibbon or Crook," he said.

"I'm not giving up yet," Benteen said. "The old man has come through tighter scrapes than this."

It was not an idle boast. The ridge on which Custer was ensconced was virtually invulnerable to attack by an enemy that was lacking in sophisticated firepower. It was shaped roughly like the numeral "1" and was three-quarters of a mile long.

From its base facing Medicine Trail coulee, it extended northwest. The highest point was a hummock that formed the spur near the top of the "1." On the left the ridge sloped away to a rolling, grassy plain that offered relatively little cover for an attack force. Running parallel to it, some five hundred feet to the east, there was a lower broken ridge, and between the two ridges lay a ravine that fell away to a grassy valley opposite the high point.

The only weak point in the defenses was the approach from the northwest where there was a rise overlooking the lower slopes of the hummock to become famous as "Custer's Hill."

The only other accessible approach to the position was from due west where the ground was broken up by gullies, mounds and potholes where the Indians could hide.

The cavalrymen mounted the flaring wings at the base of the ridge and marched along the narrow crest to the spur at the far end. Here they dismounted and deployed.

"Tom, take two troops and post 'em on the high point. Brian, you go with E Troop to the end of the ridge. That's the most vulnerable spot, so you'll have the remaining two troops backing you up in reserve on the east side. We'll corral the horses there too."

There was something about Custer's heady exuberance that troubled Brian. A quality totally foreign to the confident, swashbuckling, brilliant tactician he had fought alongside at Gettysburg and Yellow Tavern.

"What happens now?" Tom Custer mused.

Custer's laughter was high and shrill. "We wait for Reno and Benteen, of course."

Brian O'Neil stared moodily across the rolling grasslands in the broad valley to the west. The Indians kept moving upstream from the ford in endless procession, filing up a deep ravine that extended northeast from the river to within three hundred yards of the middle of the ridge and about six hundred yards south of Custer Hill. At this point the ravine split up into numerous gullies out of which the warriors swarmed like ants and fanned across the valley in an uneven battle line.

Behind them near the river mounted braves were putting on a battle pageant, riding back and forth and shouting war cries.

Brian took a deep breath. "Too many of them, George. Benteen and Reno would never make it through that mob."

Custer was irate. "What kind of defeatist talk is that, Colonel O'Neil? Of course they'll come! The Seventh takes care of its own!"

Brian and Tom Custer exchanged a look pregnant with meaning.

He was pacing now, flinging out his arms as he rambled on almost drunkenly. "Oh, they'll be here, all right. One hour, two at the most." He pointed out a grassy knoll to the south, just opposite the right wing of the battle ridge. "They'll come over that slope and give these bastards the surprise of their lives. Hell! We can hold out here for ten hours if we have to. Those red bastards don't have the guts to charge a position like this. It's a veritable fortress."

"Ten hours, sir?" Adjutant Cook said grimly. "Not with only a hundred and fifty rounds of ammunition a man, we won't."

Custer was contemptuous. "You're an old woman, Cook." Yet he stalked around the ridge admonishing troopers who were taking pot shots at the Indians still a half-mile away. "Goddamn it, men! Wait until they get within range!"

The Indians were advancing cautiously and halted about a thousand feet away from the hill. Here they engaged the cavalrymen in a sniping duel. They were hopelessly outclassed; muzzle loaders and bows and arrows were no match for the troopers' modern repeating carbines. After about fifteen minutes they withdrew.

Custer was elated. "I told you so!" he crowed. "We've got them buffaloed!"

At five-thirty it looked for a time as if his optimism would be vindicated when a cheer went up from the troops posted on the tip of the ridge.

About three miles off on the high twin ridges on the east bank of the Little Big Horn, the vantage point from which Custer had first observed their present defensive position, a succession of horsemen rode into view.

Brian put the glasses to his eyes. No doubt about it, they were cavalrymen. Custer fired his pistol into the air three times.

Answering shots echoed back to them across the plain. "It's Benteen or Reno or both!" he said gleefully. "It won't be long now."

Another hour passed and the Indians evidenced no inclination to resume the attack. They had lost at least 100 braves in the initial gunplay.

Confident that reinforcements were on the way with the ammunition packs, Custer no longer deemed it necessary to conserve.

"Fire at will," he gave the order.

Brian frowned. "Colonel, I don't think that's wise."

"I don't give a damn what you think, O'Neil! I'm commanding this regiment!"

Brian's lips were narrow and tight. "There was a time when you invited advice, Colonel," he said evenly.

Custer glared at him. "That was before you became a mollycoddle like Cook and my dear brother."

The rattle of carbine fire grew heavier as the troopers snapped off shots every time a feathered headdress popped out of the grass and gullies in the valley.

"By gawd!" one young Tennessee lad exulted. "It's just like an old turkey-shoot back home!"

Soon the ridge was shrouded in gunsmoke which hung low in the still, humid air like pockets of fog.

As the smoke drifted and banked, Custer kept shifting position to keep the high twin ridges where the rest of the regiment had briefly appeared in view. He kept muttering to himself.

"Where are they? They should have reached us by now."

Meanwhile the Sioux continued to swarm across the valley. Most of them lined up southwest of the ridge. Others flanked the ridge on the south and southeast.

The Indians were divided into three classes. Front-line warriors. Behind them were the reserves, riding back and forth on their ponies whooping it up and firing their muskets into the air, lashing themselves into a battle frenzy. Behind them were elders and women and children, shouting encouragement to their fighting men.

Most of these reserves and noncombatants came up the North Medicine Trail and gathered on the ground to the south of the battle ridge behind the rise over which Custer anticipated his reinforcements would be arriving. As the build-up and firing and noise heightened out of his sight, Custer made yet another uncharacteristically irresponsible decision.

"Lieutenant Harrington, Lieutenant Smith, Tom, Cook, O'Neil, report to me at once!" he shouted through cupped hands.

When they were assembled, he told them. "I believe Captain Benteen's command is engaged with Indians back of that ridge, a half-mile to the south. I want E and C Troops to go to their support immediately. The red devils won't be expecting anything like this. We'll turn the flank just like we did at Gettysburg and Yellow Tavern, Brian me lad!" He cackled and slapped his leg in high spirits hardly justified by the hard facts.

Brian could no longer remain silent. "That's insane, George! This isn't Gettysburg! This mob doesn't even have a flank! They'll smother us by sheer weight of numbers. Besides, what makes you think it's Benteen over that ridge? Those shots don't sound as if they're fired from cavalry-men's carbines, not any of them."

"He's right, George," Tom Custer agreed, and from the expressions on their faces it was plain that the remaining officers were in accord with Brian.

Custer accepted the criticism with surprising calmness. He did chide Brian patiently. "You've been away from soldiering too long, my friend. You've forgotten that a good regiment is like a healthy human body. All the parts work in harmony for the good of the whole. The right hand gets in trouble, the left hand is right there to help it. We don't stop and question it. It's instinctive, like putting one foot in front of the other when you walk. The same way that Troops C and E are going to ride out to help Benteen."

"Colonel, it ain't Benteen," Mitch Bouyer put in his opinion. Them's Sioux and Cheyenne muskets, not carbines. God! I ought to know, I've heard enough of them."

"It's true, George," Brian tried to reason with him. "Benteen, Reno, they're not coming. They can't."

"Goddamn it! I've had enough of this insubordination! I sent a direct order to Captain Benteen to follow us downstream with the ammunition packs. Benteen is a soldier. He'll obey the order. He'll be here!"

"I'm not taking my men out there to certain death!" Tom Custer said firmly.

Custer's eyes blazed with fury. He walked toward his brother, arm raised as if to pistol-whip him. "You yellow-bellied faggot! As of now, you're relieved of your command! Lieutenant Harrington, hereafter you will be in command of C Troop."

Ten minutes later the two troops left the hill and advanced across the valley in skirmish order in the direction of the ridge where Custer believed Benteen was fighting the Indians. Greasy Grass Ridge as the Sioux labeled it. Lieutenant Smith rode at the head. Directly behind E Troop was C Troop under Lieutenant Harrington.

As Custer had predicted, the Indians in the valley, unmounted and lying in the tall grass, offered slight resistance to the advancing cavalrymen and suffered heavy losses as they retreated in confusion.

With more confidence the Gray Horse Troop pressed on to its objective, unaware that lying in ambush in a ravine blocking their line of advance were hundreds of Indians.

Before the cavalrymen reached the ravine, they were

struck on the flank by Lame White Man's crack Sioux cavalry, covering the retreat of the unmounted warriors. His braves charged up from a gully west of the skirmish line and split the loosely strung-out column at its center, turning the flank and isolating the two troops from each other.

Lieutenant Smith ordered his men forward at full gallop with the sound intention of riding out of range of the Indians' muskets and arrows, turning the troop and rallying it for a mounted charge. Tragically, they rushed straight into the enfilading fire of the Indians in the ravine. To add to their woes another force of Indians attacked them from across the open ground to the east.

Back on Custer Hill, the commander and his other officers watched the debacle unfold through binoculars.

"My God! What have I done?" Custer let the glasses fall limply to his side. He watched the carnage out of glazed eyes.

"What are we going to do, Colonel?" Adjutant Cook agonized. "The Gray Horse Troop is being cut to pieces."

Custer's mouth moved, but no words came out of it.

"He's in shock!" Brian said. "Tom, see that I have covering fire." He sprang into his horse's saddle and dug in his spurs. "Go, boy! Go!"

The troopers on the ridge fired salvo after salvo over his head, and the smoke from their carbines served as additional cover for Brian as he galloped toward the fray. As he drew near he was relieved to see that C Troop had recovered, reformed and was holding firm all along the line.

The situation of E Troop, however, was grave. Trapped between a solid phalanx of Little White Man's mounted warriors on their right flank and raked by the guns and bows of the hordes in the ravine, the Gray Horse, literally, disintegrated into small groups which were surrounded and destroyed. Some escaped across the ravine where they were shot down by Chief Gall's warriors.

Brian dashed back and forth, desperately rallying the stragglers into some form of fighting unit. He ducked an enemy arrow and shot the bowman in the heart.

Three more Sioux converged on him, two with short spears, one armed with a musket. At point-blank range the musket misfired and Brian calmly put a slug between his enemy's eyes. He got one more before the remaining attacker lunged at him with the spear. He twisted in the saddle barely in time, or the spear would have caught him squarely in the belly. As it was, the pointed fire-sharpened stick inflicted an ugly wound, just below his right hipbone at the top of his groin. He didn't give the red man another chance, shot him in the gut.

He finally integrated all of the survivors from E Troop with C Troop and emulated the strategy that Lieutenant Smith had tried futilely to bring off. He led them galloping over Greasy Grass Ridge out of range of the Indians' muskets and arrows, then turned for the charge.

"Only this time we won't try and break through their center. When I sound the word, we'll veer off to the right and skirt their flanks. That's the weakest portion of their line, the unmounted warriors."

They moved out, a solid line of troopers, straight as an arrow. Quick step, canter and into full gallop, firing as they swept down on the Indians. The carbines and Colt revolvers spreading a hail of lead ahead of them. The mounted braves had a hard time controlling their wounded horses. Many fell and their horses went berserk, spooking the other horses.

It was going to work!

Brian drew his sword, the signal to break to the right. It caught the enemy completely off-guard. The cavalrymen thundered through the tightly packed foot soldiers, scattering them in all directions.

Brian cut a swath through a pack of braves, arrows whizzing past his head. He cut down one, two, three, with a single swipe, and he decapitated a fourth. The head rolled ahead, like a polo ball, kicked by his horse's hooves.

And they were through and racing back to the ridge with the Sioux in hot pursuit. The chase ended when the enemy came in range of the troopers firing from the ridge in two ranks, one kneeling, one standing behind the other.

The other officers flocked around Brian, congratulating him.

"The finest cavalry charge I've ever seen," said Adjutant Cook.

"Magnificent," echoed Tom Custer.

Colonel Custer offered little more than a grunt and quickly got on to other matters.

"Did you see any sign of Benteen or Reno back of that other ridge?"

"Nothing back there, George, but a bunch of elders, women and children." His mouth tightened "They're staging a celebration. A victory celebration."

Custer flashed a bitter smile. "They're premature. We'll beat them yet."

Brian gazed across the sea of Indians in the valley and said nothing.

"Look, up on the ridge back by the river!" cried Captain Yates.

On the distant point where they had first seen elements of the Seventh, there now appeared a second contingent.

"That must be MacDougal with the pack train!" Custer said excitedly. "They're on Benteen's trail! That proves beyond a shadow of a doubt that Benteen and Reno are looking for us. Possibly in the coulee. We've got to get word to them."

"How?" asked Cook.

"Follow me."

Custer started up for the highest point on the ridge and scanned the terrain with his binoculars. He held them steady for a long time looking to the east.

"No sign of Indians on those ridges over there or in the gully that runs along the foot of this ridge. Keogh, can we hold this hill for an hour or two with forty men?"

"No way, Colonel."

"We could manage it if we had a barricade," Brian put in.

Custer grinned. "Right you are. Borrow a trick from old Bob Lee. The horses, dead horses. All right, get the men to drag the horses to the key defense points on the perimeter. The hummock, the tip of the ridge and the northwest approaches."

He turned to Lieutenant Calhoun and Captain Yates. "Commanders of Troops L, I and F will alert their men to move out at once. Follow the ravine on the other side of the ridge all the way back to Medicine Trail. Stay low, and the chances are the Indians won't even know what's going on."

"And if Major Reno and Captain Benteen aren't there in the coulee?" asked Captain Keogh.

"You'll find them," said Custer with a finality that would tolerate no contradiction.

Brian closed his eyes and screamed silently to himself. *"You goddamned fool! You poor damned fool! They say it gets to a man after so many years and so many battles. The cool, objective judgment gives way to hot, subjective fool-hardiness. And with each miscue that nourishes fading confidence, the mind becomes more unmalleable and isolated from the counsel of others."*

Forty-five men remained with Custer on the ridge when the three troops rode off to search for Benteen and Reno. Thirty-nine dead horses formed the main breastworks on the slope of Custer Hill. Five more were arranged on the crest to form a barricade for the seven men posted there to guard against a sneak attack from the rear. The half-dozen live horses were held in reserve.

When the defenses were completed, Custer took Brian aside. It was not easy for him to say what he had to say. "Brian, I—I've never had much experience in making apologies."

"Nothing to apologize for, George."

"Damn it, man! Don't you go telling me what is and what is not! I say that an apology is due, and I intend to tender it to you now! Is that clear, sir?"

"Yes, *sir*!" Brian grinned. Now this was more like the George Custer he knew. The real Custer.

"All right. I'm a pigheaded ass, Brian. I've gotten away with so much more than other men in my position would ever even dream of trying, that there comes a time when you feel that you're invincible. One of the men told me once that he thought of me as God." He shook his head in self-deprecation. "And I almost believed it myself. What an awakening this experience has been for me. A self-revelation. When you led that charge back to the ridge, I hated your guts, Brian. For showing me up for what I was. I should have been the one to go after the men that I sent out to near suicide for everybody. But you know something, Brian. I was too petrified to move! I was scared, my friend."

Brian did not want to see the anguish he knew was mirrored in the eyes and expression of George Custer. He looked after the three troops disappearing around a bend in the ravine.

"George, the only thing that proves is that you are indeed a mortal man like the rest of us. Not a god. Christ! The times I was afraid in the war, and you saved my worthless ass for me! Say, do you remember the battle of Brandy Station? I lost a month's wages to you because I let you sucker me into that bet, a greenhorn like me thinking he could get more Rebs than you. I think maybe I'm ready to take you on again. A hundred dollars says I'll wing more redskins than you, George!"

Custer turned, his eyes shiny with moisture, and he grabbed Brian's hand. "By God! You're on, you bragging Irishman!"

When the three troops under Captain Keogh moved down the ravine on their way back to Medicine Trail, Troop L was at the head of the column with Lieutenant Calhoun at the point.

Two hundred yards behind Troop L was Troop I. Troop F brought up the rear, commanded by Captain Yates.

The First Platoon of Troop L had just rounded the bend in the ravine when the entire column was raked by rifle fire and arrows. Once again Custer had erred in underestimating his adversaries. Anticipating just such a move by the besieged cavalrymen, Chiefs Crazy Hill and Two Moons, for over an hour, had their warriors infiltrating the gullies and smaller ridges to the northeast and east. Lying low until the three troops were well into the narrow ravine, they sprung the trap. Springing out of their hiding places, the Indians lined up on both sides of the ravine and raked the column with a murderous enfilading hail of bullets and arrows. Panicked by the noise and the sting of arrows and shots in their flanks, the horses panicked and bedlam broke loose.

Lieutenant Calhoun ordered the First Platoon to dismount and form a skirmish line, while the Second Platoon took the horses farther down the ravine and out of range of the enemy's fire. Only there was no sanctuary anywhere in the valley. The Indians bedeviled them all the way down the ravine and up onto the left wing at the end of the ridge, and, finally, around to the sweeping right wing. Here, silhouetted against the sky, they were perfect targets for

Chief Gall's braves. In minutes they were wiped out to a man.

Captain Keogh meanwhile was leading Troop I to the defense of L Troop's First Platoon which was pulling back down the ravine under withering volleys of muskets and bows.

At the rear of the column, Troop F sought to escape by veering up the slopes of the ravine and fighting their way back to the battle ridge where Custer was. As it rode over the crest, it was greeted by a volley from yet another band of warriors that Chief Gall had held in reserve in a ravine to the southwest.

Back at the battle ridge the tête-à-tête between Custer and Brian was interrupted by the heavy gunfire coming from the direction of the ravine. They rushed up to the high point and looked across the barricade of dead horses.

"An ambush," Brian said grimly. "The sneaky bastards are all around us."

"Sound the recall!" Custer screamed at the bugler. In a desperate futile gesture he climbed on top of the horses and cupped his hands to his mouth. "Keogh!—*Keogh!—Come back!*"

The words were eclipsed by even more intense gunfire.

"We've got to go to their rescue," he muttered and started down the slope to where his horse Vic was tethered. Brian followed him.

They galloped off in the direction of the ravine with twenty men. Halfway, they met Captain Yates and Lieutenant Reilly leading a smattering of survivors fleeing pell-mell back to the ridge with the Indians literally breathing down their necks. Custer ordered his squad to rein in and: "*Fire at will!*"

Hopelessly outnumbered, the small contingent of cavalrymen held their ground and poured it on the Sioux, wave after wave, turned back each time.

Brian squeezed off two bull's-eyes to Custer's three.

"One up on you, O'Neil!" he shouted gleefully.

Another volley and Brian sang out. "I got that one back and one to boot!"

And it went that way as they staged an orderly retreat to the ridge. Given a chance to regroup, Reilly and Yates were able now to lend their firepower to the fight.

There was no longer any hope for the men of the Seventh, but they were going to die with dignity and in a blaze of glory. When they reached the ridge, Custer turned his horse to meet the last determined charge of the Indians. Pistol in one hand, sabre in the other. Six more times the gun and the blade scored before it was over.

Brian had the sensation that he was at the eye of a hurricane as he had been that awful day and night on the *West Wind*.

A hurricane of flesh and blood perpetrated by human elements. A whirling blur of men and horses, red and white seen dimly through a shroud of smoke. Inhuman cries of pain and fury and hate and lust. Blood lust.

And then it was over and Gall's warriors pulled back.

In a state of shock, he dismounted and saw Tom Custer kneeling beside his brother's still body on the grassy slope. Tom lifted him gently, cradling him in his arms. The commander's sightless eyes seemed to be staring—almost in accusation—at the distant ridge by the river where, even as the troopers on the battle ridge were taking the last gasp of their lives, a row of their comrades watched from their safe observation point. Motionless. Indifferent?

Lieutenant Smith shook his fist at them and cursed: "Lousy bastards! Sitting back there like tin soldiers, seeing us die!" He looked back at Custer and began to sob. "And *you*! You stupid bastard! You died still believing in *them*! That Benteen and Reno would come to our rescue! The Seventh Cavalry!" He spat in the blood-soaked dust. "The best damned horse soldiers in the US Army! What a joke!"

Brian put an arm around his quivering shoulders. "Don't be too hard on Benteen and Reno, Smith. You know they wouldn't have had a chance of getting through to us."

"If they had tried right off, they could have," Smith said bitterly. "But they kept putting it off, procrastinating. And what about MacDougal? He was supposed to be here with the ammunition."

Brian sighed. "We're men, lad, mortal men. We make mistakes. Benteen, Reno, you and I." He looked at Custer. "And him as well. It's the one thing George never learned. Never understood. And that was his biggest mistake."

Tom let his brother down gently on the grass and stood

up. "The Seventh Cavalry—it was his god. And it failed him."

A trooper shouted excitedly, "Here they come again!"

Dispassionately Brian watched them charging the ridge, five deep in a closed circle around the ridge. A tightening noose.

"I hope there is a hereafter, George, old cock. I'd like the chance to pay you that hundred."

He picked up a rifle and went down on one knee, lining up the sights on a mounted warrior. This would be the last stand!

CHAPTER FIVE

After the Civil War the West spawned a multitude of the biggest and wildest outlaw gangs the United States has ever seen, preying on a territory stretching from Canada to Mexico along a route that became famous as "The Outlaw Trail."

Operating in small guerrilla bands they held up stage coaches, trains and unwary travelers. Operating in larger groups that were literally armies, they swept down out of the mountains and deserts like the Huns to wage war against ranches and mining camps.

Brown's Hole was the main headquarters on the Outlaw Trail. A lush valley on the Green River in the Uinta Mountains, it was walled in by sheer cliffs on all sides. Its limited approaches could be defended by a handful of men, and it would have taken the entire United States Army to comb the countless labyrinths threading through the thickly wooded forests in the mountains that surrounded it.

And that was precisely Ravena's indignant view of what should be done about Brown's Hole, where Butch Cassidy and his cutthroats had taken her.

"Surely the government will act against these—these—I can't think of a word opprobrious enough to describe them —these animals. No, that's an insult to a gentle species." She was conversing with one of the half-dozen women who lent a feminine touch to the infamous robbers' lair. Sybil Jackson, Etta Place, Della Rose and three dance-hall girls spirited away from Deadwood, South Dakota, by the Cassidy bunch, Kathy, Anne and Sue.

Etta Place, a dark pretty girl with a rather prim air about her, smiled. "Oh, they make token raids against Brown's Hole, lawmen, the soldiers, but their heart isn't in it. They know that in order to really clean out this place, a lot of their own men would be certain to die. And they have all the trouble they can handle with the cutthroats in their towns and hostile Indians. Besides, there are legal points to be considered. Brown's Hole lies squarely on the intersection of the boundaries of Utah, Wyoming and Colorado. According to law, it requires a posse made up of law officers of all three states to invade it."

Ravena was impressed by the woman, certainly not the type of alley cat one would expect to find consorting with outlaws. She was pretty, clean, and exceedingly bright and well versed.

"Where on earth did you learn that?" Ravena asked her.

"From Harvey, Harvey Longbaugh, he's the one they call 'the Kid.' He and Butch are quite intelligent, you know. They're always reading law books and every newspaper they can lay their hands on."

"You're an educated girl, aren't you?"

Etta blushed. "Yes, as a matter of fact I'm a school-teacher by trade."

Ravena was mystified. "And how did you end up here? I suppose you were kidnapped, the same way I was?"

The blush deepened and her eyes dropped. "No. I came here of my own volition. I'm from Denver. My father is influential there. One night I went to a church social and Harvey was there."

"At a church social? I don't believe it! *His* kind at a church social?"

Etta's head snapped up and her chin thrust out. "I wish you wouldn't talk about him as though he was some loathsome creature. He's really quite gentle and sensitive."

"A pillar of society, I'm sure," Ravena said dryly.

Etta's black eyes flashed in defiance. "Oh, I realize you are a grand lady, Mrs. O'Neil, and you look at all of us here down your long nose, wrinkling it up as if we all smelled bad. I don't suppose a lady of your breeding and gentility could ever understand how a woman might fall in love with a man who was wanted by the law."

Ravena was about to dismiss the poor thing with a sarcasm, and then the room caved in on her, so to speak. Her mouth hung open as she absorbed the impact of truth.

Who better than she should know about loving a man who was wanted by the law? Brian was a traitor and a murderer in the eyes of English law! And a murderer in the view of the authorities in Hawaii! It was entirely a matter of perspective—from whose point of view you considered the matter.

"I'm sorry, Miss Place. I have no right to play the snob with you. You may not believe this, but I was once in love with an outlaw myself. I still love him dearly, and I grieve still that he's dead and gone forever."

Etta's eyes were round as saucers. "You're pulling my leg, Mrs. O'Neil!"

"It's the gospel truth, and stop calling me 'Mrs. O'Neil.' My name is Ravena, Etta."

The girl smiled and took her hands. "I do believe you are truthful. Ravena, what a lovely name."

Ravena grinned. "It dates back to another outlaw far back in the family who picked up a Spanish sailor."

Etta burst into laughter. "Now you are teasing. I like you, Ravena, and I'm pleased to have your company. It gets lonely here at Brown's Hole when Harvey is away. And the other women—" She bit her tongue. "Aside from Sybil, we don't have too much in common. Oh, they're nice enough beneath their boisterous exteriors, but—see, now I'm acting the snob."

Ravena laughed. "That's all right. We can all use a lesson in humility once in a while, and I've just had mine. No matter. What do you think Mr. Cassidy intends to do with me? No doubt he's got rape on his mind?"

Etta was shocked. "Oh, no, what a thing to suggest! Butch Cassidy would never force his attentions on a lady. Perish the thought!"

Ravena spread her hands in confusion. "Then what? Ransom, can that be it?"

Etta looked perplexed too. "I don't truthfully know. It may have crossed his mind, but I think it was not a prime motivation. I think it was a whim on his part. He's given to whims." And her smile was sly. "I do know one thing. He's bewitched by you. Like a callow lad in love with his teacher, I've known that, it's a touching and fragile emotion."

Ravena's eyebrow curled. "It's difficult to think of Mr. Cassidy as touching and fragile."

"I felt the way you do when I first met Harvey and George."

"George?"

"Butch. His real name is George Parker. His boyhood hero was a Mike Cassidy, they called him Butch. When Mike died, George took on his name as a tribute. One day some other young lad in the gang will do the same. So Butch Cassidy is immortal in a way."

Ravena was intrigued. "He's an oddity, that's a fact."

"Not all that odd. Men like Butch and Harvey, there's a reason for what they are. They were born into decent homes, industrious, small-farm families. Then the large, powerful ranchers forced out the little people and took their land. The railroads, too, they're a special peeve of the gang."

Life at Brown's Hole was monotonous for the most part. The main house was a small hotel where outlaws moving along the Trail could stop over for a night or two and get a square meal and a bottle. There was a saloon and a small gambling casino for recreation. And of course there were the girls who could provide other entertainment for a lonely traveler.

Butch was shocked one night when Ravena suggested, tongue in cheek, that perhaps she should start to earn her keep like the other girls.

"You ought to be ashamed of yourself, Mrs. O'Neil," he reproved her.

"Mr. Cassidy, why did you bring me here?"

His face reddened. "Damned if I know for sure. You are the prettiest thing I've ever laid eyes on."

"So you decided to take me for a pet. Like a bird in a cage, is that it?"

"Nothing of the kind. You're a real lady, and haven't I always treated you respectfully?"

"But you have no respect for my feelings in the matter. Or the feelings of my daughter. Do you know what agony that child must be going through?"

His face reflected pain. "I'll get word to your kin that you're safe and unharmed. Where do they live?"

"Richmond, Virginia. It's far from here. How will you contact them?"

"I'll find a way, don't you fret."

"Mr. Cassidy, if you care for me at all, you will set me free."

He shook his head. "I'd never see you again."

"Under the present conditions, you might as well have a daguerreotype of me to stare at. Or a marble statue. Maybe if you get it out of your system, you'll change your mind. Do you want me as a woman?"

He was scandalized. "Don't speak that way, like one of those females."

"I'm a practical woman. I'll bargain for my freedom."

"I won't listen to any more talk like that. Go up to your room, Mrs. O'Neil."

She smiled. "Yes, *master!*"

Her laughter mocked him even from the upper floor of the building.

Late that night he knocked on her door. Ravena draped her body in a blanket and called out, "Come in."

He looked sheepish and rocked back and forth from one foot to the other. "Mrs. O'Neil, can you ride a horse?"

"I was born in the saddle."

"Then get ready to leave sun-up tomorrow?"

"You're letting me go?"

"I'm taking you home, that's what."

She was incredulous. "All the way to Richmond?"

"It's not much further than Mexico and we make that ride all the time. Etta will fix you up with some Levi trousers and a wool shirt and boots, anything else you'll need. I'll see you tomorrow."

"Mr. Cassidy," she said as he started to leave.

"Ma'am?"

"Thank you. You're a gentleman."

His grin was fetching. "I only wish it was true. Then I might stand a chance with you."

Her smile was bewitching. "Don't underestimate yourself. Shall I call you Butch?"

"I'd ruther you called me George, my Christian name."

"Good night, George."

"Ma'am."

"No, Ravena."

He gulped and exited quickly. Ravena let the blanket slide down off her shoulders. Idly she cupped her hands over her breasts and lifted them. Her nipples were turgid. She shivered, imagining that it was his hands fondling her breasts. It had been over seven months since a man had held her in bed. Caressed her, kissed her, coupled with her. She was a healthy, lusty woman and she was suffering from the lack.

Brian and she had discussed what each would do if the other passed on.

"I'd always want a woman, not the way I love you, but it's a sad thing to lie alone in bed at night without the warmth and comfort of a woman's body. I've known too many of those nights."

"I'd become an old maid," she had joked. "A chaste spinster, never to be touched by a man's hands again."

"Ho, ho! Now that's sheer blarney and you know it. A body like yours, what a waste it would be to cover it with widow's weeds for the rest of your life. No, you'd quickly find yourself another man and that's as it should be."

She turned down the lamp on the bed table and lay down again, smiling in the darkness.

The Sundance Kid and the other gang members were flabbergasted by Butch's decision to take Ravena back to Richmond.

"You go East and you'll run afoul of the law for sure," the Kid warned. "That little lady was bad news, I knew it first time I seed her."

Butch grinned and clapped a hand on his pal's shoulder. "I'll make out fine. You hold down the store while I'm gone. We got enough out of that last job to tide us over for a year. Tell you what, why don't we meet in Fanny Porter's place at Fort Worth? Skip over to Mexico and get a little sun."

"All right. But I still think you're a damned fool."

"I couldn't agree with you more."

Next morning Etta woke Ravena at dawn. "I've got your clothes and an extra shirt and Levis so you can wash things out and have a change while they're drying. Underwear too."

Etta studied Ravena as she put on the men's clothing. "Your hair's too long," she said.

"What do you mean?"

"When you're on the trail in this lawless country, it doesn't pay to advertise the fact that you're a woman. Butch is only one man."

"I see your point. All right, Etta, get to work with the scissors."

All of the gang members gawked when Ravena came downstairs. Her long, lustrous hair reduced to a shaggy thatch no longer than Butch Cassidy's.

"By God!" he exclaimed. "You've been scalped!"

"A security measure. Etta thinks it will be safer to pass myself off as a man."

Her remark elicited hearty guffaws. "That'll be the day, when you can sell that bill of goods to a man. But it is a good idea. From a distance you could pass, I guess. Needs an extra touch. Wait a minute."

He went into another room and came back holding something behind his back. "Close your eyes," he told her. Then he whisked a bowler hat and a cigar out from behind him. Set the hat on her head at a jaunty angle, and poked the cigar into her mouth.

They all laughed as Ravena studied herself in a mirror. She jammed her thumbs in her belt and struck a pose. "Now all I need is a pistol."

"You got it." He walked to the bar and took a six-gun and gun belt out from under the counter. "Think you can handle this baby?"

"Child's play."

Outside she demonstrated her marksmanship by drilling six slugs into a tree trunk in a circle no larger than a silver dollar.

Butch looked at her wistfully. "Gee, we sure could use a gun hand like yours, couldn't we, boys?"

"Amens" from all around.

They said their good-byes and mounted their horses. As they rode out onto the Outlaw Trail, the girl named Sue commented: "You know, it just hit me where I've heard a strange name like hers before, Ravena. There was a fellow in Deadwood, his girl was named Ravena. His name was Brian. Ain't that a coincidence?"

Etta shrugged. "I don't suppose it's that uncommon after all."

* * *

On the afternoon of their third day in the saddle, Ravena and Butch reached Denver.

It was sheer luxury for her to soak in a hot tub and then to crawl between clean sheets on a soft mattress. She slept solidly for ten hours and would have dreamed on but for Butch's knock on her door at six A.M.

"Time to rise and shine!" he called out.

"Come in," she said drowsily. Dazedly she sat up in bed, forgetting that she slept in the raw. Sheets and blankets fell around her hips.

Butch's eyes widened and he swallowed hard, his burning gaze fixed on her bare breasts.

"Beg yer pardon," he croaked and turned his back on her.

Fully awake now, she pulled the covers up around her shoulders. "It's all right, George. I'm decent again."

His stiff back remained the way it was. His fists were clenched. "I better see about the horses. Meet you in the dining room for coffee and buns before we set out again."

Ravena looked quizzical as he departed hastily. "As if the devil himself were after him," she mused. She smiled and ran her fingers through her short tousled hair.

The first day out of Brown's Hole, Ravena had been excited and exhilarated by the novel experience. The scenery was breathtaking. Rugged, naked beauty, virgin nature at its purest. Spectacular vertical country, cliffs soaring up from rocky brushland into the very heavens. Snow-capped peaks that seemed to hold up the sky like girders on a bridge, their summits obscured from time to time by mist.

Barren desert land, empty and stark. Challenging life and winning most of the time. Skeletons of the losers, man and animal, strewn along the trail they followed.

The sweeping plains of Kansas. The wind charted by rippling wheat and corn. Grazing cattle, seen from afar on a high hill.

"I had a toy farm as a child. From my bed it looked like this, all the miniature cows and hogs and horses arranged about the red barn." Ravena looked wistful.

He smiled ruefully. "Just as we're toys of the gods. They arrange things for us and push us around as you directed your toys on the farm."

She turned to him. "I didn't know you were a philosopher, George."

"Lots of things you don't know about me."

It was warm, and Ravena had unbuttoned the two top buttons of her shirt. She was aware of his yearning eyes on the V of her neckline where the tops of her breasts peeped out enticingly.

"We'll camp here tonight," he said curtly. "There's a stream in the wood a ways. Tomorrow we'll make Kansas City. You know, that's civilization. You could travel in comfort the rest of the way by rail and coach to Richmond."

She pretended to pout. "Do you want to get rid of me, George?"

He reached out and took her hand. "I could go on like this with you forever, Ravena. To the ends of the earth."

"That's sweet, George, but I think I'd perish from saddle sores before we were halfway there." She put a hand on her backside and winced. "Maybe before we get to Kansas City."

They made camp at the end of an apple orchard with a stream running through it. At a point beyond the orchard there was a rocky basin where the water was about three feet deep. Butch kneeled down and cupped water into his mouth.

"Ahhhhh. That's good."

Ravena giggled. "Careful you don't swallow a fish."

Myriads of small fish flashed about in the clear water like beads of quicksilver.

"I'd like to swim in here," he said.

"Be my guest." She bent over, put her hands on his back and shoved him headfirst into the pool.

He came up blowing like a whale. "Ho! Is that ever cold! You're a sneaky wench, Mrs. O'Neil!"

She doubled up laughing with her hands braced against her knees. But her laughter ceased abruptly as Butch grabbed her by an ankle and tugged her into the drink with him.

"You bastard!" she sputtered.

He recoiled. "*Mrs.* O'Neil, that's fine language for a lady."

"Who said I was a lady? Not all of the time anyway."

He looked at her in silence. Shirt and trousers plastered to her body, leaving little to the imagination. She licked water off her lips, measuring him. A warm churning in her loins and belly. Her breasts felt swollen. She walked through the waist-deep water to him, unbuttoning her shirt. Took one of his hands and slipped it inside the shirt. Her nipple hardened against his palm. Slowly she put her arms around his neck and turned her mouth up to his.

"I've wanted you since that first day," he murmured in her ear, nuzzling her hair with his lips, kissing her neck, her nose, her eyes and then pressing his mouth down gently on hers. Her mouth opened to receive his tongue.

"Ravena, my darling," he gasped as the kiss broke.

"Come along," she took his hand and they climbed out onto the bank.

As unself-consciously as if they had been lovers for years, she peeled off her wet clothing and stood naked before him. Pleased by the way he looked at her, and enjoying the experience of looking at a man's naked body after so many months. Thrilling to the sight of his hard, ready manhood. Proud that she had the power to arouse the insatiable lust she read in his expression. He embraced her. She pressed her body tightly against his, meshing her soft contours to his lean, male muscular form.

He swung her up into his arms and carried her back to where the sleeping bags were spread out. Put her down and bent to kiss her breasts. His hands all over her body. She sighed and closed her eyes, savoring the blissful sensations welling up all over her body. Breasts. Belly. Buttocks. Thighs. And then he touched the very core of her and she cried out.

"Now, George! Hurry, my darling!"

She was ready for him and he entered her smoothly.

"*My cup runneth over—*" she thought as the sweet spasms commenced.

They slept together in one sleeping bag that night under a diamond-studded sky. Lay awake for hours in each other's arms, looking for shooting stars.

"I wish I may, I wish I might, get the wish I wish tonight," Ravena recited the childhood rhyme.

"What would you wish for if you could have anything in the world?" he asked.

"That Brian was alive and with me," she said without hesitation.

He said nothing, but she could feel his body draw away from hers. It pained her.

"I'm sorry," she said softly. "I shouldn't have said that. I wasn't thinking."

"Yes, you should have. Because it's the truth. You're still in love with him."

"Brian is dead, and no wishing of mine is going to resurrect him."

"Just the same—" He lapsed into deep thought.

She fell asleep finally and didn't stir until a bird warbled its morning song in a tree over their heads.

She bent over him and kissed his bare chest, nuzzling in the curly hair the way she had done with Brian over and over again. He was like Brian in so many ways. Hard and rough but tender. A man with a cause. She wondered. . . .

He read her thoughts. "It would never work, Ravena, you and me." He kissed her hair, her ear, the nape of her neck.

She sighed. "No, our worlds are so different. I'm enjoying myself now, but I'd tire of this kind of life on a permanent basis. Running, always running. I've had enough of the fugitive life. I'm too old for it any more. And I have a child to think about."

"Of course. Let's say no more about it."

They made love again and it was good. But there was a sadness in each of them that caused them to treat each other with a special tenderness. A kind of reverence that lacked the passion of the previous day.

Butch cooked them a hearty breakfast of beans and bacon and panbread along with the most delicious coffee she had ever tasted. Ravena loved eating out of doors.

"Everything tastes so much better. I'd never touch beans and bacon back in Richmond or Ireland."

He grinned in pleasure. "That's because it's getting back to nature the way man was meant to live in the first place. I lived in a cave once for two months hiding out and loved every minute of it. Well, time we were on our way."

Ravena washed the dishes with sand down by the creek and packed them back in the saddlebags.

"They're not dishes." He laughed when she told him she was ready. "Mess kits and two rusty forks and spoons."

"I'd like to take my set with me," she said impulsively.

"That old tin junk?" he said with surprise. "What for?"

"Souvenirs of an unusual and very happy time in my life. I'll never forget you, George."

"Nor I you." He kissed her cheek and squeezed her hand. "By the way, I have a few more souvenirs for you."

He went to his horse and opened one of the two saddlebags. From it he took the ivory jewel case he had pilfered from her aboard the train.

"I want you to have this back too."

Ravena accepted it and smiled. "You are a gentleman, Mr. Butch Cassidy, and don't let anyone ever tell you you're not."

"Thank you, Mrs. O'Neil, and you are a lady I'll take pride in having known till the bullet that has my name on it ends this farce called life."

He kissed her for the last time.

CHAPTER SIX

Old men, women and children roamed the battlefield looking for souvenirs. The victorious braves whooped and danced among the dead cavalrymen, stripping the corpses and scalping and mutilating with fierce vengeance.

Three Sioux prepared to go to work on Custer but two Cheyenne women protested: "It is Yellow Hair, a good man. He was a brother to our people in the South. Do not touch him. It will anger the gods."

"It will be as you say," the leader said. "But we must have something." He kneeled down and drew his knife. "The smallest thing about him." He then proceeded to cut off the tip of the small finger on Custer's right hand.

The two women cleansed the wounds as best they could and anointed his face and head with oil. Then they laid him out across two other corpses with his hands folded on his chest. Before they withdrew from the ridge, one woman stooped and pierced both of Custer's ears with a sewing awl.

"Why did you do that?" asked another woman.

"He did not hear what our chiefs said when he smoked the peace pipe with them," the woman said sadly.

The other woman nodded. "It is well then. Peace be with him."

The next day General Terry and Colonel Gibbon arrived on the scene and relieved Reno's and Benteen's besieged commands on Reno Hill. United they went in search of Custer.

The carnage at Custer's battlefield stunned everyone from the lowest trooper to General Terry, seasoned Indian fighters all, and accustomed to violence and death in all its hideous guises.

Suddenly a corporal rummaging around the main breastwork of dead horses on the slopes of Custer Hill shouted excitedly.

"Hey, give me a hand! There's someone underneath here. I just heard a groan!"

Troopers heeded the summons from all directions, and the horses were hauled off what proved to be a man so covered with blood from head to foot that he was unrecognizable.

"Get him washed off," General Terry ordered.

A half-dozen buckets of water were sloshed over the unconscious man before Benteen exclaimed: "By God! It's Brian O'Neil! And he's alive! You medics, haul your asses over here on the double!"

Brian's wounds were ugly but not serious. The regimental surgeon took 20 stitches in his head and 30 more in his right shoulder.

"Lucky he's a thick-headed mick," Benteen joked when he and a group of fellow officers visited Brian for the first time in the hospital tent.

Brian touched his aching head and grinned feebly. "Christ! I've been scalped for sure."

To his best recollection, it had come down to the Custer brothers and himself and he had taken cover behind the main breastwork. The last thing he remembered was two Indian ponies leaping over the barricade and a fusillade of shots. Then the horses and their riders had come crashing down on him.

"Custer and Tom must have brought down a few more before they died, and by that time you were buried alive in horseflesh," General Terry theorized.

Later that day, he returned for a private session with Brian.

"I've given the men strict orders not to say anything about you. They swore an oath on the honor of the regiment. After what happened to George and his command, you can rely that no man will defile that honor."

"I appreciate that, General."

Terry paced up and down with his hands folded behind his back. "I made the decision based on two considerations. First of all there will be an inquiry into the affair by a Military Court. There is no doubt that the witnesses who testify will receive nation-wide notoriety."

"And I'll be the chief witness and then the jig will be up for Brian O'Neil, wanted for murder in Hawaii."

"Precisely, and you deserve much better than that. After all, you didn't want this job. George forced it on you, and you served him with courage and distinction. I've been through his reports prior to the battle and removed all reference to you from the official records."

"My thanks again."

"As for the second consideration, George Custer was one of the most brilliant cavalry officers I've ever been privileged to serve with. A gentleman of total integrity and incontestable bravery. It would be criminal to blemish his name any more than it will suffer from the unhappy inference we must draw that his judgment was irresponsible in almost every instance in the final battle." He cleared his throat. "Not to mention that he cracked up in the end."

"Not a crack-up, General. A lapse. In the end he was magnificent, fighting shoulder to shoulder with his men until he died."

"Nevertheless, everybody's interests will be best served if you vanish from the records."

"I couldn't agree more. I'd like to get back to Sam Schaffer's outfit and see how my investment is making out."

"You can leave any time you want, says the surgeon. I'll arrange for an escort to travel part of the way with you."

"Then I'll leave tomorrow morning."

"Fine, Brian." He held out his hand. "I'd like to offer my personal thanks for adding your weight to the regiment."

Brian's smile was pained. "Unfortunately it wasn't weight enough."

He lay there after Terry had departed, staring at the top of the tent, conjuring up ghostly images on the canvas.

Ravena.

Sabrina.

The haunted face of George A. Custer, dripping with blood as the five damned troops of the Seventh Cavalry Regiment made their last stand.

BOOK THREE

PROLOGUE

In rereading *Books One and Two* I am satisfied that I have honored my vow to the reader to present the truth as it occurs in my narratives, especially in the latter volume, without regard to the light cast upon any character, particularly Ravena Wilding O'Neil, favorable or unfavorable.

I must confess that a good many of my acts through the years do not reflect honor or glory on me. We all have our weaknesses. We all have our faults. We all have our irresistible passions and obsessions. We all make mistakes. I admit to more than my share of such sins—if they do be sins.

However, I state with unabashed candor that if I could turn back my life the way one can turn back the pages of a novel and begin all over again on page one of *Book One* at the tender age of ten years, I assure you, the reader, that scarcely one word, one line, one page of any of the three volumes would be considerably altered. In short, I would not have lived this life in any other fashion than I have lived it.

And I will continue to live it. And so will Brian. And so will Roger.

I promised there would be no happy endings to these works of mine.

There are no endings except death for any of us. Life goes on. Good or bad. Happily or unhappily. Successful or a failure.

CHAPTER ONE

As things worked out, being kidnapped by the train robbers was a blessing in disguise for Ravena. In the collective mind of Richmond society who, among other epithets, branded her as an "adventuress" and a "traitress" and an "adulteress" after fleeing from justice with the infamous Brian O'Neil, the "harrowing ordeal" to which she had been subjected was deemed a kind of penance leveled on her by the Almighty.

That sentiment, along with the notorious healer "Time," enabled those who felt she had betrayed friends as well as country to forgive and forget.

Moreover, Ravena supplied a much-needed charge of color and excitement to Richmond high society afflicted with postwar malaise. Disabused of its former narcissism that its men and women were God's chosen people, with no other mission in life but to be gallant and charming to one another and wallow in self-indulgence, by the brutal, humiliating crushing defeat at the hands of the Northern armies, the South had lapsed into brooding decadence. Her dramatic return breathed new life and verve into Richmond. Some of the old spirit was recaptured in the plantation parties. Aristocracy revived.

Ravena, on her part, was surprised. On Maui they had heard a multitude of shivering tales about the rape of the South by northern Radicals and carpetbaggers. Subjugation by military rule with vengeful Negro troops looting, raping and murdering whites with impunity.

But when she arrived back in Richmond in the summer of 1876, all of the Confederate states were back in the Union, firmly in charge of their own domestic affairs once more. And the Negroes, shockingly, appeared to be in worse straits than they had been prior to the war. Technically emancipated with the right to vote as free and equal men with their former masters, they dared not cast a ballot under threat of fast and violent punishment administered by the white-hooded Ku Klux Klan or other vigilante organizations in what was referred to as "the invisible empire." Any black who stepped out of line or "forgot his place," as Roger phrased it, was sure to be horsewhipped, beaten or even murdered. Merely looking at a white woman in a way that her white escort arbitrarily deemed as lecherous was incontestable grounds for a lynching; or if the perpetrator was lucky he might get off with being castrated.

Of the five black servants who had served them at *Ravena* before the war, three still performed their menial functions eleven years after the surrender at Appomattox. The other two, Gordon the butler and Hattie the cook, had died on the job. Lenny Freeman, once the footman, had replaced Gordon.

Emancipation had changed the happy-go-lucky teenager with the big grin to a bitter, hostile, disillusioned adult who almost choked every time he said: "*Yes, sir,*" or "*Yes, ma'am.*" But he said it because it was the best job he could find anywhere in the South. Or in the North, for that matter. Scores of his acquaintances who had rushed North to the Promised Land after the war came slinking back ultimately with their tails between their legs like whipped dogs.

Libby, the new cook, was a fat jet-black "mammy" of the old school. She resented emancipation and hated "uppity blacks" and "Northern white trash" with equal venom for disrupting what to her had been an idyllic existence.

Birdy the maid was always the practical realist: "Mr. Lincoln signs his name on a paper and says: 'All right, black folks, now you're free to do what you want and go where you please.' I'm supposed to do handsprings and go 'round singing? I've seen too many poor miserable, unhappy white folks to believe a fairy tale like that."

Vanessa Wilding no longer had a personal maid. Rose had returned to Ireland three years earlier to take care of her invalid aunt and uncle.

The Duchess had failed painfully in the years since Ravena had seen her. Ravaged by a wasting disease, her beautiful face and fine body were withered and wrinkled. But neither pain nor disease could defeat the woman's inborn nobility, as shown in her carriage, head held high and proud.

The Duke of Ulster, in his early seventies, had fared better than his wife at the hands of time. He was plagued with bronchitis and a touch of heart disease, but his health had improved remarkably, so said his physician, since the return of his prodigal daughter.

"The best medicine in the world for the two of us, right, my dear?" he chortled. And he put an arm around each of their shoulders and pulled them close to him. "You'll see, we'll all live happily ever after."

"At least we'll die happy that we know Ravena is home and safe," his wife said wryly.

"And that wonderful granddaughter you've given us," he raved on. "There are no words even in an Irishman's lexicon to express how my heart runs over with love and joy when that dreamchild walks into the room. Where is Sabrina anyway?"

"Last time I saw her she was heading for the stables," Ravena told him.

Lines of concern ruffled his high brow. "I wish she wouldn't ride that bloody black stallion."

Ravena laughed. "Father, she's been riding since she was three, just like me. You never fretted about me riding Apache when I was small."

He snorted. "Hmmrh. Can't say I recall. But this is different. Sabrina is—" He caught himself as smug smiles spread over the women's faces.

"Sabrina is your granddaughter," Ravena teased. "Your angel, your pride and joy."

"No, seriously, my dear, there's a chap visits here, friend of Roger's. Dan Butler, you'll meet him, he's abroad right now. He's in the import business with his brother. Savannah, I believe. The brother had quite a shady reputation during the war. Made millions in various illegal enterprises. The point is the older brother, Rhett, lost his only child at the time, a daughter, because she fell from her pony."

"That's a terrible tragedy, but obviously the child attempted some maneuver that was beyond her capabilities. I'm exceedingly strict with Sabrina."

"Nonetheless, I believe I'll go down there and keep an eye on her."

They looked after him with loving eyes. "Sabrina has been a breath of fresh air in this house. New life," said the Duchess.

"I'm happy she makes you happy."

"I thought she was going to shrivel up and die all those weeks those horrible outlaws held you captive. She wouldn't eat, and every night she'd cry herself to sleep."

"We're very close, Sabrina and I." She let out a sad little sigh. "We all were very close—the three of us—Brian, she and I."

Her mother bent over and patted her hand. "I know how you must feel, Ravena." She paused. "Yet I do think it's fine how well she and Roger get along."

Ravena had been uncomfortably aware of a shrewd and questioning manner on the part of her mother on matters concerning the child and the circumstances of her birth.

Casually she answered. "Well, there's no reason she shouldn't. After all, he is her natural father."

"Yes." The Duchess clasped her hands and gave Ravena that special look.

Everyone else in Richmond accepted without question that Roger had fathered Sabrina before Brian and Ravena left the country. In fact Roger—magnanimously, Ravena thought—went so far as to defend her act of desertion.

"The poor thing panicked. After all, she was bamboozled the same as the rest of you. Brian and I were twins, identical except for the color of our hair. One summer, when we were boys, we went to a military camp that required all cadets to shave their heads because of a lice epidemic. Our own mother couldn't tell us apart.

"What was Ravena to do when she discovered the impersonation and Brian threatened to implicate her in the plot if she exposed him? And that traitorous bitch, Jesse Farnsworth, she was the real instigator of Brian's escape. Poor Ravena believed her to be a loyal friend, and when Jesse urged her to leave with him, she did as she was told."

Whether or not the Richmond clan really believed his explanation is questionable. Yet there was sufficient substance to the story to persuade them to rationalize that she was innocent. As the years passed, the entire affair was forgotten.

It had never happened.

Only Ravena herself clung to every memory of her glorious years with Brian O'Neil. Brian was the only man she would ever truly love.

But she was too hotblooded to take to a nunnery. Her affair with George Parker had been brief but good. And there would be other affairs in her future.

In the course of the next four years, she had a succession of lovers just as Roger had a succession of mistresses.

Neither made a secret of it, and by 1880 they were spoken of by their friends, with affection, as "the scandalous O'Neils."

Oddly enough, their domestic life was smoother than it had been before Ravena's defection. Their relationship, though strictly platonic, evolved into a camaraderie of sorts, largely due to their mutual bond with Sabrina.

She had no doubt at all that Roger truly adored his foster daughter and lavished her with everything a young girl could desire. And as time passed Sabrina's affection for Roger grew into love. When she called him "Daddy," she was sincere. He had become her father.

Vanessa Wilding died in the spring of 1877, and the Duke of Ulster followed her just five months later. "Of a broken heart," Ravena told everyone.

A little bit of her own heart died with them, as it had the day she learned that Brian was dead.

At the burial of her father beside her mother in the little family plot behind the big white house, Roger put an arm around his wife and Sabrina. "Try and think of the great joy you brought them by coming home before they passed on."

"It was little more than a year," she bemoaned.

"It was better than no time at all with you and Sabrina."

When she tossed a handful of dirt on her father's coffin in a last farewell before the grave was covered, tears blurred her vision, but she did not cry.

"You do enough crying for the two of us, dear," she said when Sabrina questioned her about it, showing faint resentment.

She was too strong a woman to be incapacitated by grief. You lived for the day and planned for the future, but the past was no more than visions and dust.

That was the day she first paid any serious attention to

Dan Butler. She had met him at the lavish homecoming party Roger had given for her and Sabrina soon after her return to Richmond. He was accompanied by a haughty Englishwoman he had brought back with him from his last trip to the Continent. A Mrs. Cleo Bates, a thirtyish widow with a striking figure, a flawless complexion and sea-green eyes. It was common knowledge that they lived together in Savannah, but they were often seen in Richmond because of the numerous business trips Butler had to make to Washington, D.C., on government business.

He happened to be in Richmond the week her father died, and that evening he stopped at the house to pay his respects. Roger was at his club and Sabrina was attending a dance at the private school in which she was enrolled.

Freeman the butler showed him into the music room where Ravena was embroidering a black stallion on the white silk shirt that Sabrina wore with her riding habit. She put her embroidery aside and stood up to greet him.

"It was thoughtful of you to come, Mr. Butler."

"I wish I could have been here when your mother passed on," he said. "The Duke and Duchess were two of my favorite people."

"They liked you as well," she said shading the truth somewhat.

Her father's opinion of Dan Butler was that he was "a charming fellow but on the shady side."

"Please sit down, Mr. Butler. Can I have Freeman bring you anything?"

"Yes, thank you. A bit of brandy will be welcome on a night like this. I think we're in for an early winter this year."

"Yes, the chill gets into your bones." She rubbed her forearms. "I'll have brandy too, Freeman."

He sat down in the leather chair opposite her rocker. "Do you mind if I smoke?"

"Not in the least. In fact I'll join you." She opened a lacquered box on the table beside her chair and took out a cigarette.

Butler's thick eyebrows lifted and his smile conveyed admiration.

"Do I shock you, Mr. Butler?"

"No, what makes you think I'd be shocked by a woman smoking? It's quite the vogue in the Parisian *haut monde*."

He rose and lit her cigarette with a match from the onyx container on the table. His eyes met hers and he lowered one eyelid in just a suggestion of a conspiratorial wink.

"I don't believe there's too much in the world that would shock either one of us, wouldn't you say, Mrs. O'Neil?"

"No, I wouldn't say, Mr. Butler."

He appraised her boldly. Even the severe black mourning gown could not hide her voluptuous figure. He'd heard enough about Ravena O'Neil to deduce that she was not stingy with her charms. She was the most beautiful woman he had ever met; even more beautiful than Rhett's former wife, Scarlett O'Hara.

"How is Mrs. Bates?"

"The last time I saw her, she was fine. It's been several months."

"Oh?" It was her turn to lift an eyebrow.

"Yes, Cleo decided that America was too provincial for her tastes. She went back to France. By the way, last time I was abroad I met an old friend of yours. Jesse Farnsworth."

"How is Jesse?"

"Just fine. She's remarried, you know, to a French count."

"Dear Jesse, I'm so happy for her. She's always led such an adventuresome life."

"From what I've heard your own life has not been lackluster, exactly."

"That's all past history, like the war. Now I'm like any other middle-aged Richmond matron."

"Hardly, Mrs. O'Neil. There's no other woman in this city can qualify in the same race with you."

She met his challenging stare without blinking. "You classify women with horseflesh, Mr. Butler?"

"Not in a derogatory sense. I'm in love with beauty in whatever form it takes. The configuration of a blue-ribbon champion. The flesh of Aphrodite."

The message in his eyes and voice was clear. The Butler men were not shy or devious. Ravena felt a sensation she had not experienced since her encounter with George Parker. A tingling in the fine down on the hollow of her back and on her nape. She shivered.

He observed it. "You've taken a chill?"

"Yes, I believe I'll have Freeman light the fire."

She was relieved when Freeman entered the room with the brandy so that she could break off the duel of eyes without surrendering.

She took a glass from the silver tray and Butler took the other.

"Will there be anything else, madam?"

"No, thank you, Freeman."

When Freeman had left, Butler said, "I thought you wanted a fire?"

"I've changed my mind. A woman's prerogative, remember?" She warmed the snifter between her palms.

As she sipped the brandy, she examined him covertly over the rim of the glass. A good-looking figure of a man in his navy-blue frock coat, red waistcoat and fawn trousers. His nose and jaw too prominent to qualify him as handsome. She did not like "pretty" men, as Brian had once referred to certain Richmond fashionplates who preened and strutted at parties like peacocks.

He crossed his legs the way Brian had, in a wide angle, with the top of his boot resting on the opposite knee. The tight trousers molded to his muscular thighs. Her eyes were drawn to his crotch. She was not ashamed of her natural attraction to the opposite sex. Ravena admired men the way men admired women, always conscious of their physical attributes. It was a long time since she had looked at a man the way she was looking at Dan Butler. Her body had been dormant for more than a year. Now, like the sleeping princess in the fairy tale, she was stirring again. Awakening. Coming back to life. It felt exhilarating. She closed her eyes and swallowed the brandy. Savoring the liquid fire it sent coursing through her veins. Her flesh was hot now.

"You look as if you have a fever, Mrs. O'Neil," he observed.

She smiled. "I do believe you're right, Mr. Butler. I must be coming down with something."

His lazy smile reminded her of Brian. What it all came

down to was that every man she made love to was Brian.

"It must be contagious. I have a touch of fever myself. May I call you Ravena?"

"It would please me—Dan."

"Well, hello there!" Roger's voice called to them from the hall. He appeared in the doorway. "Freeman told me you were here, Dan. What a pleasant surprise."

Butler rose and the two men shook hands. Roger motioned him to sit down. "Here, let Freeman refreshen that drink."

Ravena yawned and said. "If you gentlemen will excuse me, I think I'll be off to bed." She nodded to Butler. "It was pleasant chatting with you, Mr. Butler. And thank you again for your kind wishes of sympathy."

"Mrs. O'Neil, it's been charming." He took her hand, bowed and kissed it. "I hope we meet soon again."

Roger laughed as he bit the end off a cigar. "Now there is a real Southern gentlemen for you."

Ravena left and the butler brought them fresh drinks. They spoke of mundane affairs, politics, the past racing season, business, travel.

"I hear you were in England this summer," Brian said. "Are things in Ireland going as badly as the papers say?"

"The Fenians have stepped up the insurrection, that's for sure. The landlords and government officials in Dublin and Ulster are afraid to walk the streets without police protection."

Roger scowled. "It's that goddamned bloody Parnell with his revolutionary talk about Home Rule and agrarian reforms! Inciting the ignorant peasants to commit violence and treason. Christ! Can you imagine what would happen if those dumb brutes were to run the country without English direction? They'd end up like a mob of bloody African savages, cannibalizing each other!"

Butler smiled tolerantly. "That's what the Romans said about the English back in 55 B.C."

"Don't play the wag, Dan. This is serious business. The biggest mistake the English ever made was to let that rebel Charles Stewart Parnell sit in the British Parliament. Where he should be sitting is in the Tower of London!"

"The Fenians are becoming active again up in New England, I understand?"

Roger pounded his fist on the arm of his chair. "Damned cheek of the bastards! They're up to something nasty, possibly another attempt to invade Canada. I tell you this country is in for real trouble unless we ship the Irish and the niggers back to where they came from."

"Roger, I don't mean to change the subject, but there's something you should know. I took a trip to Ireland, business in Tyrone. I saw your mother and father."

"That was thoughtful of you, Dan. How are they? The last letter I had from father, he wrote that mother was still suffering from her chronic hypochondria, but that the doctor said it was nothing serious."

"Yes, your mother has the typical complaints that come with old age, but she's all right. It's the Earl we should be worried about. I'm afraid it's consumption. He has such difficulty breathing that he must sleep sitting up."

Roger was genuinely distraught. "I say, that's rotten luck. The old boy never even hinted that he was ailing."

"That's how your father is, Roger. Never a complaint in his own behalf. Your mother asked me to give you this note." He took a small, pale green envelope from his jacket pocket and handed it to Roger. He opened it and took out the single sheet of matching stationery. Frowning as he read:

Dear Roger:
Since your last visit in '74 your dear father has failed considerably. The doctor fears he may not last much beyond Christmas. Now that you and Ravena have been united, I beg of you to grant your father and me what amounts to a deathbed request.
Dear Edward and Vanessa—God rest her soul—had the blessing of seeing their grandchild. Your father and I have yearned for a similar blessing for so many years. Our only grandchild, Roger. . . .

He broke off reading and looked up at Butler. "My mother wants us to bring Sabrina to Ireland."

Butler nodded solemnly. "I know. What will you do?"

Roger stood up. "Dan, I know you'll excuse me for being abrupt, but I must speak to Ravena at once."

"Of course. I'll see you before I return to Savannah."

Ravena was seated at her vanity, brushing her hair when he tapped on her bedroom door.

"It's Roger. May I speak to you?"

Her throat constricted at the thought that after all this time, he was going to break his vow and demand his marital rights. She stood up and put on a robe over her nightdress.

"Come in, Roger."

The instant she saw the grim expression on his face she realized her premise had been wrong.

"This is self-explanatory. I got it from Dan Butler." He handed her his mother's note. Ravena sat down on her vanity bench again and read it.

When she was finished she looked up. "There isn't anything to discuss, Roger. Of course you and Sabrina must go to them as soon as possible. I'd go with you, but someone must stay here to run the plantation."

"Yes, of course. I never thought of that. The leeches we have working for us would rob us blind if they were left to their own devices."

Ravena buried her face in her hands. "Poor Edward. Poor Theresa. How cruel time treats us, and with such dispatch. It only seems like last week when I went to my first ball."

His smile was wan. "The Viceroy's ball. Lord Clarendon. Where we met."

"I thought your father and my father were the two handsomest men in the room. So tall, so strong, so young, so invincible. They'd never die."

"Yes." He turned and walked slowly to the door, shoulders slumped in dejection. With his hand on the knob he turned, cleared his throat and said: "I've never thanked you properly, Ravena, for coming back here, for letting everyone believe that Sabrina is my own flesh and blood. My own child."

"She is your child now, Roger. You're her father and you've been a good father to her. She loves you."

"And I love her." He lifted his hand and covered his eyes. "If only—Well, good night, Ravena, and thank you again for allowing Sabrina to accompany me to Ireland."

"I wouldn't have it any other way, Roger." She started to rise, seized by an impulse to ask him to remain. But the words choked in her throat and he did not turn to see her outstretched hand.

Roger and Sabrina sailed for England from Portsmouth the following week. Dan Butler was there to wish them "bon voyage" when they boarded a Richmond river steamer.

He escorted Ravena back to her carriage. On the way he said casually: "Did you know I have a small summer place outside of Richmond? Right on the river and it's marvelous for boating and bathing. No more than an hour's ride from here."

"How intriguing."

"Would you care to see it?"

"I'd be delighted."

"Fine. I'll tell your coachman to go back to *Ravena*."

She overheard him tell Davis. "Mrs. O'Neil will be coming with me. We're going to call on Colonel Cooper."

He took Ravena's elbow and led her over to his surrey, drawn by two horses.

"I prefer to drive myself," he told her as he took the reins and slapped them gently on the horses' backs. "Giddyap."

She looked at him thoughtfully. "Why did you tell Davis we were going to visit the Coopers?"

He grinned. "Gallantry, pure gallantry. I was just thinking of your reputation."

She laughed. "There's little enough to think about, my reputation that is."

"A reputation is a reputation whether you happen to be the president's wife or his mistress. Different strokes for different folks."

"I like that. It sounds as if it might be Irish."

"No, it's unadulterated Butlerian. Brother Rhett."

She gave him an impish glance. "They say he's even better-looking than you."

"That's a rumor he started himself. Rhett's getting old and paunchy."

"You said your place on the river is fine for boating and bathing. It's hardly the weather for either."

Casually he put his arm around her waist. "I had neither in mind."

"Then what did you have in mind?"

"The fever we spoke of the other night. I have exactly the prescription to cure the two of us."

"Is that the truth?"

He leaned toward her and kissed her on the ear.

Their gay laughter rang out across the James River and echoed up and down the river valley.

It was, as he had promised, no more than one hour's ride. The horses turned off the road and stepped carefully down a steep incline through an arch of trees to the water's edge.

The house was more elaborate than she had expected. A rambling lodge built entirely of redwood imported from California and stone from Vermont and slate from the Hudson River Valley.

"I built it right after the war," he told her as he showed her through the rooms. "I've always felt that Richmond was my home away from home, so I wanted roots here as well as in Savannah."

"It's lovely. Reminds me of certain old homes in Ireland. There's a welcoming air about it like an inn."

He was pleased. "That's exactly what I had in mind when I designed it."

"Do your talents have no limits, Mr. Butler?"

"Scarcely, Mrs. O'Neil. Now, we're coming to the bedroom."

"Then why don't you fetch us something to drink? I'll find it myself, sir."

His laugh was deep and masculine, like Brian's laugh. "You do believe in calling a spade a spade, Mrs. O'Neil."

"Honesty saves so much time, don't you think?"

"I think you and I are going to be famous friends."

"Friends, I like that. Lovers would be the wrong definition. I don't love you and you don't love me. Good lusty friends is what we're going to be."

"Amen." He grabbed her roughly and kissed her. Her response was so galvanic that he pulled away, gasping.

"Hey, there! Easy, woman. There's an old saying in rugby: 'He lost the game in the locker room.' You wouldn't be wanting me to lose our game out here in the hall?"

She laughed. "I'd say you have more than a few games left in you, Dan."

"I'll see you shortly." He went back downstairs to the wine closet while Ravena went into the bedroom.

It was an appealing room, decorated in French provincial decor with a huge four-poster bed covered by a canopy. With rising excitement, she began to undress.

She was naked under the covers when he came back with a tray bearing two champagne glasses and a bottle of rare sparkling wine he had been saving for ten years for a very special occasion. And this was going to be a very special occasion. He knew it the moment he saw her clothing draped over a chair. He put down the tray and picked up her chemise, a frothy light undergarment made of silk, lace and ornamented with tiny colored bows.

He whistled. "The last time I saw anything like this was in Paris."

"I imagine you saw a lot of things in Paris?"

"Yes, indeed. Next trip I'll bring you back the very latest items. Fancy panties, barely nothing at all, thigh-high silk stockings and a black garter belt to match."

"All the best whores wear 'em. Well, don't just stand there, Dan Butler. With all your fine manners you ought to know it's impolite to keep a lady waiting."

Altogether the affair between Ravena and Butler endured for two years. There was never any question about their mutual fidelity. He was a restless man whose surreptitious business dealings took him out of the country five or six months every year. Ravena was a bored, lonely woman possessing a vast appetite for life. She was also obsessed. Brian had been brutally snatched away from her. And now Sabrina had been taken off to Europe. These deprivations had left her less than a whole woman and now she was engaged in a desperate search for something, anything, anyone that could help her regain her totality.

In the beginning Roger had written from the castle in Tyrone:

It is a miracle that Sabrina has wrought here. My father is eating again and sitting out on the terrace. Laughter is ringing through these dank corridors for the first time in years. And Sabrina is deliriously happy. It is as though Edward and Theresa have replaced the terrible emptiness in her life resulting from the death of your parents. Can you find it in your heart to let her remain here for a few more months?

Of course she could find it in her heart. Certainly she could not tear out the hearts of those two dear old people by depriving them of Sabrina in so short a time.

Six months went by and more letters, some from the child herself.

Dear Mommy,
     I love it here, but I miss you. We all miss you. Grandpa and Grandma send their love and their thanks. Ireland is the most beautiful place I have ever seen, even in picture books. I wish we could live here all the time. Why don't you come over here and. . . .

Six more months. More letters. A subtle change in the tone of Roger's letters.

     The political situation here is critical. It would not surprise me if these Irish savages were to launch a full-scale rebellion. If such a thing were to occur, it would undermine the very roots of the Empire. I stood on my honor when the war broke out between the States and did battle for a nation that was not my native land. I could not face myself in the mirror every morning if I were to pledge less for England and the queen. I must stand ready to do my duty if war is thrust upon us.

Butler paid Richmond a visit in the summer of 1879, and she solicited his advice.

"What can I do, Dan? I want my child."

"Then you shall have her, Ravena. I'll go and bring her back to you."

"That's a splendid gesture, and I know you're sincere, but I can't let you make such a sacrifice. You have too many responsibilities of your own. No, I'll give him six more months, and if he still persists in this procrastination, I'll go to Ireland myself."

That was the summer, too, that Jan Seedley's fifteen-year-old son spent the months of June and July at *Ravena* while his parents were vacationing in the Mediterranean. Roger had bought a colt from Nate Seedley two years earlier—the favorite of young John. Touched by the lad's

sorrow at losing his pet, Ravena had assured him that he
could see the future racer at any time his heart desired.
The result was that John had become practically a member of the family. So when his parents considered with
whom he should stay during their absence, the natural
choice was with Ravena.

She was only too glad to have a lively, happy boy in the
house to dissipate the silence and solitude. He was a big
help too, performing chores and assisting the stableman.

Ravena was affectionately amused by his obvious in-
fatuation with her. He worshipped her with his eyes, his
voice, his puppylike antics to show off and entertain her.

The first inkling she had that his feeling for her was
more than platonic was one morning when Birdy came to
her with a startling discovery. The maid was holding a
pair of black lace panties that Dan Butler had brought
her from Paris.

"What on earth are you doing with those, Birdy?"

"I found 'em in the young man's dresser drawer. I was
cleaning his room and putting stuff away; he's sloppy like
all men. And there they was."

Ravena accepted the panties soberly. "Birdy, I don't
want you to say anything about this incident to the other
servants, or anyone else."

"No, ma'am." She hesitated. "Mrs. O'Neil, you better
be careful. That boy has a lech for you."

"Don't be absurd, Birdy," Ravena scoffed. "He's a
child."

"He's a manchild, and he's got a man's dirty ideas, if
you know what I mean."

"It's all right, Birdy. I'll take care of it."

It was harder than she believed. Speaking of sex with a
man like Brian or George or Dan or any adult male sex
partner was one thing. Discussing sex with a fifteen-year-
old adolescent was more formidable.

She avoided the issue so long that its importance
dimmed, and she was able to rationalize it:

"Boys will be boys." At that age the new dramatic body
changes and urges were mysterious and confusing to both
boys and girls. John was fumbling his way through the
maturing process, and the filching of her undergarment
was a harmless expression of his aspirations to manhood.

Then an incident occurred that compelled her to confront John with his problem. One night she was in her dressing room preparing for bed when she heard a thump on one wall. On the other side of the wall was a linen closet, and she suspected that a rat was prowling about the house. On two occasions a servant had reported sighting the big rodents around the barn and in the storage basement under the pantry. She continued removing her clothes and slipped a nightgown over her head.

She was hanging up her dress when, as if by magnetism, her eyes were drawn to a blemish in the cedarwood paneling. It appeared to her at first glimpse that a wood knot had been dislodged from its hole. Sharper scrutiny revealed that it was too perfectly round and there were traces of sawdust around the edges.

A peephole! Intuitively the answer snapped into her mind. She dashed out of the dressing room across to the bedroom door and flung it open.

Just as the linen-closet door swung open and John emerged, cringing when he saw her.

"Mrs. O'Neil! I—I—I—"

"Stop stuttering, John. What were you doing in there?"

He was panic-stricken. Trying to answer but his vocal cords were paralyzed and he kept clutching his Adam's apple and gagging.

"Never mind. As if I didn't know what you were doing. Peeping at me through that hole you bored in the wall from the linen closet. You did bore that hole, John? Don't lie to me."

He gulped and nodded. His face was crimson with shame.

"You ought to be ashamed of yourself. And I always thought you were a friend of mine. Friends don't spy on one another."

He wrung his hands and fell to his knees, shaking his head in vigorous denial. He found his voice.

"No, no, you don't understand. I—I—I—I'm in love with you!" Blurting it out!

Ravena was nonplussed. She looked up and down the dim hall. It was almost midnight, and the servants were long in bed.

"Look, get on your feet and come into my room. This

is something that can't be talked about in the hall, John."

He followed her obediently and she closed the door behind them. She pointed to a chair facing the bed.

"Sit down, John."

He did and she put on her robe and sat on the edge of the bed.

"Now what is this nonsense that you love me?"

Before he couldn't speak, and now he babbled on compulsively: "I do love you. I do! I think about you all the time. I dream about you." His eyes filled up with tears and he covered his face with his hands. "I even stole a pair of your—your underwear, and I make believe—I make believe—I can't say it, oh, I'm so dirty!"

"Now calm down, John," she said gently. "You're not dirty. You're just growing up."

"I don't like growing up," he said miserably. It makes you want to do such terrible things."

"Sexual desire is not terrible. It's the most natural feeling in the world. When you're older and come to understand it and learn how to control your desires, then you'll discover it's one of life's richest experiences."

"I doubt it. Anyway, I'm in love with you. You're the most beautiful girl in the entire world."

Ravena smiled. "Thank you, that's one of the nicest compliments ever paid to me, John. But you see, I am decidedly *not* a girl. I am a woman. A much older woman than you are a boy. Someday you'll meet a pretty girl and the two of you will know it the instant you touch hands. You'll know it's love."

"What girl would ever love the likes of me? My ears stick out. My nose is too big. I'm clumsy. My legs are too long."

Ravena laughed softly. "At your age all boys, and girls, exaggerate their slightest imperfections. Do you know when I was fifteen I thought my legs were too long, and I was always tripping over my feet?"

"You *did*?" His eyes were round with wonder.

"Of course. It's just you're at that gawky age, John. Like the colts in the meadow. Do you think they're ugly because they're ungainly?"

"No, they're beautiful."

"And so are you, John."

He blushed. "Aw, Mrs. O'Neil, gee! I'm not *beautiful*! Girls are beautiful, the way you are."

Her heart went out to him, a warm rush of blood through her breast. As she studied him, she realized that he looked a good deal the way Brian had at fifteen. Impulsively she stood up and went over to him. She stroked his dark hair. Softly she said: "The girl who finally gets you will be very lucky, John."

He squeezed his eyes shut and shook his head. "No, it will never happen. I can't even speak to a girl without stammering and getting red, and they all end up making fun of me."

"They're not making fun of you. That's a way girls have of covering up their own embarrassment."

"You really think so?"

"Stand up, John." She had the sensation again. A sense of anticipation and some anxiety. An intuition that when she turned the next corner, there would be waiting for her —what? who? The suspense was unbearable.

The boy rose hesitantly. "Yes, ma'am."

"Why, you're as tall as I am." She put up a hand and touched his flaming cheek. He recoiled as if she had touched him with a hot poker.

"Don't be so jumpy." Her hand slid around to the back of his neck and caressed the short hairs there.

"M—M—Mrs. O—O—O'Neil," he moaned and he began to tremble violently.

She pulled his head toward her and kissed him tenderly on the lips. He would have collapsed if she had not supported him.

"Here, we can't have you falling down every time a woman kisses you. Come along." She took his hand and led him to the bed. He was a puppet in her hands and she had to manipulate his every action. She unbuttoned his shirt. Trousers. Shoes and socks. He whimpered and clutched his underpants when she tried to remove them.

She smiled encouragingly. "Maybe I can persuade you to take them off yourself." In a leisurely fashion, she untied the sash of her robe, let it fall to the floor. Still smiling she bent over and grasped the hem of her nightgown and slowly pulled it up over her body and head. She cast it aside and stood before him naked. The first naked woman John Seedley had ever seen. She held out her hands.

"The underpants?"

He needed no further encouragement after that. He was a fine, healthy young male in every respect. A veritable stud. An eager if awkward pupil. She drew him over her, cradling his still-trembling body between her thighs.

Like a thirsty horse at the water trough, he couldn't get enough, and had to be disciplined.

"Now John, I think your instruction is over for tonight."

He clung to her fiercely. "I don't want to leave you! I never want to leave you! I don't care what you say, I *love* you more than anything else in the world!"

She pulled his cheek to her breast and stroked his hair. "You only think that, John. You're running over with gratitude because of the help I gave you tonight."

"Can I come here tomorrow night again?"

"No, John," she explained gently. "You can never come here again. Don't you see, now that you know that you are attractive to females and have confidence that you can please them—you did please me, John—you can look for a girl nearer your age. You can look her in the eye without stammering or blushing, because you are a man, John. As manly as any boy you know. Maybe more so."

He lay still for a while, saying nothing; she could almost hear the wheels turning in his head. Then he pulled himself up on one elbow and smiled down at her.

"I know what you mean now, Mrs. O'Neil. No, it wouldn't be right for me to expect anything more from you than what you've given me tonight. But I tell you one thing, I will never forget you or what happened tonight. It will always be the most beautiful memory of my whole life, and that's the truth."

She touched his cheek. "Thank you, John, I like to think it is the truth. And I will never forget you either. You'll always be a symbol of—" She hesitated. "No, it's too fragile to put into words. Now you had better get dressed and go back to your room."

When he was ready to depart, she remembered something else. "John, there's a chore I'd like you to do for me tomorrow morning."

"Yes, ma'am, anything at all."

"There's a hole in my dressing room wall I'd like patched up."

He mumbled something unintelligible and rushed out of the room. Ravena laughed and lay back on the bed still warm from his feverish young flesh. She pressed a hand to the indentation where he had lain beside her.

She felt remarkably refreshed. Young, vibrant, eager to get back to the business of living. If she had performed a service for John, he, in turn, had done one for her as well. The muddy indecision that had been infecting her mind for so many lethargic months had dissipated.

She was suddenly sick of Richmond. The South was a malady in the blood. It recalled a story she had read as a child about Odysseus and his crew in the Land of the Lotus-Eaters. The magic blossom that destroyed all incentive and cast a pall of indolent euphoria over all who partook of it. In the nearly four years since she had returned to Richmond, Ravena had led a life of self-indulgence, one party after another, one affair after another, and finally she had tired of making small talk with casual bed partners. Only Dan Butler had endured, and it had been over three months since she and he had made love. No, enjoyed sex!

She had vowed she would allow Roger to keep Sabrina with her grandparents for six more months; only two had passed. She sat up with determination.

The hell with Roger! I want my child, and I'm going to get her! The sooner the better!

No more idle procrastination.

CHAPTER TWO

It was a bitter cold day in mid-January 1880 when Dan Butler arrived in New York on a bit of mysterious business that intrigued him. He took a hansom cab from Grand Central Station to a fashionable building on Park Avenue.

Stepping out of the cab, he turned up the collar of his coat to ward off the icy blast of fine snow that stung his face like needles.

He hurried into the building and walked to the elevator.

"Levi International," he told the operator.

He got out at the third floor and entered the reception room. A pretty girl wearing a black skirt and a high-necked starched white blouse greeted him.

"Mr. Butler, it's good to see you again. Mrs. Casey is expecting you. Go right in."

He went down a long corridor and turned right into a shorter hall. At the end of the hall was a massive oak door with a bronze nameplate:

REBECCA L. CASEY
PRESIDENT

He went through the doorway into another reception room where a secretary was posted at a desk in front of still another oak door.

"Hi Sally," he said jovially. "You're looking as gorgeous as ever."

The girl, wearing the identical outfit of the receptionist, smiled. "Don't butter me up, Mr. Butler. Last time you were in New York you promised to take me to Tony Pastor's Restaurant and then you jilted me at the last moment."

He bent over and pinched her cheek. "Business before pleasure, my sweet. Sorry about that. What about tonight?"

"I already have a date."

"So break it. See you later. I don't want to keep her ladyship waiting."

He passed through the door into a spacious dark paneled office, luxuriously appointed with soft leather chairs and couches. A mahogany desk sat opposite the door in front of a bay window. The dark-haired woman looked up when he entered and smiled.

"Danny boy, I'm grateful you could make it. I know how busy you must be these days."

He grinned back. "After your mysterious letter, wild horses couldn't have kept me away. You're looking wonderful, Becky."

She stood up and came around the desk, turning up her cheek for his kiss. "I'm gaining weight, too much weight." She tugged at the hem of her short mannish jacket. Scotch tweed with a slim skirt to match.

"I like my women with meat on them."

"That's what Larry always says, but I never believe what an Irishman says." She winked. "Or a smuggler."

He postured indignantly. "Entrepreneur, you mean."

She laughed. "Come sit with me and I'll tell you what this deal is all about. But first a drink and some small talk between friends. You know where the bar is. I'll have the usual, port."

He walked to a cabinet that opened into a fold-out bar with an array of bottles, decanters and glassware. He poured her wine and three fingers of scotch for himself and carried them over to the couch where she was sitting.

"Well, Becky, this is sure a far cry from the loft on Fourteenth Street."

"And Rebecca Casey is a far cry from mousy Becky Levitz." She took a cigarette from a jade box on the coffee table. He lit it for her and a cigar for himself.

"We never would have come as far if it hadn't been for you, Dan."

"Not so," he denied it. "Levitz made the best goddamned uniforms the army ever had. You did me a favor."

"So it was a mutual good fortune." She lifted her glass. "To the future."

"Amen." They drank. "How are Larry and the children?"

"Larry is in San Francisco and the girls are at college. Radcliffe. Who are you seeing these days?"

He grinned rakishly. "Still playing the field. All right, now what are you up to, my girl? And what am I doing here?"

"I want to place an order with you, Dan."

His left eyebrow curled up. "That kind of business, heh?"

"Your kind of business. I want one hundred thousand brass buttons."

He frowned. "Now that's an anticlimax if I ever heard one. What's so mysterious and hush-hush about brass buttons?"

"These buttons will be very special. The insignia on the buttons will be IRB."

It clicked into place for him. "Uniform buttons! IRB. The Irish Republican Brotherhood!"

She nodded. "What do you know about the IRB?"

"They're a radical group of revolutionaries in Ireland as well as Irish-Americans here in the United States. The IRB is dedicated to overthrowing British authority in Ireland and establishing a free republic. Right after the war they formed an army in upstate New York and Vermont and invaded Canada with the intention of applying pressure on England to restore Home Rule in Ireland. It turned out to be a damned fiasco. Don't tell me these buttons are for the uniforms of a resurrected IRB army? If so, you'd better get your money up front."

"Don't be cynical, my friend. In the past fifteen years the IRB had been quietly growing and consolidating its membership. They've inaugurated a hierarchy of leadership. The top man is the 'head center.' He's got his cabinet and then there are 'state centers' and 'district centers' and 'circles' which are the local chapters. It's all very disciplined and they hold elections and have yearly conventions to elect delegates."

He stared at her in amazement. "Since when have you been so interested in subversive organizations like the IRB? All this knowledgeable talk of 'head centers' and 'circles' and whatever! You astonish me, Rebecca."

She compressed her lips. "In a way we are brothers and sisters under the skin, the Irish and Jews. In both cases our homelands have been usurped by infidels. I am also very active in Zionism, the movement to reconstitute the Jewish nation. The Promised Land of Moses and David and Solomon."

"I can't think of two more worthy causes," he admitted. "But I hate to see these poor Irishmen marching over the border and into certain defeat."

"Not so certain and not-so-poor Irishmen. They have millions in backing."

He whistled. "Millions? I don't believe it. Some mick is feeding you blarney."

"It's true. Some of their supporters are extremely wealthy men. In fact one of them is due here right now." She consulted the wall clock. "Two-thirty, I wanted to have some time alone with you."

"Who is he and why is he coming here?"

"To deliver a cash payment for the uniforms. It has to be a cash transaction."

He chuckled. "Now, you know better than to have to tell me that. All right, I'll run over to France next time I'm in England. How soon do you need them?"

"One month, six weeks at the most."

"What's this chap's name?"

"I don't know. I've never met him in person. We've dealt through the district center. He's the regional center for the Northeastern states, and he goes by the code name Red Hugh. They dare not use real names."

"Naturally. Red Hugh. Quaint."

There was a knock on the door and the secretary poked her head into the room. "There's a gentleman here says he has an appointment with you, Mrs. Casey."

"Show him in, Sally, please."

Rebecca stood up and smoothed down her skirt. And then he came through the door grinning like a jackanapes, big as life and scarcely changed in the twenty years since she had seen him off to war.

Brian Hugh O'Neil!

Red Hugh, of course!

He'd told her once about his ancestor, the legendary Irish hero Red Hugh O'Neil, the first Earl of Tyrone.

Rebecca staggered backwards and clapped her hands to the sides of her head, leaning back against the desk for support.

"It can't be! My eyes are playing tricks with me! Or else you're a ghost!"

Brian laughed and walked toward her with his arms outstretched. "Your eyes are sound and so is my flesh and bones. Here, let's have a kiss and you'll find out for yourself."

She submitted limply to his bear hug and wet kiss on the mouth. His lips were cold and wet from the snow.

"There now, Becky, what do you think now? Did it measure up to the ones in the old days?" He looked at Butler and winked. "We've exchanged a few busses, Becky and I, isn't that so, love?"

She kept shaking her head in wonder and touching him. "It is you, my God! We heard you had been killed."

"Those reports were grossly exaggerated. How's Larry? And I understand you have a couple of young Caseys?"

"Larry's out of town, and the girls are hardly 'young 'uns.' Eighteen and sixteen."

"I know. Jenny and Rose."

"How do you know that?"

"I know a good deal about you, Rebecca. You and Larry and Levi International. You shouldn't have deleted the '-itz.' It had character. Before I contacted you about that order I made some inquiries." He glanced at Butler. "Is he cleared?"

"Dan Butler is a man who can keep a secret. Dan, shake hands with Brian O'Neil."

There was no response. Butler sat riveted to the couch, his hand clenched around his glass, staring at Brian. His expression was stunned.

"Dan, what is it?" Becky asked in concern. "Why are you looking at Brian that way?"

He swallowed a few times before he was able to speak in a weak voice. "You said he was a ghost when he walked in here. He *is* a ghost!"

"How is that, Dan?" Brian was curious.

"Because I'm a close friend of your family. Roger O'Neil and his wife Ravena. They were told you were murdered in San Francisco back in '76."

He looked grave. "Yes, I know, and I had to let them believe it. How is Ravena? And my—" he caught himself; it had almost come out: "*My daughter*." "How is Sabrina?"

"She's fine, a beautiful girl like her mother. Right now she's in England visiting with her grandparents the Earl of Tyrone and his Lady."

"With her mother?" he said evenly.

"Well, as a matter of fact, she went abroad with her father. Ravena joined them only last September."

Roger posing as her father. It hurt like a wound! His gaze fell on the open bar. "I think I could use a drink. Is it all right, Becky?"

"Let me get it for you."

From various sources he had managed to piece together some of what had transpired after he ran away from Maui. Somehow Roger had tracked down Ravena and persuaded her to return to Richmond. No doubt he had concocted the report of his, Brian's, death himself; there had been no police record. And Ravena, believing it, had concluded that the best course for her and the child would be to return to her family in Richmond.

But to let Roger pretend that he was Sabrina's father, that was something she would have to account for!

Rebecca brought him the drink. "Thanks, love." He gulped it down gratefully.

"Where have you been all these years?" Butler asked.

"Prospecting for gold, among other things."

"Did you find any?"

"The richest vein ever struck in the Black Hills. My partners and I, we're all millionaires, times over. That's not bragging. The money came from luck, not hard work. But I intend to put it to good use, not for myself, but for humanity."

"Beginning with the IRB."

"Has she briefed you?"

"In general. What are your plans?"

Brian smiled wryly. "No offense, Dan, but that information is classified. Can you supply Rebecca with the buttons?"

"Easily. I'll push up my trip to England by a month, which means I'll be sailing in two weeks."

"Good. The sooner the better."

"When is your deadline?"

"April One."

They spoke at length about production schedule, delivery

and price, and by three-thirty all of the details had been resolved. Butler mixed another round of drinks and they chatted about casual topics.

"Ravena speaks of you often, Brian. She'll be surprised and overjoyed to learn you're alive and well," Butler said. "You do intend to let them know, don't you?"

Brian was cautious. He had no way of knowing how much of the story Ravena had related. Butler had penetrating eyes and the sly, wise look of a Cheshire cat. He side-stepped the question.

"You said they're all in Europe."

"Ravena plans to return in the spring to Richmond."

"How about her parents, the Duke and Duchess?"

"They're both dead."

"I'm sorry to hear it." He looked down into his glass, thinking about his own father and mother. They couldn't have too many years to look forward to. He was happy that they had the opportunity to know Sabrina. Such a gesture was out of character for Roger.

He asked Butler, "Was it the sole reason my brother went back to Ireland, so that our parents could see their granddaughter?"

Butler saw through him, he could tell from his bemused expression. "Yes, Roger is mellowing in his middle years. Your mother requested it, and he was quick to oblige her, take my word for it. You know he dotes on Sabrina."

Another hard blow. His mouth was stiff.

"Roger, a doting—father." He could barely bring himself to say it. "Yes, he must have mellowed."

He looked at his watch. "I'm sorry to break up this pleasant conversation, but I have another appointment in a half-hour. Rebecca, I'd like it if you would have supper with me tonight. We can go to the Fraunces Tavern, for old times' sake."

"I'd love it, Brian."

He kissed Rebecca's cheek and shook hands with Butler. "Be quick with the buttons."

Butler smiled. "Depend on it. Say, maybe the next time we'll meet it'll be in Richmond."

Brian rubbed his jaw. "It will depend on a lot of things. Good-bye. Rebecca, where can I pick you up this evening, and what time?"

"I'll be ready by seven. Our house is on Sixty-Eighth Street. Just off Fifth Avenue. Tell your driver you want to go to Casey Mansion, he'll know."

Brian made a bow. "Casey Mansion, what about that, Butler? This little lady has really come up in the world."

"Haven't we all, you lowly apprentice Irishman?" she responded with affection. She turned to Butler. "Can you imagine, Dan, when we were working our fingers to the bone on the East Side, he used to tell me he was born of royal lineage, and it became the joke of the shop. And now I find out he was telling the truth. *Oy, oy, oy,* you Irishers, as my father used to say."

There was a twinkle in his eyes. "For all you know I'm pulling your leg now when I say I'm a millionaire."

"Yes, and maybe you're planning to stick me with the balance on the uniforms?"

"It's a thought." He winked. "Good-bye now. Butler, have a good voyage. Becky, I'll see you at seven."

The supper party at Fraunces Tavern was a pleasant affair. Despite the passing of twenty years Brian and Rebecca effortlessly picked up their relationship as if no more than twenty days had intervened. Reminiscences flew back and forth across the table through every course. Coffee and cordials topped off the sumptuous meal. They were both warm and mellow and Brian felt it was appropriate to introduce a topic that both had avoided up until now.

"Do you remember the Fourth of July picnic?" he asked.

Her enormous dark eyes were full of childish innocence. "Which Fourth of July? We had picnics every year."

Before she could pull back her hand on the table, he clasped it and stared deep into her eyes, through the mask of innocence.

His voice was soft. "You know the one I mean."

Two bright spots of color stained her cheeks. "Indeed I do. A gentleman wouldn't have mentioned it."

He smiled. "I've been accused of many things, but not of being a gentleman."

"Brian O'Neil, you haven't changed at all."

"Neither have you, Becky. You're still as beautiful as you were the day I kissed you good-bye at the rail terminal."

"Liar! I'm middle-aged and fat."

"Fat?" Boldly he scrutinized her, that part of her visible above the table. She wore a chic evening gown, a Paris creation, that bared her powdered shoulders and a provocative portion of her uplifted bosom. "You're perfect to my taste. Don't you remember I used to tease you because you were so skinny?"

"I was not skinny. Slender is the word."

He shrugged. "Have it your way. I like the way you are now."

"You shouldn't be speaking to me that way, Brian O'Neil. I'm a married woman with two grown children. Happily married."

Yet it was obvious to him from her radiant expression that she enjoyed the compliment.

"I'm glad you and Larry are happily married. Did he ever tell you when the two of us lived in the flat over the shop above the store that we did battle over you?"

She covered her mouth with a hand and began to laugh, her shoulders shaking in mirth. "Yes, he did. Oh, this is so embarrassing. Please, let's change the subject."

"All right, then let's go back a bit. You *do* remember *that* particular Fourth of July?"

She pulled her hand away from him. "Brian, you are outrageous!" She was blushing furiously.

He laughed and shook his head. "I am, I admit it. It was always so much fun teasing you, you were so shy and prim."

There was a hint of mischief now in her as well as him.

"It would have served me better if I had been shy and prim that day at the picnic."

His smile was quizzical. "That's not true. The both of us were served well that day, and many days after it."

"It's getting late, and I have four morning appointments. Do you mind?"

The game was over. Not permanently he vowed.

"Of course." He signaled the waiter. "Our check, please."

It was bitter cold outside, and while the snow had stopped, the fierce wind whipped what had accumulated in the streets about with the gusto of a full-fledged blizzard. Bundled up in fur travelers' robes inside the closed carriage, Rebecca was still freezing.

"Hear my teeth chattering?"

"This won't do." Brian removed her robe and his robe, folded them together and pulled the double-covering around them. Her body was pressed tightly against his. He tucked in the sides under her thighs and buttocks.

"This way we utilize our body heat to better advantage."

"Is that a fact?" She turned her face up to his and their eyes met. So close he could feel her breath on his throat.

"You're warming up, don't deny it, Becky. See, you've stopped shivering."

"Yes. I'm warmer. It feels good."

He slipped a hand under the robes and put it on her thigh. "By the time we get back to your place, you'll be warmer still. Then what a shame that you must climb into a cold and lonely bed."

"Brian, please don't talk like that."

He sensed it was a wooden protest. A muscle fluttered under his hand on her leg. She did not draw back when he bent and kissed her. Her lips were cold at first, but quickly her blood warmed them. She moaned and responded, opening her mouth to receive his tongue.

When the kiss ended, Rebecca closed her eyes and turned her head away. A tear rolled down her cheek from each eye, glistening like ice crystals in the eerie luminous light reflecting off the snow from the three-quarter moon.

"Why are you crying?"

"I feel so cheap, doing what I just did. Me a married woman with grown children!"

He repressed a smile. *Me a married woman with grown children!*

"Marriage and children have nothing to do with it, Becky. You're a mature, healthy, lovely female animal with the needs and desires that are natural to a woman. Be truthful, one of the reasons that you work so hard at the business is because hard work is a substitute for physical satisfaction, am I right? Larry spends most of the year traveling for the firm. You derive little sexual gratification from your stacks of orders and invoices, and that's a fact, my girl!"

She turned back to him again, wiping her eyes with a gloved finger. "You've a nerve speaking so disrespectfully to me, you cheeky mick!"

He threw back his head and laughed. "Now, that's the

spirit. Say, do you remember the pillow fights we used to have in the old flat? Now there's a sport that will quicken the blood on a night such as this."

She threw back the robe and slapped his hand off her thigh. "Glory be, I'm burning up as it is!" She drew away from him.

The coach stopped, and the driver opened the hatch in the ceiling and called down to them: "We're here. The Casey Mansion."

"Well?" He looked at her solemnly with his head cocked to one side, a crooked boyish expression, an appealing look.

Rebecca compressed her lips and said with severity: "Brian O'Neil, I won't have you treating me like the sluts you no doubt have been consorting with all over the world for the past twenty years. If you think for one moment that I'm going to be taken in by your blarney—if you think for one moment that I am going to let you sleep with me, you are—" He stopped the tirade with an unexpected kiss.

When it was over, he said, "Please continue. If I think for one moment that you are going to let me sleep with you, I am—"

She slumped in resignation. "You're right. Come along. We'll put you in one of the spare bedrooms and tell the servants that you'll be staying here until you leave New York. Tomorrow you can have your things brought over from the hotel. Oh yes, one other thing: Make certain you are back in your own room before dawn."

Brian laughed softly and shook his head. "Madam Executive. Yes, you are a take-charge lady. When you make up your mind to do something you make sure it's done right."

There was a bittersweet quality about their lovemaking that transcended passion. Brian felt like a prodigal returning home after a span of years, entering the home of his youth. Touching beloved objects in a bedroom that had been kept intact for him by one who never once doubted his return.

Afterward Rebecca cried softly into the pillow. He held her close. "Conscience?" he asked.

"No, God damn it! I don't feel guilty at all. I feel wonderful and terrible too. Why do things have to end, you and I, the way we were? Damn the war! Damn growing old!"

"It's only the outer layers that grow old, Becky. The heart never grows old, if you fill it with youthful desires. Don't damn what you are, Larry's wife. It was meant to be that way. You're better off with him. I never would have made the business what he did."

She pressed herself against him fiercely. "Make love to me again, Brian. I wish we could spend all the time you're here in bed."

He laughed. "I wouldn't be in very good shape to battle the British if we did that, my girl."

He pressed his lips to her left breast, and his hand stroked over the swell of her belly across her mound of love and down. Her hand found him and moved rhythmically up and down.

He remained at Casey Mansion three more days. He and Becky ate at Delmonico's, went to the theater and opera, heard the Swedish Nightingale, Jenny Lind, sing at the concert hall. Best of all, they made love.

On the last night she was frigid at first. Nothing he did could arouse her.

"I don't want you to leave," she said finally. "It's twisting me up inside."

"My darling, we both agreed this was to be a short and happy fling. Don't spoil it now. I must be in Philadelphia by tomorrow night for a meeting of the high command."

"I know. I despise myself for being the weak and bitchy clinging vine I've always held in contempt."

"You're not that at all. You're used to having your own way in matters, but in this you have no say."

She smiled. "I know, and now that I've resolved that, let's get on with what we started out to do. Tonight it must be special. You lie down and relax, that's it, on your back."

She kneeled beside him so that her big breasts dangled over his loins like ripe melons. Braced one hand between his thighs, the other on his muscle-rippled belly. Head descending until her seeking lips found him.

They ate breakfast together in her dining room next morning before he departed, served by a maid and butler.

"You have a fine day to travel," she said.

A thaw had settled over the city after the big storm and

the icicles, hanging like stalactites from the eaves outside the windows, shed torrents of water melting in the blazing sunshine.

"I'll give you an address where I can be reached with regard to the uniforms."

"About that, Brian, I'd like to make a contribution to your cause. Say, half of the balance due."

He covered her hand with his. "You're a generous woman, Becky, in more ways than one. All of our people appreciate what you are doing."

The butler appeared and cleared his throat discreetly. "Mr. O'Neil, your carriage is out in front."

"Thank you, Parker." He rose and wiped his mouth with a napkin. "Don't get up, Becky. Finish your meal." He bent over her and kissed her chastely on the forehead. "I'm sorry I didn't get to see Larry. Give him my best and maybe after this is over, we can have another reunion, the three of us."

"I'll look forward to that, Brian. I don't like good-byes."

"The Hawaiians have a word, *aloha*. It means whatever you want it to mean—hello, good-bye, and even God be with you."

She smiled. "So then 'Aloha.' "

CHAPTER THREE

It was the final meeting of the top brass in the organization. Present were the national head center; the state centers from Vermont, New York, Pennsylanvia, Delaware and Maryland; seven district centers and the regional center for the northeastern states as well as Delaware, the eminent Red Hugh.

Emulating the example established in the old days in Ireland by the disorganized rebel gangs members were never identified by their given names; only by code names such as Red Hugh.

The head center, General Cauliflower, a reference to a deformity incurred in too many brawls and too much battering around the ears, was concluding his introductory remarks. "And for the benefit of the three district centers who arrived here two days late—through no fault of their own; they had Pinkerton Agents on their trail—I respectfully request that Colonel Red Hugh repeat the briefing he gave at yesterday afternoon's session. For me own part, I'd like to review it myself. Colonel?"

Brian walked over to the situation map thumbtacked to a board and propped up on an easel. It showed the northeastern section of the United States. He picked up a pointer and placed the tip at a point on the border between New York State and Canada.

"The First Army under Captain Bandy Legs will push off from Rouses Point here on Lake Champlain at three A.M. on the morning of April One. That force will number about two thousand men.

"The Second Army led by Major Pin Whistle, numbering twenty-five hundred men, will strike across the border, same time, here at Enosburg Falls in Vermont, at the forty-fifth parallel.

"The two strike forces will converge in a pincer move-

ment on the Canadian militia. Our mission, to capture
Montreal."

He spoke for more than an hour, emphasizing that political strategy must take precedence over military strategy.

"Obviously we can't expect to overrun Canada with
forty-five-hundred men, but we can raise hell the way old
Jeb Stuart and Phil Sheridan did in the war, rampaging
behind the enemy's lines. It's the kind of action that will
give Parnell leverage in parliamentary debate."

General Cauliflower chuckled. "That man he can talk
the ears off a brass monkey. Sooner or later the British
will have to give him his way just to stop his filibustering."

"He'll need all the help he can get from us on this side
of the ocean," Brian noted. "So the real objective of
Operation Emerald Isle is to make a big splash in the
papers, scare the pants off the Canucks so they'll demand
that the British repeal their repressive policies in Ireland
—to stop such harassments from the Irish Republican
Brotherhood against Canada."

"We can't equip that many men with weapons and
explosives," one of the centers objected.

"That brings me to the other mission, Operation Gunpowder. Have any of you ever heard of the Du Pont
Company?"

There was a modest showing of hands.

"They make explosives," a center said.

"The biggest manufacturer of explosives in the United
States, and that's where our gunpowder is coming from.
We're going to raid the Du Pont factory at Wilmington,
Delaware, on March 15. It will be a lark. They've almost
no security at the plant, just one old night watchman."

A murmur of enthusiastic approval went around the
ranks.

"How do we carry the booty away?" someone asked.
"They'll have the police and the army after us as soon as
we leave. Can't move fast with wagons loaded with
explosives."

"We're not taking it overland, Mr. Spindles," Brian
retorted. "We're smuggling it out by sea. There'll be a ship
in port at Wilmington waiting to load us aboard. We'll
move the stuff on the Du Pont's own barges down Brandywine Creek to Delaware Harbor."

From a paper sack he removed a bluish-gray stick about two inches in diameter and eight inches long. "Anybody know what this is?"

All of the men present had varying degrees of skill in the gentle art of demolitions.

Mr. Cauliflower was anxious. "Jesus! Mr. Red Hugh! Colonel! Be that dynamite?"

"It is, sir. Wood pulp, nitrate mixed with nitroglycerin. The most formidable explosive ever devised."

"Yes, and I've seen the infernal stuff detonated by a strong wind!" said Captain Stout, a portly redhead with a bulbous nose.

"Aye!" the chorus went around.

"We used it in Ulster ten years back, and we killed more of our own than we did the Limeys!"

Brian smiled and held up his hands for order. "Gentlemen, gentlemen, please, this is something revolutionary that the Du Pont brothers have developed. They've succeeded in taming dynamite, as it were. Here, let me demonstrate."

To the horror of the assembled delegates, he threw down the stick on the wood floor as hard as he could.

"Jesus, Mary and Joseph!" uttered the head circle.

Brian laughed. "No need to panic, gentlemen. The only thing that can set this little gem off is a fuse on a percussion cap."

Now they all flocked around him excitedly.

"Do the English have it?"

"Nobody has it yet. There's just this one batch they made up for the War Department, but it hasn't been shipped yet. One of our circles is an employee of the Du Pont Company. And it will never be shipped if we have anything to say about it. Do I make myself clear?"

"*AYE!*" The ovation was thunderous.

On the evening of March 14, 1881, sixteen men clad in the uniforms of the US Cavalry rode into Wilmington, Delaware, and headed for Brandywine Creek.

It was seven o'clock when the Du Pont plant came in view. Row upon row of squat stone structures with walls three feet thick.

As they advanced at a trot up the dirt road that led to the main gate, a watchman armed with a shotgun stepped out of his sentry box.

"What in tarnation is happening?" he demanded. "Are we at war again?"

Brian O'Neil dressed in the uniform of a full colonel addressed him: "Army Intelligence has uncovered information that the Du Pont warehouses are the target of a band of saboteurs."

"Saboteurs!" The old man was goggle-eyed. "None of the Du Ponts said anything to me about it."

"Security reasons, Mr. Hester. The Du Ponts are fully aware of the threat and they requested the War Department to post a military guard around the plant until such time as the vandals have been captured."

The guard shook his head. "I'll be a buzzard's butt. Who in hell are these saboteurs?"

Brian's eyes twinkled. "Rowdy members of the outlawed Irish Republican Army."

"You don't say? The same bunch that invaded Canada after the war?"

"The very same. A dangerous bunch, let me tell you. But don't worry, Mr. Hester. We'll be here to back you up if trouble arises."

"That's a relief, Colonel."

"We're going to water our horses at the stream now."

Hester stood aside. "Go on through, boys."

Brian whispered to a man wearing sergeant's stripes. "Sergeant Lightfoot, better post two men here to keep an eye on the old coot. He just might be on to us and is putting on an act. I don't want him harmed, but don't let him out of their sight."

"Ride on, men," he ordered the squad.

For appearance's sake they struck a camp down on the banks of the Brandywine, watered the horses and tethered them to trees. Then Brian, Sergeant Lightfoot, Lieutenant Baldy and Corporal Brass set forth on a scout of the plant.

They established the location of the warehouses where both the gunpowder and the recently invented "tame" dynamite were stored.

The lock on the door of the first building was simple to

pick. But the thick stone walls of the windowless building where the dynamite resided and the heavy oaken door posed difficulties.

"I can't solve this lock at all," conceded Corporal Brass, the breaking-and-entering expert, after struggling with it for a half-hour.

Abruptly Brian laughed. "I'll be damned! What a bunch of ninnies we are! We can't see the forest for the trees! They've gone and put the hinges on the outside, can you imagine?"

It was then a simple matter of knocking out the hinge pins and lifting off the heavy door.

At nine o'clock with darkness fast settling over the wood, Brian visited the gate. The watchman and the two IRB members were engaged in a game of mumblety-peg with a hunting knife. The shotgun was propped up against the side of the shack. Casually he picked it up and examined it.

"Nice piece you have here, Mr. Hester."

"Yup, I bagged myself plenty of ducks with that li'l ol' girl. Betsy Sue, I call her. She's like a pet to me."

Brian brought up the muzzle in his direction. "Behave yourself and you won't get hurt, Mr. Hester. All right, boys, tie him up."

"What in tarnation!" He gaped at Brian. "You ain't soldiers, are you? Them uniforms are phonies."

"You're a very astute fellow, Mr. Hester."

"Then who are you?"

"The rowdy bunch of Irishmen who are going to sabotage this factory. Will you please tell the Du Ponts to arrange with the newspapers to print an itemization of what we're taking from here. I assure them that they will be reimbursed in full."

Under cover of darkness the operation was executed with neatness and dispatch. When three barges had been packed to capacity with cases of dynamite and drums of gunpowder, they proceeded single file downstream to the Delaware River.

It was three A.M. when the three laden barges sidled up to the square rigger anchored outside of Port Penn.

"Ahoy!" Brian called out to the lookout. "Will you tell your skipper that Colonel Red Hugh has arrived and requests permission to come aboard with my men."

"Aye, aye, Colonel. We been expectin' yer."

A fine Irish brogue. Brian grinned.

Soon after, while the crew was unloading the barges, Brian sat in the master's cabin with his old friend Captain Casey.

"More than five years it's been, Brian, me lad, since you walked off the *Nelly Bligh* in Frisco. I'm hearing you've done very well for yourself."

"I've done well indeed. How about yourself? You could have floored me with a feather when I learned that you were a member of the Brotherhood."

"Aye." He sucked his pipe. "I got to thinkin' after that voyage from Maui to Frisco. All the talkin' we did about Ireland and England. Now, I never was one to meddle in politics. I minded my own business, live and let live."

Brian smiled. "With a name like Casey, Ireland is very much your business."

"Aye. I came to realize that. And as a ship's captain I've been able to make a modest contribution to the cause."

"It's you who's modest, not your contribution. You've been invaluable to the Brotherhood. Look what you're doing now. It wouldn't have been possible without you and your ship on our side."

"I'm grateful to have the chance to help. How is that wonderful wife of yours? Surely you're reunited?"

"I'm afraid not, Captain. It's a long story and I'll save it until we're underway. Let's go on deck and see how the loading is progressing. I'd like to clear Delaware Bay by dawn. Once the alarm is out for us, it'll be safer for us if we're outside the United States territorial limits."

"We'll sink the barges in deep water," Casey said. "That way they'll have no cause to link the robbery to a ship as a means of escape."

"Excellent suggestion. You're learning fast, Captain. It'll appear as if vanished into thin air."

Captain Casey put on his cap. "C'mon, we'll go topside."

The *Emerald Isle* rounded Cape May as the sun traced a silver-red border along the horizon. A steam-powered naval vessel saluted her with a blast of its whistle, and the lookout returned the greeting on his bull horn.

"That's timely," Captain Casey said. "It proves they're not looking for us."

"Not yet," Brian said, spitting into the sea.

"Aye. Let's go below and have a toddy of rum, and you can tell me about your Ravena."

"Did you ever get to see her again on your way back to the Orient?"

"No, I stopped over at Maui in the summer of '77, but she'd already sold the plantation and left for home. I talked with George Deal then, and he told me what had happened. Poor George, last I heard he'd passed on. Now what's happened to her since?"

"She and the child are over in Ireland visiting with my parents."

Casey's face darkened. "With your twin brother as well?"

"I fear so, Captain."

"Then you should reclaim her as soon as possible."

"That's easier said than done. Perhaps the time is wrong in any case. This present venture of mine holds very small promise of longevity."

The captain nodded and lit his pipe. "Aye, it's a point. It's not a good time for Ravena and the girl to be in Ireland. This agrarian movement has set off a wave of terror not seen since the days of Cromwell's massacres. Mindless atrocities committed by both sides. Some say another Armageddon is at hand."

Brian scowled at the rising sun. "And here I am an ocean away."

"You're doing your part here."

"It's not the same."

They went into Captain Casey's cabin and he poured them tumblers of dark brown English rum. He lifted his glass.

"To your success."

"God willing. It's funny, I never used to consider God at all in my destinies. But age is the universal apocalypse. We're not alone in our battles for justice and righteousness. If we were, the English would have erased Ireland off the face of the globe by now. God knows they've tried hard enough."

They drank and the ship pursued her northeast course with a stiff wind ballooning her canvas and snapping the sheets.

They set a good pace for the next two days and were approaching their destination on the afternoon of March 17: Portsmouth, New Hampshire, a shipbuilding town since 1800, right across the border from Maine. While they were still in international waters, two sleek navy cutters fell in, one on each side of the *Emerald Isle*.

On the bridge, Captain Casey and Brian studied them with the naked eye and with binoculars.

"What do you make of it, Brian?"

"Trouble."

The lookout sang out: "There's a launch approaching from the starboard, she's north by northeast!"

The cutters made no effort to intercept the newcomer as she drew alongside the square-rigged brig.

Captain Casey ordered the *Emerald Isle*'s sails furled. The bosun cast lines to the launch as soon as she sat dead in the calm water. A rope ladder was put over the side and the launch's passengers clambered aboard.

"General Cauliflower, Major Bandy Legs, Captain Pin Whistle," Brian greeted them. "What's happening?"

The general inclined his head at the navy cutters circling the *Emerald Isle* now. "They're on to us, my lad. There's been a leak in the organization."

"Damned spies!" Brian muttered. God, how he loathed them, even though he'd been one himself. The informers on both sides. "What happens now?"

"There's not much choice. We've had to cancel the invasion. Temporarily, of course, until the heat is off."

"My God! What about us? This ship is jammed to the gunwales with explosives. We can't stay at sea forever."

"There's a contingency plan. It came over the telegraph this morning from headquarters in Dublin. Code, naturally. All hell has broken loose in Ireland. The revolution is about to erupt. The English have declared martial law. They can shoot you or jail you on mere suspicion of treason. Parnell himself is going to be taken into custody as a traitor! The Brotherhood is calling for a general mobilization. It's do or die from now on. Our men need gunpowder and arms badly. Most of all they need men trained in the arts of war. Battlefield leaders."

Brian inhaled deeply, feeling the oxygen pounding

through his veins and tingling in his extremities. He was lightheaded.

"We're sailing to Ireland then, that's the contingency plan?"

"That's it, but not directly. Captain Casey, the council has decided you're to sail the *Emerald Isle* to Nova Scotia. The IRB has a training base there on Cape Sable Island. The French Canadians are sympathetic to our cause, and have given us asylum as well as material assistance. Can your ship carry another hundred men?"

"More if we can bunk them on the hatch covers. We'll string canvas awnings over them to keep them dry."

"Excellent. Colonel Red Hugh, you'll be in charge of the Nova Scotia Expeditionary Force. They've got rifles, but are short of bullets."

"If we can get casings, we're in business. There's enough gunpowder aboard this ship to make a million shells."

"Shell casings they've got aplenty on the island."

"Good, then we'll have something to keep the men busy on the voyage."

"What will be our heading after we take on the troops in Nova Scotia?" Captain Casey asked.

"Dingle Bay on Slea Head. At last report the insurgents hold a portion of County Kerry. With the reinforcements from Sable Island, your command will number over five hundred men, many of them cavalry."

"By God! We'll show those English dragoons a trick or two!" Brian exulted.

"That's what we're hoping, Colonel. Your second in command will be a Major Maple. A good man who served two years with the infantry himself before defecting. But he knows only the uninspired Continental style of battle tactics."

Brian nodded. "They fight like close-order drill. We've had the benefit of a war under our belts, many of us. The men who were on the Du Pont raid with me, Lieutenant Baldy and Sergeant Lightfoot, they were with Jeb Stuart at Yellow Tavern. Corporal Brass, he was with Phil Sheridan for two years. We've got a seasoned cadre to whip our greenhorns into shape."

"Many of the men you'll pick up from Nova Scotia have cavalry experience. Most have some war experience."

The Navy cutters had pulled off now and were headed shoreward.

"They hope to trick us to sail into US waters," Captain Casey said.

"What of you?" Brian asked General Cauliflower. "Will they pick you up on your way back to Portsmouth?"

"Without a doubt," the general said. And with a smug smile. "But it's no more than a formality. The New England States have no love for the British. Too many Irish that part of the country. Still, the official view must be that we are a tribe of rogue radicals, and so the Navy goes through the motions to keep relations harmonious with the Crown. The United States can not condone arms smuggling, that's for sure. Oh, they'll interrogate us and let us go and file the report with all the others they have on us. Nothing to fear, my lad. Now it's time for you to be on your way. Literally, every second counts."

"When we reach Dingle Bay, what's the plan of action?" Brian wanted to know.

"You'll stand far off the coast until it's dark. If a British patrol ship spots the Emerald Isle, they'll blow you out of the water. At nightfall you'll proceed slowly and look for the signal lights on Slea Head. The middle one will mark your landing site." He and the other men shook hands with Brian and the captain, then clambered down the rope ladder into the waiting launch.

"Good luck and God speed!" the general shouted as they cast off from the ship.

"Freedom for Ireland!" Brian said in Gaelic and raised a clenched fist in a victory salute.

"Prepare to make sail!" shouted the captain.

"All hands aloft!" the bosun yelled.

A brisk wind from the southwest snapped the canvas full and the spars creaked as the slim ship surged forward in the water like a greyhound straining against the leash, impatient to get to its destination.

"Are you a gambling man, Captain?" Brian inquired as he and Casey stood on the bridge gazing out across the Atlantic Ocean.

"I've been known to wager a shilling or two on occasion."

"A good gambler has a sixth sense that tells him when

he's on a lucky streak, and he knows he can't lose. I have it now, that special feeling. Everything is going to go right for us, I feel it in my bones."

"Ireland, we're coming," echoed the captain. "Keep the faith."

"It's been over twenty years since I had my feet planted on the Auld Sod," Brian mused. "And now at long last, the heart turns homeward."

The confidence Brian felt about the mission was rewarded by fine weather and strong favorable winds. They cruised into Clarkes Harbor a half-day ahead of schedule and by nightfall the men and shell casings were all taken aboard from Cape Sable Island. The full training coterie numbered two hundred thirty, but only one hundred twenty could be squeezed onto the *Emerald Isle*. Every available cubic inch of space had been utilized, and the small square-rigger rode so low in the water that Captain Casey observed, "If a rat were to slink aboard now, I do believe we'd sink under its weight."

Once again nature favored the voyage across the North Atlantic to Ireland. The weather was unseasonably warm, to the benefit of the men sleeping on deck. Seas were moderate, and it only rained twice for the duration of the voyage. At the end of the first week in May Captain Casey plotted their position on the charts and announced, "We're forty nautical miles off Slea Head."

They scanned the horizon with glasses for some sight of land in vain.

"But it won't be long now before she pokes up over the horizon," he said. "I think we'll furl sail and lay over until it's dark."

All afternoon Brian paced the deck restlessly. The men felt it too, the impatience, the anticipation, the throat-lumping passion to lay eyes on the green hills of home which most of them had not seen in five, ten, twenty years or, as in Brian's case, even more.

They seemed to generate an electric charge that crackled along the bare masts and spars, up and down the sheets like St. Elmo's fire. There was nothing to ease the tedium. All of the shells had been filled, and their weapons were sparkling from so many cleanings and polishings.

Brian circulated among them discussing the landing

procedure with his noncomissioned officers and exchanging jokes with the enlisted men.

"I hear tell they have the sexiest wenches in all of Ireland in County Kerry."

"Aye, that's so, Flat Foot, but the sexiest wench in all of Ireland resides at present in County Tyrone."

He turned away quickly so they wouldn't note the shine to his eyes. He gripped the rail and strained his eyes eastward, as if by some optical miracle he would see Ravena. She was there no more than sixty or seventy miles away. Closer than he had been to her in over five years. Tomorrow the distance would be halved. The day after that? Two days? A week at the most. Either she would be in his arms or he would be dead from a dragoon's bullet.

They made a safe run into Dingle Bay, and, no sooner had they cleared the mouth of the harbor, three signal fires erupted on Slea Head.

"Set course three degrees to starboard," the captain ordered the helmsman, "and hold her steady." The *Emerald Isle* anchored three hundred feet offshore as the ship's bell tolled seven times.

"Three-thirty," Brian observed. "We made good time."

The crew put the dinghy over the side and Brian, the captain, Sergeant Lightfoot, Lieutenant Baldy and Corporal Brass were rowed into shore.

Brian stepped out of the boat and when his foot struck the beach he was overcome with euphoria.

"Home at last," he murmured. He stooped and gathered up a handful of wet sand and inhaled deeply of it. From it emanated all the lovely airs of Ireland.

The welcoming party of twelve men was led by Major Maple. The sobriquet suited him perfectly; he was built like a sturdy maple and bearded like Methuselah.

"You be Colonel Red Hugh, sir?" he inquired in a thick brogue that Brian placed as County Cork.

"Aye, I am."

The big man grinned. "The O'Neil himself; the circle has come full 'round. Himself risen from the grave to lead *Everio* out of bondage."

Brian grinned back. "That's a poetic vision, Major Maple. I take it you be he," he said, mimicking the brogue.

"Aye, let me shake your hand, Colonel."

His grip was iron.

"I want the ship unloaded before daylight. Captain Casey must sail before the British patrol ships spot the *Emerald Isle*."

"No problem. We've got three barges and fifty men standing by to get the job done."

"Good, they may begin at once. Where are your headquarters?"

"Come along, there's much to speak of."

The revolutionaries' lair was in a spacious chamber in one of the larger caves that laced the limestone cliffs like the labyrinthine tunnels of an ant hill, virtually undetectable from the sea or from the bluffs above and ideal for defense. Exposed since the beginning of time to the fury of the Atlantic, the land was penetrated by long, deep valleys and fissures carved out by the sea.

Off the main chamber were smaller tunnels and chambers, storehouses, armory, lodging for the four-hundred-odd IRB members who inhabited the natural fortress.

After the tour, they returned to the main chamber appointed with tables, chairs, and maps and charts fixed to the stone walls with pitons.

"You've done a splendid job, Major," Brian complimented him.

"I've done the best I know how, but it's been marking time mostly. I'm not a military man, least not up here." He tapped his head.

"Well that's my job." He pointed to a keg of whisky in a corner. "I think we could all do with a wee nip of that elixir."

"Private Tits," Maple called to a stout, pasty-faced fellow who unhappily had been endowed with a chest that would please most women, "pass the tankards around."

They sat around the table poring over a situation map of the southwest section of the country.

"Counties Cork, Limerick and Kerry, they'll be our objective. How many men do the English have policing this part of Ireland?"

"Two battalions, I'd say, grenadiers and dragoons of equal numbers. Mainly they keep watch on Cork Harbor and the port of Limerick. It's been mostly peaceable down South. Most of Her Majesty's troops are stationed up north around Belfast and Dublin where the big troubles have been happenin'. There's been scores killed on both sides. It really blew up when they kicked Parnell out of Parliament."

"Well, it's about time we gave the British a kick in the behind down here and give 'em something to think about from Red Hugh's Raiders."

Major Maple slapped the table gleefully, showing snaggled teeth through his red brush. "Aye, Colonel, we'll all drink to that!"

"How many horses do you have? I mean smart mounts fit for cavalry maneuvers?"

The major's brow rippled. "Say maybe one hundred scattered over the three counties. It's not easy to keep good horses from the British."

"Not as many as I had hoped, but it will have to do." He put a finger on the map over Cork Harbor. "Our first strike will be here. At dawn. During the night our horse soldiers will circle around to the east of the port and take up positions behind the hills here. The attack will be launched from the west by foot soldiers. We'll cut the English up the way we made mincemeat of the Rebs at Gettysburg and Yellow Tavern."

"When do we go at them?" Major Maple asked with eagerness that made Brian smile.

"Not so fast, Major. It'll take considerable training before this ragtag mob of ours becomes a unified army. An army must be like a clock, all the wheels and parts working together in harmony."

They commenced the following day. Rifle practice on the beach in the lee of the highest bluffs to muffle the reports from inland ears. Close-order drill.

"What's all this marchin' got to do with fightin' Limeys?" a callow youth complained.

Brian walked over to him and confronted him, bearlike, with a fierce scowl and his hands cocked aggressively on his hips.

"You're the reason, the kind of greenhorn who questions a superior's orders. Discipline, it's the life's blood of an army in battle. I don't like it any better than the next man, but you can't win without it, not against professional soldiers like the British. Now step out of line and run down to that big rock." He pointed to a boulder on the beach some thousand yards away. "Double time, mate, and if you question this order, it'll be five times around and back instead of one."

Mounted drill was held after dusk when the British patrols made their final rounds of the day before returning to their camps. He chose the men carefully with an eye to their experience with horses. A good many of the volunteers for the rebel cavalry had been former horse soldiers either in the United States or the British Army. But the number of seasoned men still fell short of the required hundred. Former stableboys or grooms made up the next preferred group.

Dog-tired that night, Brian fell onto his sawdust mattress and slept like the dead, until Private Tits, who served as permanent orderly for the quarters, woke him at six A.M.

On the third day, the men began to shape up. Undetectable to the untrained observer, perhaps, but Brian sensed the coming together of the multitudinous parts. The gears were beginning to mesh.

By the end of the week the men themselves were infected with the team spirit and morale as well as initiative prospered.

Brian now felt confident to delegate authority to his subordinates. While Major Maple was nominally second in command, Lieutenant Baldy had been one of Jeb Stuart's sergeants, and Maple was more than ready to defer to his military experience. Sergeant Lightfoot was as solid as a rock too.

"Gentlemen, I'll be gone for a few days," Brian announced at supper. "I'll depend on you to keep up with the rigorous program we've put together, and by the time I return, let us hope, we'll be ready for some action."

"Where are you off to, Colonel?" Maple inquired. "To meet with the IRB leaders in Dublin?"

"No, we are an independent unit at this time responsible only to our own authority. If the council decides otherwise, they'll let us know, you can be sure. I don't mind telling you, I'm going north to see my mother and father." He left it at that, not wanting to bring Ravena into the picture at this time. The men might consider he was jeopardizing his own safety and the success of the whole mission for something as inconsequential as a female. There was truth in it too, but the obsession was too powerful to deny. He could not wait longer. One night with Ravena was all he asked from Providence before he went into battle.

"Good luck, sir, and be careful," Maple said.

"God be with you," said Corporal Brass, and he crossed himself.

He chose a horse he had christened Big Red II—a black stallion with white star on its forehead. At midnight he left the "Roost" as the men called their hideout and headed north.

Heading home.

CHAPTER FOUR

Ravena arrived at Tyrone Castle in early November. A strange butler admitted her.

"Yes, ma'am, to whom do you wish to speak?"

She smiled and indicated her luggage stacked on the steps. "Anyone will do. I've come to stay."

He looked stricken. "Madam. I—I—"

"It's all right. I'm Mrs. O'Neil."

"Mrs. Roger O'Neil?"

"Correct. Recently arrived from America."

"My word!" He was *veddy* English, an import.

"May I come in?"

"By all means. I beg your pardon, Madam. It's just that no one told me you were expected."

"I wanted to surprise everyone."

"I'll have the maid prepare your room, and I'll bring up your bags shortly."

"Thank you—I didn't catch your name."

"Sanders, Madam."

He escorted her into the library where the Earl and his wife were seated before the crackling fire. Edward O'Neil looked like a death's head, all skin and bone. But he had surivived far beyond the expectations of his physician.

"It was Sabrina who did it," he said in a weak voice. "That marvelous child breathed life into this old manse."

"My father said the same thing when I brought Sabrina back to Richmond."

Theresa O'Neil wiped her eyes with a handkerchief. "Dear Edward and Vanessa. I knew we'd never see each other again when they sailed away."

The Earl, swathed in blankets, reached out a bony hand and patted her plump arm. "You're wrong, my love. We'll all be together again very soon. At least I'll be with my old friends."

It was curious, Ravena reflected, how little Theresa had changed over the years. Odds were, she, the one who was always ailing, would outlive them all.

Sabrina was in the music room with her tutor. "I'll have Sanders call her," Theresa offered.

"No, please, let her finish her lessons. I've waited this long. Another few minutes won't matter. How's Roger?"

There was an uncomfortable silence before Theresa said in a quick, nervous voice: "Roger. Roger is just fine. He's at the armory today. He keeps very busy. Yes, we scarcely see him any more."

Ravena smiled. "How nice." Translation: Roger was up to his old tricks boozing and whoring.

"He's joined the militia, you know," the Earl said.

"I'm not surprised." So that was it. All the lies about keeping Sabrina in Ireland because of his father's health, when all the time Roger was indulging his obsession with military life and war.

"He's a full colonel," Theresa told her. "Due to be brigadier in a few more months."

"How nice for Roger."

"Ravena—" Theresa said hesitantly. "Did you come here to take Sabrina away from us?"

"Mother O'Neil, you make me sound like an ogress. Don't be alarmed. We'll stay on a few more weeks, maybe a month. But then we must return to America. The plantation cannot run by itself forever."

"Oh dear!" Tears rolled down Lady Tyrone's round cheeks.

"Mother, she's been away from me far too long as it is. After all, I am her mother."

The Earl's laugh was like the rustle of dry leaves. "Don't fret, Theresa, my darling. Ravena won't take Sabrina away."

She frowned. "Why do you say that, Father?"

His dying eyes were bright. "A premonition. I can see things you can't. It's a gift God bestows briefly on those he is about to claim. Ireland's in your blood, Ravena, the way it was in Brian's blood, God rest him. You two, you were always the rebels. Not the Crown's lackey that Roger is!"

"Edward! What a thing to say!" Theresa O'Neil was

shocked. "Roger's cause is different than yours. But it's every bit as vital to him as Home Rule is to you rebels."

He sighed. "Theresa, I am not a rebel. Neither was Brian. Not in the sense of the meaning you and Roger attach to it. We *rebel* against tyranny. But we are the true patriots. An Irishman owes no allegiance to the English and they have no right to claim so."

Ravena clapped her hands. "Bravo! Brian couldn't have put it any better!"

He winked. "Ha! There, you see, my girl, your blood heats up at the very mention of the Irish struggle for freedom! No, your home is here in Ireland. Your heart is in Ireland, and it always will be!"

"Mother!" A cry from the doorway.

Sabrina rushed into the room and threw herself upon Ravena. Mother and daughter embraced, kissed, danced around together.

"Oh, what a wonderful surprise!" the girl cooed. "Now we'll have the best Christmas ever! All of us together again! I'm so deliriously happy I could cry!"

Ravena pushed her off and looked her up and down. "I don't believe it! You've grown so in just the past months. You're almost as tall as I am."

Sabrina straightened up and thrust out her bosom. "I've grown all right, and not just straight up and down."

Ravena cocked her head and lifted an eyebrow. "Yes, I can see that plainly."

Lady Tyrone was shocked. "Such talk from a fifteen-year-old young lady!"

Sabrina laughed. "Grandmother, things have changed since you were a girl. I even know about sex."

Her ladyship almost went into a swoon. "Please, child! Have mercy on an old lady. I've never used that word in my life."

The Earl was staring at the two of them, Ravena and her daughter, with wonder in his eyes.

"It's uncanny, the resemblance. You could be sisters."

"That's flattering to me," Ravena laughed, "but hardly to this nymph."

Sabrina hugged her. "I wish we were sisters."

"Then you'd be out a mother."

"One day back and your Irish wit and lilt of speech is

coming back to you," the Earl said, not altogether in jest. "You're hooked, my girl."

"Do you know what I'd like to do, dear?" Ravena said. "I'd like to change and go for a ride. You still have a stable, Father?"

"A fine one," Sabrina answered. "My favorite is Shamrock. He's the blue-black color of a merle. You'll love Shannon, I'll wager. He's a monstrous roan."

"I owned a roan when I was your age."

"I know. Apache."

"How is Donny?"

"Oh, he's getting on in years, but he's fine. He's devoted to Shamrock and sleeps in his stall every night."

"He's certainly the most traveled dog in the world," Ravena said. She thought of the tiny puppy he'd been when they first got him for Sabrina on Maui. Nostalgia seized her. She patted her daughter's cheek. "Remember how he used to sleep under your bed when you were little?"

"I'll never forget. Come on, Mother. Hurry up and change."

Sabrina's riding habit was made of navy blue velvet, almost the same color as Shamrock's coat. It was leanly tailored and showed off her womanly endowments more boldly than had the gown.

"I'm amazed your grandparents allow you to parade around in such a risque outfit," Ravena declared.

Sabrina laughed. "It took a while to train them. Grandmother insisted at first that I ride sidesaddle with an ankle-length skirt and a bustle."

"How I used to hate those outfits, all that cloth and crinoline and bone. Do you know what I did? As soon as I was out of sight of the house I'd take off the skirt and ride in a pair of trousers filched from my brother."

Sabrina reacted with peals of laughter. "I did the same thing, only I didn't have trousers."

"So you rode in your drawers?"

"How on earth did you guess?"

Ravena giggled, feeling young again, a sister to Sabrina exchanging girlish confidences.

"I was fifteen myself, young lady. And they say the apple doesn't fall far from the tree. We're two of a kind."

She wondered if there was a boy in Sabrina's life.

"Do you have any friends here?"

"A few. There are the Cavendish girls, Sissy and Louise. And then there's Glenn Burke."

"His father's Sir Gordon Blake, I'll bet. We were childhood friends."

"I know. Glenn says his father had a terrible crush on you."

Ravena said slyly, "And Glenn has a crush on you?"

The girl blushed. "He does, poor thing. I feel sorry for him, no more."

"Of course, nothing more."

She's mad about him!

Sabrina said with revealing shyness, "You know who he reminds me of? Father—I mean my real father."

"Is that so?"

The saints preserve us! A boy like Brian! Riding about the landscape in her underdrawers with a boy like Brian! Lord, how our sins come home to haunt us!

At the stables, Donny came bounding out of a stall and leaped all about Ravena, licking her hands and her face and whimpering in sheer ecstasy.

"See, he didn't forget you."

"He's getting fat. You're feeding him too much."

"He eats Shamrock's oats."

Buttons, the former stableboy, was now the middle-aged groom. His red, curly hair thinning, but he still had the impish look of a leprachaun.

"It does me heart good to see you again, Lady Ravena," he said. "Sorry, Madam, *Mrs.* O'Neil. It's just that it seems like only yesterday."

"A lot of yesterdays, Buttons. Or should I say *Mr. McClean?*"

"I'll always be Buttons."

"Yes, and Ireland will always be Ireland. With its seasalt, sweet-grass, sky blue, emerald-green air. I've never breathed an air like it anywhere in the world."

Not even Maui, her second favorite place in the world.

It troubled her what she was feeling and she thought of what Edward O'Neil had said. *"Your heart is here in Ireland and it always will be."*

Five months went by so quickly she couldn't believe it. Roger and she resumed the platonic relationship they had maintained during the years after her return to Richmond. The only time they exchanged anything other than casual words was when they clashed over the English policy toward Ireland.

"The Queen's own Prime Minister speaks out for Home Rule," she reminded him.

"Gladstone's a fool!"

"The English people don't think so. He was reelected this year."

"He and Parnell, that son-of-a-bitch agitator, the two of them are traitorous!"

"That's a fine thing to say about your English PM," she taunted him.

He was away from the castle for weeks at a stretch, leading his regiment of royal dragoons in relentless "rat hunts" for Fenians and guerrilla fighters of the Irish Republican Brotherhood.

He was happiest when he came back covered with blood. "Enemy blood," he'd snarl with satisfaction. "I won't wash this uniform, I'll retire it."

And he was true to his promise. Prizing battle-worn gear the way hunters mount the heads of their kills on library and study walls.

As the end of May approached, Ravena made a resolve. "This is no good, I'm stagnating here. There's so much to be done back in Richmond. We must make plans to leave, Sabrina."

The girl rebelled. "I don't want to leave here. Please. Not until Grandfather is dead. The doctor says he can't last through the summer."

Ravena was grim. "That's what they said about him more than a year ago."

"This time there is no doubt," Roger joined the discussion. "It would be cruel to take her away now."

"That's fine talk now. But you know as well as I that when he goes, your mother will use that excuse to keep her here."

"I'll make a proposition to you," he said. "As soon as my father dies, you sail back to the States and take my mother with you."

"Your mother leave Ireland?"

"Yes, she's worried sick with all the violence and bloodshed. She'd welcome the chance to go. Especially if she's with Sabrina. I'm not joking. Within the next six months this whole bloody island is going to explode like a powderkeg!"

"All right then, Roger. We'll remain until—I hate to say it. It's almost as though we were wishing him to die."

That night Ravena had a difficult time sleeping. Her brain raced around and around like a squirrel on a treadmill wheel, getting nowhere. In exasperation she got up, put on a light negligée and walked out onto the bedroom balcony overlooking the garden. It was a glorious night with a low, full moon that was balanced on the crown of the forest to the west, an immense golden sphere. And yet the moon's radiance did not eclipse the brilliance of the stars. She counted Orion's diamond-studded belt; the Morning Star, a small moon in itself; the Big Dipper brimming over with light; Cassiopeia rocking in her celestial chair.

Ravena shivered and drew the wrap tighter around her naked body. Her heart beat faster. She turned quickly sensing another presence behind her. Nothing. Reverting to a phobia of childhood when hobgoblins lurked in dark corners of the bedroom, and shadowy shapes of chair and dresser were transformed into preying beasts. Even the bushes and trees in the garden came to life, creeping toward the house. Frightened, she ran back into the room and closed the French doors to keep out the night.

With her heart still running wild, she lay down on the bed and pulled the covers over her head. Yes, a child once more.

Terror mounted. She heard distinctly the creaking of the French doors as they swung open. It was upon her now and she was petrified and helpless. Soft footsteps prowling from door to bed. And now it was on the bed. *My God! It was calling her name!*

"Ravena?" A ghostly whisper.

No way but to face it now. She pulled back so slowly one corner of the sheet, peeking out with one eye. It was standing over her, a faceless, featureless form.

She gasped as a match flared, the dim light shattering the darkness like a cannon shot to her high-strung ears and eyes.

No beast, a man! He lit the candle on the bed table and the brighter light illumined his face.

No man, a ghost! The ghost of Brian O'Neil. The fear drained out of her and she filled up with exhilaration. So many times in the lonely night she had prayed to God for this:

Oh, Holy Father of the Universe, send him back to me in spirit. Phantom though he may be I will find peace and comfort in his incorporeal presence.

She sat up now, adoring him with her eyes. "Brian, you've come back to me at last," she said softly.

"Aye, lass, you don't seem surprised to see me."

"Oh no, it's the answer to my nightly prayers. I knew your spirit would never desert me, Brian, my darling."

"Neither body nor spirit, love." He sat down on the edge of the bed and reached out for her. She braced herself for the icy touch of the grave.

Stunned! His fingers against her cheek were warm with the feel of flesh and blood and bone. She put a hand on his arm. Hard and real as the sturdy limb of an oak tree.

"It's a miracle!" she gasped. "Or a dream."

"No dream, I'll vouch for that. As for a miracle, well, that depends on how you look at it. No, no ghost either. I see the look of awe on your sweet face. Here, I'll prove it."

He took her in his arms and pressed his mouth to her mouth. The squirrel caged in Ravena's head careened madly off its wheel. No sense, no rhyme, no reason left in her. Alice stepping through the magic glass.

The body laughed at the mind. He was peeling off her robe. His hands were on her breasts. Hot and kindling heat in her. She helped him remove his shirt and her fingers worked frantically on the buttons of his trousers, caressed him lovingly. Now *that* was real enough!

To be or not to be!

Be damned!

He slipped between her entreating thighs and went into her as naturally as a staple receives the bolt. Locked together. One entity.

"I'm whole again," she whispered as the boiling blood

blinded her and deafened her to the world around them. At this instant he and she were the nucleus of the universe.

"Roger said you were dead," she told him later as she lay in his arms.

"Roger is a lying bastard. But you always knew that. Why did you go back to Richmond with him?"

"Because I did believe him. And I had to consider Sabrina. He convinced me she should be educated in the States. That she should enjoy the privileges of her station. And then there was my mother and father. I felt, I still do, that she should know the love of grandparents. And I was right about that. Just as I was right to let her come to Ireland to see your mother and father."

"Aye, I understand."

"And what about you? You could have let us know you were alive. You're a thoughtless man, Brian O'Neil."

"My word of honor. I wrote faithfully for three years and assumed you were getting the letters in Maui. It came to me through the grapevine eventually that you had sold off the plantation in Hawaii and returned to the States, but I never imagined you'd live with the likes of *him* again."

"Roger and I don't *live* together. We reside in the same house and pretend we're a family for the sake of Sabrina. Incidentally, he's been very good to her, and she thinks a good deal of Roger."

"Son of a bitch!" He punched the mattress. "Posing as her natural father! My daughter!"

"It was for the best, Brian. Can you imagine how she'd be treated if people knew she was a bastard? Don't look at me like that. It's true. She was born out of wedlock. Do you want that on the records?"

"For myself I don't give a damn! A priest saying words over a man and a woman means nothing to me nor to God, if there is a God."

She smiled. "So you've temporized too? There was a time when you wouldn't have given Him that acknowledgment."

"God's just a name for a superior immortal force, the power plant of the universe. I believe in that, not a man in white robes with a stone tablet under one arm."

"No matter, what's done is done, and I'm not sorry about

any of it. It brought us together again, didn't it?"

"Aye, that does make sense." He kissed her. "Now I'd like to see my daughter."

"Don't be a fool, Brian. She's a child. She couldn't keep the secret. He'd find out, Roger. You'd be in prison by morning. How did you get back into Ireland anyway? You're still on the infamy list of the British. Stamped DECEASED. But they'd open the file fast if they suspected you were alive."

"You're right again, as usual."

"As usual. Now tell me what you're doing here."

He did as succinctly as possible.

"It's even worse than I envisioned," she lamented. "Leading an army against the British. To certain death, that's a fact, you're so hopelessly outnumbered."

"Aye, outnumbered, but we're not about to march into the British Lion's jaws. We'll tweak his nose and kick him in the arse, and fade away into the landscape like wraiths."

"You must go before morning."

"Where's Roger?"

"On patrol, seeking the likes of yourself. He'll be back by eight."

"Then at least I can see my mother and father. I hear the old man is ailing."

"He's dying. Yes, I suppose that's a risk you must take. You can't walk off without seeing them. Him in particular. Come along, but be quiet. We don't want to wake the child."

"Our child." He pulled her close one last time before they arose and he dressed.

They left the bedroom and walked down the long dim hallway.

"Can I see her at least?" he asked plaintively.

"I don't see why not. She's always been a deep sleeper. Come along."

She took his hand and turned the corner into the west wing of the castle. Sabrina's room was at the end of the corridor. Ravena put a finger to her lips and opened the door quietly. They walked on tiptoes into the dark room. A muted *burring* sounded from underneath the bed. Brian struck a wooden match on the leg of his corduroy trousers.

The balloon of light revealed the dog slinking towards them on his belly, fangs bared.

"It's all right, Donny," Ravena soothed him. "You remember Brian, don't you?"

Brian lit the candle on the dresser and kneeled down on the rug. "As I live and breathe, it's Donny! And still the brave protector."

"He's never left her side since you brought him home that day on Maui. Though he has a habit of deserting her sometimes for Shamrock, that's Sabrina's horse."

As he drew closer the dog's ears stood up and his tail began to wag. With a joyous yelp he hurled himself at Brian, his long wet red tongue flapping like a banner in the wind.

"Shhh, boy!" Brian hissed and gathered the animated bundle of fur up in his arms. He held Donny's head against his chest and stroked him, all the while cooing Gaelic words whose sound the animal could take comfort in. He put him down at last and walked over to the bed. Ravena held the candle over her daughter.

She lay there as serene as the fable's Sleeping Beauty, dark hair fanned out over her pillow, one hand bent up to rest against her cheek. Her expression of innocence made his throat lump up.

"She's as beautiful as you," he said with emotion. "I've never said that about any other woman." He hugged her to him. "I can't express how much I love you both."

"No need to," she told him. "I know the feeling well."

"I'm coming back to you, my love," he whispered. He kissed his fingers and touched them to her forehead.

Sabrina stirred and moaned in her sleep. "Why is Daddy going away?"

Brian drew back in alarm. "Damn! We've awakened her."

"No, she's dreaming," Ravena assured him. "What a coincidence that she should say a thing like that. In her heart she knows you're here. Come, we'd better go before she does wake."

They carried the candle down to his father's room. It was eerie entering the old familiar chamber confronted by the massive oaken bed with head and foot posts reaching high into the gloom of the cathedral ceiling, spanned by the silken canopy. As vividly as if it was yesterday he remembered creeping into that warm haven as an infant when his mother and father still shared the marital bed.

"I'm frightened of the thunder, Mummy. Roger says it's going to kill me."

The sight of his father lying stiff with his hands folded over his chest as if he were already dead was shocking. A withered doll.

"Christ!" he muttered. "I'd never know it was he if you hadn't warned me. Oh, Lord, why don't you be merciful and take him?"

Ravena bent over the old man and shook him gently by the shoulder. He was awake at once, feverish eyes reflecting brightly the candle light.

"Yes, my dear, is it morning already? Why do you have a candle?"

"No, Father, it's not morning. I woke you because you have a visitor."

He rolled his eyes and groaned. "Oh, no, now the doctor plagues me in the middle of the night. Tell him to go away. Tell him I died."

Brian chuckled softly. "I'm pleased you haven't lost your sense of humor, Father."

The Earl cackled and struggled up on his elbows, squinting at him with myopic eyes. "Is that you, Brian?" As casually as if they had seen each other the day before.

It was that kind of an experience, this night, time warped and bent together. Years were no more than days.

"Yes, Father, it's me." He sat down on the side of the bed. "Don't tire yourself. Lie back."

"Lie back, when my favorite son visits?" He reached out a bony arm and hand and touched Brian on the arm. "Yes, it's you all right, and very much alive. You know, I never did believe that yarn about you burning up in a peasant's cottage. Not you, you're too wily to get trapped that way by doltish British mercenaries. What brings you back, Brian? Have they given you amnesty?"

Brian laughed. "You think my brother would abide with that? Forgive the black-sheep brother?"

"Aye, it was a stupid question. He'd cut off your head

and mount it on the top of the flagpole in the court. He doesn't know you're back, does he?"

"No fear of that."

"You still haven't said why you're here."

"Among other things to tell my father and mother that I love them and they've been with me always in heart and mind to give me comfort in times of crises."

"That warms my heart. What else?"

"And to claim my darling wife and daughter."

The old man cackled again and slapped his pitiful hands together in glee. "As God is my witness, I've always known it. Sabrina is your child! There's so much of you in the child, I've never been able to quite define what it is. It's *you* in her, my son. Just as I used to marvel looking into you as a boy and seeing myself."

Ravena was astonished. "It's unbelievable! He hasn't showed such strength and lucidity in weeks!"

She hadn't meant it for his ears, but they were sharp. "Hah! What did I tell you, my girl? God endows us with omniscience, we who are about to enter his kingdom. It makes the passing over easier." His eyes were cunning. "There's more, isn't there, what brought you back to Ireland?"

"There is. I've come back to pay my dues to my motherland. I've dallied too long as it is. Ireland will be free."

The hand, inhuman in appearance, closed weakly on his hand, and in the touch there was all the humanity and love in the world.

"Thank God, you've come home. Home."

"Brian must see Mother now, Father," Ravena told him. "It's almost light, and Roger will be home any time now. You go back to sleep."

"Yes, yes, yes." He closed his eyes, still grasping Brian's hand, and the smile on his face was beatific. He shuddered and was asleep, softly sighing.

Brian disengaged his hand and folded the old man's hand back across his chest.

Ravena fully expected a display of hysteria and histrionics on the part of Theresa O'Neil when she confronted the son she had believed was dead for over twenty-five years. Brian expected the same. It was a revelation to both of them that the timid, ailing woman, the spineless hypochondriac they had come to know her as, possessed a backbone after all.

She wept, that was nothing, and caressed his face until he complained. "Mother, you'll rub all my skin off if you keep it up."

"My son, my son, why have you done this to us, allowing us to mourn you all these years?"

"I had no choice, Mother. I was badly wanted here in Ireland and in the States. I'm a bad apple, as brother Roger always said I was."

"Roger! Roger!" She threw her hands up to her face in dismay. "My God! What if he should find you here?"

"I'll tweak his nose."

"It's no matter to joke about, is it, Ravena? He'd have you trussed up and on the gallows before sundown if he found you here alive."

"I'd hate to be the poor devil elected to do the trussing. Have no fear, Mother, I'll leave at once."

He embraced her a last time and said good-bye. "I'll see you again, Mother, before too long."

"Don't risk it, Brian. I'd rather never see you again than see you dead at the hands of the British police."

"Next time I come here, it will be with the blessing and forgiveness of Queen Victoria."

"Do you really believe that, Brian?" Ravena asked as she bade him farewell at the rear entrance of the castle.

"Oh, the day will come, I guarantee you that. I may not be here to see it, but one day Ireland will be free."

They embraced and kissed, not with passion but with bittersweet tenderness.

"My love," he murmured in her ear.

"My dearest darling." She kissed his neck.

She stood at the half-open door and watched him stride to a grove of trees where his horse was tethered. He disappeared into the shadows and moments later she heard the receding hoofbeats. Ravena closed the door and went back inside the house.

She was on her way up the staircase in the front hall when Roger came swaggering through the main entrance. His boots were muddy and his trousers and tunic were rumpled and there was a rent in his left sleeve. He carried his plumed officer's hat under his arm.

"What on earth are you doing up at this ungodly hour?" he demanded.

She thought quickly. "I heard hoofbeats a while back. It made me nervous. I thought it might be one of those rebel rowdies."

He frowned. "I thought I heard hoofbeats as I came up the drive."

"You must have frightened him off."

He unbuckled his sword belt and placed it, the sheathed sword and his hat on the marble table beside the door.

"I don't like it, Ravena. They may have this house marked for a raid. My name is spoken like a curse in the ranks of those cowardly bastards! I think I'll have a guard posted here while I'm away."

"Oh? Where are you going and how long will you be gone?"

"Through informers, we've learned that there's trouble brewing in the South. Limerick, Cork and Kerry. I'm taking down my regiment to reinforce the garrison there. Her Majesty's Royal Navy is sending two men-of-war to join the coastal patrol as well."

Ravena's heart accelerated and her face grew hot. Brian's men had been betrayed! *Damned informers!* Her face and voice disclosed nothing of the anguish she was feeling.

"When will you be leaving?"

"Day after tomorrow, but I'll have to spend tonight, tomorrow and the next night at the post. Catch up on my paperwork before we go. I can't say for certain when I'll return. It will depend on how much resistance we encounter down there. One day or two weeks, it won't make any difference. Sooner or later we'll stamp the vipers to death!"

"Well, if you'll excuse me, Roger, I'll try and catch a few more winks before breakfast."

"I could use a catnap myself. I'll see you later."

Ravena lay on her back staring at the ceiling, her mind striving to thread the labyrinth that she and Brian were lost in. It was imperative that he be informed that there was a traitor in the IRB's midst and that the English were sending reinforcements to the south. Otherwise Brian and his army might well be marching into another Valley of Death.

Into the valley of death,
Rode the Six Hundred. ...

Ravena shivered. Could Tennyson's grim poem contain a prophecy?

What was it Brian had said?

"We've got close to six hundred good men now. We'll give Johnny Bull a run for his money."

CHAPTER FIVE

On the second night after he had returned from O'Neil Castle, Brian was awakened in the middle of the night by the charge of quarters, Private Tits.

"The outposts have picked up a spy. At least they think she's a spy."

"She?" Brian sat up wide awake and alert.

"Yup, a woman. And she says she knows you're here. So she must be a spy."

Brian leaped off his cot and put on his trousers. "Have her brought into the HQ at once."

He walked through a corridor into the main chamber of the cave. Minutes later, two sentries brought her into the cave.

"Ravena!" he exclaimed. "What on earth are you doing here?"

"I had to come and warn you. There's an informer in your midst. The English know there's going to be a big revolt down here. Roger told me so. He's coming down with his regiment to reinforce the garrisons at Limerick and Cork Harbor."

"The hell you say!" Brian whistled through his teeth.

"That's not all. The British Navy is sending two men-of-war to patrol off the coast."

"Damn! That's a nasty bit of news! Tits, tell Maple, Lightfoot, Baldy, Brass and Boots I want to see them at once!"

"Yes, sir." The big flabby man waddled off, his rolls of flesh wobbling like jelly.

Ravena's eyebrows lifted. "It's easy to see where he got his nickname from."

Brian laughed. "He's a chubby all right, but a good, willing fellow. Now, tell me, how did you find me?"

"I know this country well. We used to come here in the

summer. I played on these very bluffs and explored many of the caves. I never did find this big one, though."

"It's well concealed. When the men first came here, it was nothing more than another grotto, that was sealed off at high tide. Maple and a crew took soundings of the walls and discovered that one wall indicated that there was a chamber on the other side of the rock. They broke through and discovered this enormous cave. When do you think Roger and his regiment will get here?"

"Day after tomorrow, according to what he told me. The warships should arrive about the same time."

"That's something. We have a little time, at any rate."

When his staff was assembled around the table, he detailed the crisis confronting them.

"What can we do?" Major Maple asked.

"There's only one thing to do. We've got to move up our schedule. We strike Cork Harbor at dawn on Tuesday."

A murmur of mixed emotions greeted his announcement, but after some debate they were all in accord that it was the only reasonable decision.

"If we wait till the reinforcements get here, we may as well chuck the whole idea," Maple expressed the common view now resolved.

"Major Maple, you'll lead the infantry assault from the west. I'll command the cavalry, attacking from across the hills after you engage the enemy."

He turned to Sergeant Lightfoot. "Lightfoot, you are about to take on an assignment that will make you think of old times when you rode with Jeb Stuart. I want you to take a detachment of thirty horsemen and ride northeast, raiding and raising hell as you go, every village you pass through. Shoot up the police stations. Don't wait around to engage the police or soldiers. Ride like the devil once you've made your presence felt. Take the fastest horses. That kind of a diversion should elicit prompt attention from the British troops in the area. I'll wager half the garrison in and around Cork will be drawn off to chase you. You'll leave at once. The rest of us will follow as soon as we can get organized. It's almost two days' forced march to Cork Harbor, the way we have to make it, out of sight in valleys and woods."

"Yes, Colonel. I'm on my way." Lightfoot saluted and left to pick his detail.

"Is this English colonel really your brother, Colonel?" Maple asked.

"Yes, Mrs. O'Neil is married to my brother," he admitted reluctantly. He stared hard at the rock wall in front of him; through the wall into outer space. "My twin brother."

The major recoiled in awe. "Aye, so that's it! Of course, he's well known, this Colonel O'Neil, with the IRB. He's on the Brotherhood's ten-most-wanted enemies list. The son of the Earl of Tyrone." His eyes went round. "Then that means that you are—"

"I'm Red Hugh, and that's all," Brian snapped.

"Aye, sir." He shook his head. "The saints preserve us, brother fighting brother."

Brian's mouth twisted in sour irony. "And what's new about that, Maple? Brothers have been battling brothers ever since Cain and Abel. All right, gentlemen, it's time we got our army mobilized."

And what a ragtag army it was. The only evidence that it was an organized military unit was the uniform green-dyed stocking caps worn by the enlisted men with shamrocks of darker green emblazoned on the front. The officers wore comfortable campaign hats of the type worn by the US Cavalry in the Civil War.

Leggings, boots, workmen's shoes characterized the footwear. Trousers were tough corduroy or denim. Shirts, sweaters, seamen's pullovers covered hard-muscled torsos.

At four A.M. as they were preparing to move out from the beach, luminous in the light of the moon brilliant on the rim of the ocean, Brian expanded the scope of his battle plans.

"One of our scouts just reported that a small frigate anchored this evening off Valentia Island to take on water, gunpowder and repair a split spanker. I think we might have a chance of capturing her."

Loud dissent was voiced from officers and enlisted men alike. Brian explained: "She's not one of the big men-of-war headed here. Just a small three-master with one deck of thirty-six guns. Except for a dozen or so men on watches, the rest of the crew is ashore, still swilling rum and wench-ing at this hour, no doubt. Corporal Whaler, check out that longboat stashed away in the grotto."

"It's in fine shape. I was lookin' at it only day before yesterday."

"Good. Then rig up a small mast at her stern like the British Navy has on its dinghies and run up one of the British Navy guidons we have in the booty barrel.

"Lieutenant Baldy, it'll be up to you to command the cavalry attack on Cork Harbor. I want to command this boarding party myself. I'd like about a dozen agile volunteers with some knowledge of seamanship."

Warming to the idea now, scores of hands went up. Brian chose twelve, including Whaler. "Now see what else we have in the booty barrel? British seamen's caps and shirts. Just to add a touch of authenticity to the men up in the front of the boat."

Sufficient articles of apparel were found in the booty barrel to outfit four of the men with enough genuine British naval gear so that in the dark they could pass as Limey sailors.

For his key role in the operation Brian donned skin-tight black shirt and black trousers. Before climbing into the boat he shook hands with Major Maple, Lieutenant Baldy and his other officers.

"We won't meet again, gentlemen, until it's all over. If all goes well we'll rendezvous back here on Thursday night or Friday. Good luck."

As they watched the dinghy pull away from shore heading past Slea Head, Maple remarked to the others:

"Well, we'll surely miss him up at Cork, but he can't be everywhere at once. Personally, I think this adventure is madcap, but—" He hesitated.

"But we got our orders," finished Lieutenant Baldy.

"Amen!" was the chorus. With or without their leader, they formed a disciplined army and would get on with the mission as best as they knew how.

The team in the boat rowed close to the shore in the shadow of the bluffs, away from Slea Head, out of Dingle Bay, 'round Doulus Head, heading for Valentia Island.

It was the perfect time for a covert operation, just before dawn when it is darkest, the moon gone now and even the stars seemed to wane.

The lapping of the waves against the high banks dulled the sound of the oars.

The British frigate lay in the snug harbor between the island and Bray Head, a dark ghost in the water. The longboat gave her a wide berth, holding to the shadow of the headland, and made a three-quarter circle around her, making its final approach from the direction of the village where lights were still twinkling in some of the homes and shops.

About one hundred yards away, Brian slipped over the stern into the water, hanging onto the gunwale. Aboard the frigate the ship's bell rang out two bells. A silver band ringed the horizon. Dawn would burst on the world suddenly.

A silhouette stood at the rail by the boarding ladder. He called out to a shipmate and now there were two figures at the rail.

All of the way the IRB soldiers kept up a charade as Brian had ordered. Drunken, raucous laughter. A medley of bawdy sea chanteys. Loud arguing. When they were twenty-five yards from her side, Brian let go of the boat and struck out underwater for the stern of the warship.

"What are you doing back here at this hour?" the lookout called down to them.

Whaler answered him. "Blimey, mate, we done run out of girls and rum, so we thought we best come back to the ship and catch a few winks."

"Damn few. It'll be daylight soon."

"Well, we're here." The longboat scraped the side of the frigate. "Throw us a line, mate."

The line dropped down and they moored her. Whaler grasped the rungs of the ladder and started up, holding his head down so that his face would not be seen too soon.

"What about the others?" the second man on board shouted.

"Luckier than we'uns. They're all bedded down with nice Irish lassies."

The captain's small private boat was moored at the stern. Brian tested the line that held her and it was strong. He pulled himself up out of the water and climbed hand over hand up the rope until he could grasp the stern rail. Silently he swung himself aboard and surveyed the deck.

It was deserted except for the two sailors amidships occupied with Whaler and the other rebels in the dinghy. He moved in their direction along the port rail, picking two belaying pins out of their racks as he went.

Corporal Whaler reached the top of the boarding ladder, and one of the Englishmen held up a lantern to his face.

"Who the hell are you?" he demanded.

Whaler brazened it through. "It's too late for jokes, mate. I'm comin' aboard."

"No! Bosun, sound the alarm!"

He shoved at Whaler with one hand and drew the pistol from his belt with the other.

The second man turned and ran. Ran straight into Brian who decked him with a swipe of a belaying pin. The one battling Whaler had his pistol free now and pointed it at Whaler's face, point-blank. Brian cocked his right arm and let another pin fly. It struck the Englishman on the side of the head and he crashed to the deck. Brian rushed over to the ladder and helped Whaler aboard.

"Come on, the rest of you, be quick about it!"

Whaler gave a hand to the man behind him as Brian stooped and picked up the fallen pistol. None too soon, either. The other sailors who had been asleep in the forecastle, aroused by the commotion, came tumbling out on deck. Whaler raised his pistol, but Brian knocked it down and shoved the requisitioned pistol into his belt.

"Don't, Corporal, they're not armed. Twelve good Irishmen can take double their number in Englishmen with their fists. Come on."

He and Whaler rushed the groggy, bewildered sailors as the rest of the rebel crew poured over the railing.

The man in the fore of the sailors' ranks was a big fellow with arms like a gorilla. Brian ducked two roundhouse whistlers that would have decked a bull and drove his right hard into the man's gut. It was like punching a brick wall. Patently, other measures were called for. He danced out of harm's way, circled, feinted with his left, and, when the brute grabbed for his arm, he chopped at the side of his neck with the flat of his hand, an axlike blow that landed flush in the angle of neck and collarbone where a network of nerves and veins joined. It was a paralyzing blow. He reared up and back stiffly, staggering backwards until his back hit the rail. He hung there, braced, swaying from side to side, arms limp at his sides. Brian stepped in and brought up an uppercut to the lantern jaw. Up and over he went and down into the water.

"Colonel, look out!"

Brian whirled, dodging to one side, as an attacker swung at his head with a belaying pin. It missed by a hair. The momentum of his charge carried him into the rail, and the bar struck his gut, knocking the wind out of him. Before he could recover, Brian stepped behind him and grabbed him by his shirt and drawers and heaved him over the side.

All around him the other rebel raiders were doing their part as well. The Whaler, the Swordsman, the Card, each flattened one Limey and Whaler got another. There were eight to account for not counting the two in the drink and the two Brian had felled at the boarding ladder.

"I din't even work up a sweat," said the corporal as they admired their handiwork.

"No time for flattering ourselves," Brian said. "Come on. we'll run up those cases of dynamite from the dinghy. Then we'll set the English navy afloat in a somewhat smaller craft."

"String 'em up to the yardarm, Colonel!"

There were all sorts of irate protests against showing leniency to the foe.

"Quiet, all of you!" Brian snapped at them. "There's one lesson you blockheads must learn if you ever hope to achieve a lasting victory. When a side stoops to the indignities practiced by the other side, even the most noble of causes loses its luster. No, we set free the Englishmen. Let them go and tell their captain to let this be a lesson to him and to all English sailors and soldiers. Don't tread on us. We Irish, we sting like St. Patrick's snakes!"

He propped one fellow who was recovering up against the cabin and asked him, "Where is your captain, and your other officers?"

"They're partying ashore with a lot of whores."

"Screwing, is that what they're up to? Aye, that's fine. You tell them too from Colonel Red Hugh that how they were screwed in the village is nothing to compare with the royal screwing we're giving them. All right, let's move."

The cases of dynamite that lined the bottom of the

dinghy were hauled aboard and the English sailors, still in a daze, were ordered to descend the ladder into the dinghy. They picked up their two shipmates who were conscious now, swimming about the ship, bellowing for help, and rowed back toward shore in dejection.

Brian slapped his hands together in glee. "All right, me hearties, let's see what we've got here. He toured the frigate from stem to stern, above and below.

Her thirty-six cannon, eighteen on each side of the ship, were of the smooth-bore muzzle-loading variety mounted on truck carriages.

"She's of the old line," he noted. "One of the original coast defense warships. But she's sturdy enough. All right, men, all hands aloft and make sail for a race!"

"Aye, sir, but where are we going?" asked Whaler.

"To Cork Harbor, where else? We'll give our lads a fine reception when they arrive. I dared not reveal my plan to 'em, in case we failed. Not finding us at Cork, it would have spoiled their morale. This way, it'll fire 'em up beyond all expectations when they see the green flag of Ireland flying from a British frigate!"

A loud huzzah went up from the men, and they ran to the sheets and climbed hand over hand into the rigging.

Later on, down in the captain's cabin, Brian studied British naval charts of Ireland and the sea environs surrounding it. "Aye, we're a small crew, but with every man pulling twice the load, we'll manage."

"Aye," replied Whaler. "And the wind is with us."

"When the wind is with you, as it has been with us since we left Wilmington, it's a sign of God's favor. Providence. Fate. Call it what you will. The gambler's lucky streak isn't mere chance. He's been smiled on."

He studied the chart and grinned. "Ay, yes, we have been smiled on indeed. This chart has the British installations around Cork Harbor clearly indicated. I wish Major Maple had the advantage of this knowledge. Well, we mustn't be the greedy dog who saw his reflection in the water and dropped his own bone to snap at the other dog's bone.

"See here, they're concentrated here between Cobh on the harbor and Cork on the mouth of the river that empties into the harbor. Hmmm. See how narrow the mouth of the harbor is? That suggests some interesting possibilities. Who's our demolitions expert aboard, Corporal?"

"Private Powder. He's apprenticed to Sergeant Bang."

"Good. Have him report to the cabin immediately."

Private Powder was a skinny, long-limbed man with sparse sandy hair, a squint, and a pockmarked face. A second-generation Irish-American, he had been born in Birmingham, Alabama, and had enlisted in the Confederate Navy at the onset of war.

"If memory serves me correctly, Powder, you served under Admiral Buchanan at Mobile Bay?" Brian inquired of him.

"Yes, sir, aboard the *Tennessee*. I still don't know how the Yankees got inside the bay to sink her. I helped lay those defenses, the cement pilings and the torpedoes."

Brian repressed a smile. The irony of life, the absurdity of it all. He wondered what Powder would say if he informed him that it was he, Colonel Red Hugh, who had fed the secret information to Washington that enabled Farragut to penetrate the bay and get the drop on the formidable *Tennessee*? And now the two of them, former foes, were plotting to sink two British men-of-war!

"How would you like to mine another harbor entrance?" he asked.

Powder shrugged his hunched shoulders. "My fingers are itching." He held up his hands. Good hands, Brian thought, long, slim fingers, dexterous, steady as stone.

"Can you manage it with the new dynamite we have?"

Powder pondered on it and finally said, "I don't see why not. It'll take some improvising with them percussion caps, but I'll give it a go."

"I want the mouth of Cork Harbor strung across with submerged torpedoes. Once we get there we may not have much time to work on it, so get done what you can on the ship."

"Aye, Colonel."

"Get all the men you need to help you when they've got slack time. The ship is pretty much sailing herself now. Get busy."

The strong west wind held through that day and night and all the next. At dusk on the second day the lookout in the crow's nest scanned the sea in all directions through the spyglass. Then he bawled out:

"There she is, Colonel, Cork Harbor!"

"Good! Corporal Whaler, let's shorten sail. I don't want to get in before dark."

By the time HMS *Kent* crept through the narrow inlet into Cork Harbor the lamps had been turned on in the village of Cobh. They passed a fleet of fishing boats going out to sea to lay their nets.

Brian hailed the captain of the lead boat. "Have any other warships been here lately?"

"Two cutters, night before last," was the reply.

The fishermen regarded the frigate sullenly. Naturally, she was flying the hated Union Jack from her mainmast. Brian was certain they had been spotted by British lookouts stationed on either head at the mouth of the harbor. They wouldn't have paid much attention to one more warship in these waters in such times of crisis.

"The trouble is, they've no doubt got cannon up there to guard the harbor," he theorized.

"Then how can we lay the mines?" asked Corporal Whaler.

Brian winked. "You'll find out. Whaler, Wood and Powder, we're going to a costume party. You other men, lower the captain's boat."

Not much later Brian, attired in a dress uniform he had taken from the captain's locker, descended the ladder into the waiting boat. Whaler wore a first mate's uniform, while Wood and Powder on the oars were dressed like ordinary tars.

They were met on the dock at Cobh by a detail of grenadiers, all over six feet tall and looking smart in their red coats and dark trousers. The lieutenant in charge touched his cocked hat in a salute.

"Welcome ashore, Captain. This is a pleasant surprise. We were expecting two men-of-war within the week, but there was no mention of your frigate."

Brian snorted in derision. "That's the War Office for you. Inefficiency, carelessness. We were originally bound for Belfast, then at the last moment the orders were changed. We're to mine the mouth of the harbor."

"Mine the harbor?" The lieutenant was shocked. "Against what? The insurgents don't have any navy."

"I'm sorry, Lieutenant, but I can't discuss it any further. Would you please take me to see your superior?"

"Certainly, Captain. The commander in this district is General Laccy, Robert Lacey. This way, sir." They were escorted to the Blue Boar Inn on the edge of the village which had been commandeered by the occupation forces and turned into a corps headquarters.

The general was eating supper when they arrived, and he graciously invited the captain and his first mate to join him.

"Forbes, take the seamen to the enlisted mess and see they're taken care of," he ordered his orderly.

"You're very generous, sir," Brian said. He and Whaler took their places on either side of General Lacey.

They had taken the identities of the captain and mate gleaned from the ship's roster: Captain Lewis Halstead and First Mate Samuel Tate.

"So you're here to mine the harbor," the general said with grave concern. "I knew things were bad, but not so serious as to warrant a step like this."

"It's only a precaution, sir, and I have no doubt a needless one, but the War Office doesn't want to take any chances. Our agents have passed on an ugly rumor that radical factions both in France and Spain are conspiring —with the tacit consent of their governments, mind you— to send an expeditionary force to invade Ireland and support the revolutionary Irish Republican Army in its struggle for independence."

The general dropped his fork. "I am flabbergasted! I've never heard anything so audacious."

"It's not all that improbable. Remember, Spain and France are both Catholic countries and have no love for the British in any case."

"Yes, when you consider it from that point of view. What cheek! Bloody Latins, you can't trust 'em."

"No more than the bloody Irish," Brian said archly. "With your permission, sir, we'd like to get started laying out our torpedoes at once."

"In the dark?"

"Our orders state we are to commence the operation 'upon arrival.' "

"Yes, well, that doesn't leave you much choice. Can I detail some men to assist you?"

Brian smiled. "More of your generosity, General. I'd appreciate it, and could we have two small launches assigned to us? It will quicken the work considerably."

"By all means."

They shook hands warmly and Brian and his crew departed.

They began work at eight that evening. The launches each had two powerful lanterns, and with four British military assignees and four men from his own crew, the mission was accomplished by two the next morning.

The torpedoes had been assembled during the voyage from Valentia Island. Metal drums rigged with bundles of dynamite packed in guncotton. The detonators were attached to the dynamite through metal pipes extending through the sides of the barrels. The detonators, primed by fulminate of mercury mixed with potassium chlorate, were attached to the pipes after they had dropped anchor in Cork Bay. Then the drums were sealed watertight with lead and pitch so that they would float. Strung across the mouth of the harbor at ten-foot intervals, they were anchored to the bottom by nets weighted down with stones and anchor chains. They floated beneath the surface at a level that would pose no danger to the fishing boats of the village with their shallow draught. Only warships laden with armor and cannon would ride deep enough in the water to detonate the torpedoes.

They were all joined together by light, waxed line so that, as Brian explained to the curious British helpers, "We can easily clear a channel for the passage of HMS *Kent* or any of our other warships by posting details on either side of the inlet to pull on the towline at one end and to let out slack at the other. That will have the effect of depressing the torpedoes in the water to permit the passage of vessels with a deep draught."

It satisfied the soldiers, but later, when Brian and Whaler were sitting around the mess table of the frigate, swigging the English captain's captured whisky with the rest of the crew, the corporal challenged Brian. "Where did you come up with that one, Colonel? I never did hear anything like it before."

"Nor I," Private Powder agreed. "And my job was laying mines in the war."

Brian chuckled and swished amber scotch whisky around in his tumbler. "It came to me in a revelation. But now when I consider it, it is in accord with the basic laws of physics." He hefted his glass. "A toast to Private Powder. He did a bang-up job on those torpedoes."

"That's only right," Whaler said. "After all, he learned his craft from Sergeant Bang."

"He added a lot to me bag of tricks I learned in the navy," Powder conceded.

"Well, gentlemen, it is now three o'clock," Brian announced. "And Major Maple and Lieutenant Baldy will be attacking in another three hours if all's gone well on the march. I suggest we get an hour's rest or two before sun-up. We'll stand shortened half-hour watches so that every man gets a chance to sleep."

They were all in agreement.

For himself, Brian had no desire to sleep. Every nerve and muscle in his body was tuned up for the battle to come. He lay in the dark on the captain's bunk and conjured up pictures of Ravena and their daughter to distract his mind from its restless thrashing. What was she doing now back at the Rebel's Roost in the cave off Slea Head?

He had seen her alone before leaving for Valentia Island.

"Another good-bye, is it?" she said, clinging to him with a fierce tenacity. Her head was bent and he put a hand under her chin and tilted her face up to his. Her eyes were wet.

"Don't!" she protested. "I don't want you to see me crying."

"Lord knows I've shed plenty of tears over you," he joshed her. "And it's not good-bye. Don't you remember what we used to say on Maui?"

"*Aloha*," she said with irony. "Personally, I'm partial to the German: *Auf wiedersehn*."

"Till we meet again," he said. "Yes, that's what I'll say to you. Till we meet again, and may it be soon."

She sighed. "One of these days you won't be coming back to me. Ever. It could be this time."

"It won't," he said firmly. "I will come back. To you and to Sabrina."

His confidence had not waned. They would succeed. This morning the sun would rise over a victorious IRB army. He dozed briefly and dreamed of Ravena's dark, haunting beauty. Her mouth moving soundlessly, but he could read her lips.

"I love you."

"And I love you, my darling."

At five o'clock they all gathered on deck to watch the sun rise. Brian made a scan of the shoreline within the harbor through the telescope. The streets of Cobh were silent. The only signs of life were the sentries manning the cannon guarding the mouth of the harbor. Overhead, seagulls traced loops and whorls against the blue sky. A dog barked in the distance.

The men moved about uneasily. "I don't like it," Whaler complained. "It's too damned quiet. Major Maple should be attacking by now."

"Easy does it." Brian lowered the spyglass.

It happened so quickly they were rudely startled even though this was what they had been anticipating with such anxiety all night.

Ashore hell broke loose!

A column of smoke and fire erupted high into the air from the location of the Blue Boar Inn, General Lacey's corps headquarters. In swift succession other flaming geysers shot high, one hundred feet or more, accompanied by billowing mushroom clouds of jet-black smoke. The sappers had done their jobs well, planting bundles of dynamite at strategic locations around the bay area: the HQ, the police station, ammunition dumps, warehouses and under barracks.

Brian counted at least fifty explosions, the shock waves from the blasts rattling the ship's masts and spars, flapping the furled sheets. The men on deck were buffeted as if by an invisible giant hand.

"Blimey!" Whaler exclaimed in awe. "I never seen nuthin' like it before! That dynamite sure is brute powerful!"

With the last echoes of the explosions still ringing back and forth among the mountains and through the valleys, the din was joined by human voices, gunfire and the thunder of horses' hooves, shouts, screams. The countryside around the harbor abruptly was teeming with life. Terrified civilians fleeing into the hills and forests. Bright-coated British grenadiers and mounted dragoons. A sea of green hats. The swirling mass of humanity locked in mortal combat. On a knoll to the west a troop of dragoons driven to retreat was reforming for a countercharge.

"Man the cannons!" Brian shouted. "And run up the Irish flag!"

The night before he had anchored the frigate so that her cannons were broadside to the east and west shores of the harbor, calculating that the nature of the terrain must inevitably steer the battle there. Natural ground for cavalry fighting to the east, broad plains and rippling ridges. To the west the uneven ground, furrowed with dry stream beds and gulleys, could be defended by a small force against an enemy far superior in numbers.

"Fire!" he bellowed.

The eighteen cannons on the portside were right on target. Six men manned the gundeck on the portside; six on the starboard side. Each man responsible for three guns.

Brian jerked the lanyard of one gun and moved on to the next, then the next.

The shells fell short of the hill where the British cavalry troop was regrouping.

"Elevation by ten degrees!" Brian ordered. The correction was made and the cannons reloaded, the hooks of the lanyards snapped in place on the breeches.

Three more cannonades, this time on the mark. The British officer leading the counterattack against the flank of a group of IRB cavalrymen already sorely pressed by another British troop brandished his sword in the air. A hurtling missile cleaved off his raised arm at the shoulder. A shower of iron and steel fell amidst the men and horses, creating panic. The attack was broken. Demoralized, the dragoons who survived the barrage fled in all directions.

Whaler yelled from the starboard side near the prow: "Men-of-war off the head!"

Brian rushed forward with the telescope, aimed it at the mouth of Cork Harbor. Out to sea but closing fast were two big British battleships, side by side.

He read the names on the hulls:

HMS Prince of Wales

HMS Victoria

Nearing the mouth of the harbor, the *Victoria* fell in behind the *Prince of Wales*. Slower now they came as, one by one, sails were shortened. Brian studied their approach through the spyglass. There was bustling activity aboard both vessels as gunners scurried to their posts at the cannons bristling from two gun decks one above the other.

"They spotted our shamrock flag!" he announced. "Let's give 'em a show, my hearties!"

He cocked his right arm, elbow bent, fist upraised, and slapped his left hand hard against the biceps in the universal language. *Fuck you!*

Brian studied the oncoming warships through the spyglass. "The newest capital ships. Two turret guns on one, four on the other. That means they won't have to wait for a broadside. Damn!"

An instant later the battleships opened fire with their forward turret cannons. Two geysers of water shot high into the air far off the port side of the *York*. The Irish rebels along her rail leaped up and down, shouting obscenities and making scornful gestures.

"A hundred yards to go before they strike the line," Brian said. "Jesus, hurry!"

The warships' big guns belched smoke again. One shell burst off the stern. The second whistled through the rigging, splintering spars and the top of the mizzenmast like matchsticks.

The *Prince of Wales* was almost abreast of the heads on either side of the inlet.

"Fifty!" he marked it off.

"Twenty!"

"On the line!"

The warship was obscured by a wall of fire as torpedoes exploded on either side of her prow. The *York* reeled and canted from the aftershock. Through the smoke they saw her now. Stem gone, one-third of the ship almost. Her bowels lay bare, deck upon deck, like an architect's sketch showing a cross-section of a ship.

Behind her the *Victoria* trying desperately to sheer off and away, but too close to effect the maneuver. Scraping along the side of her sister ship and pushing the *Prince of Wales* sideways into another torpedo and plunging forward to disaster herself. Simultaneous explosions. Towering spires of flame. The thunderous blasts detonating other torpedoes down the line. A tidal wave of flame spanned the inlet from head to head.

Brian pushed back his cap and threw a casual, disdainful salute at the flotsam of what had minutes earlier been twin prides of Her Majesty's Navy.

A chorus of cheers went up from the rebels. They jigged about the deck, slapping one another, whooping gleefully and waving their green shamrock caps.

"Time to celebrate later on," Brian cautioned them. "This isn't over yet. Now's the time to go hit the beach."

The captain's boat was moored at the stern. "She's only built to carry eight," Brian said, "but we'll manage."

He was the last to leave the frigate. Before he climbed down the rope ladder into the overloaded boat, he lit a delayed fuse that Powder had rigged up to the remaining cases of dynamite.

On afterthought, he went to the mast and ran down the Irish flag. Then he ran up the Union Jack again.

"It's only proper that the lady should sink under her own colors," he explained to the others. "She's been good to us."

They cast off from the HMS *Kent* and rowed northeast toward Cobh. The village appeared deserted now, the battle having spread out into the countryside surrounding the harbor.

"Don't nobody sneeze," warned Corporal Stone. "Ain't no more than an inch between the gunwales and the drink, and I can't swim!"

They landed on a sand spit near where the river emptied into the harbor and struck north into the woods, then northwest heading for Cork. Armed with Colt revolvers and English rifles confiscated from the frigate's armory.

Along the way they encountered heavy casualties, dead and wounded, English and too many of their own men.

Baldy.

Brass.

Boots.

All dead.

Sergeant Terrier with a broken leg.

Brian told him as he told the other wounded, "Lie low, stay out of sight, and we'll be back for you."

On the outskirts of Cork they joined up with Maple's infantry force. They were in good spirits despite the loss of fifty men.

"We saw what happened in the harbor, Colonel," Maple gloated. "Gor! What a magnificent sight. I almost wet my pants for joy! We couldn't believe our eyes! I still can't believe it's you! How? What? Why?"

Brian laughed and slapped his shoulder. "Later, Major, later. No time for talk now. I want a litter detail to go back the route we came from and carry back the wounded."

"Aye, right off. We saved those we could, but we didn't scout the woods."

"What's our position now? Where are the British?"

Maple grinned. "Still running, I suppose. It went off like clockwork. The opening salvoes with the dynamite shook them bad. They've never encountered anything like it before. That set the tempo of the rest. And Baldy's horsemen were holy terrors. Rolled up the dragoons' flank after we attacked like a ball of string. They're nipping at the Lion's heels now so's he won't have a chance to pull himself together. Of course what made it possible to start with was Lightfoot's diversion. Half the garrison around Cork Harbor is out looking for him."

"Good work." He did some critical thinking. "Let's not push our luck. We've accomplished what we set out to do, and much more. I think it's time we withdrew to our base."

It took them three days to make their way back to Dingle Bay. All of Cork, Limerick and Kerry Counties were swarming with British troops on foot and mounted.

"The reinforcements have arrived," Brian deduced as they lay low in a wood after narrowly avoiding an enemy patrol of more than a hundred dragoons.

After dark they moved west once more.

"We're too conspicuous," Brian told them. "We'll split up into parties of ten and fifteen and put fifteen-minute intervals between them. It's easier for a small group to find concealment than it is for more than three hundred."

Brian's group of fifteen was the last to leave the wood at midnight. They struck out along a dried-up streambed that offered good cover, but as morning broke they entered a stretch of rolling, open country that expanded as far as the eye could see. Brian surveyed the terrain with a pair of British military fieldglasses he had taken from a dead grenadier captain.

"Looks clear to me," he observed.

They did not spot another British patrol all that day and all the next.

"It appears they've given up on us," Major Maple rejoiced.

"I don't like it," Brian brooded. "Suddenly it's become too easy to give 'em the slip."

The misgiving stayed with him even after they were safely back to their subterranean hideout off Slea Head.

CHAPTER SIX

Brian and Ravena enjoyed a reunion so touching that some of the men choked up and walked out.

"I think we'd better leave these two alone," Major Maple said finally. His voice was gruff but his eyes were moist. "Get on with yer, yer lazy Irish louts!"

When they were alone, he kissed her the way he'd craved to since his return. Deep, mouths open, her tongue teasing his. His hands adoring her breasts, her buttocks, the nape of her neck.

She gasped. "If you keep this up, me lad, I'll demand you take me like one of them Dublin whores, standing up with my bare butt braced against the table here."

"That sounds like good fun to me."

They might have given it a go, too, but for the mighty explosion that rocked the stone chamber and sent pebbles clattering down on everything from the roof. Brian thought at first the chamber where they kept ammunition and powder had gone up.

But Private Tits came waddling in as fast as Brian had ever seen him move, white and wheezing. "The English are here! They've got the cove surrounded!"

Brian, with Ravena on his heels, pushed past Tits and ran to the cave's entrance. From the bluff above there sounded busy riflefire. He walked to the edge of the rock ledge overlooking Dingle Bay, stunned to see two British frigates and a gunboat standing offshore.

He pulled Ravena back and shoved her back into the cave just as the lead ship's cannons belched smoke. The volley raked the stone abutments on either side of the cave and above the entrance. Rocks rained down on their heads and a crack opened in one wall of the grotto. Brian ran to the opening that led into the main cave.

429

"Tits!" he yelled. "Come out of there before the whole damned mountain comes down on you!"

He spied the fat man far down the corridor waddling as fast as he could. Too late. Another barrage from the warships strafed the bluffs, and this time the grotto's domed ceiling began to tremble like an inverted bowl of jelly.

"Get out!" he shouted to Ravena and ran for the entrance. They squeaked out an instant before the grotto was wiped away by an avalanche of rocks.

"Come on!" He took her by the hand and climbed a flight of steps carved out of the soft stone up to a narrow defile, no more than two feet in width, that ran back a hundred yards to a higher ledge. From there they traversed a zigzagging route up to the top of the bluff. Through thick woods to the far side where the rebels had erected breastworks out of thick logs across the peninsula to guard against just such a contingency as was befalling them now.

The firing was only sporadic now.

"What's the situation?" he asked Maple.

"We stopped 'em this time good. See for yourself." He indicated the score of British grenadiers strewn about the clearing in front of the barricade. He swept the terrain with his fieldglasses. The British had withdrawn to a ridge much like the one where Custer had made his ill-fated stand.

"No wonder we had an easy time of it getting back from Cork," Brian said. "They were playing cat-and-mouse with us. They're bringing up artillery along with the dragoons. We're not equipped or trained to fight in a stationary position like this. Hit-and-run is our specialty."

To make matters worse the ships in the bay began to lob projectiles onto the bluff. They fell into the woods, far short of effective range, and several trees came crashing down.

"They're firing blind," he said. "But sooner or later they'll get lucky."

"What are you going to do?" Ravena asked.

"Damned if I know," he admitted.

And now the artillery was moved up and the cavalry formed a line behind the guns.

"Brace yourself!" Brian told the defenders. "Fire at will."

"Wait!" Ravena said with sudden inspiration. "I know a way out of this."

"The hell you do!" He and the men around them stared at her in wonder.

"I do! I do! Quickly bind my hands in back of me!"

"You must be daft, woman!"

"It's the only way to save our necks. Brian, run up a white flag and tell them you want a truce so as to speak to their commander. Tell them you're holding hostage Brevet-Brigadier-General Roger O'Neil's wife."

"The saints preserve us!" Maple said in awe. "Mrs. O'Neil, you've got more brains and courage than any man I've ever fought alongside of!"

"I won't let you do it," Brian said.

"Don't you try to tell me what I can do and can't do, Brian O'Neil. You should have learned that by now."

Laughter eased the tension somewhat.

Brian wore a silly grin and scratched his head. "I guess we don't have any choice. All right, let's truss her up and rig up a white flag. Pebbles, tear up a white shirt. You, Dancer and Pignose, go down to the pen and move the horses back into that gulley in the rocks."

The barrage from the warships was creeping eastward in the direction of the pens, tearing up big chunks of virgin forest, but posing no danger to the troops as yet.

Brian hoisted the makeshift flag on the barrel of a long rifle and waved it high over the barricade.

"Cease fire," he told the men. When he was sure the British officer in command had ample opportunity to see it, he stepped up on top of the breastworks. When his appearance did not draw fire, Ravena was hoisted up alongside him, hands bound behind her back.

"Here I go," he murmured. "Keep those pretty fingers crossed."

He stepped down in front of the barricade and advanced across the clearing, carrying the truce flag high.

A party of three came out to meet him from the British lines. A captain and two lieutenants. As they drew near him, their expressions projected utter astonishment. He found it comical.

"My word!"

"It's uncanny!"

"I don't believe it!"

"They're identical!"

Brian inhaled deeply. So that was it. They were under Roger's command.

The captain confirmed it. "Mr. O'Neil, the general prepared us for this possibility. Our spies are as efficient as the IRB's. It was known that you'd come back to Ireland."

Brian smiled. "My congratulations to you, Captain. And how is my dear brother, Roger?"

The captain, a saturnine man, smiled back. "Much better than he has been now that you're in tow, I'll wager."

"You'll lose. You see I am not in tow. Not yet."

"If you're procrastinating to gain time, sir, it won't work. You have two choices. Either unconditional surrender or we'll blow you to kingdom come."

"You're forgetting about the lady." He jerked a thumb over his shoulder in Ravena's direction. She played the role of subjugated captive well. Head hung low, shoulders slumped. Clad in rough shirt and trousers borrowed from one of the smaller rebels.

"Is that a woman?" the captain squinted.

Brian scoffed. "My men don't wear their hair in braids, sir."

Brian took the field glasses out of their belt pouch and handed them to the captain.

"Look for yourself."

The captain did. "By God! It is a woman. A lovely wench at that."

"I don't believe General O'Neil would appreciate that remark. The 'lovely wench' is his wife."

"His wife? That's absurd. What do you take us for, fools?"

"You'll be worse than fools if you dismiss me and attack us. She'll die with us. Ravena O'Neil, daughter of the Duke of Ulster as well as the general's wife. Don't take my word for it. Ask the old cock to come down here and have a look for himself."

"But how? I mean, the general believes his wife is safe in Tyrone Castle."

"That is for the general's ears alone, I'm afraid, Captain. Look, why not take me to the general's quarters right off. I assure you I can convince him."

The three withdrew a ways and conversed in low, troubled voices. At last they concurred on a decision.

"O'Neil, all right. Come along with us."

"At your service." He lowered the truce flag and handed the rifle to one of the lieutenants. "I don't believe my brother would care to have me walk into his tent carrying a loaded gun. Oh yes, one other thing, Captain. Get word to those warships in Dingle Bay to stop firing. If one of those missiles lands near Mrs. O'Neil, those captains might as well resign from the navy."

Brash talk, but it was working. He could read the respect in their new attitude toward him.

"Yes, sir. Lieutenant Hemmings. Attend to it at once. Double time!"

Regimental Headquarters of the Royal Tyrone Dragoons was located about five hundred yards to the rear, behind the rocky ledge on which the dragoons had regrouped.

Atop the center pole of the general's tent two guidons flew, one emblazoned with the regimental colors, red, gold and blue, the higher inscribed with the Tyrone coat of arms.

A guard, six-foot-four or over, stood spraddle-legged at parade rest. He snapped to attention at their approach and brought his rifle diagonally across his chest in a salute.

The three officers returned it and the captain said: "I'd like a few words with General O'Neil, Sergeant."

The sergeant turned and pulled aside the tent flap. Roger O'Neil was seated behind a table strewn with maps and charts.

"Captain Pearce would like to speak with you, sir."

"Send him in." He leaned back in his campaign chair, wood and canvas. His expression was surly.

"Well, be quick about it, Pearce. I'm a busy man. I hope you're here to report that this rat's nest has been cleaned out."

The captain reddened. "Not quite, sir. There are complications."

"Complications!" Roger roared. "Goddamn it, man! Can't I trust a small operation like this one to my subordinates? You've even got naval support. What the hell are these so-called 'complications'?"

The captain gulped, speech coming hard. To have to

tell this martinet that his brigand brother was holding his wife hostage, God, what an unenviable task!

"Speak *up*, man!"

"General—sir—it pains me to tell you this, but there's someone outside to see you."

Fury fanned briefly in Roger's face, his body tensed as if he was about to spring to his feet and demolish poor Pearce. Then to the captain's amazement, he sat back in the chair again and a smile—sinister as it was, it was a smile of sorts—spread slowly across his handsome face.

"Is there now? And who might that be who persuades you to indulge in such insolence as to disturb me when I gave you distinct orders that I did not wish to see your simpering face until you had completed the mission to my satisfaction?"

He blurted it out. "The commander of the rebels, sir. He's here under a flag of truce, Sir." The worst to come. "Sir, it's your brother."

"My brother? You can't be serious." His tone deceptively amiable now.

It frightened Pearce more than when he shouted. "I—I'm afraid so, sir. No mistake, he's the image of you."

To his further amazement, the general began to chuckle softly, shaking his head like a man who'd won at the races and couldn't believe his good fortune. He had to be daft, thought Pearce.

"Brother Brian. Well, well, well. We had information that he was back in Ireland, but I never dreamed it would be this easy to catch that slippery eel. You say he asked for a truce? I assume then that he's going to surrender?"

Pearce gritted his teeth. "No sir, he has no intention of surrendering. There's something else, sir. I don't know how to tell you this—"

"Pearce!"

He blurted it out. "Sir, they've got a woman hostage out there on the barricade. He claims it's your wife, General."

He recoiled and resisted an impulse to throw up an arm to protect his face against the clap of emotional thunder the revelation produced in General O'Neil. He sat rigid as a statue first, hands clenched on a thick ruler, knuckles drawn white. Face pale too. Eyes ablaze. Mouth twisted in a cruel grimace. Still he managed to control his inner fury.

"My wife a hostage." Voice brittle as untempered glass.

"Maybe it isn't she, maybe he's lying," Pearce said with an eagerness to please.

"You saw her?"

"Yes, through field glasses. A lovely woman, black hair, her eyes. Even at a distance, you had to notice those eyes."

The ruler snapped in two with a loud *crack* that made Pearce start.

"Bring the man in, Captain." The voice dangerously calm.

Before the storm!

Pearce went outside and nodded to the guard. "It's all right, the general wants to speak with him."

"I'd better come along." The guard held his rifle at the ready. Mesmerized by this vandal who was the spitting image of his general. A phantom!

When he entered the tent, Roger looked quite composed, sitting forward in his chair with his hands clasped in front of him on the table. Alongside them a service revolver. His expression was impassive.

"You may leave, Captain. You too, Sergeant."

"But, sir!" the guard protested.

"You heard me. *Out!*"

When they were gone, Brian walked slowly to the front of the table and the two men stared at each other in silence. It had been—how long—twenty-five years or more since last he had set eyes on his brother. It never ceased to amaze him when he appraised his mirror image. If anything the resemblance was more precise than when they were youths because both were graying.

"You're looking well, Roger," he broke the ice.

"I understand you have Ravena?"

"She's a hostage."

"Damned liar! The whore came to warn you we were on our way to comb this country and stamp out you traitorous lice once and for all."

"That's not true. She—she—" It had an empty ring to it and he stopped.

"Incidentally, I knew you were at the castle. Your

memory betrayed you. You should have known better than to trust our mother with a secret. Poor soul, since we were infants, she's labored under the delusion you and I can be reconciled."

Brian smiled and shrugged. "No matter, let's get to the point. No matter what you think about Ravena and myself, the fact is these are desperate men. I vow they'll kill her as well as myself because I'm bound to defend her. Roger, she is your wife."

"She was never my wife," Roger said bitterly. "Vows and a gold band mean nothing. She's always belonged to you, damn her!"

"Sabrina's mother then. I know you love the child."

"Sabrina—" A perceptible softening in his tone.

"She cares for you too, Ravena told me so."

"More lies?"

"I swear on Sabrina's life, it's true. You know it is. She calls you 'Daddy.' "

Roger's head bent and he said nothing. Deep in thought.

Brian pressed what he was sure was a gain. "I've come here to bargain, Roger. The lives of my men for my life. And you get Ravena and the child."

Roger stood up straight and the brothers confronted each other across the table, no more than two feet apart.

"You filthy, stupid, *blind* swine." The quiet voice of doom. "Do you think I'd make bargains with a devil like you in the name of the Crown? Do you think I'd let your vermin go loose to kill more honorable British soldiers? Do you think I'd lift a finger to save that harlot's life? Damn the lot of you! I'm going to see you all blown to hell where you belong!"

They both lunged for the pistol. Neither could get a hold on it as they grappled fiercely over the table. He pulled Roger forward and the table collapsed in shards and splinters of wood. Roger chopped a hard right behind his ear, and he was staggered. He threw up his hands as Roger attacked him like an enraged animal. Ducked and fell in close to clinch with his arms wrapped around Roger's waist. He drove a knee hard into his brother's groin, felt him go limp an instant. Enough to shove him away and measure his jaw for a right cross. It landed flush and Roger staggered back. Pursuing he drove a left hook to his gut and finished the combination with a right uppercut. Roger went down and lay there on his back glaring up at him with malevolent eyes. Eyes as bright green with hate as a tiger at bay.

He struggled up on one elbow and threw up his other hand. "No, Sergeant, don't shoot! I don't want him dead! Not yet!"

Brian started to turn, but too late. The butt of the grenadier's rifle caught him solidly on the back of the head. He blacked out before he hit the ground.

When he regained consciousness he was in chains, hands manacled behind him, ankles clamped by two metal clamps with a short chain binding them together.

"March him back to the line!" Roger said crisply. "I'll be along presently."

Brian looked across the open space at the barricade two hundred yards away. Ravena was still standing on top of the logs, playing her act to the hilt. He shouted to her, "Get down! It didn't work!"

A soldier backhanded him in the mouth. Blood gushed from his torn lip.

"She didn't hear him," Captain Pearce said, "but gag him anyway."

General Roger O'Neil arrived dressed in battle uniform, his sword at his hip, his plumed dragoon's helmet sitting rakishly on his head.

Captain Pearce came to attention as did the other men present. "Shall we inform them that the truce is over, sir?"

"Yes, indeed, Captain, and in a manner that will leave no room for misunderstanding. Shoot the woman."

"Sir?" Captain Pearce was aghast. All of the troops within earshot were stunned. A few dared show their revulsion in muttered asides.

"Blimey! Shoot a woman?"

"His own wife, no less."

"I always knew he was a brute."

The captain floundered. "Sir, might I suggest that we postpone this matter until you've cooled down a bit?"

Roger stepped up to the captain and seized the front of his tunic and shook him the way a terrier shakes a rat. "If you ever evidence such insubordination again, Captain Pearce, I'll have you cashiered out of the service! Now

I've given you a direct order. Pick a squad of sharpshooters so there'll be no doubt of the outcome and *shoot that woman!*"

Brian, held fast by two guards, used their restraining arms as a fulcrum, lashed out at Roger with both feet, kicking him in the small of the back. He grunted in pain and went down on one knee. There was choking and coughing all along the British line, as the men muffled the gratification they felt at being witness to his mortification.

"Serves him bloody right!"

Roger rose with dignity, brushed himself off and sobered the men with his glare. Then he turned to Brian.

"As soon as the woman is dispatched, put this man in front of a firing squad. Then we'll exterminate the rest of them!"

Captain Pearce was looking past him to the rear. "General, there's someone approaching."

Roger turned around and frowned with annoyance at the interruption. "What the devil?"

Three horsemen, British officers, strangers to General O'Neil. Nearby they dismounted and advanced on foot.

The tallest of them addressed Roger, saluting. "General O'Neil?"

"Yes, what is it? There's a battle going on. You have no right to be here."

"My apologies, sir, but that's why I am here. I'm Major Jennings, the adjutant for Kerry County. I have an urgent message for you from Dublin, the Viceroy himself."

"It will have to wait until this fight is won. Later, Major."

The major, unaccustomed to being treated in such contemptuous fashion, reddened and said with irritation "No, it won't wait, General O'Neil! You are to break off this fight at once and seek a truce with the insurgents."

"A truce?" He shook both fists in the air. "Over my dead body! Captain Pearce, follow your orders without any further delay!"

"If you disobey the Viceroy's order and continue with the battle, I personally will testify against you at your court martial, General!" Major Jennings warned him. "You too, Captain Pearce."

The General quite literally went mad! It would be a topic

of barrack conversation for months to come. Howling like a banshee, he hurled himself upon the manacled prisoner and seized him by the throat.

"I'll kill you, you bastard! I should have done it before when I had the chance!"

It required the efforts of four men to pull him away from Brian.

"Who is the prisoner?" Major Jennings demanded.

"The insurgent commander," Captain Pearce advised him. "He came over to talk about a truce."

"By God! That's a stroke of luck. Take that gag out of his mouth and unfetter him at once."

"I thank you kindly, Major, for your intervention, and now what is this about the Viceroy declaring a truce?"

"That's right, and if you'll throw down your arms and give your word you'll be peaceable, I am authorized to bestow a general amnesty on your forces."

Brian was flabbergasted. Wary as well. "But why? What's the trick behind it?"

"No trick, O'Neil. All of the IRB leaders, all of the factions, Fenians, what have you, they are to assemble in Dublin for a conference with the Queen's representatives to discuss a permanent peace in Ireland."

Brian threw back his shoulders and let the tears stream down his face with pride.

"We've won it," he whispered.

CHAPTER SEVEN

"It's not a clear win by a long shot," said John Redmond, one of the two emissaries speaking for the imprisoned Charles Stewart Parnell at the Dublin meeting.

"But it is a long step in the right direction," said Captain O'Shea, Parnell's other representative. "Who was it?— a Chinese philosopher I believe—said that a thousand mile journey begins with a single step. And Ireland's come a long way forward this past decade."

The Viceroy peered over the tops of his rimless spectacles from the head of the conference table. "The Land Act is the greatest and most momentous concession that the British Parliament has accorded Ireland in this century."

To be heralded in Irish history thereafter as The Three F's: Fair Rent. Fixity of Tenure. Freedom from Sale.

And in a confidential agreement not to be made public the Viceroy of Ireland, speaking for Prime Minister Gladstone, assured Captain O'Shea and John Redmond that Parnell would receive a pardon within six months.

Still, Brian O'Neil, the ranking member of the IRB, pressed for another concession: "We want greater representation in Parliament. At least two more MP's."

Captain O'Shea and Redmond backed the demand, and reluctantly the Viceroy agreed. "I'm not authorized but I'll stake my reputation that Parliament will ratify that condition as well."

"That's good enough for me," Brian said, and Redmond, O'Shea and the IRB delegates acquiesced.

General Roger O'Neil, military member of the reactionary bloc opposing any concessions at all to "the traitorous rebels," glared at his brother sitting directly across the table.

"I never thought I'd live to see the day that England

would submit to blackmail from a band of brigands! It's sheer piracy! You give them an inch, and next they demand a foot! And after that they want a square foot. Foot by foot, yard by yard, acre by acre, mile by mile, they keep on grasping until before you know it they've taken over all of Ireland!"

"Well stated, General," Brian said acidly. "One day we will take over all of Ireland! We'll kick your arse, you and your kind, across the Irish Sea, back to England where you belong."

Roger appealed to the Viceroy. "You hear the blackguard, sir? Be sure you warn the Prime Minister that when he deals with felons like these, he's nurturing a viper at his bosom."

"General O'Neil, the truth is England had no choice in the current matter. In the first day of the uprising in Cork and Kerry, she lost three warships—two of them capital ships. All this at a time when our relations with France are critical. No, sir, it was imperative to reach accord with the insurgents if they were willing to be reasonable in their demands. And I for one believe the agreements reached are fair and reasonable. And, as you well know, General, the Prime Minister is a staunch proponent of absolute Home Rule for Ireland."

Roger shook his head and sneered. "The bloody fool is undermining the entire British Empire."

"And what's wrong with dismantling an empire?" Brian demanded. "The very concept of 'empire' is restrictive, oppressive, pompous. It means financing the biggest army and navy in the world to police one's restless colonies. Britain's been at war for most of its mature history, keeping order all over the world, at an exorbitant cost in money, material and chiefly human lives! Empire be damned!"

After a few other closing remarks from the other members, the Viceroy of Ireland adjourned the session.

At the door, Brian and Roger nearly collided. Brian stepped back, bowed facetiously and made a flourish with one hand. "After you, my dear brother. You are the senior heir, after all."

"Go to hell, you bastard!" Roger raged. He shook a fist at Brian. "Let me tell you something, brother! We're not done yet, you and I. The day will come I'll see you hang!"

Brian smiled. "The day may come when I hang. But you won't be around to see it!"

Roger stalked out, followed by his aide-de-camp.

After the council Brian went directly to Tyrone Castle. His reunion with Ravena and their daughter was tearful and joyous.

Sabrina near mauled him to death with her hugs and kisses. "You must promise you'll never leave us again, Daddy."

He hugged the two of them to his breast. "Ah, lassie, would that I could make such a commitment, but I can't. Right now the government has given us amnesty, but that can all change. See, it's only one battle, and there are more to be fought. Next year, the year after that, I could be a fugitive again. We've gained, but there's much more to be gained, and we can't afford to lose the gains we've got through inertia."

She was so impressed with the sentiment that she repeated it to her young friend Glenn Blake. Already a legend in Glenn's eyes, Brian's status soared to new hyperbolic heights.

When he next called on Sabrina, Glenn literally worshipped at the older man's feet, sitting cross-legged on the floor near Brian's chair.

"Some day they'll put up a statue to you, sir, in Phoenix Park. You're Ireland's greatest national hero."

Brian fixed him with a mildly reproving look. "You forget there are a few more in the running for that honor, going all the way back to 1600 and Red Hugh O'Neil. And to name a few others, Wolfe Tone, Dan O'Connell, Will O'Brien, John Dillon, John Mitchell, Charles Parnell. Oh, I could bend your ear all night just reciting their names.

"But I tell you lad, I don't think any one of 'em would care for a hero's statue in Phoenix Park. It's a poor word, 'hero,' because it smacks of vanity and the sin of self-pride. It tends to turn a man's concentration in upon himself and he loses interest in the affairs of other men around him. No, what you construe as 'heroism' is a man with vision who champions a just and reasonable cause and who has the patience and the determination and, yes, the courage not to be distracted or frightened off from his purpose until he gets the job done."

The boy and the girl went riding that day and Ravena and Brian watched them from the terrace.

Alone at last Ravena broached the subject she had been avoiding all day. "I was told by Mother that Roger will be coming home tomorrow."

"Aye, I know." He sighed. "I'll be leaving tonight after supper."

"And we'll be coming with you, Sabrina and I."

He drew her close to him and kissed the top of her head, the once-raven dark hair less lustrous than it had been the first time he'd kissed her, streaked with gray, but none the less dear to him.

"You will be with me one day soon, I swear to you."

"Brian!"

"No, hear me out, my sweet. I can't take you and Sabrina away from this comfort to live in a cave or a tree house."

"There's no need for hiding any more."

"True, but there's IRB business to be administered all over Ireland. I expect to be traveling steadily for the next three months. London too. I've been invited to address Parliament."

"We'll travel with you. I love London."

"Maybe London, by that time things will have settled down. But for now, you must stay here. It would be unfair to Sabrina. She's fifteen. You remember what it was like at that age? A child needs permanence. Then there's Father—he doesn't have more than a few weeks remaining. I want the two of you to be here with him when he goes. For me, Ravena, please?"

She smiled and tightened her arms about his neck. "I never could refuse you anything, now could I?"

He winked lewdly and rubbed his belly against her. "Funny you should say that. I was thinkin' of askin' for something more personal."

She laughed softly and raised her lips to receive his kiss.

Afterward they watched Glenn and Sabrina from their bedroom balcony riding in a distant field.

"She's close to the age I was when I first went riding with you."

He nodded. "They make a handsome pair."

"Think what a mixing of bloodlines would mean, the benefits. Red Hugh O'Neil and Daniel O'Connell on her side. Sean Blake, the Black Blake who battled Cromwell at Drogheda."

"Yes, the Blakes are fine people." His expression abruptly brooding as he assumed the role of the protective father. "But Sabrina is much too young to be thinking of marriage." He stood up and stared hard at the young couple racing their mounts back and forth in the meadow.

"I was only fifteen that day you—"

"Stop talking that way, Ravena! She's our daughter."

Her eyes were bright with mischief. "Yes, and they say that: 'As the twig is bent, so grows the tree.' You know, he rather reminds me of you."

"Oh, Christ! What a thing to say to me!"

She came over and stood by him. "I know, I've felt the same way myself at times. It would be a fine match though. You and I can't go on bearing Ireland's standard forever."

"Aye, the job won't be done in our lifetime. Independence and peace and prosperity for all. Equality."

"Glenn and Sabrina, it'll be their generation that will carry on after us. They'll see the dream realized."

Brian was silent, thinking of Roger's parting words to him in Dublin:

"We're not done yet, you and I."

Roger was right. There was more to come.

EPILOGUE

As I inscribe these last sentences on paper (it's an odd fact not realized by the general reader that prologues are, in fact, the final summing-up of a book even though they appear at the beginning) we are awaiting news of the vote on the First Irish Home Rule Bill submitted to the British Parliament by Prime Minister Gladstone and Charles Stewart Parnell.

A majority of our people believe it will be soundly defeated. But as I said to Brian before he left our London hotel this morning:

"Whoever would have believed that such a bill would ever be up for a vote in Parliament? Not forty years ago when we first met. Not thirty. Nor twenty nor ten. Just ten years back who would have dared to hope the Independence movement could have achieved what has been achieved up until this date?"

Year of Our Lord—1886
(signed) Ravena Wilding O'Neil

ELISHA'S WOMAN
Norah Hess

$1.95

Bold, passionate, willing, Rachael Jobe came as a stranger to Devil's Ridge. She was eager to begin a new life, hungry to find love and determined that no man would hold her cheaply again. When she met Adam Warden, she thought she had found her match, but Adam believed she was Elisha's woman and contemptuously called her a whore. Insulted and enraged, Rachael resolved to teach him a lesson about women that he would never forget.

BIG NIGHT AT MRS. MARIA'S
Barney Parrish

$1.95

Everyone who was anyone was invited. And everyone came: the Hollywood starlets, the politicians, the super-jocks, the society matrons, the rich and the celebrated, the gifted and the damned. But it was an orgy that would turn into a night of terror.

HURRICANE OF ICE
H. L. Perry

$1.95

A howling inferno of a storm descended with crashing force. The mighty Trafalgar Bridge surged and thrashed like a bucking bronco, and the ultraplush Tallifaro Inn—with its curious microcosm of guests—shook to its very foundation, pitted against nature in a harrowing test of survival.

THE TRANSFORMATION
Joy Fielding

$1.95

At midnight the house was alive with laughter and the glitter of Hollywood's swingingest stars; by morning the party was over and the stench of slaughter was unmistakable. Three star-struck women, disenchanted by Hollywood, are caught in an orgy of satanism and death.